THE YOKE

A NOVEL

DARRELL DUNHAM

Halo ●●●●
Publishing International

ISBN: 978-1-61244-500-7
Library of Congress Control Number: 2016959207

Printed in the United States of America

Halo ●●●●
Publishing International
www.halopublishing.com

Published by Halo Publishing International
1100 NW Loop 410
Suite 700 - 176
San Antonio, Texas 78213
Toll Free 1-877-705-9647
Website: www.halopublishing.com
E-mail: contact@halopublishing.com

To Betsy, who loves me, and to Oliver,
who taught me so much about how to love.

Acknowledgments

This book took five years to write. I would write a draft, set it aside, ask my friends and others to read it, and then I would make changes as the process went on. The final product reads nothing like the earlier drafts. Many people helped me in this process, too many to list. I must give credit, however, to Mike Chylewski, who gave me much-needed critical advice; to Jeanette Windle, whose patience I tried but who refused to let me get by with anything but excellence; to my brother, Doug, for his advice and encouragement; to Dan Schmechel, who provided valuable insight and insisted that I get it published; and to Jodie Greenberg, who claims to be only the editor but who became much more than that. I also acknowledge the late Cord Finch, whose sarcasm I injected into the book.

Contents

PROLOGUE

"Do you have any more evidence, Mr. Mitchell?" the judge said sternly. Barnabas was staring down at his notes when he lifted his head and made eye contact with the judge. Her eyes were narrow, and her jaw was clenched. He was trying her patience. Barnabas didn't have any more evidence, but he couldn't bring himself to admit defeat. It was his twenty-seventh trial. He had lost cases before, but this loss was going to be particularly bitter.

Barnabas was standing in the middle of Judge Alice Kruger's courtroom. She was a federal district judge for the United States District Court for the Northern District of Illinois. The courtroom ceilings were a full twenty feet high. The carpet was plush, the chairs padded, and the walls paneled with red oak. The courtroom was fully automated with state-of-the-art technology. Halfway up the wall, where a jury would usually sit, hung eight oil paintings of federal judges that had previously presided over this courtroom. They were all men. Each of them mimicked Judge Kruger's stern expression. Even the retired and dead judges were displeased.

Barnabas believed that it would be a long time before he appeared in front of Judge Kruger again. He had no other cases pending in federal court. After this trial, he would be back representing clients who could barely afford to pay his fees. He had managed his finances in the past, and he knew he would manage them in the future. That was only a minor problem.

The case involved an invention that both sides agreed was worth in excess of 500 million dollars. Barnabas was convinced that the invention belonged to his client, but he had not been able to prove it. While he had been tempted to blame the sad condition of his case on the judge, Barnabas knew he would rule the same way. She really had no choice but to decide against him. Barnabas had learned that no trial lawyer had every ruling go in his favor. All he could expect was a judge who had good reasons for ruling against him, and in this case, Judge Kruger had good reasons.

Barnabas looked over at his client, who offered him a polite smile, signaling his resignation. The smile said, "It's okay. You did your best. We just had too many obstacles to overcome." But Barnabas knew it would take weeks to get over this defeat if he ever did get over it. His client had acquired the gruff exterior that came from working his whole life, but he also had a gentle heart. His client had invested his life savings in this case, and he was going to receive nothing in return. He deserved to win, but he was going to lose. Barnabas believed that he had put on a good case, but in litigation, it was not about doing your best; it was about winning. The suggestion that he was valiant in defeat gave him no comfort.

Barnabas looked over at the table across the courtroom where opposing counsel sat. Senior counsel for the principal defendant, North American Coal, looked at him with a smug expression.

In his previous losses, the other attorney had at least made an effort to demonstrate some level of magnanimity at the end of the trial, but this was going to be different.

North American's counsel despised Barnabas, and the feeling was mutual. But Barnabas was determined that opposing counsel would not get the chance to gloat in front of him. Barnabas and his client would exit the courtroom as soon as the judge announced her ruling, depriving the opposition of the opportunity to revel in their success.

Bill Cushman sat next to North American's attorney. Barnabas had known Bill for over eleven years, and during those years, Bill had become his nemesis. He sat there with his patented smirk, clearly enjoying Barnabas' anguish. With Bill, the question was not if he would gloat, it was how soon after the judge announced her ruling that he would begin. At that moment, Bill's smirk was particularly painful. There was another matter that Bill was going to gloat about, but it was too agonizing for Barnabas to even consider.

Barnabas turned to the far end of the counsel table and glanced at the attorney for Century Coal. She looked confident, even though she had previously led him to believe that she was on his side. But it didn't matter; Barnabas didn't think he could trust her anyway.

The judge repeated the question, this time with a greater edge to her voice. "Mr. Mitchell, do you have any more evidence?"

Barnabas had just gotten back to the point that he had started to believe in God again. *Why did God make his life so difficult? Why did it seem as if life was so easy for others?* When he was a child, his mother bribed him to memorize Bible verses, and for some reason, he had remembered, "My yoke is easy and my burden is light." He didn't believe that now, and he didn't think he ever would.

He had one last Hail Mary, and he might as well throw it. Although he knew that Judge Kruger would not be pleased, it was the only thing he had left.

"Your Honor, may I approach the bench?"

PART ONE

Even youths grow tired and weary,
and young men stumble and fall;
but those who hope in the Lord
will renew their strength.
They will soar on wings like eagles;
they will run and not grow weary,
they will walk and not be faint.

—Isaiah 40:30–31 (NIV)

CHAPTER ONE

It had been the worst day of his young life. Barnabas had celebrated his twelfth birthday the day before. It was shortly after 2:00 p.m. and a feminine voice came over the school's loudspeaker. "Barnabas Mitchell, please come to the principal's office."

His teacher nodded at him. Barnabas rose from his desk and slowly walked to the principal's office. He had never been called out of class before. He had never gotten in trouble. He liked school, but few people really knew him, and he liked it that way. He had no clue why the principal wanted to talk to him.

Barnabas walked into the waiting area, and a glum-faced woman softly said, "Barnabas, the principal is waiting for you. Go right in." Barnabas didn't think this woman even knew who he was, yet she called him by his first name.

Barnabas approached the door hesitantly, and as he pushed it open, he interrupted a quiet conversation. He was startled to see a man in a police uniform and a woman about his mother's age dressed in a suit. The conversation stopped, and there was an awkward pause.

The principal spoke in a slow, soft voice. "Barnabas, your mother... your mother was in a tragic accident, and she's in the hospital. Officer Canfeld and Ms. Wilson are here to take you to her."

Barnabas' voice rose. "Is she going to be all right?"

From his look and tone, the principal clearly didn't know what to say. "Officer Canfield and Ms. Wilson tell me that it was a serious accident. You should go to the hospital. They will know more there."

Barnabas remembered that meeting in the principal's office clearly. His mother's accident was to become a dominant force in his life. A day never went by that he didn't think about the moment when he learned about the accident. But the next two days had been a blur. He remembered spending that night with Nancy, his mother's friend. His dad, a trucker, shortened a road trip and was at the hospital the next day.

After that, his memory was clearer. He stood next to Nancy and listened to what his mom's doctor said. "She made it past the critical stage, and we are moving her from intensive care. But there was some brain damage, and she has no feeling in her legs. Her spine was fractured in so many places that it truly is a miracle that she survived. While it is possible that she may walk again, I'm not optimistic."

When the doctor left, Barnabas asked Nancy, "How did this happen?"

Barnabas remembered Nancy as a good-natured, cheerful woman, but she had responded with uncharacteristic anger. "A drunken young man. He decided that he couldn't wait for the next light and raced through the intersection just after the light turned red. It happened at noon, and he had been drinking for at least two hours!"

It turned out that the doctor was right. His mom did spend the rest of her life in a wheelchair. While she recovered her speech, her mind got weaker with each passing month. Prior to the accident, she had been strong, healthy, and vibrant. She was active in the church, and she and Barnabas attended every Wednesday night and twice on Sundays. She had worked in a hospital, and frequently her former patients would approach her at church or in the supermarket and thank her for the care she had given them. After the accident, she spent most of her time at home. She died nine years later.

His dad had started drinking even more than before, and each time he went out on the road, he seemed to be gone longer than the last trip. Ten months after the accident, his dad went out on a trip and never came back. When Barnabas figured out that his dad was not coming home, he wrote in his journal:

Dad is not coming home. They say that the guy who ran into Mom is now in jail. I hope they both rot in hell.

At first, Nancy took both Barnabas and his mother to church every Sunday morning. She would come over and talk to his mom two or three times a week. It was obvious to Barnabas that these visits were difficult for Nancy. Previously a woman who always had a smile on her face, Nancy now wore a perpetual mournful expression. Then, one week, Nancy went on vacation, and she never came back. Since she was their ride to church, they stopped going altogether.

Several years later, during Barnabas' sophomore year in high school, he saw Nancy when she came into a supermarket where Barnabas had a job bagging groceries. Money had become a problem immediately after the accident. After his dad left, Barnabas had gotten a paper route to help with finances. From then on, he had always held a job. He learned to enjoy working; it became his way of life. After a couple of years, his dad began paying child support, but it was not regular, and Barnabas learned that he could not depend on it.

Nancy walked up to him and said, "Barnabas, how are you doing?"

Barnabas forced a smile and responded, "We're hanging in there. Surviving, I guess."

"How about your dear mother? How is she?"

"She is doing as well as can be expected. I know that she misses your visits. She asks about you all the time." The last statement was a lie. In fact, she had not asked about Nancy in two years.

"I know. I feel so guilty about not coming over. It's just so hard on me to see her like that. I just prefer to remember her the way she was."

Barnabas paused and knew that he should have said something innocuous, but he couldn't resist the temptation. "You're fortunate that life is so easy for you." Nancy stared at him for a second and chose not to respond. He saw her on two other occasions in the supermarket after that, but she always used another checkout line.

Apart from working, the other things that kept Barnabas going during high school were his mother, his journal, and basketball. He never really had any friends. It wasn't that he disliked people; it was just that he didn't think that he had time for them. By the time his mother died, being alone had become a way of life.

His mother had qualified for Medicaid, so while Barnabas was in school, at work, or at basketball practice, an LPN would look in on his mother every three hours. At that point, she was spending more time in prayer than ever before, but he concluded that her prayers were not being answered. Instead of anger, he opted for fatalism: things were going to be whatever they were going to be, and he had no power to change them.

Before her accident, Barnabas fought his mother's relentless efforts to get him to sit through church services. It was a small church. He was pretty much at home there; he liked Sunday school but hated the main service when the preacher droned on and on in monotone. No one ever laughed during his sermons, and Barnabas couldn't understand why anyone, particularly his mother, listened so intently. Barnabas would fidget and yawn and generally do everything a boy his age could do to demonstrate that he was ready to go home.

When he was nine years old, his mother's frustration boiled over, and she took him home during the middle of the sermon one day. She didn't say a word as they drove, but Barnabas knew that his mother was furious. As soon as they got home, she went into the kitchen, pulled out a chair, and faced it toward the wall. In a calm voice, she said, "All I really ask of you is to give me an hour each week sitting in a pew without being a distraction. Sit in the chair. You are going to sit there for an hour. While you are sitting there, you decide whether you are going to give me that hour in church or here at home. But you are going to give me that hour either here or there. You choose."

It was the worst hour of his young life to that point. The next week he sat in church, afraid to move for fear that any movement would be counted as a distraction. His mother pulled out a book from her purse. The title was *Crossword Puzzles for Kids*. She handed him the book and a pencil. It took him only a few minutes to become engrossed.

By the end of the fifth Sunday, he had finished the book. On the sixth Sunday, his mother gave him another book of crossword puzzles, which was more difficult than the first. Six months later, he wrote his first journal entry:

> Hello. My mother promised me that she would give me fifty cents if I wrote something in this journal that she gave me. Goodbye.

Three weeks later, he actually started to write thoughts that reflected the events of the day. Two months after that, his mother refused to give him any more money. She said, "I only promised to pay for the first three entries. Consider the other payments a gift."

By then he was hooked. From age nine until he was in law school, Barnabas wrote in his journal every night. When he was eleven, he moved his journal writing from a notebook to a used laptop that his mother had gotten him for Christmas. When he got older, he would write before he went to sleep, and he would often think back about the wisdom his mother displayed when he was nine. His mother knew the gifts of her child; Barnabas loved to write.

When Barnabas was six years old, he got a small basketball for Christmas—no more than six inches in diameter—and a plastic basketball hoop. He spent every hour of every day playing with this simple setup. Even his father seemed to be amused by the fact that Barnabas got so much joy out of doing such a simple thing. For his eleventh birthday, his mother bought him a regulation-size ball and a ten-foot basket. They put it up in the driveway. Even from her wheelchair, she encouraged him to practice.

Barnabas would occasionally play at school during lunchtime or in gym class, but mostly he practiced alone. He even purchased cheap videos online that taught him how to shoot and handle the ball. There was something about the ball and hoop that drew him in.

Barnabas hadn't gone out for the junior high team because he was one of the shorter kids in school, but he did decide to try out as a freshman in high school, standing at a mere five feet five inches tall. Despite his height, he easily made the team. Between his junior and senior years, Barnabas had grown five and a half inches, entering his senior year at six feet two inches tall. His newfound height, combined with some of the best ball-handling and shooting skills among his teammates, made him a formidable player.

Barnabas knew that he wanted to go to college, but he could only manage it financially if he got a basketball scholarship. When a scholarship opportunity did come along, he almost didn't get it because of Bill Cushman.

Barnabas first met Bill during their senior year of high school, but he had heard of him the summer before. Barnabas had been bagging groceries when he overheard a couple of girls from his class who were waiting to check out. They giggled excitedly.

"Did you hear that Bill Cushman is transferring from Hillside Prep?" said the tall one.

"Yeah, I heard," the short one responded. "He's really hot. I hope I have him in all of my classes."

* * *

Bill Cushman woke up in his seat in first-class on his direct flight from Anchorage to Chicago. It had been a good two weeks of vacation. He had never been to Alaska before. He caught a twenty-five-pound salmon, and he saw Mount McKinley on a clear day, a mere twenty miles from the base. It was magnificent. In the higher elevations, it was covered with pure white snow, and it dominated everything around it. That was the way Bill wanted everyone to think about him.

The man he admired most was his father; a man whom Bill knew was rich and powerful without him ever saying so. The last two presidential candidates from his dad's political party had dined at their house. His father was on a first-name basis with the governor, and Bill frequently heard them talk on the telephone.

While he revered his father, Bill could only pity his mother. In her wedding pictures she was strikingly beautiful, but the aging process had not been kind to her. At forty-two years old, she was prematurely gray with wrinkled skin, and she looked like she was almost sixty. Bill didn't begrudge her that, but he couldn't understand why she put up with his dad's affairs. She never talked about it, and she acted like she didn't know, but even his friends at prep school would make snide remarks about it.

When his parents married, his dad was laden with debt, but from what Bill was able to surmise, his mother had money from inheriting a fortune. The two had met two weeks after his dad graduated with his MBA in finance, and they were married two months later. His dad had taken his mom's inheritance, doubled it within the first three years, and never looked back.

Bill didn't have any siblings, and he never asked why. At times he wondered if he had siblings from some of the other women his dad had affairs with, but he supposed that if any of them had come up pregnant, his dad would have insisted on an abortion.

He respected his dad. His dad always set the rules. He did whatever he wanted whenever he wanted to. He wanted to be like his dad. He didn't want anyone telling him what to do.

It turned out that Bill was in Barnabas' English class, but he didn't make an appearance until the fourth day of school. Barnabas later learned that Bill had been on a fishing trip in Alaska, causing him to miss the first three days of school.

Bill walked in during the middle of class. He had been permanently expelled from his former prep school when he was found in the back seat of his sports car with the daughter of the school's algebra teacher the evening of junior prom. Bill was already on probation from when the school found out that his English paper had been written by one of his friends. His dad had tried to get Bill into other prep schools, but he had become too notorious.

Leonard Aspinall, the English teacher, stopped class and took the papers Bill was carrying with him. "Take a desk," Aspinall instructed in a surprisingly surly tone of voice as he pointed to the back of the room. Barnabas guessed that Bill already had a reputation among the teachers, and that reputation was not good.

Bill winked at two girls wearing cheerleading uniforms sitting in the front row. Enthusiastically, they smiled back. Bill had reddish-brown hair, an easy smile, and was a natural athlete. He enjoyed the attention that came with money, good looks, and graceful, athletic moves.

At eighteen years old, Bill stood at six foot four. Later, in the spring semester, he was elected class president, but he was a poor leader. He made it a habit to delegate all of his duties, and he shirked responsibility. Nothing ever seemed to get accomplished with Bill in charge, but no one except Barnabas ever seemed to care.

At the start of the semester, Barnabas liked Leonard Aspinall. His politics were strongly liberal, but Barnabas leaned to the liberal side as well, so he enjoyed listening to Aspinall's homilies. Eventually, however, Barnabas became annoyed with the class altogether. Aspinall's speeches became tiresome, and Bill's constant wisecracks made Aspinall look like a fool. Bill was usually good for a minimum of three quips per class.

"Mr. Aspinall, you're starting class two minutes early."

"Mr. Aspinall, you need to straighten your tie."

"Mr. Aspinall, did you say 'deer' or 'beer'?"

The only time that Aspinall rebuked Bill was when Bill said, "I hate that expression 'when the rubber meets the road.' It gives me the creeps."

If Barnabas had been teaching the class, he would not have tolerated Bill's disruptive comments. It made Barnabas wonder if Bill actually had something on Aspinall.

During Barnabas' junior year, the basketball team had gone 18-10, with all the starters coming back. The local papers rated them fifth in the state. When Bill showed up for team tryouts senior year, it was evident that Coach Martinson had already been briefed about him. Bill loved to shoot, but he didn't rebound, and he especially didn't play defense. He made the team anyway. Barnabas thought that Bill could have been a great player if he worked at his game, but Bill didn't work at anything.

The first game of the playoffs, Bill cost the team a victory, and their season ended. They lost by one point. Bill gave up a layup in the last twenty seconds of the game. He just waved his hands as his opponent drove past him. The coach immediately called a time-out and spent most of it in animated conversation with Bill. Bill just stood there and smirked.

Coach Martinson then called for a play where Barnabas was supposed to pass the ball to Bill on the wing and then go over to Bill's man, fake a screen, and break for the basket. Bill was supposed to pass the ball back to Barnabas for an easy layup. Coach Martinson liked to call the play only once a game, but it always worked. The coach used it only at critical times; this was the most critical time of the team's entire season.

Barnabas let the clock run down to six seconds, passed the ball to Bill, and ran over to Bill's man, faking a screen. Barnabas then broke for the basket, leaving his man behind. He was wide open. Bill, however, decided not to pass and instead took a twenty-five-foot jump shot while he was closely guarded. The shot didn't even come close. The other team got the rebound, and the season was over.

Barnabas purposely avoided Bill after that last game. His career had ended after the first game of the playoffs because of Bill. The team was 22-3 prior to the game.

Early in the basketball season, Bill had attached himself to Barnabas. *It's probably because I'm the point guard, the one who can feed him the ball,* he assumed. He would have preferred that Bill leave him alone altogether, but Coach Martinson preached team unity.

During lunch, Barnabas liked to eat quickly and then spend time studying or practicing free throws in the gym. But Bill would always come over and spend at least half of the lunch break talking with him about girls. Virtually everyone in the school would have enjoyed Bill's attention, but Barnabas could have done without it. Barnabas would normally listen unresponsively, hoping that Bill would get the point and leave him alone. Bill would usually move on after fifteen minutes or so, but in Barnabas' mind, that was fifteen wasted minutes.

Eventually, Bill seemed to sense that Barnabas was annoyed, but that only seemed to encourage Bill even more. One lunch period, Bill called Barnabas "Barney," and Barnabas made a mistake that he soon regretted.

"Don't call me Barney," he said. "I don't like that name." Barnabas didn't even like his given name, but he especially despised "Barney." His mother had named him after a biblical person, but the name wasn't a popular one, and Barnabas was afraid that people would think of him as a television cartoon character. Bill then knew that Barnabas hated "Barney" and could use it to get under his skin. And if Bill wanted to goad Barnabas further, he would address him by his initials—B.M.

* * *

When Bill started school, he was pleased. Most people admired him, and he was able to get by borrowing other people's notes and copying their papers. He learned quickly that if he were going to make a name for himself on the basketball team, however, he needed to get close to Barnabas Mitchell. Mitchell was only two inches shorter than he, but he played point guard. He was not vocal, but he was a leader by example. Mitchell could do it all on the basketball court: handle the ball, play rugged defense, rebound, and shoot. If Bill was going to get the ball and eventually the glory, Barnabas Mitchell was going to have to pass it to him.

Bill spoke to his dad, who said, "Don't worry about it. I'll talk with the coach." Bill never did learn what his dad said, but it seemed to work. During practice, Coach Martinson was constantly yelling at the team to feed Bill the ball.

Bill began sitting next to Barnabas in their two classes together, and he regularly sat with Mitchell during lunch, but nothing seemed to work. Unlike virtually everyone else in the school, Mitchell could barely disguise his contempt for Bill, and Bill didn't know why. He had never done anything to offend Mitchell. Mitchell was not rich, was not in the popular group of cool kids, and didn't have a girlfriend. Bill had heard that his mother was seriously injured and that he was devoted to her. Bill thought that Mitchell, by trying to ignore him, believed that he was better than Bill, and it irritated him. What seemed to set the two apart even more were Mitchell's precious values. He didn't cheat, he worked hard, and he seemed to pride himself—without saying so—on his honesty.

Bill couldn't understand it. Mitchell had the opportunity to become popular if only he had been willing to submit to Bill's guidance and tutelage. Bill began to despise Mitchell and probed for soft spots in his personality. He quickly learned that Mitchell did not like being called "Barney," and Mitchell almost took a swing at him one time when, at the end of basketball practice, Bill called him B.M. From then on, whenever Bill wanted to put Mitchell in his place, he called him Barney, with the lingering threat of B.M. being next.

* * *

By the middle of the first semester, Bill began sitting sat next to Barnabas in the back row of Aspinall's class. Barnabas would have preferred that he sit somewhere else, but it was not worth saying anything about it. Bill didn't study, and as the semester wore on, Aspinall was growing less patient with him and his antics. There was a big mid-term coming up the last week before Christmas vacation, and Barnabas didn't know how Bill was going to pass. Secretly, he hoped that Bill would take an F in the course, which would disqualify him from playing on the basketball team in the coming spring semester.

The morning of the test, Barnabas walked into the room, and he was surprised that Bill was already there. Bill was typically the last one to arrive. Barnabas sat down next to Bill and noticed that the tests were already on the desks. In a stern voice, Aspinall said, "You have fifty minutes to complete the test. As soon as you sit down, write your name at the top of the paper, and you may begin."

Barnabas noticed that Bill had his left hand in his lap with his fist clenched. He also saw Aspinall looking intently at the class as he began patrolling the aisles. They had had quizzes in class, but Aspinall had never demonstrated this level of commitment to exam security before. Barnabas suspected that Bill did not figure on Aspinall monitoring the exam that closely.

As Aspinall made his way down the aisle, Barnabas heard the sound of rustling paper coming from Bill's direction. Aspinall slowly approached Barnabas and Bill. He stood beside Bill for a full minute. Barnabas was trying to concentrate on the test, but it was impossible. Finally, Aspinall spoke. "Open up," he instructed Bill.

There was a long pause.

He spoke again, this time in a louder and more adamant tone. "Open your hand."

Barnabas couldn't help himself. He dropped his head and glanced under his arm at Bill's desk. Bill's left hand was open, which revealed crib notes. Aspinall grabbed the crib notes and returned to his desk. He sat there for the remainder of the period with a satisfied expression on his face. But Aspinall did let Bill finish the test.

During lunch, Barnabas asked Bill, "What are you going to do? Is he going to flunk you? What will that do to your eligibility to play on the team?" Barnabas immediately regretted asking, because it implied that he thought Bill was an important player.

Bill responded, "Don't worry about it. I have it handled."

When Barnabas arrived at school the next morning, he saw Bill, Bill's father and mother, and Coach Martinson coming out of the principal's office. He caught Bill's eye, and Bill gave him his signature smirk, turning his right thumb upward. Bill had it under control as promised. As he sat down later that morning in Aspinall's class, Barnabas wondered if Aspinall was going to say anything. Aspinall bore an angry countenance, but he said nothing.

The next day, Barnabas talked to Bill. "So, you dodged a bullet. I guess that's the difference between you and me. I would rather take an F than cheat, and with you it's the other way around. One day this is going to catch up with you."

Bill slowly looked up. "You do what you have to do. A man wiser than me once said, 'Nice guys always finish last.' You may be a nice guy, Barney, but you're always going to finish last."

* * *

After high school, Bill went to an elite college on the East Coast where his father had gone to school. Barnabas assumed that Bill's father had used his connections and made a large donation to the school to secure Bill's admission.

CHAPTER TWO

Barnabas figured that a college education was not in his future, but the week after his high school basketball career ended, the coach for Illini College came to his house and offered him a scholarship.

After Bill had cost the team a victory in the first game of the playoffs, Barnabas was devastated. He had missed the chance to play in front of some important scouts who would be attending games throughout the rest of the playoffs. Barnabas had received a few letters of interest during the year, but they were all from schools that would require him to live away from home, and Barnabas was not about to leave his mother. No local college had shown any interest, so Barnabas assumed that his education would be over after graduation. Needless to say, he was grateful that Illini had come along.

Illini College was an NAIA school, and in his junior and senior years there, Barnabas led the team to a fourth-place—and later, a second-place—finish in the national tournament. A scout for the Trailblazers talked to Barnabas after his final game, giving him a chance to play at the pro level, but he would have to go to Europe and work on his game over there. He thanked the scout for showing interest but explained that the health of his mother prevented him from leaving home. Besides, he had never been farther east than Indiana. The idea of living in Europe was truly frightening.

On January 1, at the start of his final semester, Barnabas' mother suffered a major stroke. Her physician had warned him that given her condition, she was susceptible to strokes. The entire right side of her body was paralyzed from the neck down. She had to be fed intravenously. For two years he had already had to bathe her and help her while she was on the toilet. Now, given her condition, he was required to put on sterile plastic gloves to assist with her bowel movements.

In the abstract, Barnabas' circumstances appeared extremely trying, but he always adjusted relatively quickly. The most stressful part was the pain she had to deal with. One month after the stroke, he wrote:

> Mom is in a lot of discomfort. She can't sleep more than a couple of hours, and she groans a lot when her system is stopped up. The medication helps some, but she is paralyzed on her left side, and she even needs help with her natural bowel movements. The day nurse taught me how to help. At first I thought it would be difficult for her to pass the waste, but as long as you are gentle, it's not so bad. When you're finished, you can tell that it has relieved a lot of pain. She is able to sleep, and she can regain comfort for several hours. The slight inconvenience is worth it. It is the very least that I can do for her. I fear that she is not going to be with me much longer. I suppose I am being selfish, but I don't want to let her go.

On April 1, his mother died. The funeral was sparsely attended. He got the minister at her old church to preside. There were some neighbors and a few of her older friends from work. His college basketball coach was there, along with Coach Martinson. Barnabas didn't notify Nancy because he was afraid that she might attempt to offer words of consolation, and he didn't want to hear them from her.

During the service, he looked around and saw his dad in the back. By the time the service was over, he had left. Barnabas wondered how his dad had learned that she had died.

Several people came up to him and offered trite consolations: "Well, she's now in a place where she is not suffering," "She is in a better place now," and the one he hated the most: "At least your ordeal is over now." Barnabas knew that these people were well-meaning, but they couldn't understand that it was more than his mother dying. She was the reason he got up each morning and persevered. Now she was gone, and there was a huge void in his life. The more she needed him—relied on him—the stronger his attachment to her grew. The loss was devastating, and no one seemed to understand. That evening, he went home and wrote five pages in his journal.

Barnabas fell into a deep depression that lasted a month. He had no real friends. He had no real goals. His life was his mother. Four weeks later he was home alone going through the house, deciding what to keep and what to throw away. He was cleaning out his mom's closet, and on the shelf above the clothes rack, he found a handgun. He put it down on the pile of things to take to the pawnshop. The only things he kept were some completed crossword puzzle books that his mom had saved and her wedding band and engagement ring. She told Barnabas that her grandmother had worn them. That evening, he wrote in his journal:

> I was cleaning out Mom's house when I found a gun in her closet that Dad must have left there. I almost used it on myself. I do enjoy writing and playing basketball, but I don't think those things are enough to give life any meaning. I have friends but no close friends. If there is a God, He certainly has abandoned me. I look around, and I see people my age living for their own desires. But that seems to be a life that is as empty as mine. So why didn't I pull the trigger? The only reason I have is that it would dishonor my mother. So, if I'm ever asked what meaning I have in my life, I would have to say it's to honor my mother.

Barnabas spent the next week lying around the house doing nothing. He had to decide what to do with his life. Despite caring for his mom and his work schedule and basketball, Barnabas had been able to carry a B average in college, and thanks in part to his basketball scholarship, he had less than $20,000 in debt.

He majored in English since he enjoyed writing and literature, but he didn't know what field he was going to pursue. He knew he didn't want to be a teacher, and there was little else he could do with an English degree. He thought about graduate school, but his grades were not strong enough for anyone to pay for his education. His mother had had no estate to leave him. It turned out that she had put a reverse mortgage on the house, but at least she did not leave Barnabas burdened with her debt.

Out of exasperation, Barnabas went to the college placement department and took a career aptitude test. "Attorney" came out on top by a substantial margin. On advice from a counselor, he took the LSAT and scored in the top three percent of all test takers. He surprised himself. He applied to three law schools and got into all three, but the scholarships offered covered only a fraction of the cost. He knew that he couldn't work if he were going to do well in law school. With tuition, fees, rent, food, and other expenses, law school was going to cost him $30,000 a year.

He decided to enroll at Midwestern College of Law because it offered him the most money. Midwestern was one of six law schools in the city. By reputation, it was not the best, but it was not the worst either.

Law school started the third week in August. Barnabas was waiting in line to enroll when he heard a familiar voice in back of him say, "Well, Barney, how the hell are you?"

Barnabas turned around, but he already knew who it was. "Bill, what brings you here?"

"Just like you, Barney. Going to law school."

Barnabas chose not to greet him warmly. If he had the choice of going through law school with no friends or with Bill being his only friend, he'd choose the former.

"Why aren't you at some elite school on the East Coast, Bill?" Barnabas already knew the answer. Bill's father's influence was not strong enough to get him into Harvard or Yale.

But Bill gave a good answer. "I was told that if I was going to come back to Illinois to practice, it was a good idea to go to a law school here."

Typical Bill, claiming that he had a choice when he didn't. There is no way he got into an Ivy League law school.

Barnabas elected to part on a softer note. "Well, best of luck to you, Bill. I guess we will be seeing a lot of each other." *And the less time the better,* thought Barnabas.

In the first year of law school, Barnabas and Bill were in all of the same classes. While Barnabas took the advice of the second- and third-year law students and prepared detailed outlines for each of his courses, Bill frequently missed class. And when he was in class, he usually was not prepared. Barnabas thought that Bill was smart enough to do well if he simply applied himself, but that just wasn't in Bill's nature.

Barnabas liked law school—unlike most of his fellow students—and he got good grades. He had a natural aptitude for it, and he had more time for studying than he'd had in undergrad. He started to make friends, and he thought about Bill as little as possible. There were several single girls in his class. The wives of his married friends frequently invited him over for dinner, and there always seemed to be a single girl who had been invited as well. But Barnabas decided not to get serious with anyone. He wanted to finish law school first, and since he was going to graduate with almost $100,000 in debt, he didn't want to even think about marriage until he had substantially reduced that amount. Otherwise, how could he afford to support a family?

During his second year of law school, Barnabas took an evidence class with Professor John Paulus. Out of 120 students in the class, Barnabas received the highest grade on the final exam. Barnabas had rarely spoken in class, but Professor Paulus was impressed by the analytical quality and writing style of Barnabas' final examination paper. After the grades were posted, Paulus asked Barnabas to be his research associate. Barnabas was delighted.

The last week of the fourth semester, Paulus called Barnabas into his office.

"Barnabas, as you know, I'm the faculty advisor to the school's moot court team, and I would like you to try out for it."

"Really? I'm not sure I would be any good."

"I know that you didn't have any debate experience in college, but your mind is quick. You will make an excellent trial lawyer. I am confident that with practice you will be able to make exceptional oral arguments. But the brief is fifty percent of the competition. Your writing skills are the best I have seen in a long time. If you get the right partner, you could go far."

Twenty students tried out for the team. They were given one week to write a legal memorandum, and each student then gave an oral argument in front of a faculty panel that pretended to be the United States Supreme Court. Two days later, the team members were posted outside of Professor Paulus' office:

Bill Cushman

Barnabas Mitchell

Barnabas looked at the names and sighed. It shouldn't have surprised him that Bill tried out. And he had no doubt that Bill had been very glib with the judges, but he was shocked that Bill's memorandum had measured up. He went to Professor Paulus' office an hour later.

"I don't think I can do this. I haven't told you this before, but I knew Bill in high school. He's lazy. He will not spend any time working on the brief. I'll have to do it all by myself."

Paulus was surprised to learn of their history but pressed Barnabas to stay on the team. "Barnabas, regardless of your issues with Cushman, I think that the two of you will be our best team. His memorandum was mediocre at best, but he did very well on the oral argument. The two of you have the potential to win this thing. You are about to become a professional. This means that on occasion you'll work with people you don't like. Frequently, you will be in front of a judge who you don't like. I honestly think that Cushman and you are our strongest team. You need to do this. It will be an excellent experience for you."

Barnabas looked at him plaintively. Professor Paulus looked back resolutely. Barnabas decided to forge ahead. He wanted to do it, and he didn't want to disappoint Paulus.

Each August, the national moot court organization sent out a comprehensive record of a hypothetical case to every law school in the country. Barnabas would have to write a brief that would count for fifty percent of the score. He and Bill would then participate in a tournament, giving oral arguments the weekend before Thanksgiving. There were eighteen schools in the Midwest, and each school sent one team to the competition. That meant that in order for Barnabas to go to nationals, he and Bill would have to defeat seventeen other teams.

When the case arrived, Barnabas began his research. He had no illusions about Bill's involvement. The day after the problem came in, he met with Bill.

"Bill, why don't you let me take a crack at the first draft of the brief, and you weigh in after that. I expect to have a first draft done by the first day of school."

Bill nodded and smiled. They both knew that he wouldn't do any work on the brief at all, and that was fine with Barnabas. Any contribution from Bill would only make it weaker.

That semester, Barnabas let his studies slide, spending sixty hours a week writing the brief. The organizers had assigned Midwestern the petitioner's side of the argument, which meant that Barnabas' hypothetical clients had lost their case in the supreme court of a hypothetical state.

Two regulations were being challenged by a Christian school: All non-public schoolteachers were required to attain a teaching certification from the State Board of Education, and all public school students were required to receive sex education at the fifth-grade level. It was apparent that the legislation was aimed at Christian schools in particular.

As Barnabas researched the problem, he fashioned an argument that justified the first regulation, but there was a dearth of authority to support the second regulation. Defending mandatory sex education in public schools only—and for eleven-year-olds—proved difficult. Quickly, Barnabas became fascinated with the problem, and in the end, he produced a brief that surpassed his own expectations.

Predictably, Bill showed up the day the brief was to be mailed out and signed his name to it. Barnabas intentionally put his name above Bill's on the signature line, even though Cushman came before Mitchell in the alphabet. Bill had done nothing, and Barnabas was not going to let it appear that Bill's contribution was in any way greater than or equal to his.

* * *

The brief was sent to the regional competition sponsor in the middle of October. That meant that Barnabas and Bill had five weeks to prepare for the oral competition, which would be held at Lincoln University College of Law located in the middle of the state. Each team was expected to argue both sides of the case.

Barnabas was surprised that Bill made all of the practices. He had never seen Bill work so hard at anything, but after the first week of practice, Barnabas figured out why. Barnabas reread the competition rules, and he learned that the regional competition sponsors would be awarding a medal to the student who gave the best oral argument. Bill wanted to win that medal.

Barnabas conceded that Bill worked hard on his style and his poise, but he unfortunately gave little effort to learning the intricacies created by the drafters of the problem. Barnabas worried that Bill's lack of diligence would come to haunt them both.

Barnabas tried to talk with Bill about his concerns, but Bill wouldn't listen. Barnabas enlisted Paulus' help, but that yielded only marginal results. There was no way to avoid the fact that both of them would have to argue.

To make it as easy as possible on Bill, Barnabas planned to take on the most difficult arguments and leave Bill the easier ones. This meant that when they would argue the petitioner's side—the side of the State—Barnabas would defend the sex education regulation while Bill defended the teaching certification. When they would argue the respondent's side—the side of the Christian school—Bill would argue that parents should not be forced to have sex education taught to their kids in public school while Barnabas argued that the State could not force Christian schoolteachers to obtain certification.

During the practice rounds, the judges, acting like they were sitting on the United States Supreme Court, peppered them with questions, asking why parents shouldn't reserve the right and responsibility for their children's sexual education. The questions became even more difficult when the judges learned that the mandatory sex education would take place in the fifth grade.

Inevitably, a judge would ask something along the lines of, "So this would mean that most of the children would only be eleven years old. Don't you think that's a little early to mandate sex education? Why couldn't a reasonable parent say that is too young while also contending that they want their children to learn about sex from them?"

After two practice rounds, Barnabas knew that he had to come up with a plausible response that would at least let him continue with his argument. So, in the third practice round when one of the judges predictably asked about the grade level of the mandatory sex education, Barnabas was ready.

"Your Honor, the most recent statistics show that more than five percent of the female population between twelve and fourteen years of age will become pregnant. More than half of these pregnancies will end in abortion. There is every reason to believe that many of these pregnancies go unreported. This education would come at a time in the child's life when he or she needs to know the facts about this important subject."

"Mr. Mitchell," the judge followed up, "that may be true for many children, but why not an exception for religious families where there is every reason to believe that their children will be informed and it is unlikely that the parents will permit such relationships to develop?"

Barnabas responded, "Your Honor, the statistics indicate that this problem is not exclusive to non-religious individuals. Anytime you have a rule with a uniform application, you are going to catch some people that don't need it, but you have to make it uniform in order to solve the problem. It is similar, if you will, to our rule that you cannot run a red light, even though you know that there are no other cars near the intersection. In many instances, you can run the light without consequence, but the danger posed by eliminating the rule surpasses the minimal invasion on a person's right to drive their car. This regulation represents a reasonable attempt to curb an epidemic."

His response satisfied the judge, so Barnabas used it in all of the subsequent practice rounds and in the competition later on.

One week before they left for the competition, Bill asked Barnabas to stay a few minutes after practice. "Barnabas, we have to decide who is going to do the rebuttal when we argue the petitioner's side. I want to do it. I am stronger on the oral argument than you are."

"Bill, I'm going to be blunt. You may be a flashier speaker than I am, but you don't know the problem. If you ever get a tough question, we're screwed."

"Look, we generally don't get that many questions in rebuttal anyway. It's only for five minutes. I'll be fine." Against his better judgment, Barnabas relented. Later, he would regret the decision.

CHAPTER THREE

On Friday at 9:30 p.m., the week before they were supposed to leave for the competition, Barnabas was tired and decided to go home after a long night of preparation. As he was leaving school, Bill and three of his friends were leaving as well. Bill insisted that Barnabas join them at a bar.

Barnabas called the four of them—Bill, Rick, Ted, and James—"the studs." Barnabas considered "studs" to be a derisive name, but the four of them actually liked it. They got to the bar and ordered five beers. Barnabas did not intend to stay long, just long enough so that he didn't seem rude.

After discussing where they were going to look for jobs after law school, the discussion turned to Virginia. Virginia was five foot ten and blonde and blue-eyed with Scandinavian features. She was a college cheerleader. She headed the Christian Legal Society at the law school, and she had the reputation of not sleeping around. Bill was strangely quiet, and then he made a proposal. "I have a wager for you."

The four others turned their attention to Bill.

"I say that we each throw five hundred dollars into the pot, and the first one of us that bangs her collects the full twenty-five hundred."

Immediately, Barnabas said, "I'm out."

The studs guffawed at Barnabas' quick decision. Barnabas was curious why Bill even proposed the bet.

"Bill, why are you doing this? Virginia will be difficult, if not impossible, for you to sleep with. As head of the Christian Legal Society, I think she'd be the one that you wouldn't want to bet on."

"Barney, it's not like I have any money at risk. If no one gets the job done, I'm not out any money. But if anyone can do it, it will be me."

Bill paused and then said something that surprised Barnabas. "Barney, I know that your pristine ears cringe at four-letter words, so in deference to your Puritan sensibilities, I'll say that she won't be the first Christian girl that I've slept with, and she won't be the last."

Barnabas didn't know if Bill was sincere in his purported concern about four-letter words or was just taking the opportunity to call him a Puritan, which Bill obviously thought was an insult.

At that point, Rick—who seemed to be looking for pointers—asked, "So, what's your trick?"

"I'm not going to give away all of my moves, but my grandmother was a devoted Christian, and I learned all of the jargon from her. First, you have to get them to believe that you share their beliefs. After you've done that, ask them where in the Bible Jesus condemns premarital sex. They won't be able to find a passage for you. After you have them thinking, then you share something with them that is highly personal. That is a good way to get their trust."

This piqued Barnabas' interest. "But I do remember when I was going to church that the Bible talks about fornication. I'm sure that I'm right about that."

"Well, Jesus never expressly condemned it. But if they want to talk about other passages, simply ask them to define fornication. Convince them that there's a difference between being promiscuous and really loving the person you're sleeping with."

Rick, Ted, and James chortled their approval. That was Barnabas' cue to leave. As he got up, he heard Bill say, "How am I going to prove that I'm the winner?"

Typical Bill, thought Barnabas.

He was tempted to warn Virginia about the bet, but he knew her only casually. She had invited him to attend a Christian Legal Society meeting once, and he had been somewhat gruff in declining. If he did warn her and no one attempted to seduce her, she would think he was messing with her. He reasoned that if Virginia were so shallow that she couldn't figure out what the studs were up to, she would be forced to learn one of life's difficult lessons. Barnabas had no further occasion to think about the bet until the following March.

The next day, Barnabas read the seventeen briefs that had been submitted by the other schools. He was particularly impressed by the brief submitted by Trinity Christian Law School.

CHAPTER FOUR

Stephanie Schultz called her father, Sam Schultz, and he picked up after the third ring

"Dad, are you and Mom still planning on going to the competition to see me argue?"

"Of course. Wouldn't miss it for the world."

"I'll have to drive down with the team, but I'm sure that win, lose, or draw, I can ride back with you."

"How do you think you're going to do?"

"I've read all the briefs, and I think we are in good shape in every case but one."

"But one? What do you mean?"

"This brief from Midwestern Law School is exquisite. The research is thorough, and it is beautifully written. It's almost like poetry if you can believe that. If their oral arguments are anything like that brief, the best we can hope for is second place."

"Stephanie, maybe you are giving them too much credit. It's natural to see the flaws in your own efforts and excellence in the efforts of others."

"Dad, I'll fax it over to you. You'll see what I mean."

"Just because they wrote a great brief doesn't mean that you will ever see them in competition," responded her dad.

"I hate to say it, but I hope they are gone early so we never will."

Stephanie tracked the progress of the competition, and as her team won every round, so did the Midwestern team. As her team marched to the finals, so did the Midwestern team, just as she had feared. She had not even bothered to look at the program for the finals. Her heart skipped a couple of beats when she saw a name on the final argument program: the Honorable Oliver Kraft, Seventh Circuit Court of Appeals.

She sought out her father. "Dad, do you know who is going to preside over the final round?"

Sam Schultz replied, "Didn't bother to look. Who?"

"Judge Kraft. Is there any chance that he will remember me?"

"Pretty good chance. When I see him, he asks how you're doing."

"You know what that means?"

"Stephanie, I agree. You're going to have to disclose it."

* * *

It started out as one of the worst days of his life and ended as one of the best.

Barnabas and Bill had made it to the final round of the regional moot court championship. It was scheduled to start at 6:00 p.m. on Saturday and Barnabas had arrived thirty minutes early. The winner was going to advance to the national championship in Washington, D.C., with the championship round argued before an actual justice of the United States Supreme Court.

Barnabas was in the courtroom, sitting alone at the counsel table. Ten minutes later, one of the organizers approached him. "Are you Mr. Cushman or Mr. Mitchell?"

"Mr. Mitchell."

"Mr. Mitchell, you need to come with me. We have a development, and we need your input."

"Professor Paulus, our faculty advisor, is in the building. Let me get him."

"Okay. Meet us in Room 343, and hurry please."

Barnabas located Paulus, and the two of them approached Room 343. Barnabas knocked on the door.

"Please come in," a voice said.

They entered the room, and Barnabas saw a middle-aged man and a slightly younger woman with a nametag standing behind a desk. Barnabas assumed that she was part of the organization team. On the right, he noticed a man about Professor Paulus' age, a younger man about Barnabas' age, and the most striking young woman that he had ever seen.

They all smiled, but the young woman's smile had a warmth to it that he had not seen before. It was almost apologetic, like she was saying, "I'm sorry to have created this problem."

The woman with the nametag opened the conversation. "Mr. Mitchell and Professor Paulus, first let me congratulate you on making the finals.

I would like to introduce you to Stephanie Schultz, William Beeson, and Professor Kratz from Trinity Christian Law School."

They all extended their hands and exchanged the proper greetings. The organizer then got to the issue. "Ms. Schultz indicates that there may be a problem with one of the judges. Before anything was done, we thought that your team should be notified and given the opportunity to provide us with your input. Ms. Schultz, please tell them what you perceive to be the problem."

Barnabas thought it odd that the organizer used the word "perceive." It was like she was put off by the fact that Stephanie Schultz had raised an issue at all.

Stephanie Schultz explained. "I have met one of the judges. Judge Oliver Kraft sits on the Seventh Circuit Court of Appeals, and my dad is one of the lead agents for the FBI in Chicago. When Judge Kraft was sitting at the district court level, my dad regularly appeared as a witness in his court. The two of them got to be friends. When I was in my first year of law school, my dad took me into Judge Kraft's chambers and introduced me. I don't know if he will remember me. He certainly will know the name 'Schultz,' and it is very possible that he will remember that I am Sam Schultz's daughter. Given the nature of the competition, I am not comfortable if he judges the final round."

The organizer didn't seem to think that it was that important of an issue, and it was apparent to Barnabas that the organizer was hoping we would agree with her.

Barnabas studied Stephanie as she was talking. She had auburn-brown hair that curled under just above her shoulders. She was about five foot eight and had sparkling, hazel-green eyes. There was something different about her that he could not articulate. Although she was very attractive and clearly took pride in her appearance, he was drawn to her for other reasons. She had a wholesome confidence. She smiled easily and naturally. He was impressed with her honesty. She could have argued the round, and no one would have been the wiser about her association with the judge. Even if it was learned later that she knew the judge, there was nothing in the competition rules that prohibited him from being the judge. And she had no obligation to tell anyone about her relationship. Her honesty and forthrightness were compelling.

It was Barnabas' turn to talk. "I admire Ms. Schultz's candor and honesty. If we don't substitute the judge and she wins, she will always wonder if she won for reasons other than merit. If she were to lose, she would always wonder if Judge Kraft, in an effort to be more than fair, held her to a higher standard than my team. Under the circumstances, I think it would be best if we found another judge."

The organizer frowned, but she had no choice.

"Judge Greg Palmer is a local state judge, and he judged two rounds last night. He didn't sit on either of your rounds. He can come here, but we'll have to start ten minutes late. The final round will begin promptly at six ten p.m."

Paulus and Barnabas were the last to leave. "What an honest woman. How many law students in her position do you think would have done the same thing?" Barnabas asked as they walked to the courtroom.

"Not very many, Barnabas. I agree with you. It was a classy thing to do."

They arrived at 5:55 p.m. and the courtroom was packed. Seated immediately behind Stephanie Schultz were a man and a woman in their early fifties. The woman had the same color hair as Stephanie, and she appeared to be only an inch shorter. Barnabas assumed that the couple must be her mother and father.

Bill made his entrance at 6:08 p.m., a mere two minutes before the start of the round. Paulus was obviously perturbed that Bill had chosen to wait to make his entrance until the last moment. It was a purposeful move. He was perhaps hoping to break the opposing counsel's concentration, but it was certainly so that everyone would notice him. There were easily 200 people in the audience.

Bill went over to the opposing counsel's table. William Beeson and Stephanie both stood. Bill smiled at them and shook their hands.

Paulus had already briefed Bill about the situation with the judge, and Bill scolded Barnabas for agreeing to the change.

"Barney, it isn't going to make any difference. I have never felt better about a competition. I don't think I can lose."

That morning, Barnabas had warned Bill that Trinity Christian's brief was extremely well written, that Barnabas' brief would not necessarily carry the day if the oral arguments were a draw. But Bill had been dismissive. "They're a new school, they're Christians, and their academic standards are not that high. They won't be a problem."

At exactly 6:10 p.m., the side doors opened, and a clerk pounded the gavel. They all rose, and the clerk announced the judges. On the left was Judge Palmer, in the middle was Judge Sally Gibson, who sat on the state appellate court, and on the right was Judge Thurston Gilmore, who sat on the Seventh Circuit Court of Appeals.

Barnabas and Bill were going to argue for the petitioner, which meant that Bill would argue a five-minute rebuttal after the other side finished. The judges sat down, and the chief judge nodded to Barnabas and Bill. At the time, it was the most important hour of Barnabas' life.

Bill argued for the first ten minutes and—as promised—he rose to the occasion. It was the best that Barnabas had ever heard Bill argue. He exuded confidence and anticipated all of the questions. It was a relatively simple argument for Bill to make, but he had done it well. Barnabas was pleased.

Then Barnabas argued for fifteen minutes. Three minutes in, the judges besieged him with questions. Of course the judges were well prepared, but so was Barnabas. He had a more difficult argument than Bill, and the judges appeared to admire his ability to answer them in a precise, cogent manner.

However, his worries returned when William Beeson began his arguments. He demonstrated a superior understanding and clarity of thought. Barnabas kept checking his watch, hoping that time passed quickly so Beeson would sit down. Finally, he was through.

As Stephanie stood, Barnabas hoped that she would wilt under the pressure; she was tackling a very difficult argument. But she was stronger than Beeson. He shouldn't have been surprised. She was on point with each question, citing the relevant authority. She could not be rattled. It was a highly impressive performance.

As Bill stood up to give the rebuttal, Barnabas predicted that the final result would be determined by the brief. If the judges thought that Trinity Christian's brief was better than his, they deserved to win. If his brief was stronger, he and Bill had a good chance of going to the national championship.

One minute into his argument, Bill got the dreaded question from the Judge Gibson. "Mr. Cushman, I understand that the mandatory sex education class is required for fifth-grade students. Why can't Christian parents, or all parents for that matter, reserve the right—for personal, moral, or religious reasons—to provide sex education to their own children as they see fit, particularly at such an early age?

Bill had never been asked that question in the preparation rounds. It had only been given to Barnabas. Bill paused too long as he struggled for words. As he sat, Barnabas hoped that Bill had been listening in the rehearsal rounds when Barnabas was asked the identical question. But Bill had not been listening. He offered one of his quips. "Your Honor, we believe that the more anyone can learn about sex, the better."

Judge Palmer chuckled, but the other two were not amused. Both frowned at the response. They were lost, and Bill didn't seem to know it.

When the round was over, Barnabas and Bill shook hands with Stephanie Schultz and William Beeson, and all exchanged the ritual "good job." Barnabas returned to the counsel table and sat there glumly, waiting for the inevitable bad news. Professor Paulus approached him and put his hand on Barnabas' shoulder. Leaning over, he said, "You were right. Bill's laziness cost you a chance to go to the nationals. I'm sorry."

"You called it the way you saw it. If it hadn't been for your encouragement, I never would have tried out, and I never would have pursued being a trial attorney."

Fifteen minutes later, the judges returned. Before they announced the winner, all three judges offered critiques of the young law students. All were given the usual accolades of what great lawyers they were going to be.

Ten minutes later, Judge Gibson announced the decision. "First, I have been asked to announce the winning team for the best brief. We are advised that the winning team is here tonight. In fact, both the first-place and second-place winners are represented in this final round. Now, without further statement, I have been asked to announce that, out of eighteen teams in the competition, the team from Midwestern Law School won this year's best brief award."

The audience applauded, and Barnabas looked at Bill. Bill smiled at him, signaling his approval with both of his thumbs up.

Maybe this is a good omen, Barnabas hoped.

The applause subsided, and Judge Gibson continued. "The winner of this year's Midwest Regional Moot Court Tournament is Trinity Christian Law School."

The applause was stronger, and Barnabas sat dejectedly. It meant that they had won on the brief but lost in the oral argument.

Bill leaned over and whispered into Barnabas' ear. "If only you had been stronger in the oral argument," he said and stormed out of the courtroom. Bill didn't even realize that he had screwed up. Barnabas wanted to leave as quickly as possible and head for home.

Professor Paulus came down to the table. "Barnabas, I know how much you wanted to win this. It wasn't your fault. I should have heeded your warnings and kept Bill off the team."

"I'll admit I'm depressed. Let's get out of here."

The three had driven to the competition in one car, but Bill wasn't ready to leave. "They're going to announce the medal winner for best advocate at a reception in the student lounge," he explained, "and I would like to see who's going to get it."

Barnabas should have known. Bill didn't have any idea that he had no chance of getting that medal. And, of course, Bill wouldn't be willing to miss any opportunity to attend a social function and hit on the girls from the other schools.

Frustrated, Barnabas went over to the lounge where they were serving drinks. He got himself a diet soda and sat in the corner. He was tempted to try and get Paulus to overrule Bill and force him to leave early, but then he saw Paulus in the corner, happily engaged in conversation with a couple of professors from the other schools. He sat alone in silence.

Barnabas ruminated about how it had gone wrong. He kicked himself for not doing a better job drilling Bill on the questions. He castigated himself for even letting Bill do the rebuttal. He then looked up and watched in amusement as Bill went to each girl in the room, attempting to woo them with his good looks and charm. After ten minutes, Stephanie Schultz walked into the room with her parents, and Bill made a beeline for her.

This is going to be interesting, thought Barnabas.

Bill approached Stephanie, ignoring her parents. She extended her hand as he approached. Bill had his back turned to Barnabas, and it was difficult to read Stephanie's lips. Barnabas guessed that she was congratulating him. Bill put his hand on her shoulder, and she frowned slightly and backed away.

Undaunted, Bill stepped forward and grabbed her lightly by the elbow. Clearly, either Bill did not know that the older man and woman behind her were her father and mother, or Bill did know but didn't care. Meanwhile, her father was about to step forward and intervene when Stephanie glanced at him with a stern expression, as if to say, "I can handle this."

She firmly grabbed Bill's hand and removed it promptly. At that point, Bill got the message and started to back off.

At least there is one attractive girl who is not interested in Bill's bullshit.

But then, something even more surprising occurred. Her father asked Bill a question, and Bill turned and pointed in Barnabas' direction. Immediately, Stephanie Schultz and her parents walked toward his table. The closer they got, the more obvious it was that they wanted to talk to him. As he stood to greet them, he wondered what they wanted to talk about.

Stephanie spoke first as she extended her hand. "Mr. Mitchell, can I call you Barnabas? I would like you to meet my parents, Sam and Ruth Schultz."

Barnabas smiled, and they all shook hands.

"Stephanie, please call me Barnabas."

"Barnabas, I just wanted to congratulate you on that exquisite brief you wrote. My father and I both enjoyed reading it. My dad went to law school and works for the FBI. He was a big help going through law school."

Barnabas was impressed that her father had read his brief. He smiled. "Well, I did get some help," he felt obliged to say.

But Stephanie Schultz would have none of it. "If you are referring to your partner, I may be young, but I have read enough briefs to recognize that yours was written by a single person with a special style. Besides, I don't think your partner is capable of writing something like that given the way he argued."

Stephanie Schultz's mom quickly interjected. "Stephanie!"

But Stephanie would not back off. "Why object, Mom? It's true."

Barnabas smiled. They sat down and began talking. Ten minutes into their conversation, they were interrupted by the announcement that Stephanie had won the prize for best oral argument. Her smile was gracious and infectious as she accepted the award, and she made a few polite and cordial remarks about how she and Beeson would do their best to represent the Midwest region at the national competition. She returned to their table, and they resumed their conversation.

Ten minutes after learning he had not won and having struck out with all the women, Bill, along with Professor Paulus, came up to Barnabas and announced that he wanted to leave. But now Barnabas was not ready to go.

Barnabas attempted to buy a few more minutes. "So soon, Bill? I've never known you to be the first to leave a party. Can you hold off another few minutes?"

Bill, not accustomed to having others make decisions for him, objected. "Look, I'm tired, and I need to get home and into bed."

Sam Schultz offered a solution. "Where do you live in the city, Barnabas? We don't mind giving you a ride."

Bill frowned but could not object. Barnabas was not looking forward to riding back with Bill anyway. Barnabas didn't want to relive the events of the competition with Bill, nor did he want to put up with Bill's claims that Barnabas was responsible for their defeat. Barnabas would have to either say nothing or defend himself, and Professor Paulus might feel obliged to referee any arguments. As it was, there was an illness in Paulus' family, and he hadn't wanted to come at all to begin with.

Barnabas accepted Sam Schultz's offer. "I'd love to ride back to the city with you."

Barnabas, feeling a little better after having rid himself of Bill for the time being, lingered at the party with the Schultzes, enjoying the drinks and food and good conversation. During the ride back later that evening, they discussed law school and Stephanie and Barnabas' plans after graduation. The Schultzes were unpretentious people, and their sincere interest quickly overwhelmed him.

Thirty minutes into the trip, Sam Schultz asked, "How did you develop your writing ability?"

"Do you want the long version or the short one?"

Ruth Schultz laughed and said, "How about the medium one?"

Barnabas smiled and told them the story of how his mother got him hooked on journal writing.

"Do you still have your journals?" Stephanie asked.

"Yes, I guess they are my most precious possession."

"Do you still write in your journal?" she followed up.

Barnabas, feeling embarrassed to answer, said, "Yes."

Ruth said, "Keep writing. Your grandchildren will want to read them."

That assumes that I will ever have any grandchildren, Barnabas thought. He was grateful that there were no follow-up questions.

Ruth changed the subject. "It sounds like your mother is an extraordinary woman. What is she doing?"

"She died three years ago."

There was silence in the car for a few seconds, and then all three of the Schultzes simultaneously said, "I'm so sorry."

"I had a rough patch there for a while, but I'm doing much better now."

"And your father, is he still alive?" Ruth asked.

"You know, I assume he is, but I'm not really sure. The last time I saw him was briefly at the funeral."

The silence grew deeper, and Stephanie elected to change the subject. "Tell us how you met your partner. Have you known him long, or did you meet him in law school?"

"I have known him a long time. I met him in high school." Barnabas did not want to pursue that conversation further.

Ruth sensed the change in the mood and attempted to break the tension. "Tell me more about your mother. Was she responsible for your decision to go to law school?"

"Yeah, I have to give her the credit. She instilled a love of learning in me. Toward the end, she wasn't really coherent, but I do remember her insisting that I continue in school for as long as I had a desire to learn."

He had never talked about his mother in detail to anyone before, but for some reason, for the first time in his life, he actually wanted to talk about her.

Barnabas talked for almost an entire hour, the others interjecting only an occasional word. "I feel like I am dominating the conversation."

"No, please go on," they insisted. For some reason, they seemed fascinated by what he was saying. He talked for another thirty minutes. At one point, Stephanie remarked that Barnabas had been aptly named. She did not go into detail, and Barnabas wondered what she meant. As the car approached his apartment, Barnabas realized that it had been the best two hours of his life as an adult, but sadly, it was over.

As he got out of the car, Stephanie, Ruth, and Sam did also. Barnabas smiled at them and said, "This was great. It was fun. Thank you for the ride, and Stephanie, good luck at the national competition."

Stephanie smiled and grabbed his hand. "It was fun for me, too. I'll pray for your future."

Barnabas later learned that Stephanie's team placed a respectable fourth out of sixteen teams at the national competition.

* * *

"Such a beautiful but sad story," said Ruth as they got back into the car.

"Why sad?" asked Stephanie.

"He was robbed of his childhood. Doesn't seem fair."

"Why beautiful?"

"Because he persevered. He developed a strong character. He got a good education. He emerged with all the tools to do well."

Sam joined in. "And I read that brief. He writes beautifully."

"But he has no relationship with God," Stephanie said.

Sam replied, "He does. He just doesn't want to admit it. We never met his mother, but I know she prayed for him every day. She must have prayed that the Lord would protect him, and her prayers were answered."

"Do you think I'll ever see him again?" Stephanie asked.

Ruth responded, "If it's the Lord's will, you will. In the meantime, let's fill the prayer void left by his mother's death."

CHAPTER FIVE

Barnabas and Bill avoided one another until they came back for their final semester of school in January. Both had to take a seminar and write a lengthy paper as a graduation requirement. Only three classes were offered when Barnabas started the semester, and two of the three were filled. Barnabas knew why only Professor Eastman's class had openings. It was a seminar in constitutional law, and they were required to write a sixty-page paper on the scope of the tenth amendment. Professor Clyde Eastman was a graduate of the Naval Academy and had been the number-one student in his law class when he graduated from the school fifteen years earlier. Eastman had the reputation of being a stickler.

When Barnabas attended the first class, he grinned when Bill entered the room. *For once in his life, Bill is going to have to do his own work,* he thought.

Eastman made it clear that first day what the ground rules were going to be. "Absolutely no collaboration on this paper," he said, "and your work must be solely your own."

The first draft of the paper was due on April 1. The week leading up to the due date, all Barnabas did was go to class, work on his paper, and sleep four hours a night. He finished on Saturday night and actually slept in on Sunday.

The Friday evening before the paper was due, Barnabas was in the computer room in the library finishing up his paper when Bill came in.

"Barnabas, I'm in a world of hurt with this paper. I'll come right to the point. I need your help."

It was the first time Barnabas had ever seen Bill demonstrate any measure of contriteness or humility, so the level of his desperation must have been extreme.

"Have I ever done anything to suggest, in all the time that I've known you, that I would be okay helping you cheat? On this one you're going to have to figure out a way to get this done by yourself. If you are going to get help from someone, I don't want to know anything about it. Don't put me in the position of having to tell Eastman that you got help. This Eastman guy seems serious about this. If he catches anyone collaborating, there'll be hell to pay."

"I'm sure that I could go to someone else, but the problem is deeper than that. I let my grades slip, and I'm going to need a strong grade or I won't graduate."

Barnabas looked at him but did not respond.

Bill pressed ahead. "Look, I know that you're always short on cash. I can pay you." Bill reached into his wallet and pulled out what appeared to be over $1500 in cash.

Barnabas gasped. "What in the world are you doing? Do you think it's safe to walk around with that much cash? Where did you get it?"

"You know that bet you passed on last semester?"

Barnabas nodded.

"I won the bet last weekend."

Barnabas was stunned. Clearly, Bill was desperate if he thought that telling Barnabas about winning the bet would impress him.

"My answer is firm, and it's no."

At that moment, Professor Paulus appeared in the window outside of the computer lab, and he beckoned Barnabas to join him. It was past 8:00 p.m., and it was unusual for Paulus to be in the building at that hour. Barnabas closed the document he was working on, leaving his thumb drive in the computer, an oversight that he would regret.

Barnabas followed Paulus to his office.

"Barnabas, I know that you have wanted to interview with the Frederick firm. I called a friend there by the name of Richard Oxnard, and you can have an interview if you'd like. Is this what you really want to do?"

"Professor, three years of law school with no scholarship. I only worked during the summers so that I could get top grades, but I now have a hundred thousand dollars in debt. I have to make some money."

"Barnabas, I'm afraid that you are going to spend most of your time doing transaction work and will spend very little time in court. You are a natural litigator. If you go to the state's attorney's office or even the public defender's office, you will learn to try cases. In a few years, the firms will seek you out because of what you have learned."

"Professor, it is only an interview. That firm will only take one of our graduates each year, anyway. There is no guarantee that I will even get an offer."

"Well, you've got a point. You don't have to make a decision until you have a decision to make."

As Barnabas walked back into the computer room, Bill was leaving. His look of desperation had disappeared as if he had solved his problem.

Barnabas wrote in his journal that evening:

> Bill is in a bind about his paper for the con law seminar. He asked me for my help. He even offered me money. He says that he has to have an A on the paper to graduate. Things finally may have caught up with Bill.

On April 1, the following Monday, Barnabas handed in his paper to Professor Eastman. The following Friday morning, he checked his mailbox at school, and there was a note inside:

> Please see me after your 4:00 class. Professor Eastman.

Barnabas was naturally curious what Professor Eastman wanted but didn't think much of it until he arrived at his office. Eastman had a stern expression on his face.

Barnabas sat down, and Eastman pulled two papers out of his desk drawer and put them in front of Barnabas. Barnabas recognized the first one as his and saw Bill's name on the cover page of the second.

"Take a look at Cushman's paper, and give me an explanation as to why you shouldn't be dismissed from school."

Immediately, Barnabas became sick to his stomach. He picked up Bill's paper and slowly began to read. On several of the pages, Eastman had written comments in the margin, underlined phrases, and highlighted certain citations. Bill had not been so stupid as to copy every word, and he plagiarized Barnabas word-for-word infrequently, usually no more than seven or eight words at a time. But the organization of the paper was virtually the same, and it appeared that Bill had cited only one case differently from Barnabas.

It was clear what had happened. While Barnabas was seeing Professor Paulus, Bill had copied the files on his thumb drive and helped himself to the contents of Barnabas' paper. Bill had badly underestimated Professor Eastman's ability to identify the similarities. Barnabas' anxiety and stress deepened. *How could I have been so stupid? So careless? Of course Bill couldn't avoid the temptation.*

Professor Eastman spoke again. "Do you have an explanation?"

Barnabas chose his words carefully. "My work is solely my own, and I didn't knowingly share it with Bill. But I know how he did it."

"Mr. Mitchell, I should advise you that Mr. Cushman was here an hour ago, and he claimed that you plagiarized from him. I have scheduled a meeting with the dean, you, and me for one p.m. on Monday. It is best that you not talk with me further. You can bring an advisor with you. I will be urging the dean to set up a hearing date for the Student Conduct Board to convene and take up the question of whether you should be expelled from school. If it is any consolation to you, I am proceeding against Mr. Cushman as well."

Barnabas sat quietly with his head down. Suddenly, he realized that he was acting like a guilty man. He looked up and felt the anger rise. *How could Bill have stooped so low as to jeopardize my professional career?*

Barnabas left, mumbling something to Professor Eastman. He headed directly for Professor Paulus' office, but he had left for the day. He was desperate, so he called Paulus on his cell phone.

"Professor Paulus, this is Barnabas."

"What's up, Barnabas? You sound worried."

"I am. I've got a big problem, and I need to talk to you as soon as possible."

"Come out to the house. I'll have my wife put out an extra plate for you for dinner."

"Thanks, but I am not interested in eating. What time do you expect to get through?"

"We're usually done by six thirty."

"I'll be there at six thirty-one."

Barnabas arrived at 6:35 p.m. They went to Professor Paulus' study. "What's the problem?"

"I've been accused of plagiarism, and I'm in danger of being expelled." Barnabas told Paulus what had happened in Professor Eastman's office.

Professor Paulus assessed the situation and offered his support. "Anyone who knows the two of you knows that you're not a cheater. But the problem is that you are your own worst witness. You are going to have to convince the dean that you left your memory stick behind unwittingly when you knew that Bill was desperate. If you had been thinking clearly, you wouldn't have made that mistake. I can, of course, prove that you talked with him that evening, but I would advise against getting into how he showed you the cash or offered you any money. If you do, it's not likely that the others will back you up about the bet and all of that. You will also have to get the lady involved, and it will be too messy."

"Professor, Bill has been a master of getting out of jams all of his life. He has shown that he is willing to throw me under the bus to save himself. When it comes to saving his own skin, he is formidable. We have to take this seriously."

"Of course we will. We'll be prepared. Go home and try not to worry." *Easier said than done!*

As Barnabas was driving home, he realized that the paper was not the only thing that Bill had access to. *Has he been reading my journals? Most people probably wouldn't go that far, but Bill would enjoy it.* Barnabas pulled his car over to the curb and began to throw up.

CHAPTER SIX

His hands were shaking. At five minutes after the hour, the door opened, and out walked Bill's dad, Bill, and a man whom Barnabas didn't recognize. He was about seventy years old, his hair had turned white, and it appeared that he was cultivating a distinguished image. Professor Paulus whispered under his breath, "That's trouble."

"How so?" Barnabas whispered back.

"The third man is Justin Frost. He is the law school's biggest donor. He gives a minimum of two hundred fifty thousand dollars each year."

As Frost was walking out the door, they heard the dean's voice. "Justin, can you spare a moment?"

As Bill walked by, he looked at Barnabas and whispered, "Good luck, Barney. You're going to need it."

Barnabas stood to confront Bill, but Professor Paulus grabbed his arm and restrained him. A moment later, the door to the dean's office opened, and Frost left without looking at either of them. The dean stood in the doorway and summoned Barnabas inside. "Mr. Mitchell, Professor Paulus, I am ready for you."

As they walked inside, they saw Professor Eastman standing next to the dean's desk with a stoic expression.

The dean looked at Barnabas. "Mr. Mitchell, I have been briefed about what happened. In essence, Mr. Cushman claims that you copied from him, and you claim otherwise. Can you explain to me how he got access to your paper?"

"Yes, I can. I was finishing up my paper on the Friday night before it was due. I was in the computer lab in the library, and Bill came in. He knew I was working on the paper. Professor Paulus came in. I left the lab to talk with him, and I made the huge mistake of leaving my memory stick in the computer. I talked with Professor Paulus for fifteen minutes or so, plenty of time for Bill to copy the entire memory stick. He must have copied it onto the desktop and sent its contents to himself over the internet."

Barnabas' explanation appeared to startle the dean as if he had been expecting a confession, and a frown betrayed his unhappiness. The dean then assumed an advocate's role.

"Mr. Mitchell, you want me to believe that Mr. Cushman copied your computer files and sent them to himself because you left the memory stick unprotected with Bill while he was alone? Do you really expect me to believe that you were that stupid? Did you check the computer for evidence that Mr. Cushman did this?"

"I did check, dean, after all this came to light. But all of the memory on that computer was erased on Friday evening, at the very time I was in Professor Paulus' office."

The dean grunted, showing that he was unconvinced.

Professor Paulus broke in. He turned to Professor Eastman. "Clyde, is that Mr. Mitchell's paper in front of you? Ask him any question about any of the cases cited in the paper."

The dean's expression turned worrisome, and Eastman smiled. For the next twenty minutes, Professor Eastman acted like he was conducting a class and quizzed Barnabas about the cases. Barnabas was able to answer all of his questions. Ten minutes into the session, it was obvious to Barnabas that the purpose of the exercise was not only to convince the dean that he had written his paper but also to convince him that neither Paulus nor Eastman was going to let Barnabas be the scapegoat.

The dean finally said, "I understand the point. Is there anything further?"

"Yes," said Professor Paulus, pressing the advantage further. "Dean, did you ask Mr. Cushman to discuss his understanding of the cases when he met with you earlier?"

There was a long pause, and the dean declined to answer. Professor Eastman looked at Barnabas and gave him a slight but perceptible smile.

Then Paulus upped the ante. "Barnabas, if the dean requests it, are you willing to take a polygraph?"

"Of course, as long as Cushman is willing to do so as well."

The dean frowned and then stood, signaling that the meeting was over.

"I will let you gentlemen know shortly how I am going to proceed."

The three of them—Barnabas, Paulus, and Eastman—adjourned to Professor Paulus' office.

As soon as Paulus shut the door, Barnabas spoke. "Thank you, both. On Friday, I thought that I was going to be expelled from school. Now there is hope."

Eastman spoke next. "Cushman overstepped his position. He would have been better off claiming that you agreed to let him see your paper and that he had simply forgotten about the no-collaboration rule. By claiming that you copied from him, it forces the dean to decide which one of you copied the paper from the other. Now it's obvious who did that."

Barnabas turned to Professor Paulus. "Do you think that Bill is going to get off by bringing in his father and Frost?"

"I don't know. It puts the dean in a difficult position. He knows that Bill has cheated, but he is not going to want to alienate either Frost or Cushman's father. But he knows that he can't claim that you plagiarized. If he does that, both Clyde and I will raise living hell with the faculty. He won't do that. The dean may be powerful, but he's not that powerful."

"Neither of you had to stand up to the dean that way," Barnabas responded. "After all, he is your boss. Are there going to be consequences?"

Professor Paulus put his hand on Barnabas' shoulder and said, "It makes no difference what the consequences are, but I'll be surprised if there are any. If you can't do the right thing, you have no business being a lawyer, much less teaching them."

And Eastman responded, "Well said, John."

Barnabas got the answer from the dean two days later:

Mr. Mitchell:

I have reviewed the situation, and I have concluded that there is insufficient evidence to proceed against either you or Mr. Cushman. I have instructed Professor Eastman to grade the papers as if they had been written without collaboration. This concludes this unfortunate incident.

Sincerely,
Dean Hopkins.

What was particularly grating was that Bill was going to get his cherished A based on Barnabas' work. *Is there anything that Bill can't get away with? The dean could've at least made it pass-fail. Bill's dad must have made it clear to the dean that that would not be acceptable,* thought Barnabas.

That evening, Barnabas was heading for his car in the parking lot when Bill suddenly appeared, startling him.

"I was caught off-guard by Eastman. If I had had more time to think it through, I would have given him a story that didn't make you look so bad. I think you should just move on with your life and forget about all this. We both know that I know things about you that you are not going to want everyone else to know. I never knew just how unstable you could be."

So Bill had read his journals! *Unstable? He must have read the entry I wrote after my mother died.*

Barnabas decided that this time he was not going to let Bill get the last word.

"Bill, did you ever think about telling the truth? How about trying that for a change? But you never considered it, did you? I'm glad our connection, if you can call it that, is over. Whenever I'm around you, I feel dirty. Don't ever come close to me again. If I were you, I would get rid of the evidence that you stole that data off my memory stick. If I ever get any evidence that you stole that data, I will sue you for invasion of privacy. It will also prove that I was telling the truth and that you were lying. And I will go to the law school and insist that your diploma be revoked."

Barnabas turned and walked away before Bill could respond.

* * *

Bill, of course, graduated on time. Barnabas interviewed with the Frederick firm, but, predictably, Bill got the job. Professor Paulus was informed by Richard Oxnard, his connection in the firm, that they had been very impressed with Barnabas, but the possibility that Bill would be a rainmaker through his father's connections and bring new, well-connected, well-monied clients to the firm was the decisive factor.

Barnabas stopped writing in his journal; the thought that Bill had read it was so disgusting that he lost his desire to continue.

CHAPTER SEVEN

Barnabas spent the month after he graduated from law school interviewing for jobs. He did get a couple of offers from small firms, but in the end he took a low-paying job with the public defender's office. He preferred the state's attorney's office, but they had filled their last vacancy the day before Barnabas' interview. His job offer with the public defender's office was contingent upon his passing the bar exam.

He was now over $90,000 in debt, and reluctantly, he paid $800 to attend a six-week-long bar refresher course. Most of his classmates opted to take the course. It was an intensive program designed solely to prepare him to pass the Illinois State Bar Exam. The class met every weekday for six hours. His days were spent going to an auditorium at another law school, listening to lectures presented on a video monitor, eating lunch during the forty-five-minute break, returning for the afternoon session, studying, eating dinner, and studying again until midnight. He didn't even play any basketball—his sole source of exercise.

Barnabas reviewed Stephanie's Facebook posts weekly to see where she was going to start her legal career.

* * *

Stephanie began interviewing for jobs in her final semester of law school, not knowing how to begin her career. She wanted to get experience trying cases. She had enjoyed her moot court experience, which gave her the appetite for trial work. Her first choices were the United States attorney's office and the state's attorney's office, but they had no vacancies. She did get three offers from mid-level firms. She picked the Clausen-Ferguson firm because they promised her that she would do some trial work, and they asked for only a three-year commitment. The offer was contingent upon her passing the bar exam. She began to pray for a study partner who would challenge her to do her best while preparing for the bar.

* * *

The first bar review class began on the last Monday in June at 9:00 a.m. He was talking with one of his friends when a familiar voice caught his attention. "Is this seat taken?"

Barnabas turned around. It was Stephanie.

Barnabas smiled. "Of course not."

He had, of course, kept up with her on Facebook, but he didn't know that he would ever see her again. It was more than a pleasant surprise that she was not only attending the same course at the same location but that she also wanted to sit next to him.

They spent just about every waking moment studying with one another. Stephanie only took off Sunday mornings.

Three days into the course, several of Barnabas' law school friends asked him who "the fox" was.

He responded neutrally. "Just a friend I met during moot court competition." They wanted to know more, but he didn't have much more to say. Of course, he would have liked it to be more, but Stephanie wasn't giving him any signals to that effect, at least not that Barnabas could detect.

One week into the course, while they were eating lunch, Barnabas did ask, "Why are you doing this? You could study with anyone you want to. Why me?"

"Like you, I can't afford to fail. When I walked into the room and saw you sitting there, I knew you were the answer to my prayers. I know that spending my time with you will push me to learn this material. You are my insurance policy that I'm going pass. Besides that, I like you. Why is that so hard for you to understand?" As she finished, she gave Barnabas a light punch on the arm.

"Did you actually pray about how you were going to pass the bar exam?"

"I try and pray about everything that is important to me. I believe that if it is important to me, it is also important to God. I asked for a study partner who would challenge me to study hard. Do you think my prayers were answered?"

She smiled in a way that made it difficult to tell her no, but Barnabas would not back down. "You asked for something, and I'm flattered that you think that I'm what you asked for, but why couldn't it be a coincidence and not that big of one? We are both in the same year of law school in the same city. Why is it so surprising that we wound up in the same building to get ready for the bar exam?"

Stephanie shot back. "Did you hear about the new movie that the Atheist Society is going to release this Christmas season?"

Barnabas said, "No, tell me."

"It's called *Coincidence on 34th Street.*"

He chose to smile but not laugh. "One man's coincidence is another woman's answer to prayer."

The truth was that initially she was a distraction. He had never spent an extensive amount of time studying with any female, much less an attractive one, but very quickly his competitive juices started flowing as she asked increasingly difficult and challenging questions. Not to be outdone, he returned her questions with his own. While it was fun, it was also intense. By the end of the experience, the both of them had become so focused on passing the exam that there was no time to think about anything else. Nevertheless, for the first time in his life, he began to wear a touch of cologne.

When they got to constitutional law, Barnabas and Stephanie started to butt heads. They had spent hours talking about the establishment of religion, abortion, and gay rights cases. Barnabas generally agreed with the decisions, as they seemed to be about increasing freedom and divorcing the Constitution from Christian doctrine.

Barnabas tried to reason with her. "You are free to believe and act how you want to, but why should your point of view be binding on other people?"

But Stephanie gave compelling responses, forcing him to go back to the text of the document. She was also well versed on the content of the history. Barnabas soon realized that he was overmatched. Stephanie had clearly spent more time studying and thinking about those issues.

Two weeks before the exam, they took some practice tests. They did well, and one day, ever-competitive Stephanie proposed a bet. "If I beat you on the practice test, you have to come to church with me the first Sunday after the bar exam, and if you beat me, I will come over to your apartment and clean and organize your kitchen."

"I don't think you want to make that bet."

"Why? Are you that confident that you are going to win the bet?"

"No. You haven't seen my kitchen."

She smiled. "I'm willing to take that risk."

They took the test the next day. Their scores were identical. They checked three times just to be sure, but the scores were the same.

Barnabas said, "I guess it is a 'no' bet—no one wins."

"Or," responded Stephanie, "we could declare both of us winners. I'll clean and organize your kitchen, and you have to come to church."

"It's truly amazing what lengths you're willing to go to in order to get me to church." But Barnabas didn't want their relationship to end, so he agreed.

The bar examination ended on a Friday, and the next day, Stephanie arrived at 8:00 a.m. with a plastic bucket filled with a scrub brush and other cleaning materials. Barnabas helped her, as he didn't want to just sit on the couch and watch her work.

It took them four hours, but the kitchen did look immaculate when she was done. She actually appeared to enjoy cleaning it. Barnabas was impressed.

The next day, he met her at her church promptly at 9:00 a.m. Barnabas wasn't expecting a large church, but this one was no bigger than a large house. The place was packed. Stephanie met him at the front door and introduced him to the pastor, a gentleman by the name of Luke Davidson. Luke Davidson was Barnabas' height with a full head of brown hair. He appeared to be in his mid-fifties and was slightly overweight. He was naturally friendly and projected a warm smile.

Barnabas and Stephanie went to the Sunday school with six other young adults. They were the only two single ones, and Barnabas wondered what, if anything, Stephanie had told them about their relationship. He didn't say anything during the discussion, but he was surprised at how much he still retained from his childhood. He was able to track everything that was said. He listened to the sermon in the teaching service wherein Davidson gave a forty-five minute message from the book of Romans. It reminded Barnabas of his time sitting in a pew with his mother.

He had been sleep deprived for the last several weeks as a result of studying for the bar exam, so it was all he could do to stay awake. He noticed Stephanie watching him out of the corner of her eye, and he knew that he dared not embarrass her by falling asleep. He resorted to one of the tricks he used to stay awake when he'd get drowsy on a long drive—he held his breath until he got an adrenaline rush. That gave him several minutes of clarity before it wore off and he was forced to hold his breath again. It was crude, but it worked.

After the service, Stephanie walked him to the car. She tried to hide her disappointment, but he had gotten to know her well, and he was able to read her mood. Her head was down, as she didn't want to make eye contact.

He decided to make it easy on her. "I guess this truly is goodbye, isn't it?"

She looked up at him with a forced smile. "Barnabas, I just can't be in a deep relationship with someone who doesn't share my beliefs."

"I know. I'll never ask you to do that." He then opened his arms, and while giving her a hug, said, "Goodbye."

* * *

Stephanie went back into church after saying goodbye to Barnabas. She walked over to her dad and started to tear up. He put his arm around her shoulder and said, "So?"

"Daddy, I just don't think it's going to happen. He could barely keep his eyes open during the message. He's such a good guy. Am I doing the right thing by letting him go?"

"You will never look back and regret holding to your principles. You can't force this to happen. If the Lord wants it to happen, you have to believe that the Lord's going to make it happen. Trust me, that boy has too much character not to figure it out. Just be open to the Lord's leading. Maybe, just maybe, he is not supposed to be the guy God wants for you. Maybe your job is only to water a seed. Let the Lord decide."

She frowned at him and said, "I knew you were going to say something like that. I've never liked it when I'm told that I am supposed to be developing patience," and she laughed at her own joke.

* * *

They continued to track one another on Facebook and exchanged an occasional post, but for the next two years, Stephanie and Barnabas never saw one another.

CHAPTER EIGHT

Barnabas had had a good weekend. He spent the prior three weeks in trial, and his last trial concluded on Friday with not-guilty verdicts on three of the four counts. Not a bad result for a public defender; getting rid of three beefs out of four was good. His client had not seen it that way, but Barnabas reasoned that when his client calculated the difference between three years in the penitentiary versus fifteen, his attitude would change.

Before he left on Friday, his supervisor apologized for overworking Barnabas and promised him that he would reduce his workload for a couple of weeks so he could recharge his batteries. Barnabas had spent most of the weekend sleeping and lying in the bathtub reading spy novels. Boring, but needed; stress it was not.

He was at his desk at 9:00 a.m. Monday morning, two hours later than his customary arrival time. He had two new files stacked on his desk, far less than usual. One was a felony drug charge—nothing out of the ordinary—but the other one caused his stomach to turn. The defendant's name was Jessie Nicks.

As Barnabas read the file, he noted that Nicks was presently a resident of the state penitentiary, and he was about to celebrate his twenty-first birthday. The file revealed that one year earlier, Nicks rear-ended a vehicle while the driver was waiting for a light to turn green. Nicks seriously injured a young woman named Alice Capshaw, putting her into a coma. The accident occurred at 10:00 p.m. on a Friday. Nicks was arrested the following Sunday evening.

While investigating officers believed that Nicks was drunk at the time of the collision, the prosecution couldn't prove it. Nicks had driven off without waiting for the police. When they tracked him down two days later, Nicks had dried out; he was stone cold sober. He had no memory of what he had done. Nicks pled guilty to a felony count of leaving the scene of an accident. He had now been in the penitentiary for over a year. Barnabas concluded that the penitentiary was where Nicks belonged.

Nicks' rap sheet showed juvenile violations stemming back to age twelve. Beginning at age fourteen, the convictions and dispositions all indicated that Nicks was either drunk or high on drugs. Nicks had been sentenced to seven years, but with good time, he could be out in less than two.

Then, Alice died.

Now Nicks was charged with vehicular manslaughter. As an assistant public defender, Barnabas had the honor of representing him. It was Barnabas' duty to do everything in his power to keep Nicks' stay in the penitentiary as short as possible.

Up to that point, Barnabas had continually represented folks like Nicks with few qualms of conscience. But Nicks' case was different. Barnabas went to his supervisor. "Give this case to someone else. It hits too close to home. I don't think I can represent this guy."

His supervisor was not sympathetic. "Everyone else is set to go to trial. You're the only one whose schedule can handle it."

"But it's obvious that this guy belongs in jail."

His boss looked at him incredulously. "That's true of everyone we represent. Is this news to you? Where have you been?"

His boss was a good guy, especially for someone that had been working in the PD's office for twenty years. Barnabas understood that the public defender's office was no place to work if one couldn't handle sarcasm. And he had become skilled in his own right in dishing it out, so he chose to ignore the comment.

Should I tell him the story about my mother? Would he understand? No, it would be too painful. Better to tough it out, spend as little time as possible on the file, and move on to the next case.

CHAPTER NINE

The depth of the Capshaw family's loss transcended the page. They were deeply religious people. Alice's parents, Ivan and Danielle, owned a construction company, and her brother, Jay, was a chaplain in the Navy. Danielle's description of her daughter was poignant:

> Alice was a very sweet-natured girl. She loved people, and she loved life. I don't recall her ever saying a harsh word about anyone, even when she was a young girl. I am no longer a complete woman; I feel like a part of my heart has been ripped out of me. With God's help, I have to believe that I will recover, but I have no idea how He is going to do it for me.

Barnabas hadn't even met Nicks, and he already hated him. Barnabas drove out to the prison to make the obligatory visit to see his client. He had been to the penitentiary several times before, but this time, the trip was more dreary and depressing than usual. The dark gray sky threatened rain, but it never happened. *What purpose is there to a day that is covered with dark gray clouds if it doesn't even rain?* The weather matched his mood.

After Barnabas arrived, he parked his car and went to the visitor's gate. It took him less than fifteen minutes to clear security and make it to the attorney conference room. He had been there before, and it hadn't changed. It was a drab place. Everything was metal or concrete. Barnabas sat down on a gray metal chair and spread Nicks' file out on a table, waiting for him to arrive.

Ten minutes later, Nicks arrived, escorted by two prison guards. His hands were shackled. Nicks looked even worse than Barnabas had imagined. He was no more than five foot eight, easily weighing 240 pounds, but he was all muscle and no fat. The file indicated that in his idle time, of which he had plenty, Nicks lifted weights in the prison yard. He had tattoos all over the visible portions of his body, with the exception of his face. It seemed that he had a preference for snakes. Barnabas counted seven of them on Nicks' left arm alone. Nicks was a spectacle, and the spectacle was appalling.

Nicks did nothing to change Barnabas' first impression when they started to talk. Immediately, he took a shot at Barnabas. "I can see from the looks of you that they've brought in the third string. Are you just out of law school? Have you ever tried a case before? How long have you been shaving, kid?"

This guy is a real nice piece of work. He calls me "kid" and I'm six years older than he is.

Barnabas was tempted to ignore him, hoping to spend as little time with Nicks as possible, but instead he chose to fire back. "Look, I'm no more impressed with you than you are with me. But I have to find out what happened the night you ran into that girl's car. What do you recall?"

Nicks smiled, showing his teeth. Two of his upper teeth were missing. The remaining were a disgusting off-brown color. "Honestly, nothing. I was too drunk to remember." Nicks said it proudly. Barnabas began to get angry.

"Mr. Nicks, did you learn how to be an ass after you got here or does it come to you naturally?"

"Look, kid, don't come in here with some kind of superior, high-and-mighty attitude. We both know I'm going to spend a lot of time in here. It's just a job to you. So don't put on some kind of act like you're a professional and that you really care what happens to me because I know that it's all bullshit. So why don't you put your papers back into your briefcase, move along, and let me get back to the yard. I would rather spend my time with the felons that inhabit this place than the likes of you. With them at least you know where you stand as opposed to cheap lawyers like you. You can't be very good or you wouldn't be working for the PD. Look at it this way—if it weren't for guys like me, guys like you wouldn't have anything to do."

Barnabas was actually amused by Nicks' bravado. He rose and started to put his papers away, and Nicks gave Barnabas a smirk because it appeared that he was obeying him. But as Barnabas put the last paper into his briefcase, he said, "Yeah, you're right, Nicks, and if it weren't for guys like you, morticians wouldn't have anything to do. You should be real proud of yourself. After all, look at all of the great things you've accomplished in your life."

It appeared that Barnabas hit a nerve. "Kid, I don't care what you think of me. You just do your job. Your job is to get me off. Go do it. Make me a happy man."

Barnabas pondered saying nothing but decided to put Nicks in his place. "Well, this kid is all you got. Regardless of how this turns out, I'll spend the rest of my life only coming here to visit. And unless you're nice to me, I may decide to let you rot in here rather than try and do anything for you. Like me or not, I'm the only hope you've got."

As Barnabas drove back home for the evening, he hoped not to ever see Nicks again. He found it hard to believe that Nicks was actually proud of what he had done. He hoped that Nicks had some modicum of humanity that he chose to bury deep inside. Regardless of whether Nicks' bravado was fake or real, Barnabas concluded that he should be judged by his behavior, and the judgment should be severe.

He wondered if he had made a mistake by going into law. Given his present state of mind, he would have been happier doing something else. He turned his thoughts to college and law school.

Maybe I would be better off if I had never gone to law school. At least I wouldn't be over ninety thousand dollars in debt, and I never would have met Nicks. What good am I accomplishing? Would my mother be proud of what I'm doing? As for God, even if He does exist, it's obvious that He doesn't care.

When Barnabas reached his apartment, he thought of the young man who ruined his mother's life. The man must be in his mid-thirties by now. *Was he like Nicks when he was younger? By now he must be out of the penitentiary. Has he ruined anyone else's life since then?*

Barnabas was at his desk at 7:00 a.m. the next morning, and he picked up the Nicks file. He detested Nicks, and he hated himself for what he knew he was going to do.

His thoughts returned to Professor Paulus' criminal procedure class. It had been one of those few classes when he actually volunteered to discuss the cases with the professor.

He had forgotten the name of the case, but he remembered the facts and the holding. Barnabas turned on his computer. He pulled up Westlaw, entered his password, and the search screen popped up. He typed in "double jeopardy w/16 scene w/5 accident w/12 homicide."

Fifteen seconds later, three cases popped up. He immediately recognized the first case; it was the one he had read in law school. Four years earlier, the Illinois Supreme Court had ruled that once the prosecution had convicted a man of leaving the scene of an accident, it could not prosecute him for vehicular manslaughter. Double jeopardy attached when the State rested in the first case. Barnabas printed out the case and started to draft his motion. As he typed the motion, he became progressively more nauseated.

Twenty days later, the motion to dismiss was heard. The night before, Barnabas prayed for the first time since he was twelve years old. "God, if there is a God, please keep the Capshaw family away from the courtroom tomorrow. It is going to be painful for me, and I just can't imagine how painful it will be for them."

His prayers were not answered. He had never met them, but he spotted them in the second row behind the prosecution table. Ivan and Danielle looked to be in their early to mid-fifties. Jay looked like he was in his late twenties. They looked apprehensive, but Barnabas suspected that they were not anticipating what was about to happen.

Last night was my last prayer. How can I expect God to answer my prayers when I don't even believe in Him? Maybe God, if there is a God, is punishing me for even presuming to pray at all. Perhaps they wouldn't have come if I hadn't prayed.

Nicks was brought out in orange prison garb, and the officer removed his chains. He didn't take the smirk off his face for even a moment. The guard motioned for him to sit down next to Barnabas.

"What's going on? They come and pick me up this morning and tell me I'm going to court. Why?"

"Look, you're about to get a break you don't deserve. Wipe the smirk off your face, and don't do anything to piss off the judge. I think he is about to dismiss the manslaughter charges. If you don't blow it, you could be out in less than six months. So sit down and keep your mouth shut. Try and act like someone who knows that he doesn't deserve a break, like someone who really appreciates getting one—if that's possible. But I suspect that in your case it isn't possible, is it, Nicks? You don't have an ounce of decency in you, do you? So one side of me hopes that you continue to act like the asshole you are and that the judge will tack on another six months for contempt of court."

Nicks grunted and attempted to change his expression. It was better, but if you looked at him closely, he still showed attitude.

Three minutes later, the judge entered.

"All rise," the clerk yelled. "The circuit court is in session. Judge Warren Sedgwick presiding."

The judge mumbled, "Be seated, please. Mr. Mitchell, this is your motion. I have read the briefs. Do you have anything to add?"

"Nothing has happened in the last two weeks to change the law. The case is still good law."

The judge nodded at the prosecution.

A senior prosecutor stood and addressed the court. "Your Honor, in this case, the victim died after the leaving-the-scene case was brought to trial. In the cases Mr. Mitchell cites, the victim was dead at the time of the first prosecution."

Barnabas was about to rise, but the judge held out his hand, signaling him to stay seated.

"But doesn't the case make clear that that is a distinction without a meaning, Counsel?"

"Well, Your Honor, the case could be read that way."

The judge looked at both tables. "Anything further?"

Barnabas stood and said, "Nothing, Your Honor."

The prosecutor stood. "Nothing for the State."

The judge paused a full thirty seconds, composing his thoughts. "I have no choice but to dismiss these charges. Our supreme court has ruled that double jeopardy is attached to the leaving-the-scene charges. Mr. Nicks cannot be charged with the crime of vehicular manslaughter. The charges are dismissed."

At that point, Nicks couldn't contain himself, and he clapped his hands and guffawed.

The judge looked at Nicks with a contorted face and addressed him in a loud voice. "Mr. Nicks, you are a most fortunate man today. I am advised that you could be out in less than a year, and by all rights, you should be in there for another fifteen. Don't test my patience. I would love to hold you in contempt. Say one more thing, and I will. Please make my day and do it."

Nicks stared at the judge and said nothing, but his eyes still conveyed his contempt. The judge stood, and everyone else immediately stood on cue.

Nicks swaggered out of the courtroom without showing any remorse. The judge was right; Nicks was one of the last people who deserved a break. And Barnabas had been the one to help give it to him.

Barnabas' emotions shifted from shame to anger. As he was leaving, he looked over at the Capshaw family. They were hugging each other and weeping, except for Jay, the Navy chaplain. He was praying.

Praying for what? Barnabas thought. *Strength and self-control are what I'd ask for.* But Barnabas sensed that he was praying for something else. *There's no way he's praying for forgiveness. Forgiveness for whom? Surely not for Nicks.*

Barnabas went to his office, turned on his computer, and wrote his letter of resignation. It was effective immediately. He put all of his own possessions in a small box. As he left, he dropped his letter of resignation on his supervisor's desk. He didn't know what he was going to do, but it was no longer going to be representing people like Nicks. He was through.

CHAPTER TEN

Barnabas went home that night, drew himself a hot bath, and assessed his circumstances while lying in the tub. On the financial side, he had $5000 in savings, $75,000 in educational loans, and no job. His most valuable asset was a 1996 Honda with more than 250,000 miles on it. The thought of bankruptcy ran through his mind, but he knew that bankruptcy was useless against educational loans.

On the social side, he had no social life. He had no close friends or people that he could talk to other than Professor Paulus and perhaps Stephanie, and he hadn't talked with her in months. Girls generally seemed to like him, but for him, marriage was out of the question until he was out of debt. He was twenty-six years old and had no marriage prospects, and he didn't want any. His most immediate problem was finding a job, not a relationship. He didn't want to get married and be saddled with over $75,000 in debt at the same time. Other guys might have done it, but not him.

Having no social life left Barnabas time for physical pursuits. He was six feet two inches tall and weighed 180 pounds. He managed to keep his weight down by playing basketball four to five evenings a week in pickup games at the local YMCA. His law school friends had told him that he was blessed with the ability of consuming vast quantities of food without gaining any weight.

When he got out of the tub, Barnabas picked up his cell phone, dialed Professor Paulus' number, and asked what he recommended. Barnabas wanted him to say that he would use his contacts to get him placed in a law firm. But Barnabas was surprised by Paulus' advice. "Barnabas, I usually don't say this to young attorneys, but you have the skills to go out on your own and do an excellent job representing your clients."

"But where will the clients come from?"

"You have friends in both the public defender's office and in the prosecutor's office. You can get on the list, and you can take some court appointments when the public defender's office has a conflict. I'll have no problem recommending you. You continue to do good work and you'll be making money before you realize it. If you go for a firm, the partners will control your professional life, and it will be years before you reach the top. Try not to think so much about how you are going to pay your bills as opposed to what you can really achieve."

"But there are tons of lawyers out there. Why are you so confident that I will even be able to pay my bills?"

"Barnabas, from what I hear you are already a very good trial lawyer. People know that. I don't care how crowded the field is. There is always room for good people."

He trusted Paulus. He was the closest thing he had ever had to a father.

With considerable reservations, Barnabas decided to open up his own practice. If it failed, he could look for a job in a firm or on the civil side of government work.

His first task was to find office space. He found a modest, four-room suite on the third floor of an office building erected in 1949, just three blocks from the state courthouse and six blocks from the federal courthouse. He was able to sign a three-year lease for only $650 a month, but he had to promise the landlord that he would completely clean the space. The prior tenant had been there for twenty-five years and died unexpectedly, and the place was a mess. But the rent was right. It took Barnabas three full weeks—days, evenings, and weekends—to make the space presentable. By the time he was ready to open, he had used up most of his savings.

Six days before he opened his practice, he placed an ad in the "Help Wanted" section of the newspaper: *Legal secretary, no experience required, salary negotiable.*

His cell phone began to ring. Barnabas told everyone that called that he wasn't certain how long the job was going to last, and most didn't bother to come in for an interview.

Three days before his office was supposed to open, he still hadn't found a secretary. But then, Jennie called, and they arranged an interview for later that afternoon. He hired her on the spot. He usually didn't trust his intuition, but he liked her immediately. He was in work clothes painting the office when she walked in.

"Hello? Is anybody here?"

"Back here, in the office. I'll come to you. I don't want you to get any paint on your clothes."

Barnabas got down from the ladder and walked into the front office. He was wearing blue jeans and a paint-stained T-shirt, and she was wearing a conservative business suit.

As soon as she saw him, she laughed.

Jennie was five foot five, had red hair, and she seemed almost too slender. She was somewhere between forty-five and fifty years old. Barnabas liked her laugh. Clearly, if a cartoonist drew a picture of the scene, he wouldn't have had any trouble coming up with punch lines.

They sat down on the only two chairs in the office, and the interview began.

"Why are you looking for work?"

She answered directly. "I'm divorced. I have two children, ages fifteen and seventeen. My former husband is not regular in his child support. I need the work."

He was expecting a longer answer. The others he had interviewed had included a statement along the lines of having always wanted to work in a law office. Barnabas hadn't had time to prepare his second question because her answer was so short and direct.

He pressed ahead. "What skills do you have?"

She gave a slight smile and responded, "I have been told that I am smart. I always got good grades in school. I'm a problem solver, I'm honest, and I've always worked hard."

"But have you worked in a law office before?" Barnabas probed.

"I haven't worked in twenty years."

"But do you have any computer skills?"

"We have a computer at home, and I know how to get on the internet. I use the word processor on our computer."

She gave quick, non-evasive answers. He liked that. She was transparent. He felt compelled to ask the next question. "It's none of my business, but do you mind telling me why you're divorced?"

"Ten years ago I started going to church because I wanted my children to be exposed to religion. My husband didn't want to go, so he didn't.

Along the way, I became a believer. We just drifted apart. He started to ridicule me in front of the children. It wasn't a healthy situation. I used to spend most of my time worrying. Then he began to insist that I stop taking the children to church, but I refused. One day, he walked out, and he never came back."

"Tell me about your children."

"Emily is very bright and is a leader in her youth group at church. We are praying that she will get a scholarship so that she can go to college next year. Matt is very serious, more of a loner. He loves to read. He only has two friends, but they're good friends. At first I thought he was just trying to be different from his sister, but I now know that it's just the way he's wired."

Barnabas smiled. "This fellow Matt seems like my kind of guy."

Jennie responded, "I think you would like Emily also."

He decided to hire her. "Look, I can't afford to pay much, and as I said on the phone, I really don't know how long this office is going to stay open. The most I can promise to start is $24,000 a year. I am down to $1300 in my bank account, but I expect to meet my first client on Monday. Do you want to take a chance on me?"

Jennie gave him a warm, inviting smile. "What do you say about me going home, changing my clothes, and helping you finish? We want the office to be ready for your first client. I'll bring the kids with me. We can get this knocked out by the end of the day."

"It's a deal," Barnabas said, offering his hand, but he withdrew it just as quickly, realizing that it was covered with paint.

As he watched Jennie walk out of the office, he realized why he had offered her the job. She reminded him of his mother.

The three of them—Jennie, Emily, and Matt—returned ninety minutes later in their work clothes. He was impressed with both of the children. As described, Emily was vivacious, and there was nonstop chatter, laughter, and singing as she worked. Matt went into a separate room and finished painting it by himself. As predicted, they finished by 6:00 p.m.

Barnabas decided to spring for pizza at a nearby Italian restaurant. As they were waiting, Emily started to cross-examine Barnabas.

"So, Barnabas, why did you decide to hire my mom? She's never worked in a law office, and as far as I know, she has no office skills."

"Emily!" Jennie interrupted. "What are you doing? Are you talking me out of a job?"

Barnabas laughed. "I liked her honesty. I believe her when she says that she is a good worker and a fast learner. She has a certain cheerfulness that I suspect you got from her. She'll be just fine."

Emily continued. "Where are you from?"

"I have always lived in the Chicago area."

"Do your parents still live here?"

"My mother died seven years ago, and I haven't seen my dad since I was in junior high."

There was an awkward pause, and Jennie apologized for her daughter. "Emily is not always the most tactful."

"It's okay. She just wants to make sure that her mother is in good hands while she's at school."

Emily gave him a relieved smile and ignored her mother's words of caution. "So, Barnabas, do you have a girlfriend?"

Barnabas studied Jennie from the corner of his eye, and she was starting to turn pink. He decided to play along. "Why do you ask? Are you interested?"

Emily giggled. "Well, I don't think you're my type, but I'm sure that I can fix you up if you give me a little time to work on it."

"Hold off for the time being. I need to get out of debt. Girlfriends can be kind of expensive, and my creditors may not appreciate me taking one on at this time."

"Well, I am going to add that to my prayer list. With my mother helping you and with our prayers, you are going to be out of debt sooner than you think." He studied her expression. She wasn't joking. She was serious.

CHAPTER ELEVEN

For the first three weeks, the firm—Jennie liked to call it the firm—struggled, and the day after Barnabas' bank account dwindled to less than $150, three clients came in the door, giving him a total of $5500 in retainers. All it meant was that Barnabas could practice law another month. But as Professor Paulus had predicted, he started getting referrals from attorneys and from Professor Paulus himself. Nevertheless, it did not appear that Emily's prayers were going to be answered anytime soon.

Barnabas was a full three months into his practice when the intercom buzzed. It was toward the end of the day, and Jennie was getting ready to go home. Jennie hit the intercom button and with her usual cheerful voice said, "Professor Paulus, line one."

Barnabas always took Professor Paulus' calls. In fact, he rarely turned down any calls, but Professor Paulus' referrals accounted for more than fifty percent of his income. Professor Paulus had lived in the city for over fifty years and had many contacts. Barnabas did not think he would survive without Paulus' goodwill and fatherly support.

"Professor, are things still going well at the law school? How is the moot court team going to do this year?"

"Barnabas, I turned over the faculty advisor's position to a younger professor this summer. But I am sure that the team will never be able to write a brief that surpasses the one you wrote."

The moot court experience was still a sore point with Barnabas, and Paulus knew it. But Barnabas chose to take the bait anyway.

"Well, all it got me was second place." And he derisively added, "If I had just done a better job arguing the case, who knows what would have happened."

Paulus chuckled. "Now, now, Barnabas, what is that adage about crying over spilled milk?"

He felt he needed to put Professor Paulus on the defensive and distract him from the moot court days.

"Well, if you are calling to send me another client, I hope that it is someone who can pay his bills, unlike the last fellow."

Paulus laughed and then got serious. "Barnabas, I recommended you to Michael Abbott. He is the son of a dear friend of mine. He needs a good attorney, and he needs one now. And yes, he does have some money. I told him that you were the best student I've ever had."

"Thank you. That is a huge compliment. What is the case about, Professor?"

"He got served with papers three days ago. Midwest Disposal has him noticed up for a temporary restraining order in federal court on Monday at nine a.m. in front of Judge Kruger. Midwest is attempting to enforce a non-compete clause that was in Abbott's employment contract. If they win, he will have to move from the area if he wants to stay in his chosen field. He is willing to pay you to avoid it."

"Who is on the other side?"

"I'm sure you remember Richard Oxnard of the Frederick firm?"

"Sure I do. I think that if it were up to him, I would have been hired." Barnabas avoided conversation about how Bill had gotten the job. "Does Abbott have a defense?"

"I think so, but you'll have to talk with him yourself."

Abbott was scheduled to come into the office right after lunch the next day. Abbott arrived promptly at 1:00 p.m. He was five feet seven inches tall, had a portly figure, and was dressed in a coat and tie. He talked 300 words per minute, making it impossible for Barnabas to take any notes. After five minutes of attempting to listen, Barnabas finally lifted both of his hands and put the left hand on top of the right, forming a T and said, "Time out."

Barnabas was underwhelmed by his first impression of Abbott, but he did not trust first impressions. He had been burned relying on first impressions too many times in the past. His mother used to say, "Any ex-con can impress anyone for an hour." But he had to do something to get Abbott to slow down.

Abbott was startled by the gesture. He looked at Barnabas and smiled. "Am I talking too fast again?"

Barnabas grunted and nodded. "It would work better for me if you let me ask the questions, and you give me the answers rather than just giving me a narrative. I promise you that I will let you fill in the blanks if my questions overlook something."

Barnabas learned that Abbott had started a waste disposal business aptly named Abbott Disposal when he was only twenty-five years old. In fifteen years, he had built it up into a very good business with gross sales of eight million per year. He sold out to Midwest Disposal for $1.1 million in cash, and Midwest agreed to keep him on at an annual salary of $100,000 per year plus a ten percent commission on all sales he generated in excess of $250,000 per month.

After working for Midwest for only two weeks, Abbott had regretted his decision to sell. The corporate suits in the head office made all of the important decisions, but they didn't understand the waste disposal business. Abbott was forced to clear everything he did with people who were more concerned with not making mistakes rather than expanding the business. Four years later, he quit and started up his own business, taking with him all of the customers he'd had when he was operating Abbott Disposal.

Barnabas asked Abbott to give him the papers that had been served to him. The motion for a temporary restraining order was to be heard the following Monday, and the Frederick firm was seeking to have the judge issue an order prohibiting Abbott from continuing to operate his new business. Attached to the motion was the original contract from when Abbott sold Midwest his disposal business. Barnabas carefully looked over the document, which was over thirty-five pages, while Abbott fidgeted. On page thirty-two, toward the bottom, Barnabas found the standard-form, boilerplate language:

> Abbott shall not contact any present customer or former customer or any individual or company that has been a customer with Midwest Disposal for two (2) years after the date of Abbott's termination of employment.

Barnabas frowned. Hundreds of courts had looked at this type of language and ruled that it was enforceable. Every court would grant a temporary restraining order on the face of that language. It appeared that Abbott was going to be required to shut down his business. While the restraining order would be good for only ten days, full-scale injunctive relief prohibiting Abbott from competing with Midwest would inevitably follow. Unless Abbott had a good story to tell, it looked dim.

Barnabas returned to the complaint. Midwest was also contending that when Abbott left Midwest, he knew its trade secrets, especially the prices that it charged its best customers to dispose of their trash. Barnabas knew that Midwest had a right to protect its trade secrets. Typically, pricing information was considered a trade secret. Abbott seemed like a smart fellow; surely he understood that he was violating the covenant not to compete.

Barnabas sighed. "You must know that these covenants are enforceable. It plainly says that you cannot compete with them for two years after you leave. Why did you think you could immediately start competing with them?"

"Because I left the company over three years ago, and the clause is no longer enforceable."

"But the complaint alleges that you left only three months ago."

"That is true, too."

"How are both possible?"

"Because three years ago I left the company and moved to Arizona to start a company down there."

"How long were you gone?"

"Four months."

"You were really gone or you were just on leave?"

"I left. They even threw a retirement party for me."

Abbott opened his briefcase and smugly pulled out an envelope with a card in it. "Read this."

Barnabas took the card from the envelope, opened it, and read the card congratulating Abbott on his retirement. Barnabas paused. "Why did you come back?"

"I didn't like the climate, and the Midwest folks kept calling me and reminding me that I could have my old job back. Finally, I agreed, but I made it clear to them that I would not sign any contracts with a non-compete."

"Who did you deal with when you came back?"

"Gary Ross, the local branch manager."

"So you are saying that the contract they are suing on is no longer valid because you resigned your job and then came back later?"

"Precisely."

Barnabas pondered what Abbott had been telling him. The more he talked with Abbott, the more certain he was that Abbott was an easy guy to underestimate. His nervousness and motor mouth notwithstanding, it was clear that Abbott had thought about the situation carefully before he left the company.

"Okay, I understand why you think that the non-compete clause doesn't apply, but they also claim that you are using their trade secrets against them. If that is true, you are still going to lose. Do you know what a trade secret is?"

"I think I do. It is something that Midwest has developed that it wants to keep private, something that enables them to compete with its competitors."

"Yes. They claim that as their primary salesman, you know the prices they charge their best customers, and you can therefore routinely undercut their prices."

"Look, their best customers are the same folks that were my customers when I sold out."

"That may be true, but when you sold out, you gave those folks to Midwest."

"Well, their claim that their pricing is some kind of super-secret is a joke. Don't worry. Richard Adams will prove that for us. I have already told him to come to court."

Barnabas quickly recalled how much money he had in his operating account. It was down to less than $900. When he started his solo practice three months before, he vowed that he would start borrowing money to keep his doors open only as a last resort, and he knew that moment was almost upon him.

"Why did you go to Professor Paulus for a referral? Surely you could have found a lawyer some other way."

"I'll be honest. You are the fourth attorney I have talked with. One, without admitting it directly, was afraid of the Frederick firm. One didn't seem competent to me, even though he was highly recommended, and one wanted to charge me twenty-five thousand dollars to take the case. My father recommended that I talk with Professor Paulus, and he recommended you."

"Well, although I haven't been doing this that long, I have yet to run into a lawyer that causes me to quake when I see him in court. I haven't litigated against the Frederick folks yet, but they are not supermen. They had better have the law and facts with them, or they should expect to lose like any other lawyer. I am not going to pretend that when a judge sees the Frederick firm on one side and Barnabas Mitchell, solo practitioner, on the other that the intangibles are for us. But one thing I will assure you is that these guys are going to be in for a fight."

Abbott smiled. "Okay. What are you going to charge?"

Barnabas pondered his answer. He could not afford to let Abbott walk out of the office without leaving a check. This was also his chance to go against a litigation partner in the best firm in the city, and if the judge were open to following the law, Barnabas could actually win the case.

He also knew that he was going to spend every waking moment between Friday afternoon and Monday morning researching the law, preparing a legal memorandum, and preparing his witnesses. Abbott had balked at $25,000 for a more experienced attorney, and Barnabas knew that he needed at least $5000 to keep the next financial crisis away. Ten thousand was the most he could hope for under the circumstances. He decided to split the difference.

"I will be working the entire weekend without sleep. I will not do it for less than seventy-five hundred. I will need to talk with Adams on his cell phone, and you will need to spend the day with me tomorrow."

Abbott responded much too quickly. "Will you take a check?"

"A check will be fine."

Abbott wrote out a check for $7500 and handed it to Barnabas. As he stood, Abbott offered his hand. Barnabas was grateful for the money, but he knew that he should have asked for more given Abbott's quick response.

"I will be back tomorrow at ten a.m. to go over my testimony. Professor Paulus recommended you highly. Don't screw this up."

Barnabas escorted Abbott out and returned to his desk. He took a second look at the complaint, and as he turned the last page, a name jumped out at him. Just below the signature line for Richard Oxnard, the senior partner, was the name of the second lawyer on the case: Bill Cushman.

Barnabas had hoped that he would never see Bill again, and on Monday they were going to be opponents in court. He hoped that Oxnard wouldn't bring Bill, but he knew in his heart that Bill would be there.

Barnabas sighed. *Am I ever going to be rid of him?*

CHAPTER TWELVE

Barnabas spent the entire weekend writing his memorandum of law and preparing Abbott and Adams for trial. The hearing was set for 9:00 a.m. and the three of them walked into Federal District Judge Alice Kruger's courtroom at 8:40 a.m. just as the courtroom deputy was unlocking the doors. Barnabas was dressed in what he thought was his best suit. Abbott settled for a shirt and tie, and Adams wore a work shirt, his best jeans, and work boots, claiming that those were the best clothes he had available. Barnabas had neglected to instruct Adams about courtroom attire, but he was consoled by the fact that at least everything Adams wore was clean.

They went inside, and Barnabas chose not to sit at the counsel table because he was not sure whether other cases were going to be taken up that morning. Three minutes later, the deputy appeared with a docket sheet. Barnabas was relieved to see that "Midwest Disposal v. Abbott, Motion for Temporary Restraining Order" was one of the only matters pending that morning. He did not want the courtroom to be packed with other lawyers.

He took a seat at the counsel table while Abbott and Adams waited in the spectator pews. The last time he was this nervous was the finals in the moot court competition.

At 8:55 a.m., the courtroom doors opened, and in walked two men wearing expensive suits and a guy in a sport coat and tie. Of course, Bill was one of them. All three ignored Barnabas.

Barnabas flexed his finger and motioned Abbott to come sit at the counsel table. As soon as he sat down, Barnabas whispered in Abbott's ear. "Do you recognize any of those guys?"

"The guy in the coat and tie is Gary Ross, the branch manager."

Barnabas smiled and said, "I'm glad they brought him."

Immediately, a booming, very familiar baritone voice pierced the silence. "Barney! What the hell are you doing here?"

Barnabas looked up and forced a smile. He was not going to let Bill intimidate him.

"I'm here to beat you in court, Bill, and I am looking forward to it."

Bill attempted to get the advantage. "Well, you are going up against Richard here, and he is very good at what he does."

Barnabas opted for sarcasm. "I'm not worried. After all, I was trained by you."

Richard Oxnard observed the exchange with a perplexed expression, and Ross looked confused.

At that moment, the courtroom deputy, a woman in her mid-forties with a stout frame, reentered, smiled, and waved at Oxnard.

"So nice to see you here again, Richard. Did you bring an associate with you this time?"

"Clara, this is Bill Cushman. He will be assisting me this morning."

Looking over at Barnabas' table, Clara said, "The judge would like to see the attorneys in chambers. I am assuming that you are representing the defendant?" She eyed Barnabas condescendingly.

Barnabas leaned over and whispered to Abbott, "Don't let them shake you up. They may have been here before, but they are going to have to prove their case. This is probably going to be a session where the judge will pressure me to agree to their motion. But it's not going to happen. Don't worry."

Barnabas wasn't sure how to get to the judge's chambers, so he elected to follow Bill and Oxnard.

Oxnard paused and offered his hand as they approached the judge's chambers. "Richard Oxnard, and obviously you know Bill. Didn't you interview at our firm a couple of years ago? I remember your interview. You did well."

Barnabas extended his hand. "Yes, I did interview for a position. As for Bill, he and I go all the way back to high school, don't we, Bill?"

Bill smirked, but Oxnard smiled. Oxnard had a warm personality, a valuable trait for a trial lawyer. Bill was two inches taller than Barnabas, but Oxnard was no more than five feet eight inches tall. He looked like he was approaching fifty, and his brown hairline was starting to recede. He wore a dark-blue, pinstripe suit, an off-white shirt, and a blue silk tie with shades of yellow. Bill was wearing a dark-gray suit, a light-yellow shirt, and a red tie. He still had his nicely chiseled frame. Barnabas could see Bill's biceps through the sleeves in his suit when he raised his arms. Barnabas was wearing the best suit he had purchased off of eBay. It had cost him twenty-five dollars.

Barnabas was the last one to enter the judge's chambers. As soon as he entered, he was so overcome with cigarette smoke that he had to stifle a cough. The smell was overpowering. Judge Kruger was standing behind her desk smoking a cigarette, and behind her, at an appropriate distance, was a young woman in her mid-twenties with a pen in her right hand and a blank yellow pad in her left. She was obviously the judge's law clerk.

Judge Kruger was short and appeared to be a good forty pounds overweight. She was wearing a blue pantsuit, having not yet put on her judicial robe. Her face was heavily wrinkled, and Barnabas guessed that some of the wrinkles had developed because she spent most of her day with a frown on her face.

Barnabas was trying his best to ignore the smell, but it was difficult. Because she didn't have her robe on, Barnabas concluded that the judge didn't expect to hear any evidence in the case that day.

Judge Kruger took command of the room. "Everyone, please sit."

As they sat, she turned to Oxnard and said, "It is nice to see you again, Richard. Who is this with you?"

"This is Bill Cushman. He has been working on this case from the beginning. You're looking well, Your Honor. I understand that you have been on vacation. I hope that you didn't take any work with you."

Obviously Oxnard was pressing his advantage by getting familiar with the judge. Barnabas stifled a smile. By ingratiating himself with the judge, Oxnard was also sending Barnabas a signal: *I've been here before, and you haven't.* Judges, especially federal judges, did not publish their vacation plans in the newspaper. Oxnard assumed that Barnabas had only limited courtroom experience. But Oxnard could not have known that he had spent the last two years doing little else but trying cases, one right after another. Barnabas remained confident.

The judge turned to Barnabas. "And who are you, young man?"

Barnabas paused briefly. He could have read all sorts of things into the "young man" comment, and none of them were favorable for Abbott.

"My name is Barnabas Mitchell. I represent the defendant."

"And why haven't you entered your appearance before now?"

"Your Honor, I just got the file on Friday. I have been struggling to catch up."

The judge frowned and turned to Oxnard. "Richard, what is this case about?"

"It is very simple, Your Honor. At the time the defendant was hired by my client, he signed a covenant not to compete, which prohibited him from competing with us for two years after he left. Less than a week after he resigned, he set up his own consulting business, began calling our customers, and they started shipping their waste material to our competitors. As our lead salesman in the area, he knows who our customers are and what prices we charge. Our pricing is a trade secret. The court should enforce the covenant and enjoin him from disclosing our trade secrets."

Judge Kruger didn't want to let Barnabas give his own narrative, and that was fine with him. Instead, she began to cross-examine him. "Mr. Mitchell, do you plan on filing any counter-affidavits, putting an issue of fact in dispute?"

"Your Honor, I would like to call some witnesses after they rest their case."

"Well, did your client sign this covenant or not?"

"He did, but it is not enforceable."

Judge Kruger started to roll her eyes, but she caught herself. Apparently she had concluded that she was dealing with a naïve young lawyer with limited experience. The judge pressed on. "What about the trade secrets? You do agree that if these are trade secrets then Richard can get his TRO, even if there were no covenant."

The judge was coming close to patronizing him, but Barnabas was not going to let her distract him from his case.

"That is true, Your Honor."

"So then why can't I enter the TRO on the trade secrets count and we can dispose of this matter now?"

"Because they're not trade secrets. I have prepared a thirty-page memorandum setting forth our position if you would like to read it."

Barnabas was hoping that the judge would decline his offer because he didn't want to give Oxnard time to read it as well. It was evident that there was going to be a hearing because Barnabas would not agree to

Midwest getting an order by agreement.

Judge Kruger showed her impatience. "I'm not going to spend the entire day on this case. I am well aware of the law, and I don't need to read any lengthy memorandums. It seems clear to me that the plaintiff has made out a prima facie case when it filed the motion with the affidavits. Young man, I am going to give you one hour only to convince me that I shouldn't grant this motion. I am going to enter the courtroom in five minutes. That is when your hour is going to start."

The judge started to stand, and on cue, everyone else did as well. As Barnabas stood up, he glanced over at Oxnard and Bill. Bill looked confident, but Oxnard looked worried. Oxnard seemed to understand that there might be problems without knowing why. Perhaps the judge had underestimated Barnabas, but Oxnard had not. If Barnabas was reading the situation correctly, Oxnard had marvelous instincts. If Oxnard played poker for relaxation, he had to be good at it.

As Barnabas walked into the courtroom, he glanced over at Abbott. Barnabas gave him a smile and a slight nod of the head, and Abbott's worried expression changed instantly.

Barnabas sat down next to Abbott and whispered, "The judge is going to hear evidence. I will try to get this over with without having to call you as a witness. Try and make as much eye contact with Ross as possible without making it obvious. I am going to call him first, and I want him to be uncomfortable."

Five minutes later, the judge walked into the courtroom. The clerk banged the gavel and yelled, "All rise! Oh yee, oh yee, oh yee, the Federal District Court for the Northern District of Illinois is now in session. All who have business before this court may be heard at this time."

As Judge Kruger sat down, she cleared her throat and said, "Please be seated."

Barnabas sat on the edge of his chair, as he knew he would be putting on his evidence first.

The judge then spoke. "This is the case of Midwest Disposal versus Abbott, and we are here today on the plaintiff's motion for a temporary restraining order. Will Counsel state their appearances?"

Having just sat down, Oxnard stood up again. "Richard Oxnard for the plaintiff, and I am here with my associate, Bill Cushman. Here with me at the counsel table is Gary Ross, who is the corporate representative for Midwest Disposal."

Barnabas stood up. "Barnabas Mitchell for Michael Abbott, the defendant. Mr. Abbott is here with me."

Judge Kruger briefed the courtroom on the ground rules. "We had a discussion in chambers. Because we are here on an emergency petition, I informed Counsel that the plaintiff has made out a prima facie case with the affidavits that were filed with the motion. Mr. Mitchell claims that there are facts in dispute, and I am going to let him call some witnesses before I rule. But I have already admonished Counsel that we are not going to spend all day on this. Mr. Mitchell, call your first witness."

Immediately Oxnard stood, and Judge Kruger nodded in his direction.

"Your Honor, Defendant moves to exclude witnesses."

Judge Kruger asked Barnabas, "Counsel, do you intend to call any witnesses other than your client?"

"Yes, Your Honor, we do."

"The motion is granted. Mr. Mitchell, your client is permitted to remain, and Mr. Ross, the corporate representative, can remain as well. All other witnesses are excluded."

Barnabas turned to Richard Adams and said, "You are going to have to wait outside the courtroom until you are called."

Adams got up and walked out of the courtroom. As the door closed, Barnabas looked up and noticed that the judge was not pleased. He assumed that the displeasure was with Adams' attire.

"Call your first witness," Judge Kruger instructed.

"Gary Ross, Your Honor," announced Barnabas.

Oxnard and Bill looked surprised. Oxnard glanced at Bill, and Bill shrugged. Neither of them seemed to know why Ross was being called, but it was apparent that Oxnard expected Bill to know how Ross could possibly help Abbott. At this point, even Bill looked worried.

The clerk gave Ross the oath, and he sat down.

Barnabas looked at the judge, and he sensed that she was curious what the line of questioning would be.

"You may inquire, Mr. Mitchell."

"You are Gary Ross, and you are the branch manager for Midwest's local landfill, isn't that correct?"

"True."

"And you have known the defendant, Michael Abbott, for several years?"

"Also true."

"Now, the contract that includes the covenant not to compete that was signed by my client involved the sale of his business, Abbott Disposal, isn't that correct?"

"I believe so."

"Well, as local manager before Abbott left four months ago, he reported to you, correct?"

"Yes."

"And as his supervisor, can you identify any other contract with Abbott that contains a covenant not to compete other than the one signed four years ago when he sold the business?"

"No. That is the only contract."

"And you would agree that the covenant expires two years after Abbott leaves Midwest Disposal?"

At that point, Oxnard made what Barnabas thought was a weak objection. Oxnard wanted to break the flow of the cross-examination. "Objection, Your Honor, calls for a legal conclusion as to the meaning of the contract."

Judge Kruger responded sharply. "Overruled. It is clearly foundational only. I will give it whatever weight it deserves."

Barnabas read her tone to mean that she wanted the hearing to move rapidly with a minimal number of objections. Barnabas repeated the question.

Ross responded, "I am not aware of any other covenant than the one in the original contract."

Barnabas proceeded to drive home his first point. "When was the first time Abbott left the company?"

Barnabas looked at the judge out of the corner of his eye. She clearly picked up on the "first time" reference.

Ross attempted to evade the question. "He left us four months ago."

"But that was not the question. I want to know when he left the first time."

Ross started to squirm, and he looked over at Oxnard and Bill. Oxnard stared at Ross. "Well, he left us briefly, but that was only for a few months," said Ross.

Barnabas went to his briefcase and pulled out the card given to Abbott at his retirement party three and a half years prior. Barnabas first showed it to Oxnard. Oxnard attempted to keep a straight face, but Barnabas guessed that Abbott's prior retirement was something that Oxnard was just learning about. Oxnard looked over at Bill and arched his right eyebrow. Oxnard handed the card back to Barnabas, and then Barnabas presented it to Ross.

"Handing you Defendant's Exhibit 1. Do you recognize that card?"

There was a long pause. Ross didn't want to answer the question. Barnabas could not resist. He looked at Oxnard and gave him a small smile. Oxnard did not respond.

"Well, let me help out, Mr. Ross. Do you recognize your signature on the card?"

"Yeah, it's here."

Ross' response was barely audible, causing the judge to admonish him. "Mr. Ross, you are going to have to speak up. Even with the microphone, neither the court reporter nor I could hear you."

This time Ross spoke too loudly. "Yeah, it's mine."

"And you recognize some of the other signatures, don't you?"

"Well, they appear to be the rest of the folks working in the local office at that time."

"And that was more than three years ago when you and the others signed the card?"

"It was about then, yes."

"Please read the card so that the judge can hear what it says."

Ross read it aloud. "You are going to have to accept this card instead of a gold watch."

Barnabas saw the judge as the corners of her mouth arched slightly upward.

"You all chipped in and bought a cake, isn't that true?"

"Yeah."

"And Abbott went to Arizona the next day, isn't that true?"

"Yeah."

"And he didn't draw a paycheck for another four months?"

"Yes."

"But you kept in touch with him even though he was in Arizona?"

"Well, we did talk on the phone."

"And during that four-month period, he wasn't a Midwest employee, was he?"

"Not technically, I guess."

"Well, Mr. Ross, how can one be an un-technical Midwest employee?"

Oxnard finally had something he could object to, and he rose. "Objection, argumentative."

Judge Kruger agreed. "Sustained, Mr. Mitchell. I get your point. It is time to move on."

"Of course, Your Honor. Now Mr. Ross, I would like to turn to the issue of your customers. When Abbott sold his business to Midwest, he brought between twenty and twenty-five customers with him, isn't that true?"

"Yes, and we paid over a million dollars for those customers. Does he expect us to pay that kind of money just so he can take them back?"

Barnabas chose to ignore the response. "Can you name any additional customers that were brought to your landfill after Abbott sold it to you?"

"Well, the three largest ones would be Phillpott Manufacturing, Suncrest Coal, and Bear Creek Engineering."

"And Abbott brought those three to you, correct?"

"That was what he was paid to do."

"You have two other competitors in the region, those being Great Lakes Disposal and Fortran Waste, true?"

"Those are the main ones."

"And Phillpott, Suncrest, and Bear Creek are not your secret customers. Great Lakes and Fortran know who they are, don't they?"

"I don't know."

Barnabas glanced over at Oxnard, who was clearly pleased with the answer.

"Mr. Ross, have you and Abbott ever camped out outside of Fortran's and Great Lakes' landfills in order to find out who their customers are?"

"I don't know what you mean by 'camped out.'"

"Okay. You and Abbott parked your vehicle on public property just outside of their landfills and wrote down the names of the trucks that hauled waste into those landfills."

"We have done that before."

"In fact, you made a habit of doing it at least once a month."

"About that."

"And the reason for spending that time was so that Midwest could go to those folks and try and get their business."

"I guess."

"And on several occasions you have seen people parked in vehicles just outside your landfill writing down the names of the trucks that were taking waste into your landfill, true?"

"I don't know what they were doing."

"But you believed that they were doing the same thing you had been doing to them, correct?"

"I don't know that."

Barnabas decided not to press the point.

"Now, as to your prices, you post your prices for dumping trash on a board as people enter your dump, don't you?"

"Yes, but as to large jobs, we keep the price secret."

"Have you ever had a potential customer tell you what the competitor has quoted them?"

Ross paused for more than ten seconds. Barnabas' confidence rose as Ross apparently groped for an answer that was acceptable to Midwest. "Yes, that has happened."

"When you quote a price to a customer, do you make them sign a statement promising to keep the price confidential?"

Again there was a long pause. "No," Ross answered.

"No more questions."

Oxnard did not attempt to rehabilitate Ross, choosing to let the matter rest.

"No questions from the plaintiff."

Barnabas then asked the bailiff to bring in Richard Adams. The judge eyed him again, showing her displeasure with his courtroom dress. He was sworn in, and Barnabas rose to begin his questioning.

"You are Richard Adams. Tell the court what you do."

"I'm a trucker."

"How long have you been a trucker?"

"Over forty years."

"Do you know Michael Abbott?"

"Yes."

"How do you know him?"

"He's in the trash business, and I haul a lot of trash."

The judge chuckled, which gave permission for everyone else to chuckle as well.

"Do you know Gary Ross?"

"Same answers as with Michael. He's in the trash business as well."

"Do you haul into the Midwest landfill?"

"Do you mean the dump?"

"Dump or landfill, whatever works for you."

"Yeah, I haul into his dump every day."

"How about Fortran, do you haul trash there?"

"Every day."

"And the Great Lakes dump?"

"Every day."

"Are there other truckers that haul trash?"

"Sure, I've got competition, but I still haul more trash than any other trucker in the region. We have thirty trucks. We operate two shifts, six days a week."

"Why is that?"

"For some reason I like to haul trash. My wife says it suits my personality."

This time Judge Kruger guffawed.

"Do you know of any customers that use only Midwest?"

"None. They're always shopping for prices."

"How about Phillpott Manufacturing, Suncrest Mining, Bear Creek Engineering?"

"I hauled trash for all three to the Great Lakes dump last week."

"Now, you are not an employee of Midwest, are you?"

"Nope, never worked for anyone else a day in my life."

"Do you know what price Midwest charges for trash compared to Phillpott, Suncrest, and Bear Creek?"

"Sure do."

"Why is that?"

"Because they print the price on the invoice."

"Explain to the court how that works."

"When you bring in a load, they weigh the truck before and after you dump the trash. They print out an invoice using carbons, keeping one for themselves and giving two to me. They multiply the weight in pounds by the price. The total charge is right on the invoice. I give the customer's copy to him when I return for the next load."

"Why do you keep a copy?"

"Because I don't get paid unless I can prove that I dumped the trash."

"Did you bring any of your copies with you today?"

"Sure did. I gave them all to you."

Barnabas then reached into his briefcase and pulled out a six-inch stack of carbon copies. He handed them to Oxnard, who spent three minutes studying them. His frown deepened as time passed. While Oxnard was looking at the invoices, Barnabas looked over at Bill, but Bill avoided his gaze. Oxnard grunted and handed the papers back to Barnabas, who approached the witness chair and gave them to Adams.

"From these invoices, can you tell me what Midwest's prices are to dump trash?"

"Sure can."

"Please show the judge."

Looking at Judge Kruger, Adams picked up the first invoice. "This is from Phillpott last Friday, and the price was $1.27 per pound. The second is from Suncrest, and the price was $1.27 per pound. The third one is from Bear Creek, and the price was $1.27 per pound. Going through this stack last month, Midwest was charging $1.33 per pound, but on the first of the month they dropped their price to $1.27."

Barnabas glanced over at Oxnard, who was looking at the witness, keeping his poker face. But Bill was looking down at the table.

Judge Kruger said, "It's time for a break. I want to see Counsel in chambers."

Five minutes later, Barnabas, Oxnard, and Bill were sitting in front of the judge's desk. She had already taken off her robe, signaling that there would be no more evidence taken that day.

She looked over at Oxnard and Bill. "Richard, you know how I'm going to rule unless you have something that convincingly rebuts this. Your pricing is clearly not a trade secret if the truckers know what it is. You can't enforce the covenant because you didn't get him to sign a new contract when he came back. I suggest that you go into the jury room and get this settled."

Five minutes later, Ross and Oxnard met Barnabas and Abbott in the jury room. Bill was not there.

Oxnard opened the discussion. "Okay, Barnabas, what do you want?"

"Dismiss the complaint with prejudice, and pay us seventy-five hundred dollars in attorney's fees."

Abbott tugged Barnabas' coat sleeve and whispered, "What does 'with prejudice' mean?"

"It means that they can never file suit against you again," Barnabas whispered back.

Abbott nodded and resumed his taciturn pose.

"I can understand the dismissal," Oxnard responded, "but you have to give me a good reason why we should pay attorney's fees."

Barnabas smiled. He was enjoying hitting up Midwest for money because of Bill's mistakes. "Because it is clear that you guys filed this without fully investigating the facts of the case. Given the judge's mood, I think there is a fair chance that she may give us sanctions. Even if she doesn't, we have a good appeal on the sanctions issue. If we win the case on appeal, we could get sanctions for the costs and fees in the trial court as well as costs and attorney's fees on appeal."

"Look, you got a good result, but don't press your luck. I'm prepared to recommend that we split the difference. We'll pay you thirty-five hundred. Your client will be overjoyed with the result, and we both know it."

Barnabas smiled. Of course, Oxnard was right. Abbott would be happy without getting any of his money back. Barnabas turned to a delighted Abbott who quickly agreed to the terms while Oxnard privately discussed the matter with Ross.

Ten minutes later, Oxnard said, "Okay, it's a deal. We will dismiss with prejudice and cut you a check for thirty-five hundred dollars within the next five days."

Barnabas was impressed with Oxnard. He had handled it professionally. He knew his client was going to lose, and he minimized the losses immediately. Barnabas was tempted to feel sorry for Bill, but given their history, he couldn't do it. Either Bill hadn't asked his client the right questions or his client had lied to him. He had gone into court thinking that he had a slam-dunk winner and walked out completely embarrassed. He had also embarrassed his boss.

It was a good feeling for Barnabas; he had beaten the best firm in the city, and he had $7500 in his operating account, which meant he could practice law for another month. It felt even better that he had thoroughly trounced Bill. Bill had been with the Frederick firm for more than two years. *Bill's work ethic must be catching up with him*, Barnabas thought.

Barnabas, Abbott, Oxnard, and Ross went back into the courtroom. As Barnabas and Oxnard were reciting the agreement before the judge and the court reporter, Barnabas noticed a stir in the courtroom but chose to keep his eyes forward, focusing on the judge.

"Thank you, gentlemen. I want to congratulate you both on doing a good job representing your clients." She then smiled at Barnabas, conveying that she had a newly acquired respect for him.

Judge Kruger then called the next case. "Okay, United States versus Boyd, Motion to Suppress. Is everyone ready to go?"

Barnabas turned and saw the defendant in prison garb and a young lawyer seated next to him. He assumed that the lawyer was from the federal public defender's office. Barnabas looked at him and gave him a knowing smile. *Been there, done that.* He turned to the prosecution table and saw a familiar face in a suit and tie seated next to the United States attorney. It was Sam Schultz. He gave Barnabas an expansive smile and beckoned him to come over.

Barnabas approached the table. Sam rose, extended his hand, and Barnabas took it.

"If you have time, why don't you stick around and come to lunch with me?" Sam said. "I have lunch set up with Stephanie, and I'm sure that she'd like to catch up with you."

Barnabas responded immediately. "I'd love to have lunch. I'll hang around and wait. It will be fun to catch up."

Barnabas had had the whole day set aside for court, and he was feeling good about the $7500 in his account. He looked forward to having lunch. He even had enough money that he could offer to pick up the tab.

He went out into the hallway to say a final good-bye to Abbott and then walked back into the courtroom, taking a seat in the back pew. Sam was already on the witness stand. He had been the arresting officer, and the question seemed to be whether a handgun found in the defendant's closet was in plain view. Sam was very professional in the way he testified. It was obvious that he had testified hundreds of times before. The defense attorney made a cursory attempt at shaking his testimony but gave up after ten minutes of questioning.

If there were anything approaching the routine, this hearing was it. In a bored monotone, Judge Kruger ruled. "I find Agent Schultz's testimony to be credible. Motion to Suppress is denied."

CHAPTER THIRTEEN

Sam Schultz and Barnabas went to a small café near the courthouse that served burgers. Stephanie came in five minutes later. It had been more than two years since he had seen her, but she was even more beautiful. Her hair was longer, and she was wearing what appeared to be an expensive suit. As his mother had taught him to do when one of his elders or a woman approached, he stood up and gave his best smile.

Stephanie extended her hand and said, "Barnabas, it is so nice to see you again."

She looked over at her dad and said, "Where did you bump into Barnabas?"

"He was just finishing a case in federal court in front of Judge Kruger. It sounds like he did really well with the Frederick firm on the other side."

"Congratulations," Stephanie said. "It sounds like you are spending quality time in court. Most of my time is spent behind a desk writing memoranda or drafting contracts."

The first and only time Barnabas had been with Sam and Ruth, the conversation had centered on him, and he vowed not to have that happen again. He started in with questions. "So it sounds like you're still at the Clausen-Ferguson firm?"

"Yes. Still there."

Before he could ask a follow-up question, she turned it back on him. "And you left the PD's office and went out on your own?"

Barnabas paused, planning his next step to direct the conversation back to her. "Yeah, I couldn't handle the PD's office anymore, but how about you? Did I make a mistake in not trying to get into a firm?"

"Oh, Barnabas, I have no doubt that you will be successful at anything you do. How many cases did you try when you were in the PD's office?"

Is she doing this on purpose or is this something she does naturally? It had become a challenge. He was not going to give in; he was determined to get her talking about herself.

"After the first four months, I lost count," said Barnabas. "Were you being facetious? They are not letting you go to court?"

"Most of my time has been arguing motions or attending case management conferences. I did try one case without a jury that took less than a day."

Before she could ask him another question, he quickly followed up. "Tell me about it."

She looked directly at him and smiled. She seemed pleased that he really wanted to know how she was doing.

"My client had signed a five-year lease, but she left two years early and moved her business to a new location. She got sued for the additional two years in rent."

"How did the judge rule?"

"He didn't give the plaintiff anything."

"So you won your first case. Congratulations. What arguments did you make? It seems like the landlord would have had a strong case."

"The landlord had a duty to seek another tenant, which he did not, and he admitted that he had agreed to let my client leave early."

"Was the agreement in writing? Why wasn't there a problem with the statute of frauds?"

"There was part performance, and I made an estoppel argument that the judge seemed to like."

Stephanie turned to her father then back to Barnabas. "We're not going to talk about the law this whole time, are we?"

Barnabas shrugged. He was proud of having not spent the first part of lunch talking about himself. It was only a small victory but a victory nonetheless.

Sam Schultz decided to take his turn. "How have you been, Barnabas? I had been meaning to track you down and get caught up."

"I'm flattered by that, sir. I tried to get a job in the Frederick firm right out of law school, but that failed. I learned how to try cases in the state public defender's office, but I couldn't take it anymore, so I started a solo practice."

"How are you doing? Keeping your head above water?"

"I'm paying my bills, including my school loans. I've only been doing it three months, and each month seems to get a little better."

"It looked like a big win today to me. You've gotta feel good about that."

Stephanie interjected. "Big settlement?"

Barnabas smiled. "We got a good result. The evidence went in well, but we had both the facts and the law. I was worried about the case getting political, but Judge Kruger, although crusty, was fair."

"Judge Kruger is a straight arrow," responded Sam. "She will not let politics influence the outcome."

Barnabas turned to Stephanie. "Do you really dislike the firm?"

"Oh, I tolerate it. I am getting good experience, but I don't see myself staying there for a long time."

"What don't you like about it?"

"I have no control over what clients I represent or what law I practice."

"Well, at least you know that you are going to get a steady paycheck."

"Barnabas," Sam cut in, still wanting to redirect the conversation, "I think about you quite often. Like I say, I should have done this sooner."

"I didn't know that I made that kind of impression on you, sir."

"Barnabas, you remind me of myself when I was your age. I had to work for everything I had. If you are like me, I'm sure there are times when you just want to give up. But in the end, guys like us, we just don't quit. We always hang in there. You have to trust me when I say that in the end, you are going to be a winner."

"Why are you so confident, sir?"

"You have good character. You work hard. You are not a selfish person. You continue to persevere, and I believe that God will reward you in the end."

"But sir, I don't believe in God."

Sam Schultz paused and chuckled to himself. "I really do not mean to be condescending, but once I was where you are. You do believe in God, you just don't know it, much less want to acknowledge it."

"That's an interesting thought, sir. Someone believes in God but doesn't know it."

Sam Schultz smiled and put his hand on Barnabas' shoulder as they got up. "Trust me, one day you will know what I mean."

As they walked out of the café, they promised each other that they would meet again. Barnabas buttoned up his overcoat, and he noticed a leaf fall from a maple tree that was growing out of the pavement. It had been a good day. For once he had gotten the better of Bill. He had beaten what was reputed to be the best firm in the city. He could practice law another month. And Stephanie and Sam Schultz had promised to meet him again.

CHAPTER FOURTEEN

The following Monday night, Barnabas' cell phone rang. "Barnabas, it's Sam Schultz. We want you at our house for Thanksgiving."

"Oh, I don't think I can," Barnabas lied. Barnabas thought that Thanksgiving was such a personal family holiday, and he wasn't sure he would feel comfortable.

"Look, we've cleared it with Ruth, and my boys are here for the week. They are anxious to meet you. Stephanie wants to see you again. I know that you have to be ready for a home-cooked meal. When is the last time you've had one?" Sam continued without letting Barnabas answer. "Everyone will get here about noon, and we'll eat around four p.m. In the meantime, you can sit in front of the fireplace with the boys and me and watch football and eat Ruth and Stephanie's rolls. You have to come. I will pick you up at eleven thirty Thursday morning."

Sam paused and then asked Barnabas a question. "By any chance do you play basketball?"

Barnabas found himself smiling. "I've been known to shoot a few hoops now and then. Why do you want to know?"

Sam chuckled. "Basketball is a big thing in our family. You had better bring your gym bag. I'll get crucified if Stephanie finds out that you play basketball and I didn't tell you to bring your gym bag. You will have no choice. You are going to be drafted to play."

"Okay, I'll bring it if I really have no choice."

"You don't." And Sam laughed again.

Sam hung up without Barnabas having actually said yes. He was surprised that Sam was so insistent.

When they drove home together after the moot court competition, the Schultzes had made it clear that they believed in God. The division between them was made even clearer when they had lunch together. He did not share the Schultz family's beliefs, and they knew it. But they wanted to be his friend. He was curious why.

On Thursday morning there was a knock on his apartment door at 11:30 a.m. Sam was there as promised. Barnabas was about to leave without his gym bag, but thankfully, Sam reminded him.

As they drove to the Schultz family home, Barnabas thought about Stephanie's brothers, and he was curious what they were going to be like. He hadn't heard much about them. He was also curious who would be on the basketball teams. Clearly the two brothers would be playing, but did Sam play as well? Should he understand Sam's remarks to mean that Stephanie was a player?

They arrived shortly after noon. Barnabas immediately looked for Stephanie. She was there, of course, standing next to her mother. Barnabas did not think she realized how compelling her beauty was. He quickly looked away because he didn't want to be caught staring. Her two brothers, Robert and Mark, were there, along with an attractive blonde woman who was introduced as Molly, Robert's wife.

Everyone was friendly, but Barnabas felt uncomfortable. He was afraid of what would happen, but he wasn't quite sure why. It was more than the fact that he felt like an intruder. He also thought that spending several hours with such a close-knit family was new to him, and he wasn't sure whether he would fit in.

Robert was the oldest, three years older than Stephanie. He had been recently married and was finishing his residency as a pulmonologist. Molly worked as a CPA. Mark, the middle child, was an electrical engineer. He was engaged to a woman named Ashley, but she was with her family for the holiday. During the drive over, Sam had warned Barnabas that all of the Schultz men loved football.

After he had been introduced to the whole family, Ruth approached Barnabas. "Do you have a cell phone with you?"

"Yes," Barnabas said, perplexed.

Ruth reached out her hand, palm up. "Give it to me. It is a family rule. I confiscate all cell phones during family time. And Thanksgiving is family time."

With no remorse, Barnabas gave his phone to her. It never rang on Thanksgiving anyway.

Sam put his arm around Barnabas' shoulders and started to drag him toward the room where the television was blaring. He heard the announcer declare, "It's time for football!"

The room was a men-only place, and Barnabas wasn't sure whether the women had chosen to give the men some male bonding time or they didn't care about football or both. The truth was that he was as indifferent about football as the women seemed to be. He had not watched much TV in his life, but he settled into a comfortable chair next to a warm fire going in the fireplace, watching with amusement as Sam, Mark, and Robert got emotionally involved in the game. The Cowboys were playing the Bears, and Barnabas quickly learned that Sam and Mark were avid Bears fans while Robert rooted for the Cowboys. Robert had taken a residency in Texas, and he had treated one of the Cowboys coaches. Sam and Mark good-naturedly labeled him a traitor. While they enjoyed the game and enjoyed being with one another, it was also clear that they were heavily invested in seeing their teams win. There were constant high fives between Sam and Mark whenever the Bears had a good play.

After an hour, Barnabas decided to join in. Just to make it even, he became a Cowboys fan. There were simultaneous groans and high fives for the rest of the game as Barnabas celebrated or groaned in lockstep with Robert.

Five minutes after the game was over, Stephanie entered the room dressed in basketball shoes and shorts. "Okay, the game's over. Time for basketball," she said, looking at her brothers. "I don't suppose the two of you are willing to break up the team, are you?" Barnabas noticed her emphasis on "the team."

"No way!" they said simultaneously.

Evidently there was a history among them that Barnabas would have to learn about later. Barnabas was curious. Who usually played with Stephanie? How serious was this rivalry? He was surprised at his level of anxiety. He didn't understand why. He changed into his gym clothes.

They went out the back door, and the basket, which was on the edge of the driveway, appeared to be exactly ten feet high. The driveway clearly had been poured to accommodate basketball playing. The driveway next to the basket was flat with no slope at all and was about twenty by thirty feet. It extended well beyond the edge of the garage. Barnabas smiled.

They had obviously spent hours on this court.

The four of them warmed up, and Barnabas noticed that Stephanie, Mark, and Robert were all sizing him up. He decided to have a little fun and took several shots from the grass off the court, more than thirty-five feet away from the basket. He missed them all, knowing that he would. He sensed fear and disgust in Stephanie's eyes. Reluctantly, she said, "Okay, let's start."

Robert said, "Okay, first team to twenty-one wins. Have to win by two."

He pulled out a coin. "You call it," he said to his sister as he flipped the coin.

"Heads," called Stephanie.

The coin landed. "Tails," Robert announced proudly.

Stephanie moved over to Barnabas and with obvious nervousness said, "You and Robert are the same size, and Mark is only two inches taller than I am. Can you guard Robert?"

Barnabas was surprised at the intensity in her voice. He thought this was going to be a friendly game, but her voice told him otherwise.

"Sure, I'll take Robert."

Mark and Robert moved away from the basket. Mark passed the ball to Stephanie, and she looked around, assuring herself that Barnabas was in a defensive position, and passed the ball back to Mark. The game was on.

Mark passed the ball to Robert. Robert faked a pass, got Barnabas to shift his weight, and as Barnabas was recovering, Robert drove right past him and made a layup for the first basket.

Barnabas was embarrassed. He looked at Stephanie. She did her best to disguise her disappointment, but from her demeanor, it was obvious she didn't think Barnabas had the skills to make the game competitive.

Quickly, Robert and Mark got off to a 5-0 lead. Mark played Stephanie tightly, and Robert played off Barnabas. Barnabas missed his first four shots that were all twenty feet away. He didn't think he had ever been so nervous in a basketball game, even playing in college.

At that point, it seemed that Stephanie was just going through the motions, resigning herself to losing. They scored a point here and there, but then Barnabas started to find the range, and he hit five shots in a row. Stephanie made four shots, and all of sudden the game was tied at twelve.

Barnabas looked at the house. The rest of the family had gravitated to the family room bay window to watch the game.

The game got even more intense. All four of them started to play tight defense; they might as well have been playing for the NCAA championship. The Schultz kids had obviously played before and at a very high level at that. All three of them wanted to win so badly, and that intensity had been transferred to Barnabas. Stephanie didn't want to lose, and Barnabas didn't want her to lose. He started to play as if his life were at stake.

After the twelfth point, Robert started to press Barnabas, but Barnabas was able to drive around him when he did. Mark would pick him up to prevent a layup, and Barnabas was then able to pass the ball to Stephanie, who would lay it up. On defense, Barnabas played Robert just tight enough that he would be able to interfere with his shot but back far enough so that he couldn't drive. Robert would pass the ball to Mark, who would attempt to back his way under the basket for a shorter shot, bullying his sister. But Stephanie was surprisingly strong, and she did a good job standing her ground.

After forty-five minutes, they were exhausted, but no one was willing to ask for a break.

When the score was tied at fifteen, Mark missed a shot badly. "Foul. I'll take the ball," he said. Barnabas was surprised by the intensity of Stephanie's response. "You're crying foul? You've been backing into me on offense in a way that you could teach Shaq lessons, and you are tapped lightly on the wrist and you cry foul?"

Mark was not going to be intimidated. "You bothered my shot and you know it. Give me the ball. If you think you are being fouled, call it, but remember this is a man's game. Now give me the ball."

Barnabas looked at her. Sweat had broken through her T-shirt and was all over her forehead. Her hair was tied tightly behind her head. But as she was arguing with her brother, she looked incredibly sexy.

The game went on for another ten minutes. Stephanie hit a fifteen-foot shot, and they were ahead 20-19. Mark missed a turn-around shot, and Stephanie grabbed the rebound. On offense, Stephanie passed the ball to Barnabas. She went over to Robert, faking a screen, and then broke for the basket. It was the same play that Coach Martinson had used back in high school. They performed it as if they had been playing with one another for years. Mark was caught flat-footed. Barnabas passed Stephanie the ball, and she made the layup. They had won.

Immediately, Stephanie shouted, turned, ran toward Barnabas, and jumped into his arms. Barnabas was shocked. It was as if she had won a major championship. Robert and Mark looked down, dejected. When they regained their composure, they came over and shook his hand.

"Great play," said Mark.

"Good job," Robert said. "You'll have to give us a rematch sometime."

Barnabas said, "Thanks. Good game yourself." But he was still confused about what had just happened.

He went back in the house and waited for his turn in the shower. They ate dinner at four. Barnabas could not recall ever seeing so much food, and all of it was good. He had never eaten that much in one meal.

Toward the end of the meal, Barnabas could not contain his curiosity any longer. He chose to address his question to Sam. "Sir, if I could ask you a question?"

"Certainly."

"It is a wonderful family that you have here. And I know that you would give a large portion of the credit to God. But how can you be so certain that there even is a God, much less that Christ was His son?"

Sam smiled. It was obvious that he liked the question and was pleased that it had been asked. "It is a difficult question to give a short answer to, but generally, I have found that the claims made in the Bible are true. The Bible tells us humans how to live our lives, and when we are true to the way we were created, then there is great joy in life. Our family accepts the Bible as the Word of God." Sam paused and then asked, "What do you think?"

Barnabas decided to answer the question with a question. "But how do you know the Bible is true? None of us were there. How do you know that it is not a book of fiction?"

Robert weighed in. "The Bible has been shown to be a reliable historical record in cases when it can be verified."

"But I am told that there are many inconsistencies in the Bible. The text that is used for the English translations was written three hundred years after the events were alleged to have occurred."

It was Stephanie's turn. "The same can be said about Homer, Aristotle, and Plato's writings, but no one doubts that they wrote those works. Why a different standard for the Bible?"

Barnabas knew that he was arguing points that they had thought about and he hadn't, but he was truly curious what motivated them. They had a confidence and joy that he usually didn't see in people.

As Barnabas paused, Sam returned to his point. "God is not going to be measured by any human standard. If one were to read the Bible and truly examine the teachings of Christ, he could see that this is divine teaching."

Molly seconded the thought. "It is the only way to live your life."

Then Stephanie took another turn. "Barnabas, you were such a good son to your mother. What motivated you to do that? Where do you think that love comes from?"

At that moment, Barnabas felt a hand grab his right hand and gently squeeze it. He looked at Ruth, who was sitting to his right. There was a nervous smile on her face that conveyed her concern that Barnabas was feeling ganged up against.

"Family, you are not going to convert him in one sitting. He is much too careful a young man for that."

Barnabas marveled at her gracious act and supportive statement. But he wanted to show that he did not resent the discussion. "It's all right. After all, I asked the question. All they are doing is answering it. It is obvious that you have created a nice environment here. I am just curious whether it is based on the truth or what you want to be the truth. In my mind, there is a big difference."

They chose to give him the last word and honor Ruth's injunction.

Robert, Mark, Sam, and Barnabas retired to the TV room after dinner. As he sat in the chair next to the fireplace, Barnabas got comfortable. Before he knew it, he fell asleep. The sleep had come on suddenly, and he'd had little opportunity to fight it off.

He awoke at 6:00 a.m. the next morning, lying on the couch with his head under a pillow with two blankets on top of him. He wasn't sure how he had made it from the chair to the couch.

Barnabas felt embarrassed. His mother would have been appalled. But he felt so natural and comfortable with them that he gave into the temptation to fall asleep.

He found the bathroom, and when he came out, Ruth was in the kitchen making coffee and starting breakfast. She smiled at him. "Come sit at the kitchen counter. We didn't get a chance to talk yesterday. Did you sleep well?"

"I am embarrassed. My mother would have been horrified by my behavior."

She laughed. "Oh, it's okay. You should always feel welcome here. My grandmother told me that one of the sincerest forms of flattery is when a guest falls asleep at your house. It means that they are comfortable in your presence, and that is why we want you to come. Have you always been an early riser?"

"Ever since junior high. I always seem to wake up at six a.m. no matter what time I go to bed the night before."

"It is a nice time of day, isn't it? It is quiet, and you can think about more important things early in the morning, can't you?"

Barnabas understood what she was saying. "I guess that's true, but I have never thought about it that way. Can I ask you a question?"

"Of course."

"You have to explain what happened on the basketball court yesterday. At first I thought it was going to be a friendly game. Where did they learn to play like that, especially Stephanie?"

Ruth laughed. "Pretty intense, wasn't it?"

Barnabas nodded.

"They got it from their dad who played in college. All three of them played in high school, and college too."

"But what is this about Robert and Mark not letting Stephanie play with them?"

"She was always the younger one. Kind of shameful about how they would do it. She would have to find some neighborhood kid or cousin before she could play with them. This is the first time she's had a capable teammate that could give Mark and Robert a run for their money. It's a historic moment in our family. We are not supposed to have favorites with our children, but I was secretly rooting for you and Stephanie."

Barnabas smiled. Ruth had provided him with much-needed perspective.

She changed the subject. "Would you be willing to tell me more about your mother? She must have been a wonderful woman."

"She was. She was very patient. Always had a good attitude. When she was healthy, she loved to go to church and read her Bible. You would have liked her."

"I think I would have. When did you stop going to church?"

"Shortly after her accident. I know she missed it, and I feel guilty about depriving her of the opportunity, but her church drifted away from her as well. At the end, I think she was disappointed with her church, but as she got worse, she never wavered in her faith. That I'm sure of. If there is a heaven, she is there."

"How old were you when she had her accident?"

"I was twelve."

"I remember you telling us that your father left. Do you know why?"

"I never talked to him about it. Eventually, he was forced to pay child support. But as I got older, I wondered why the two of them got married. He drove a truck, and he was gone a lot. When he was home, he never went to church. I have no reason to believe that he cheated on her, it was just that when the crisis came, he didn't have the foundation to handle it."

"But you did, and you were only twelve years old."

"Well, I'm not sure that I handled it as well as you are giving me credit for."

She smiled. "Nonsense. You persevered. You didn't give up. Your mother did you well, and you did your mother well."

As Barnabas sat at the counter and watched Ruth prepare breakfast, he thought about the Schultz family. They had a way of making a person feel wanted. He had fallen asleep on their couch, and she considered it a compliment. *Wouldn't it be great if the world had more people like this?*

Ruth directed him to a shower in the basement, and when he was finished, he found a change of clothes on a chair outside the bathroom door. The smell of bacon had drifted down to the basement, and his mouth started to water.

How could I be hungry after yesterday? When he opened the door at the top of the stairs, he saw Stephanie sitting down at the breakfast table. She smiled. "Please, sit down. You were here most of the day yesterday, and we barely talked. Mom tells me that she briefed you on the history of the Schultz family basketball tradition. Where did you learn to play basketball like that? You were fantastic!"

"When I was growing up, I was interested in four things: my mother, working, writing in my journal, and basketball. I spent hours every week practicing my skills and learning to shoot. I love the game."

"Well, you gave me something that I never thought I would ever see—a victory over my brothers. They can never take it away from me."

"I was surprised about how intense it got."

She laughed. "Yeah, there are two things that we are intense about—God and basketball, not necessarily in that order." But her smile was just guilty enough that he knew she didn't really mean it.

Stephanie continued. "So, how did you like being a football fan?"

Barnabas chuckled. "Well, I'm obviously not really much of a fan, but by the end of the day I kinda got into it." He decided to change the subject. "Have things changed any at the firm?"

"Not really. They seem to be happy with my work. The people are okay. I like the law. It's just that I feel like I should be making a greater contribution than I am now. How about you? When we had lunch, I was concerned that you wanted to be doing something else."

"It's all right, I guess. I would like it better if I were making more money. At this rate, it will be another five years before I pay off all of my debt. It's not easy wondering where the next check is going to come from to pay the overhead. I would take a job with a good firm if someone offered me something, but I'm not going to look for one."

"Maybe we can try to work out a deal where we could switch for a month. Perhaps that would make us better appreciate where we are," she said with a twinkle in her eye.

As they were finishing breakfast, Sam strolled into the room. "Nice to see you this morning, Barnabas. We were tempted to wake you up, but you were sleeping so soundly and peacefully that Ruth won the argument and we left you on the couch. I hope we made the right choice."

Barnabas laughed. "You know, it really is embarrassing. If you ever invite me back, I'm not going to sit next to the fireplace."

"I suppose you need to get back to the city," Sam said. "As soon as I am finished with breakfast I'll give you a ride."

"Let me do it," Stephanie interjected. "I'm finished eating, and I need to go back in and do some work today."

Sam looked at her with a stern expression. "All you seem to be doing is work lately. Do you see this changing anytime soon?"

Barnabas came to her defense. "Sometimes, sir, you have no choice. If anyone can keep her perspective under the strain of a big-city practice, I'm sure it's Stephanie."

It took forty minutes to reach his apartment. To Barnabas, it felt like five minutes. They talked about their cases and reminisced about law school, particularly the moot court competition.

As they pulled up to his apartment, Barnabas decided to take a chance. "Stephanie, I really enjoy being around you. Can we meet again sometime?"

She paused—a bit too long—but he pressed ahead, anticipating her concern. "Look, after the bar exam, you made it clear that we have differences that prevent us from being any more than friends. But we did have fun getting ready for that exam, didn't we?"

She smiled. "That would be fine, Barnabas. I've missed our time together, too."

He did his best to conceal his excitement. His mother used to say, "Half a loaf is better than no loaf at all." Now he fully understood what she meant.

"How about a week from tomorrow for lunch, you pick," Barnabas suggested.

"That will be fine, as long as we go dutch."

PART TWO

And Lord I have come to know
The weaknesses I see in me
Will be stripped away
By the power of Your love.
—Don Moen, "Power of Your Love"

CHAPTER FIFTEEN

She picked a restaurant midway between their apartments called Bella Italy. They decided to meet at 11:45 a.m. in case the restaurant drew a large Saturday lunch crowd. Because of his finances, Barnabas had limited himself to only two restaurant meals per week. This was going to be one of them. He arrived five minutes early, and the place was only a quarter full. He picked a table in the corner.

Barnabas started to read the newspaper, and at 11:50 a.m. he was starting to get worried. Stephanie arrived a minute later. He waved, and she smiled and came over to the table. She was wearing jeans and a sweatshirt, but she still looked stunning. He was determined not to spend the hour talking about himself.

As soon as she sat down, she said, "Sorry I'm late. I thought I knew where this place was, but I didn't. What are you reading?"

"Just looking at the basketball scores."

"You know, Thanksgiving was a once-in-a-lifetime experience. Thanks for taking over the game. It was a sweet victory for me."

"Your brothers seem like good guys. Were they tough to grow up with?"

"They are good guys, but they are passionate about their basketball. My earliest memories are of Robert and Mark doting on me, but by the time I hit the fifth grade they starting teasing me. I thought it got out of hand sometimes. I ran to Mom a couple of times, but she refused to intervene. She wanted me to develop my own defense mechanisms. Looking back, I'm glad she did."

"So what did they do to get under your skin?"

"It was mostly verbal. If they saw me talking with a boy at church, they would try and make it more than what it was. I am kind of a tomboy, and I got that from them, but they wouldn't cut me any slack. None of this 'let her win so she'll feel good about herself' stuff."

"Do you consider yourself a tomboy just because of basketball, or is there something more to it?" asked Barnabas.

Stephanie smiled and paused. "I guess it was mostly the basketball, but if you are going to grow up as the youngest with two older brothers, you learn quickly how to survive in a male-dominated culture. You have to learn how a boy thinks. You know what I mean?"

"I think so. You mentioned that they would tease you when you talked to a boy at church. Did that happen a lot?"

She paused, and he thought that he might have probed too deeply. But then she smiled again and responded, "You know, that is an interesting question. I had a complexion problem that didn't go away until my senior year of college, and I was a little on the chubby side until I started to get serious about basketball when I was thirteen, so I was not used to having a lot of attention from boys. Looking back on it, I think that was a good thing."

Barnabas studied her, and he found it difficult to conceive of her as an overweight thirteen-year-old with acne. He couldn't help but voice his surprise. "I hope you understand why it's hard to imagine that. You know that most guys are attracted to you, right?"

She shrugged. "A couple of times I've been told that I'm pretty, but your self-image is always, to some extent, fashioned by your childhood. I don't think I will ever see myself as a beauty queen, but I do see myself as a competitive tomboy." She then decided to embarrass him. "So, Barnabas, do you think I am an exceptionally beautiful woman?" she asked, smiling at him coquettishly.

He knew that she was teasing him, and he wasn't confident how he should answer. She seemed to enjoy putting him in an awkward position. Realizing that he was on dangerous ground, he opted for honesty. "You know, I am not adept at giving out lines to women, and I know that you are teasing me, but in my opinion your beauty is extraordinary. But I admire your character even more. How's that for a response?"

Barnabas saw surprise in her eyes.

"It was unfair for me to ask you that, even if I was teasing, but it was nice to hear, especially when I am not used to hearing it, so thank you."

Barnabas needed to change the subject. "Tell me more about learning to play basketball."

"We always had a basketball hoop hanging off the garage. If they had a friend over, they would let me play. Whoever got me was at a decided disadvantage, and we always lost. It was not long before I developed this dislike of losing. I inherited my competitive nature from my brothers."

"So how long did you play basketball competitively, barring the intra-family competition of course?"

"I started for my team the last two years of high school—point guard. But that's not saying much. I went to a small Christian high school. There were only ten girls that went out for the team. But I was good enough to get a scholarship to play in college. And so were Robert and Mark."

"I thought I was in the finals of the NCAA tournament."

She laughed heartily. "You were the first partner that I've had that was better than both of them. I'll confess, I thought you were going to be a disaster. What was with those thirty-five-foot warm-up shots anyway? But when you started hitting your shot, it was clear that I had a chance to win. That's when things got real intense. Was it unfair to throw you into that? You do know that you are going to be my hero forever, don't you? You need to understand that they are going to want a rematch. Now that I mention it, how did you learn to play like that?

"I fell in love with the game when I was a small kid. I practiced every day for fifteen years. Basketball put me through college." Barnabas wanted to change the subject. "Why aren't you a football fan?"

"Oh, I like football and I root for the Bears, but on Thanksgiving it is time to be with Mom and Molly. You can hear everything going on in the TV room in the kitchen. If I were in the room, it would spoil the dynamic. So, how long have you been a Cowboys fan?"

Barnabas smiled. "I'm not really. I just decided to even things out."

She laughed out loud a second time. "That's what we thought. You are always going to be for the underdog, aren't you?"

"What else would you expect?"

"Nothing else. That is one of the things that makes you so charming."

Barnabas decided to pivot again, keeping the conversation on her. "Were you really the one left out all the time?"

"My mom and dad are good people. I am very fortunate. I am very attached to my brothers even though they were not perfect. My mom and dad taught me good values. There is very little I would change about growing up."

"What little would you change?"

She tilted her head, paused, and three small lines appeared on her forehead. She was deciding how much she was going to reveal. She turned and gave Barnabas a slight smile. "We moved a lot. When I was younger I didn't like that. But it forced me to learn how to make friends, and that turned out to be a good thing. It was tough being the only girl and being the youngest on top of that. But it made me resilient. Also, as I got older, I learned that Dad got passed over for some promotions because he supposedly was not a team player. I didn't like that at all."

She paused again, collecting her thoughts. "No one has a perfect childhood, Barnabas, but I know that I am more fortunate than most people. I have no complaints."

"What do you mean he was not a team player? He seems very easy to get along with."

She gave him a knowing smile. "The FBI is no different than any other bureaucracy; it is not always about merit. Sometimes it is about catering to the higher-ups. Dad would never do that. But he likes his work, and he likes to spend his time in the field as opposed to being at a desk."

It was nice getting her to open up, and he wanted to know more. "Okay, what defense mechanisms did you develop?"

"When the teasing got really bad, I would prank them."

"You like to prank!"

She laughed. "Still do."

"What would you do to them?"

"Telephone pranks, short sheets, and sometimes if I was really angry, I would get them good."

Barnabas was amused and fascinated. "What do you think was your best prank?"

"After they went to bed, I filled up their hair dryer with flour. Robert got out of the shower, turned it on, and got a face full of flour. You could hear him scream throughout the entire house. Mom came running out of her bedroom, thinking someone had broken a leg."

"Would they let you get away with this stuff? I can't believe they would."

Stephanie shook her head. "The last big one was my sophomore year of high school. They pulled one on me. Mark put purple hair dye in my shampoo. When I got out of the shower and saw that my hair had turned purple, I lost it. I have never cried so loud and so long in my entire life." But Stephanie was smiling as she said it.

"Why are you smiling?"

"I was devastated at the time, but looking back it was kind of funny. It wasn't like I didn't deserve it. That turned out to be the last big one."

"Why was that the last one?"

"Mom let me stay home from school. She went to the drug store, got some dye, and she dyed my hair back to my natural color. That night, Mom and Dad called a family meeting. It didn't last long. Dad sat us down, looked at all three of us, and said, 'No more.'"

"So did that stop it?"

"No," she smiled, "but it was much tamer after that. We understood that the teasing and the pranks couldn't be cruel."

Barnabas wanted to know about her frequent moves when she was a child. "So, you learned how to make friends because you moved a lot?"

"We were never in one place for more than two years. When a field office was in trouble, they would always send Dad to clean up the mess. Finally, because of his experience going to all of these offices that were in trouble, he was able to negotiate a deal so that he could finish his career in Chicago."

"So, tell me how to make friends."

"It is not that hard. When you get into a new school or a new church, identify people that you would like to get to know, and then you decide which direction you are going to go."

Barnabas gave her a slight nod and raised his hands, asking her to expand.

"You either do something nice for them, or if you can, ask them to do something nice for you. My mom taught me that. It is better to do the latter if you can. Mom says that she learned that from Benjamin Franklin."

Barnabas' face showed his admiration, so Stephanie turned the conversation to him. "Ever do something like that, Barnabas?"

"Not really. With my mom, work, and basketball, I didn't really have time for much else. I guess I became kind of a loner. I got along well with everyone in the public defender's office. People liked my work ethic, and I helped out quite a bit. The PD's office is where I first developed friendships."

"Have you had many girlfriends?" Stephanie was surprised that the question had just come out, but she was glad she asked.

"Not really."

"Why not?"

"I learned very quickly that girls cost money, and I've never had any."

She laughed. "You know, not all girls are digging for gold. You must have had your opportunities."

He shrugged. "Between caring for my mom, school, work, and basketball, there just wasn't time for much else. Some girls made it obvious that they were interested, but I just didn't want to go down that road."

Barnabas decided to avoid talking about girls who had been interested in one-night stands.

"How about after your mother died?"

"I wanted to do well in law school. When I graduated, I had over a hundred thousand dollars in debt, and I still have most of it. In law school, most of my classmates were either looking for a serious relationship or were married. I don't want anything serious until I'm out of debt. My mother and I were always short on money, and it is no way to live your life."

"Barnabas, you must know that most people don't let that stop them from forming serious relationships."

Barnabas gave some thought to trying to explain how life was when his mom was alive, always scraping for dollars, but he didn't want to look weak and forlorn.

He leaned forward slightly and said, "Well, I guess that I'm not one of them." He moved the conversation back to her. "So, do you have a lot of friends now?"

"Oh sure. Most of them still live near my family's house or go to our church. Not so many in the firm."

"Why not in the firm?"

"I don't know for sure. I plan on leaving next year, and I don't want anyone to feel like I am abandoning them."

"That's interesting. Why are you so sure that you are going to leave?"

"I gave them a three-year commitment when I hired on, and my commitment is up next year."

"Why do you want to leave?"

"Like I told you, I don't have the control that I would like. I am not in court nearly as much as I want to be. I was promised a lot of work in court, but it just hasn't worked out that way."

Their hour was up, and it was time to go. As they paid their checks, Barnabas looked at her. "Same time, same place, next week?"

"Sure, Barnabas. I would like that."

CHAPTER SIXTEEN

The following Saturday, Stephanie arrived promptly at 11:45 a.m., and Barnabas was sitting at the same table. She was wearing a business suit, and he couldn't help but call attention to it. "I didn't realize that this was going to be such an important meeting or I would have worn a suit as well."

She gave a mock frown and stuck her tongue out at him. "I'm going to a wedding this afternoon."

"Really? Who is getting married?"

"The pastor's daughter."

Should I take this opening or is it too early? It really is too early, but she brought the subject up last week. It won't be that big of a faux pas. If she thinks it is too soon, she can dodge the question. She has to know that I am going to ask it eventually.

"Since you asked about my girlfriends last week, what about your boyfriends? I'm sure the boys started to notice when you went from having a teenager's complexion to that of a young woman. Do you mind me asking?"

She smiled. "I don't mind. No, I have never been close to getting married."

"I find it hard to believe that you would have trouble attracting guys. Why didn't any of them pan out for you?"

"Let me tell you something that you already know. I am an independent person, and I think that the Lord has blessed me with a good brain."

"So?"

"Many guys are intimidated by independent women who are as smart as they are."

Barnabas nodded, hoping that she would provide more details.

And she did. "There was one guy that I started to get serious about, but after two months, it was clear that he wasn't the one."

"And what were the issues that separated you?"

"He had just gotten out of the Navy and was starting graduate school. He started attending our church. We dated some, but it became clear that there were some things he was not willing to give up that I thought were essential to a successful marriage."

"And those were?"

"He had some buddies that were left over from his days in the service. It was made clear early on that if I was going to marry him that I was going to marry them as well."

"What's wrong with him having friends?"

"Nothing was wrong with him having friends per se, but they had just as much influence on what he thought as I did. I do think it is healthy for my husband to have good friends, but his first loyalty has to be to Christ and then to me. Finally, there was one thing he promised he would do, but he was very uncomfortable about it and started making excuses not to."

"And that was? If you don't mind telling me."

"No, I don't mind. It's not private." She paused and then said, "He would not pray with me."

Barnabas was surprised. "I would never have guessed that. Why was that important?"

"My mother believes that it is one of the most important things that marriage partners can do. She says it increases the level of communication. You will learn what is on your partner's mind, and prayers are the most honest form of communication. No one who believes in God will lie to Him. They may lie to other people, but they won't lie to God."

Barnabas decided to make his case. "Surely there must be some guys out there that are willing to respect your beliefs even if they don't share them completely. Is praying together a deal breaker?"

Stephanie knew where he was heading, but she rejected the argument. "Barnabas, the Bible I read tells me that Christ is supposed to be an equal partner in marriage. I don't see how that is possible if my husband doesn't even believe in Christ. I could never be yoked to someone who does not share my faith."

It was an interesting choice of words—yoked. Although he was not completely sure what she meant by it, what it did mean was that he did not qualify.

But he still wanted to know more. "This fellow who was in the Navy, did you love him?"

She smiled again. "Barnabas, what do you mean by 'love'?"

He was stunned. Surely, she knew what he meant by love. "I don't know. You had strong feelings for him. You thought he was special. You thought you could have a relationship with him that would be stronger than with other men you know."

"Most of the time, when the English Bible uses the word 'love,' the root word in Greek is 'agape,' which means to respect the other person. Treat him the way you would want to be treated. I had those feelings for him, but I wasn't entirely sure whether he had the capacity to treat me that way," Stephanie explained.

"But a marriage must require more than that."

"I agree. The Bible also talks about 'phileo,' which means the kind of love that exists between friends. He and I were friends, but we were not best friends. My mom thinks that her children should marry their best friend. That is what Robert did. That is what Mark is going to do. But I didn't think I was ever going to get there with him. His Navy buddies were always going to be his best friends."

"Don't you want to be attracted to him physically?"

"Of course I do. The Greek word in the Bible for it is 'eros.' But I think that too many girls focus on that aspect only, and that is one of the reasons why their marriages fail."

"What did your parents think of the Navy guy?"

"They didn't say anything, but I knew that they had issues. I guess I've been spoiled. I don't think I could ever marry someone who is not as good as my dad. And that is a high standard. But there was another issue with him. I made it clear that I would not marry anyone without my father's approval."

Reading Barnabas' expression, Stephanie asked, "Does that seem old-fashioned to you?"

Barnabas opted for candor. "It does. If there were anyone who wouldn't need help making a decision like that, I would have thought it would be you."

Her cryptic smile betrayed amusement. "I suppose that it is more tradition than anything else. I doubt that my judgment would differ from my parents'. But I think the tradition is a good one because it makes the point that while a new family is being formed, you are still marrying into an old one. It is a request to be admitted into the family."

"I get it—agape, phileo, eros, shares your faith. Does that sum it up? It sounds like there is more to it."

"Of course there is. I hold the view that the marriage relationship is a very important one that was created by God. When a man and woman get married, a bond is established and grows. Physically they may live in separate bodies, but spiritually they are bound together and become a part of one another—intertwined if you will. That bond is created by God. At the time of marriage, your spouse is the most special person in the world, and the relationship deepens over time. Trust and faith in one another develop between husband and wife so that they truly are the same spiritually. This is a God-given thing. Do you understand?"

Barnabas was taken aback by the intensity of her statement. *Is she setting too high a standard for herself and for the men she meets?*

Barnabas nodded, indicating that he understood. He gathered his thoughts. "While I find it hard to believe that it won't happen for you, do you worry about never finding the right guy? Your standards seem so high."

"Maybe that was true a couple of years ago. My attitude is that if it happens, it happens. I don't believe that I have to be married to be happy. I am a realist in the sense that I can't be overly concerned about his past so long as it truly is in the past. It is about where his mind and heart are now."

She smiled and him, and he smiled back. Then she stood and left for the wedding.

As Barnabas drove to work afterward, he began talking to himself, working out his frustration. "The Bible this, the Bible that. The Bible, the Bible, the Bible! Am I going to have to take a course in Greek to talk to this girl? It's just not going to work. We are two different people. I might as well be living on a different continent. I'm wasting my time."

At home that night, Barnabas sat down in front of the TV and turned on something that he was not able to concentrate on.

Am I really wasting my time? No. What else am I going to do in my spare time besides work and play basketball? She is a bright person, and she is an attorney. We have a lot in common, but she has made it clear that it is never going to go beyond that. But what else am I going to do on a Saturday afternoon?

They met every Saturday for the next three weeks.

One Friday evening, Jennie's family came by the office to meet her and go to a restaurant in the city. Emily decided to interrupt Barnabas' concentration and catch up with him. As she entered his office, he looked up. "What's up, Emily? Have you been behaving yourself?"

"Not really. Life is more fun if you live a little close to the edge. How about you?"

"My life is work, sleep, an occasional game of basketball, and then back to work. I guess I should be glad that I am able to pay my rent and pay your mother."

"According to Mom you've found yourself a girlfriend. Have you been hiding something from me?"

Barnabas laughed. "She is a friend and she is a girl, but she would object to your calling her my girlfriend."

"Oh, why do you say that?"

"We agreed from the start that it must be a friends-only relationship. Her religion is very important to her, and I am not a believer. She has made it clear that she doesn't want to be yoked, to use her word, to a non-believer."

Nonchalantly, she offered a solution. "That's easy. Just become a believer."

"Oh, the innocence of being a teenager," Barnabas said. "She is too smart and has too much class for that. She would see right through it. Besides, I would be defrauding her even if I could pull off something like that."

Emily would not be derailed. "I may not know her, and I may be young, but I don't believe that she is only interested in being just friends. Something else is going on there."

Barnabas shrugged. "I doubt it, but if anything else is going to develop, the initiative will have to come from her. I enjoy being with her, and I will take whatever time she will give me."

Jennie was anxious to leave, but as Emily walked away, she offered her encouragement. "I wouldn't give up on her if I were you."

CHAPTER SEVENTEEN

They met the following Saturday. Barnabas had been mulling over his conversation with Emily. Faith was such an important part of Stephanie's life, he felt like he needed to know more.

As soon as she sat down, Barnabas asked, "How did the wedding go last week?"

"It was great, thanks for asking."

"Have you known the pastor and his family long?"

"Yes. When we arrived in the city ten years ago, we fell in love with this church. The pastor had been there for a couple years and it has been well led ever since."

"Has it grown any since I was there?"

"A little bit. One hundred fifty people are there on Sunday mornings. But there were less than fifty ten years ago."

"So, the church is growing. That's good. Why is it growing?"

"I'm not sure exactly. We liked it because the people truly love and support one another. It was like having an extended family."

The answer permitted Barnabas to raise the issue of her faith. "But you really believe the things that the Bible teaches, that Jesus is God's son, that He died on a cross, and that He was resurrected from the dead? How did you come to believe so deeply?"

"I do believe."

"I am truly curious. Why? It sounds like something out of a science fiction novel to me."

She turned her head, sighed, and looked at him again. "Okay, Barnabas, we can get into this today. But I am beginning to feel like I am one of your witnesses. Today, we are going to spend some time talking about you. Deal?"

He nodded his agreement. Most people liked to talk about themselves, and he believed that Stephanie was no different, but she obviously had her limits.

She began to explain. "Of course, I was raised in the church, so it is hard to identify a particular point in time when I knew that I believed. For me, I firmed up my beliefs the first year of college. I went to a Christian college. I had gone to Christian schools before, and some suggested that I was living a sheltered life, that I was not getting myself prepared for the challenges that would come shortly, and things like that. But there were plenty of kids at my college that didn't believe. They were there because their parents forced them to go there. It was my freshman year that I was forced to make a choice."

"What happened then?"

"My roommate was on the basketball team, but she was not a believer, and she started getting into drugs, alcohol, and sex. I had to decide how I was going to respond. Lucky for me, I was taking a New Testament class, and I read the four Gospels with an intensity that I hadn't had before. There was a power, majesty, depth, and love in those teachings that I believed had to be divine. They couldn't have come from a mere human, no matter how gifted he was. I felt compelled to believe that Christ was the true God. The great moral teacher argument didn't cut it for me."

She changed the subject as she promised she would. "Now it's your turn to talk for a while. You told me that your mother took you to church when you were a boy. You never told me her name."

He was surprised by the observation. She had always been "Mom" to him. "Her name was Alice."

"Did you like going to church?"

"I enjoyed Sunday school, but I hated the sermons."

She nodded. "I was sitting next to you on Sunday after the bar. You could barely keep your eyes open. I guess some things don't change. What did they teach you in Sunday school?"

"Mostly Bible stories. David and Goliath, Samson and Delilah, the birth of Jesus, those types of stories. I'm sure you've heard them all many more times than me. They had us memorize Scriptures. I won several ribbons for memorization."

"Really? Can you recall any of them?"

"I'm sure I could recite some of them. They are firmly embedded into my memory."

She smiled encouragingly. "Give me one."

He hadn't expected her to ask him. It brought back memories that he preferred to leave undisturbed. "Do I have to do this?"

She seemed to realize that she was taking him where he didn't want to go. "Yes," she responded firmly.

He paused. "I guess Isaiah chapter forty was a favorite. 'Do you not know? Have you not heard? The Lord is the everlasting God, Creator of the ends of the earth. He will not grow tired or weary, and His understanding no one can fathom. He gives strength to the weary and increases the power of the weak. Even youths grow tired and weary, and young men stumble and fall; but those who trust in the Lord will renew their strength. They will soar on wings like eagles; they will run and not grow weary, they will walk and not be faint.'"

He thought he noticed a tear in her eye. Stephanie pressed him for more. "It's amazing that you still remember that after all these years. Your memory is even better than I would have imagined. Are there others that you still remember?"

He eyed her suspiciously. He didn't want to recite anything else, but he relented. "One more, but this is the last one, okay?"

"Okay, I won't ask for more."

"This one I used to recite at night when I was in junior high. 'Come to me, all you who are weary and burdened, and I will give you rest. Take my yoke upon you and learn from me, for I am gentle and humble in heart, and you will find rest for your souls. For my yoke is easy and my burden is light.'"

She was silent, and he didn't have anything to say. He decided to wait for her. Finally, she asked, "Do you still believe that?"

Barnabas looked down. "No," he quietly said.

He was worried that she would follow up with a "why not" but was relieved that she didn't.

Barnabas disguised his anxiety by challenging her. "My mother was the best person I've ever known. She was devoted, even at the end. But she spent the last years of her life in a wheelchair. The last couple of months she was in a lot of pain, and she was abandoned by her husband. How do you explain that?"

"There are some things that I will never be able to explain. Life has been easier for me than it has been for you—I'll concede that—so I am in no position to judge any choices you have made. But wouldn't you agree that your mother had a faith that she never abandoned?"

"Yes, she was true to the very end."

"And it sounds to me like even in difficult circumstances she remained a loving person."

"Yes, I think so."

"How do you think her life would have been without her faith?"

Barnabas paused, wanting to give an accurate response. "That would have made it even more difficult. But as I have already said, just because her faith propped her up doesn't mean that her faith was based on something real."

Stephanie softened her voice. "But I believe that the Spirit was with her and she knew it."

"Stephanie, how can you be so sure that she knew it? Does God talk to you?"

"All the time."

"You know what I mean. Have you ever had an audible conversation with God, Jesus, or the Holy Spirit the way we are talking now?"

"No, I can't say that. But I can say that God does answer prayers, that He wants me to be happy, and that when I surrender my will to His there is a joy in my life that can come only from God. I do not believe that we were created to live for ourselves. We were created to love God and love others. There is great joy in living your life that way, and I have no doubt that your mother understood that, even when she was in considerable pain."

Barnabas felt compelled to respond. "It is kind of inspiring to hear you say that, and it is obviously working for you, but I just hope that you don't wake up someday and discover that it was all based on fiction."

"And Barnabas, someday I pray that you wake up and realize that your lack of belief was, indeed, a fiction." But then she broached an even more delicate subject. "Tell me about what happened with Bill Cushman. There is a history there, isn't there?"

He was surprised that she remembered his name much less bring him up. He had three options: He could dodge the question, he could give her the short version, or he could give her the long version. Dodging the question would make him appear fragile. He rejected the long version because he was afraid that his bitterness would become evident. So, he opted for the short version.

"We go all the way back to high school, but when I was in law school, Bill plagiarized one of my papers, and when he got caught, he attempted to blame it on me. He almost got me thrown out of law school. On top of that, I had kept my journal on my memory stick, and I later learned that he had read it. After that, I did everything I could to avoid him."

With a gentle tone, Stephanie asked, "Was that before or after you competed at the moot court competition?"

"It was after."

"That must have been very painful for you, but I'm glad he didn't get you expelled. Otherwise, I'm not sure we would have ever met again. Why didn't he get expelled?"

"Bill comes from a rich, well-connected family. I'm sure that his father made a sizable donation to the law school."

"It must have felt good to get out from under Bill's yoke. So why did you start with the PD's office?"

"At first I tried to get into the Frederick firm. Every year they hire one graduate from our school, and I was one of the top two who interviewed that year, but they gave the job to someone else."

"I'm surprised you didn't get the job." There was another pause. "They gave the job to Cushman, didn't they?"

"How did you know?"

"I am involved in a case now where the Frederick firm is representing one of the parties. Cushman is also working on the file. If they only hire one graduate and the two of you graduated the same year, he must have gotten the job."

It was time to go.

"Same time next week?" asked Stephanie.

"It's a deal."

As he drove to his office, Barnabas replayed their meeting in his head. It was interesting how Stephanie cleverly insinuated that he had been under Bill's yoke. He hadn't thought about it that way before. He was glad he had given her only the short version of his falling out with Bill.

Each time he had lunch with her, he felt closer to her. While he did want her to find someone to marry that met her standards, he also hoped that it would not happen anytime soon.

CHAPTER EIGHTEEN

Two days after his fifth lunch with Stephanie, Barnabas was sitting at his desk when Jennie buzzed him. "Richard Oxnard, line one."

Barnabas picked up. "Mr. Oxnard, I hope that we haven't run into a glitch in the Abbott case."

Oxnard chuckled. "No, not at all, and please call me Richard."

Barnabas wondered why he was calling.

Oxnard continued. "I will cut to the chase as I know that you must be busy."

Actually, Barnabas wasn't particularly busy that morning.

"Our firm is looking to expand its litigation department, and I would like to give Frederick your name. Are you interested?"

Barnabas attempted to conceal his excitement. "Well, as you know, I interviewed with your firm three years ago, so of course I am. But there may be one issue."

"What is that?"

"You will need to check with Bill Cushman. It is possible that he may oppose your taking me on."

Barnabas wasn't really worried about what Bill would say, but he thought it would be a good political move. If Bill's performance in the Abbott case were an example of his work, he wouldn't be there much longer.

"Barnabas, you may not remember, but Professor Paulus and I have known one another for years, and he briefed me about what has gone on between you and Bill. Frankly, Bill has been worthless around here except for one case he brought in, and it has brought in millions. Many days he doesn't even come into work, and when he is here, it is only for a few hours. That is the way most of us like it."

Barnabas interviewed with the Frederick firm three days later and found himself waiting for his final interview with Mr. Frederick. He believed that the interview had gone well, and he was confident that he would be hired.

Barnabas looked again at the oak-encrusted grandfather clock standing next to the executive secretary's polished mahogany desk. It read 5:12 p.m.; he had been waiting seventeen minutes for his 5:00 p.m. meeting. The chair was comfortable, and Barnabas was prepared to wait for as long as necessary. *Take your time, Mr. Frederick. I've got all the time in the world.*

Barnabas studied the nameplate on the oak-paneled office door. The polished brass letters, approximately four inches high, read "Christian L. Frederick III." Surreptitiously, Barnabas moved his left hand over the arm of the chair. He asked himself if he had ever sat in a leather chair before, and he could not recall. If he had, it certainly was not one that so perfectly conformed to his body.

As he surveyed the room, he examined the nameplate on the secretary's desk. It read "Mary Davidson." Initially, he guessed her age to be around forty, but as he examined her closely during his wait, he conceded it was possible that she might be a very well-preserved fifty-five. Her hair was a shade of light brown with three barely noticeable yellow-blonde streaks. It curled out just above the neckline. Although it was late in the day, not a single hair was out of place. As she sat, he estimated that he was no more than four inches taller than she was. Her eyes appeared to be sky blue, but he guessed that she was wearing contact lenses.

Barnabas knew that her pinstripe suit was easily ten times more expensive than his. He took pride in the fact that his business wardrobe consisted of exactly five suits, seven shirts, and ten ties. All had been bought in a lot purchase from an estate on eBay for a total of $111. He had been the only bidder. He paid a tailor $75 to make the alterations.

As he admired her suit, Barnabas chuckled to himself, wondering whether her salary was closer to three times or five times his current earnings.

An eager associate approached Mary Davidson's desk with a file in hand. As he extended the file to her, he said in a somber tone, "Mr. Frederick insisted that I complete the memorandum and get this file back to him by the end of the day." Barnabas was curious how long it would take for the one-inch purple plush carpet to return to its original form after someone had stood on it. As the associate walked away, Barnabas observed a half-inch depression clearly delineating where his shoes had been. Barnabas silently counted. *One one thousand, two one thousand, three one thousand.* Before he got to four, he could see no evidence of where the associate had stood.

How do they keep it clean? Barnabas wondered. Barnabas had purposely picked a tan color for the carpet in his office. From prior experience, he knew that tan did a good job covering up dirt and stains. *These folks must shampoo this carpet weekly and vacuum it every night.* The dark purple would show even the smallest piece of white lint, but Barnabas saw no lint anywhere in the waiting area.

Are the oil paintings behind Mary Davidson's desk hers, or are they owned by the firm? They were mountain landscapes. *Perhaps I will learn one day that they were only paint-by-number creations.* Barnabas began to laugh at his own joke, and Mary Davidson looked up. Quickly he recovered his somber mood and returned to his courtroom poker face.

Regardless of how trite the paintings appeared to be, Barnabas understood that Christian L. Frederick III would not tolerate anything less than the best on the wall outside of his office. The walls themselves were neither wallpaper nor paint. They were adorned with some kind of brown-colored tapestry with an ornate, red-and-purple design intermittently woven throughout. Most importantly, it all matched: the color of the chair he was sitting in, the purple carpet, the colors on the landscape, the color of the tapestry, and the color of Mary Davidson's desk. Even the colors of her suit, her jewelry, and her hair somehow matched the colors in the waiting area. *Does she actually color her hair and pick her suits to match the colors in her office? Does she consider it a part of her job description to have her apparel and hair coloring blend in? Hopefully not.*

Barnabas did not mind waiting for Frederick. The chair was very comfortable, and it was nice to sit in luxury. Besides, it gave him extra time to review what he was going to say to him. For such an important interview, Barnabas was surprisingly relaxed. This was the moment that he had been waiting for since his mother's accident. It was the moment he had been waiting for from the time he and his mother realized that his father was not coming back. It had been fifteen lean years. It had been a long, arduous struggle, but it was about to be over. He was going to be offered a job with Frederick, Thurston, and Klein, LLP, the most prestigious firm in the city.

The Frederick firm represented rich clients, had plush offices, and the lawyers had large expense accounts. Most of the best, brightest, and beautiful people used the firm. The firm had box seats for all of the important sports and cultural events that the city had to offer. Most importantly, the firm's lawyers made lots of money.

His thoughts turned to Bill. Barnabas had felt reassured by Oxnard's comments. He doubted that he would see much of Bill in any event. He hoped that Bill had not intervened, because only Bill could cause him not to take the offer. *Surely even Bill understands that we can't work together.*

He went over the lines he would say to Frederick. Barnabas had never seen Christian Frederick in the flesh, so it was difficult for him to anticipate what Frederick would say in response. Of course, he had seen Frederick's picture frequently in the local newspapers, on the local television stations, and in the city's *Legal Times* newspaper, which catered to Chicago's 35,000 attorneys.

As he further prepared his thoughts, Barnabas admitted that he admired Frederick. While it was true that he came from fifth-generation old money, he had built the firm from scratch by the force of his intellect, his work ethic, and his dogged insistence that he was going to be the best. Along the way, it was obvious that he had developed an enormously large ego, but Barnabas conceded that he would probably have one himself if he had Frederick's accomplishments on his résumé. Barnabas thought that Frederick must enjoy the reputation of being the best lawyer in the city. And he was about to offer Barnabas a job, and Barnabas wanted to take it—financial security at last. It would be a nice feeling to wake up every morning and not have to worry about how he was going to pay his bills.

A black box buzzed on Mary Davidson's desk, and a bass voice said, "Mary, please show Mr. Mitchell in." The moment had arrived.

Mary Davidson nodded at Barnabas without speaking, signaling that she knew he had heard Frederick's summons. Barnabas was about to enter the room from which all power in the firm emanated. He rose slowly, walked the twenty-five feet to the office door, and followed Mary Davidson through it. As soon as Barnabas walked in, Mary Davidson closed the door behind him and left him alone with Frederick.

Frederick was at his desk, pretending to be engrossed in some paperwork. *He must know I'm here,* thought Barnabas. *How could he not hear the door open and close?* Barnabas concluded that Frederick was purposely delaying looking up. The pause seemed to drag on. Obviously Frederick wanted Barnabas to understand that he was an important and busy man who worked in an impressive office. *Okay, I'll bite.* Barnabas took the opportunity to examine the room.

It was the corner office on the seventy-fourth floor. Half of the walls were windows. The north window overlooked the river, and the east window overlooked the lake. Frederick's office was a full thirty-five feet in length and sixteen feet wide. On the south wall hung what appeared to be a Persian rug, twelve feet in length and six feet tall. It was perfectly proportioned for the wall. *Is it possible that Frederick took a special trip to Asia and contracted with a skilled craftsman to stitch him a rug with precisely the wall's proportions?*

On the west wall, where the office door was located, hung diplomas and several oil paintings. Barnabas glanced at one over his shoulder. It was some kind of abstract work that he knew he would never understand. He guessed that it was worth thousands of dollars for no other reason than it hung on Frederick's office wall. Barnabas decided that he would not have paid a hundred dollars for it.

Frederick looked up, rose from his chair, and reached for Barnabas' hand. "Mr. Mitchell, it is so nice to meet you."

Barnabas moved forward and shook Frederick's hand. "It is an honor to meet you, sir." Prior to the interview, Barnabas had decided that he was going to stick with "sir." Frederick's handshake was perfect. Clearly not limp, but not too firm either. Just right. Barnabas wondered if he had applied the right amount of pressure in return. Worried that there might have been some moisture on his hands that he couldn't detect prior to entering Frederick's office, Barnabas surreptitiously put his right hand in his pocket and wiped it on the inside just in case he was actually more nervous than he felt. He was confident there had been no moisture, though, and if Barnabas hadn't applied the right amount of pressure, Frederick's face did not betray any disappointment.

Frederick motioned to one of the three leather chairs in front of his spacious desk and said, "Please sit down, Barnabas," and he talked without permitting Barnabas to respond.

Barnabas studied Frederick. He was more impressive in person than he appeared on television. He was two inches shorter than Barnabas. Barnabas estimated his weight to be approximately 180 pounds. Frederick was wearing a dark-gray suit, silk shirt and tie, and cuff links. Even though it was past 5:00 p.m., Barnabas couldn't see any wrinkles in Frederick's suit—as polished as Mary Davidson's attire. *Will I have to replace my wardrobe with wrinkle-free suits?* Barnabas tried to remember if there were any wrinkles in Oxnard's suit at the end of the Abbott trial, but he couldn't.

Barnabas already knew, after researching Frederick on the internet, that he had recently celebrated his fifty-eighth birthday. But the most noticeable thing about his appearance was his tan. It was January in Chicago, but he had a tan. *Does Frederick frequent a tanning salon? There's no way.* Barnabas guessed that Frederick's light-brown tan had come from playing tennis last weekend at some resort vacation home, most likely in Florida, but perhaps in the Caribbean or even Mexico.

"Barnabas, can I get right to the point?" Frederick again continued without permitting Barnabas to respond. "Two of my favorite people in this firm—Oxnard and Cushman—say that I should hire you."

Barnabas should not have been surprised by Bill's endorsement. Barnabas wondered how many briefs Bill expected him to write on his behalf. But he doubted Frederick's statement that Bill was a favorite. Surely Oxnard had briefed Frederick about Bill's performance in the Abbott case. If that were so, then it meant that Frederick was either shallow or ill-informed. Neither was possible. Frederick had to have been lying to him. Either that, or the millions that Oxnard had mentioned truly were millions. *Is it possible that by bringing in only one case Bill has made himself indispensable?*

"If you are willing, we would like you to start within the next ten days."

Barnabas was pleased that Frederick tactfully phrased his statement in such a way that it appeared that Barnabas could turn the offer down, but both of them knew that whatever Frederick was going to offer, Barnabas was almost certainly going to take it.

Frederick sensed that Barnabas liked the offer, so he went on. "We offer complete health insurance of course, and we will cover your spouse and family. We can start you out at $210,000 a year. If the Christmas bonus is the same as last year, it will put another $40,000 into your pocket."

Barnabas was thrilled. It was $10,000 a year more than he was anticipating. He had already done the calculations. In his present solo practice, he was taking home a little over $3500 a month after paying the overhead. He had been making an extra payment on his educational loans, but he still owed $71,334.12. He knew this because his last statement had come in the mail the day before.

Barnabas had already decided that he would not move from his apartment and still pay $515 a month for rent. He would not buy a new car. He'd continue to drive his Honda, which ran fine when he needed it, but he would continue to take the bus. He would still limit himself to two restaurant meals a week. After taxes, he would be taking home slightly more than $10,000 a month from his new job. If he continued his present lifestyle, he would be out of debt in just under six months by living frugally and by making triple payments on his educational loans. Then he could think about moving and buying a new car. He could even start to think about finding a wife and starting a family.

Frederick pressed ahead and voiced what Barnabas had feared. "Cushman has asked that you start in his section, but you will be given the opportunity to transfer out after the first year if you want to and if we like your work."

While the offer was a better deal than what he was hoping for, it was the one condition that Barnabas knew he could not accept. He hated Bill and could not work for him. Frederick paused, noticing the sour expression on Barnabas' face. "Is there a problem?"

Barnabas paused, gathered his thoughts, swallowed, and opted for dignity rather than his financial security. It was the most difficult decision he had ever made in his life.

"Sir, Bill and I have a history. I am willing to work with anyone but him. I don't want to go into detail, but personally, I cannot bring myself to trust him. And as you know, trust is extremely important in this profession."

Frederick frowned. "Oxnard warned me that this might happen. He prevailed upon me to let you go right into the litigation section with him and start working. That's what we will do, but I want you to understand that this is the first and only favor that you are going to be granted. Understand?"

Barnabas was relieved. "Understood, sir."

Barnabas had researched the firm's salary schedule, and he knew that Bill would be making $20,000 more than him. It rankled him, but Barnabas suppressed his anger. His own financial security was all that mattered. He was confident in his abilities. Within two years everyone would know that he was among the best—if not *the* best—young lawyer in the firm. He was used to eighty-hour weeks. In fact, he enjoyed them. He loved the law, and for the first time in his life, he was going to be well paid for what he was doing.

Barnabas was tempted to take the offer on the spot, but he wanted to take care of Jennie, who had been loyal and patient with him during the last three months. Hiring Jennie had been one of his smartest decisions since deciding to start a solo practice.

"Sir, can I bring my secretary with me?"

Frederick showed some concern. "What are her salary requirements?"

"Currently, I can only afford to pay her $24,000 a year with no benefits. But if I am going to move, I would like to reward her with a raise."

Frederick smiled. "We'll start her out at $60,000 a year and give her complete insurance and a 401(k) match, but counsel her that we have a rule here about discussing salaries with other people in the firm."

Barnabas liked the rule. If ever Bill dropped the fact that he was making more than Barnabas, Barnabas would warn him about the rule. Maybe Barnabas would develop a line implying that he started at a higher salary than Bill. *Bill, I was thinking of moving into a condo that has a lake view. Do you have any ideas?*

But Barnabas, always cautious, asked Frederick, "How much time do I have?"

"How much time do you need?"

"Sir, I will be honest. I am very impressed with this offer. But I do not like to make hasty decisions. Can I let you know in forty-eight hours?"

"That will be fine, Barnabas. Call me directly with your decision. Now, there is one thing I forgot, but it is important."

Barnabas' anxiety level rose because he knew that the last issue always seemed to be the deal-breaker. Frederick paused for effect. "We don't expect you to bring clients into the firm. We have all of the clients that we need, we bill our associates' time at four hundred dollars per hour, and we like clients that need an attorney. If we can't bill them three thousand hours a year, we don't want them. We don't want our associates spending any time soliciting new business unless they can handle four hundred dollars an hour and we can bill them three thousand hours a year. Just concentrate on keeping the ones we have happy. Unless the client or case is going to be seven figures or more, don't try and bring it to us."

Barnabas smiled. Selling himself to prospective clients was one part of being an attorney that he disliked. Because he was young, it was one of the most difficult parts of his job.

The meeting took no more than ten minutes. On his way out of the building, Barnabas decided to begin the amity process with Bill by attempting to say something polite. He stopped by Bill's office, but as Oxnard had described, Bill had left several hours earlier. It was not yet 5:30 p.m. Every other lawyer in that section, along with many of the secretaries and paralegals, were still working.

Bill then located Oxnard's office, and of course he was in. Barnabas knocked lightly on the door. A baritone male voice responded, "Enter."

As soon as Barnabas opened the door, Oxnard stood and smiled. He got up from behind the desk and shook Barnabas' hand warmly.

"Mr. Oxnard, I wanted to come say hello before I left."

"Please, call me Richard."

"Richard, I want to thank you for the recommendation."

"Did Frederick make you a good offer?"

"Yes, it was very attractive. And it is even more attractive because you intervened so that I didn't have to work with Bill. Thank you. I asked for a couple of days to think it over."

"Well, I hope you come on board. This place can be a little stuffy at times, but we can always use another good lawyer."

"Like I say, I wasn't disappointed with the offer. Right now I can't think of any reason why I wouldn't take it."

"We'll hope to see you again soon. Bill pressed very hard for you to go to his section. He also insisted that he supervise you, but I want you in this firm. I was not about to let your problems with him keep you out."

"I have known Bill a long time. He is not a friend. But don't worry,

I'll steer clear of him and there will be no friction, at least none caused by me."

Oxnard laughed. "Barnabas, I know that we can do good things together."

"Thank you. That makes me feel better about taking the offer."

Barnabas left the building, knowing that starting the following week he would be an associate in the Frederick firm and his financial problems would be over. He would be working on big cases and associating with important people, and he could rise in the legal profession as far as his drive and intellect would take him. He also felt good about the fact that he was going to take Jennie with him.

As Barnabas drove home from his interview with Christian L. Frederick III, he reviewed the events of the day. The offer was a good one, and he could think of no reason why he shouldn't take it. As far as he was concerned, it had come three years too late.

He pushed Bill out of his mind and continued to think about the offer. He had promised his mother that he would never made important decisions precipitously. When he got home, he decided to call Stephanie and Professor Paulus to get their advice. He called Stephanie first.

She picked up after the third ring.

"Stephanie, it's Barnabas."

"Barnabas, you don't have to identify yourself. I will always be able to tell it's your voice. What's up?"

"I was offered a job at the Frederick firm today. You have made it clear that you don't like working for a firm, so I thought I would run it by you."

"Barnabas, why are you interested?"

"I know that I can do well there. You know that I won't mind the hard work and long hours. The job pays four times what I am taking home now, and I can be out of debt in less than a year. I will be able to actually plan a future and start acting like a normal human being."

There was an uncomfortable pause, and Barnabas pressed for a response. "Look, you know I trust you. You can always be honest with me."

"Barnabas, I am starting to look forward to the day when I can leave the firm I am at now. And my firm is nothing compared to what the Frederick firm is like. I know that for you the issue is not the hard work and long hours, and by the way, I don't consider that acting like a normal human being. And I know that it may be hard for you to accept, what with being in debt and spending all those years struggling financially, but that firm has a reputation of being a highly materialistic place. I don't think you are a materialistic guy."

"But how am I ever going to get rid of this debt anytime in the next decade?"

"Barnabas, you are good at what you do. I have to believe that your practice is going to grow faster than you realize. There are a lot of lawyers, but there is always a need for more good ones. You are already making money, and you've only been at it three months. Let me ask you a question."

"Okay, shoot."

"If you were making as much money now as you are going to at the Frederick firm, would you take the job?"

He pondered her question. "Probably not."

"So it is about the money."

"I guess that's right."

Barnabas chatted with her some more and at the end of the conversation thanked her for her insight. But he was disappointed that she was not as happy about the offer as he was.

His next call was to Professor Paulus.

"Professor, it's Barnabas."

"Well, Barnabas, you usually don't call at night. This must be important."

"I got a job offer with the Frederick firm. I wanted to know your thoughts."

Like Stephanie, Professor Paulus paused. *Why isn't this as obvious to them as it is to me?*

Then Paulus spoke. "Look, I know I can speak with you frankly and you will take it the right way. It must seem to you that you are drowning in debt, so I can understand why you would want to jump at the offer—"

"I will be out of debt in less than a year," Barnabas interjected. "I can then actually start doing something about starting a family."

"Lots of people have gotten married and made it work with more debt than you have, but I understand, given your history, why you don't want to go through that. It sounds like you want to take it, but let me be the devil's advocate just to give you something to think about. You have only been out on your own for three months, and you are already paying all your bills and taking money home. Your practice is only going to grow."

"Why do you say that?"

"Because in my opinion, you are one of the best young trial lawyers in the city, and I'll bet that there are a lot of strings attached to that offer."

"What strings?"

"Because Frederick will now be in control of your life, and I'm afraid that sooner rather than later you will regret it."

"How so?"

"Did he tell you that he didn't want you to bring in your own clients?"

"Yeah, he said that they had their own clients."

"So the longer you stay there, the more beholden to him you are going to be. He will decide how much you are going to make, and you will have acquired no client base if you ever decide to leave. Do you think he is ever going to tolerate any attorney in the firm being anything but subordinate to him?"

"I suppose not. But after I get the debt paid off, I can leave if I don't like it."

"You will have to start from scratch a second time. The older you get, the more difficult that is going to be. And besides that, the place can be seductive. Unless you are extremely careful, the place can change you. One of my friends on the law faculty used to work there, and he describes it as a godless place. If you are patient, I think your practice will eventually surpass the present offer. And what about Cushman? You know you can't trust him. Have you told Frederick that you don't want to work with him? Just think about it before you take the offer."

Without meaning it, Barnabas said, "Well, I do thank you for your candor. I will give it more thought. I have forty-eight hours to accept the job."

"Good luck, Barnabas," said Professor Paulus, and he hung up.

CHAPTER NINETEEN

As Barnabas went to sleep that night, he weighed the arguments in his mind. In the end, he decided that he was going to take the job. Stephanie and Paulus didn't truly understand what his circumstances were. He understood what Paulus said about not being able to develop his own client base, but he did not have to work with Bill, and given Bill's work habits, Barnabas would rarely see him. The offer was just too tempting. He could even start to look seriously for a wife. He was going to take the job.

Barnabas got to work at 7:45 a.m., forty-five minutes late. He started to practice what he was going to say to the landlord, hoping that he could break the remaining three months on his lease. He opened his computer calendar and saw an appointment that Jennie had placed there for 8:30 that morning: *Kyle Williams, referral from Stephanie.*

Because she had to get her kids off to school, Jennie usually did not come in until nine, and it was unusual for her to schedule an appointment before then. Barnabas wondered what the urgency was. He opened his computer and checked his e-mail. Most of it was junk, but there was one from Stephanie:

Barnabas,

I asked Jennie to put Kyle Williams on your schedule tomorrow. He is in desperate need of an attorney. I gave him your name before I knew about the Frederick offer. He is a good guy, and his wife is a good friend of my mom's. I'm sorry to put this on you, but I do have a conflict of interest. Thanks in advance for listening to him.

Stephanie

Williams arrived at 8:15 a.m., so Barnabas decided to start the interview early. He would listen patiently and get Williams out the door as quickly as possible. Frederick had made it clear that he didn't want Barnabas taking on new clients, and in any event, it seemed obvious from Stephanie's e-mail that Williams was not going to be a well-paying client. Barnabas had over thirty active files, and he was already going to have to find other attorneys for those clients if possible. There was no way that he could take on a new client.

Barnabas went into the waiting room and greeted Williams, offering his hand. "Mr. Williams, I am Barnabas Mitchell."

Williams was approximately six foot five and looked like he was around sixty-five to seventy years old. His hair was mostly gray, and he had an Abraham Lincoln-like warm but sad face. His hands were large, engulfing Barnabas' hand in his grip. He had a large briefcase in his left hand. Unlike Abbott, Williams was a slow talker.

"It is so nice to meet you. Stephanie thinks the world of you, and I sure hope that you can use your talent to help me."

It appeared that he was choosing each word carefully.

"Come into the conference room and let's see what the problem is." As they went to the conference room, Barnabas noticed that Williams was walking with a limp, favoring his left leg.

Barnabas' conference room was small—twelve by fifteen feet. The table was twelve feet long and a full six feet wide. It barely fit. There were lines on the wall where the tops of the chairs had rubbed against it.

They both sat down, and Barnabas started. "I guess we can start by me asking how you know Stephanie."

"We moved into the suburbs eight months ago and started going to church where her family goes. My wife, Sarah, developed a strong relationship with Ruth, Stephanie's mom. Ruth told Sarah that Stephanie said I should talk to you."

"Ruth is a very nice lady. So why do you need a lawyer?"

"It is a long story. I can give you the long version or the short one. Which do you want?"

"Give me the version you are most comfortable with."

"Well, I'm seventy-three years old, and ever since I was sixteen years old up until three years ago I worked in the coal mines. I lied and told the company that I was eighteen when I first started working."

"How much education do you have?"

"I never graduated from high school. My dad died when I was fifteen, and we had a big family. Eight kids. I was the oldest, so I started working early."

Barnabas nodded. "I can relate to that. Did you injure your leg while working?"

"Yeah, I actually have an artificial leg from the knee down. They call me Scooter in the mines."

Hoping that Williams might have a worker's compensation claim, Barnabas asked, "How long ago was that?"

Williams smiled, knowing where Barnabas was going, and responded, "It was twenty-five years ago, son. The statute of limitations has run out. I already got my settlement, but it was only twenty thousand dollars. Not worth it."

"So you are not here about your leg?"

"No, not hardly. I worked for North American Coal for just about fifty-five years in four different mines, all of them underground. The last forty years they put me on the miner. Some folks call it the continuous miner. It is the piece of equipment that actually extracts the coal from the mine. You can only process and ship the coal that you can extract. Thus, the miner is the most important piece of equipment that we have in the mine. Some would say that the miner operator is the most important job in the mine."

Barnabas gave a slight nod, indicating that he was tracking Williams, but he was concerned that Williams' story was going to quickly become too technical for him.

"Most of the mines I worked in had a coal-seam thickness of no more than six feet, so the cutting head with bits in it was usually three to three and a half feet in diameter. The key is that when the miner is shut down for any reason, the mine is not producing any coal. If the miner operates continuously for the entire shift, the mine is going to produce the maximum amount of coal. The faster the cutting head rotates, the more that coal is going to be produced.

"The miner will not extract coal for three basic reasons. First, when you run into a seam of hard coal and apply too much pressure, you will definitely dull the bits and eventually they will break off. If you have to replace the bits, it is a twenty-minute shutdown. Second, you can run the cutting head into the rock outside of the seam, usually shale or limestone. Again, you can dull or break the bits and shut down the miner. Finally, if the ceiling caves in, you are going to have to back out, the other miners will haul out the rock from the cave-in, and again, you are not producing coal. It can take another twenty to thirty minutes to clear out a cave-in. You are never going to be able to extract coal for an entire shift because you are going to have to take part of the seam. The roof bolters will come in and shore up the ceiling, but you can go back from one part of the seam to the other, back and forth. In a good ten-hour shift, you might get eleven thousand tons out. If you have too many breakdowns, you may get only seven thousand tons."

The way Williams talked, it was apparent that cave-ins were a frequent occurrence.

"Isn't it dangerous for the ceiling to cave in?"

Williams smiled, betraying his amusement at Barnabas' ignorance about mining. "Not really. The miner itself is operated by remote control."

With a sense of relief, Barnabas decided to press ahead to the point of the meeting. "I think I understand what happens in the mines. So why do you need a lawyer?"

"Well, I have been a tinkerer, as my wife calls it, all of my life. Until I came up with this idea on the miner, I even installed my own solar power system on the roof of my house. My wife complains about the amount of maintenance that it requires, but it cuts down on the electricity by seventy-five percent. Sarah had some breathing problems a few years ago and had some films and scans done down at the hospital. She spent the night there. I saw the radiologist in the cafeteria, so I went over and started asking him some questions about his equipment. I asked him if he could read the consistency of rock formations by x-raying the formation. Well, the guy told me that you could read the density of the formation without much difficulty. I then asked him if I could buy a used x-ray machine somewhere, and the guy said that it was like anything else—there is always used equipment available. So, I bought one.

"It took me six months of working nights and part of my Sundays, but I came up with a device that I could install on the miner just above the cutting head. It shot a beam into the ceiling and the formation every ten seconds, and I ran the data back to a monitor on the operator's remote console. It was color-coded. Brown was limestone, green was shale, and coal was either light gray or black, depending on the thickness. The operator could read the monitor to determine when the miner was getting too close to the limestone or shale. Even more important was that the operator could tell whether the thickness of the shale on the ceiling was sufficient to avoid a cave-in. I created an automatic transmission for the cutting head so that it would automatically speed up when the coal was soft or slow down when the coal was hard."

Barnabas observed Williams intensely. *Is this guy for real? Some kind of uneducated technical genius?* Williams was describing his invention in such a matter-of-fact monotone that he was either unbalanced or he truly invented the thing.

"Of course, when I was tinkering in the garage, there was no way to truly know whether it would work until I actually installed it on the miner. I had a friend who ran one of the Illinois mines twenty-five years ago. His name was Carl Dawson. He was the best mine manager I had ever served under. Although he was management, he was good with the men, and he was very concerned about safety. He was there ten years, and we never had a fatality or a crippling accident. I had kept in touch with him over the years, and I called him up and asked if he could talk the home office managers into letting me install it on the miner I was operating and see if it worked. At first they said no, but I kept nagging him, and after three months of harassing them through Dawson, they relented."

"So did it work?"

"I installed it about three years ago, not long before I left the company. We were only operating two shifts, so I went in when the mine was shut down on the third shift. It took me eight hours to get it installed, and we tried it on the first shift. Dawson and one of the home office technical guys by the name of Silva were there for the trial. It worked like a charm. We took out almost thirteen thousand tons of coal on that shift, and we had only one cave-in. The monitor flashed a warning, but I decided to press my luck and go ahead anyway. If I had obeyed my own device, I could have avoided even that cave-in. It was almost a twenty-five percent improvement over the old record."

"So how important of an invention is it?"

"If you can improve production by even ten percent with the same personnel at thirty dollars a ton, you are looking at a thirty-thousand-dollar increase in production per shift for that one mine alone. So, for just that one mine, you are looking at an eighteen million dollar per year increase in the mine's gross profit. That's assuming a very conservative ten percent increase in production."

Williams paused and let Barnabas contemplate what he had just heard.

Is it possible that this guy, who didn't even make it through high school, could have created a contraption that increased production by such a large amount?

"Let me take a guess," Barnabas said. "They claimed that it was theirs because you had made it on company time."

Williams chuckled. "No, they were not that stupid. They knew with eight-hour shifts six days a week that I had no time to build this on their time. What they did is…they just stole it."

"How?"

"Dawson came to me and told me that the technical guy wanted to take it back to their design team to see how it worked. I was leery about it, but I knew I could trust Dawson. There was no way that they could steal it from me because he could prove that I had the idea first."

"So how did they steal it?"

"Well, for the first week I didn't think about it much, and then I started calling Dawson. At first I just left messages on his cell phone, but after two weeks, I called his secretary. And she told me that he was dead."

"How did he die?" Barnabas asked with intensity in his voice.

"He took a bullet to his head. From a handgun. I later learned that there was a police investigation, and they ruled it a suicide."

"Did he leave a note?"

"No note."

"Did he own the gun?"

"No. The gun had been stolen three weeks before from someone living in Indianapolis."

"So why was it a suicide?"

"Dawson had no family, his wife had died years before, and his son—his only child—died in a car accident fifteen years ago. The folks at North American claimed that he was depressed, but I don't believe it. I think someone put a gun to his head, fired the gun, and then wrapped Carl's hands around it. He was found at his desk the next morning. He had been dead for more than eight hours."

"Do you believe that his death was connected to your case?"

"I don't know for sure, but I think so. If you do the math, my invention was going to revolutionize production in mines all over the world. It is easily worth five hundred million dollars. Many men have been murdered for less. A week after I introduced it, I learned that Dawson was dead. Those jerks had installed it on the miner in two of their other mines. I quit and went to a law firm in the city the next day."

"Which firm did you go to?"

"I was told to go to an intellectual property firm, and I was told that a firm called Sharlot, Heller, and Plumb was good."

"I have heard of them, but I don't know much about them."

"Well, they did a patent search for me, and I found out that three weeks before I saw them—one week after the trial in the mine—they filed a patent application claiming that their technical guy, Silva, had invented it. The application showed that North American, Silva, and Silva's lawyer owned the patent. I cashed in my 401(k), which was worth ninety-six thousand dollars, and told them to file suit."

"With Dawson's testimony, you should have had a slam dunk."

"But he is dead. It is my word against Silva's."

"So what is wrong with the Sharlot firm?"

"Well, they did fine at first. They filed suit in federal court against Silva, his lawyer, North American, and another company that North American gave a license to—Century Coal. The complaint asks the court to invalidate their supposed patent, but it turns out that Silva holds a doctorate in electrical engineering. He had obviously reverse-engineered my invention and now claims to have invented it. The further we got into the case, the more discouraged the firm seemed to get. You could see it on their faces.

"After two years of litigation, they told me that they had used up my ninety-six thousand dollars, and the judge let them withdraw from the case. I have no lawyer. I have been looking for one for over a month, and you are my last resort. There is an important hearing tomorrow. If I don't get a lawyer, I am going to lose. The judge has shown a lot of patience, but she has told me that she is going to rule against me if I don't find a lawyer."

"Why don't you represent yourself?"

"Are you serious, son? I have no idea what to do or how to do it. I was candid with the judge about that. If I can't find a lawyer, I am going to throw in the towel, but I hate to do it."

Reluctantly, Barnabas gestured toward the briefcase and said, "Let me see the pleadings."

Williams pulled out an eight-inch stack of papers and said, "These are just a few of the most important ones. I have four boxes in my trunk if you want me to get them."

Barnabas chose not to respond. He started to skim through the stack, and he noticed that the first document was an order five pages in length. He turned to the last page and chuckled when he saw the signature: *District Judge Alice Kruger*.

The next document was captioned "Motion for Summary Judgment," and it was over seventy pages in length, not counting the exhibits. Barnabas' mood turned sour, and he felt his heart beat loudly when he noticed the signature of the attorney on the last page: *Christian L. Frederick III*.

Barnabas then turned to the first page of the pleading to see who the defendants were. It was the second-to-last name that caused him to gasp. The named defendants were North American Coal, Silva, Bill Cushman, and Century Coal.

Williams noticed the gasp.

"Mr. Williams, do you know who Bill Cushman is?"

"Sure, he is Silva's lawyer. Cushman agreed to get the patent issued and waived his fee in exchange for thirty-three percent ownership of the patent."

"Mr. Williams, I have known Bill Cushman for years. He is totally incapable of getting a patent issued. I doubt that he is even licensed with the patent bar."

"Barnabas, as I understand it, Cushman and Silva are golf-playing buddies. Cushman gave the Frederick firm thirty-five percent of his royalty interest, and the Frederick firm secured the patent."

Barnabas looked at the pleadings. The Sharlot firm had filed a complaint seeking to have Judge Kruger invalidate a patent that had been issued to

North American, to have Williams declared the owner of the patent and to seek damages from North American, Silva, Bill, and Century Coal. While there was no claim that Century Coal was part of the conspiracy to steal the patent, the company was being sued as a contributory infringer because they had secured a license to use the patent.

But Williams had major problems. Barnabas knew this just from glancing at the pleadings. North American had an electrical engineer with a Ph.D. from a major university file the patent application. Barnabas didn't understand any of the technical parts of the patent application, but if he didn't understand, it was more likely than not that Judge Kruger didn't understand either.

What reason could any lawyer give to convince Judge Kruger that Williams was the true inventor? Barnabas thought. Once the engineer had Williams' x-ray device, it would have been a simple matter for him to reverse engineer it. He would know almost as much about it as Williams. He certainly would know how it worked, how to make another one, and how to do the technical analysis so that a patent would issue. In Frederick's hands, the guy would be eminently credible.

But then a dose of realism hit Barnabas. *Who killed Dawson? Is Bill actually capable of doing something like that? He was willing to have me dismissed from law school to save himself. He had stooped so low as to read my journals. But is he actually capable of committing murder for millions of dollars?*

Barnabas agreed with Williams. Dawson's alleged suicide didn't make sense. There was no note, and Dawson had not bought the gun. *So who are the logical suspects for killing Dawson? It has to be Bill and Silva.*

Barnabas started to get angry, and he wasn't sure why. He believed Williams. The way he talked about his device, the fact that he had cashed in his retirement, and his natural inability to tell a lie convinced Barnabas that he was telling the truth. Dawson's alleged suicide did not seem plausible. But before Williams even came into the office, Barnabas had resolved that he wasn't going to take the case. It would have been easy for him to state that he was going to join the Frederick firm, that he had a conflict of interest, and that Williams would have to get another lawyer. But he felt compelled to show Williams why.

"Let me ask you some questions, if I may."

"Certainly."

"How am I going to get paid?"

"I'm sorry, but I have no money. I'm hoping that you will take it on a contingency. All my savings were given to the other firm. I get a small pension from the UMWA, and I am on social security. My wife is also drawing social security. We barely have enough to make ends meet."

"Why would I take it on a contingency? It is your word against a Ph.D. with an engineering degree. They filed first. What witnesses do you have who could actually testify that you made it first?"

"Well, my wife knew I was working on something."

"But you are always working on something. They are going to show that you installed it. They will simply say that they gave it to you for the installation. You are suggesting that I take on the strongest firm in the city and give up three months of my life when I know that I have little chance of winning. Why should I do that?"

Williams was deflated. "Maybe simply because it is the right thing to do."

Barnabas' anger started to escalate.

"Look, I am here alone. I am struggling to make ends meet as well. If I were to take this case, it would be a stupid business decision. Why should I take on a case when the odds are stacked against us? Lawsuits are not about the truth. Ultimately, they are about who puts on the best case. Sometimes the person who has truth on his side can't put on the best case. You are asking me to give up three months of my life with little to no chance that I will get paid, even if you survive their motion for summary judgment. It is not that I lack sympathy for your situation, but I think I would do more good by working on a case that I have a better chance of winning and give my fee to orphans or cancer patients. Your circumstances may be difficult, but you don't qualify as a bona fide Mitchell charity. Do you understand what I am saying?"

Williams just stared and tears came to his eyes. But Barnabas was not able to let up. "I have to be candid with you. I was offered a job yesterday by the Frederick firm. If I take your case, I can kiss the job good-bye. If I take the job, it will be the first time in my life that I will have any semblance of financial security. I suggest that you keep looking."

Williams paused. Then he spoke slowly, measuring his words. "I do understand what you are saying, but this is the last stop. I have been talking to attorneys for three months, and they have all told me pretty much the same thing as you have. I guess it is time to move on. I won't get any justice in this life, but maybe God will give it to me in the next one."

"Yeah, and if you ever produce something as good as this in your garage in the future, maybe you'll start with someone like me instead of going to the big firm and giving away your money."

Williams nodded. There was an uncomfortable pause, and then Barnabas, against his better judgment, offered a glimmer of hope. "Well, my mother schooled me to never make a hasty decision. I will think about it…I'm not sure why. When do you have to be in court?"

"Tomorrow at nine a.m."

"Well, you come back tomorrow at eight a.m. and I will give you my final decision. In the meantime, there definitely won't be any hard feelings here if you do find someone else. Leave me these papers in case I want to take a deeper look into it."

Williams left, and Barnabas admitted to himself that his conduct had been shameful. He still didn't know why he was so angry.

Jennie arrived three minutes after Williams left. Barnabas was staring at the wall in his office without moving. Twenty minutes later, she came into his office. "Are you all right?"

"Yeah, I'm all right. I really should be in a good mood. I got the Frederick job, and I think I am going to take it. I assume that you will want to come with me. You are going to get a thirty-six-hundred-dollar per month raise, and they are going to give you health insurance and a pension plan."

She nodded. "So what's wrong?"

"I guess I don't know. I should be happier. I guess I'm tired. I haven't taken a day off. Maybe it's time. Why don't you draft letters to all of my present clients and inform them that I am shutting down the practice here and they need to get another lawyer. We will mail them tomorrow."

Barnabas got up with Williams' file, left the building, and went to visit his mother's grave.

CHAPTER TWENTY

Barnabas had not gone to his mother's grave in more than six months. He thought about the same things that he always did: crossword puzzles, his journal, the accident, her character, her resolve, and her purity. He knew that she would have been disappointed with the way he had treated Williams. It was disgraceful, and he was still not clear in his own mind why he had been so hostile. He could have politely and respectfully said no without stating his reasons. He tried to block Williams out of his mind, but he kept coming back to him. Uneducated, hardworking, and a man of obvious high character, he had overcome, and at the end of his working life, he was being cheated. Williams would have been a great guy to have as his own father.

Barnabas woke up the next morning having decided to take the job with the Frederick firm and move on with his life. If Williams had come into his life a month ago, he might have been tempted to take his case, but this was a helpless soul that he wouldn't attempt to save. He was convinced that Williams had invented the device. While Barnabas only had a rudimentary understanding of what Williams told him, the ease with which Williams described the invention made it obvious that he was not lying. He wouldn't have given up his life savings if he were perpetrating a fraud.

The Sharlot firm must have taken the case because Williams had given them his money. When they had spent it, they were gone. But that was a year ago. The file showed that they had spent almost $15,000 on private investigators to prove that Dawson's death was not a suicide. *What does that accomplish?* Barnabas thought. *Even if it were murder, they would still have to tie it to Silva and Bill.* Barnabas believed that Bill and Silva had killed Dawson, but he didn't know how it could be proved. There was an enormous amount of money at stake, and as Williams said, people had been killed for far, far less.

Barnabas arrived at work at 7:30 a.m. and started to sign the letters to his clients that Jennie had prepared the day before. His form letter promised that he would help his clients find another attorney whom Barnabas was confident could give them good representation.

At 7:55 a.m., he heard the office door open. Barnabas dreaded what he was about to say, but it had to be done.

He walked out to the waiting room. He saw Williams and a woman about sixty-five to seventy years old with him. She was obviously his wife. *This is going to be tough enough with him alone. Why did he have to bring her?*

She was a full foot shorter than Barnabas. Her hair was half-gray and half-dark brown. She was thin, and she gave him a warm, gracious smile when she looked up. He looked at Williams, who was also smiling as he looked at his wife. He had been with her many years, and even though he must have been used to her smile, he was smiling like a teenage boy who was looking at the most beautiful girl that he had ever seen.

Williams turned to Barnabas. "Mr. Mitchell, I want you to meet my wife, Sarah."

She extended her hand to him, and Barnabas took it. Her smile widened. It appeared to consume her entire face. He couldn't help but smile in return. He dreaded what he was about to say even more.

"Why don't we come into my office and talk?"

They walked in, and Barnabas closed the door behind them. He had rehearsed in his mind what he was about to say. They sat down while Barnabas walked around the desk and started to talk.

"I reviewed most of the file you left me last night—"

But Williams interrupted him. "Son, before you start, we think we know what you are going to say, and I want to say something. I need to apologize to you."

Barnabas was surprised. "For what?"

"Sarah and I talked about it most of the day yesterday. She helped me understand why what I was proposing really wasn't fair to you. I was asking you to take on a case that was going to take hundreds of hours of your time with the strong possibility that you were not going to get anything back." Williams paused, and his voice broke slightly. Sarah reached over and grabbed his hand.

Williams cleared his throat and continued to speak. "You are a young lawyer, and you couldn't have that much money set aside. And you have the chance to get on your feet financially. We just can't ask you to do that. So, we are withdrawing our offer to have you take over the case."

Barnabas was stunned.

"What are you going to do about the case?"

"We are going over to the courthouse, and we are going to tell the judge that we are throwing in the towel."

"What are you going to do after that?"

"We'll get by. Don't worry about us, son. We have looked at our budget. We don't have a mortgage on the house, so we have enough money to get by."

Barnabas turned his head to Sarah. "Mrs. Williams, why did you come?"

She smiled broadly. "There is no way I was going to let him go into court alone, and besides, I wanted to meet you."

"Me?"

"My good friend, Ruth, speaks highly of you. I just wanted to connect the name with the face."

Barnabas was unprepared for the moment. He had been expecting to tell them no and then deal with their depression, and instead they had come to give him permission to move into the next phase of his life. But what struck him was what he saw before him. His mind searched for words to describe what he was seeing.

The two of them were strongly connected to each other. When she smiled, he smiled. When he struggled, she gave him encouragement. Her eyes sparkled when she looked at him. Although small in stature, she projected strength. Barnabas understood immediately what Williams would do to anyone who threatened her. He thought of his own father and mother and was saddened because his mom had never had something like that.

Kyle and Sarah Williams had to be an older version of Sam and Ruth. Barnabas had never seen Sam and Ruth in a similar setting, but their connection was probably similar. He had thought that Stephanie was unrealistic in her expectations, but looking at Kyle and Sarah, he was starting to understand what she had been waiting for and insisting upon.

"Can I ask the two of you some questions?" Barnabas asked.

155

"Of course," Sarah replied.

"How long have you been married?"

Kyle spoke first. "Forty-nine years. The best forty-nine of my life," he laughed.

Sarah chimed in. "For me, it was the best forty-six years. It took me three years to break him in."

They both laughed together.

"Do you have any children?"

Sarah responded this time. "Five children, six grandchildren, and praying for more."

"College graduates, every one of them," Kyle added.

"First ones on either side of the family," said Sarah. "And Scooter here was responsible."

Barnabas was surprised. "Scooter? Do you really call him that?"

"After he got injured, he went back to work in the mines, and the fellows in the mines started calling him that. Every miner we have ever known has had a nickname. He could have quit mining, but we still had three kids to go. Disability wouldn't have done it, so he kept right on working even though he had only half a leg. Not many men would have kept going, but Kyle Williams is different."

Kyle interjected. "There is a different culture in the mines. A nickname that would be an insult to anyone else is not offensive underground."

Barnabas suddenly felt like he wanted to know everything he could about them. "How did you two meet?"

"Extending a single into a double. She was late with the tag."

"You were out and you know it. The ump was out of position, and besides that, he was from your church."

Barnabas smiled, but he looked confused.

"Church league softball game," Kyle explained. "She was playing second base, and she missed the tag. She griped about the call the whole time I was on second base. And I couldn't resist the opportunity to needle her."

"You were acting like a jerk. I should have written you off on the spot."

"Don't kid me. You were enjoying it, and you know it, but you're never going to admit it."

156

Barnabas wondered how many times they had had that argument. It was almost like their lines were rehearsed.

"Anyway, I switched churches the next Sunday, and the rest is history," said Kyle.

"Oh, really! It took him six months to ask me out, and when I told him he had to have permission from my parents, it took him another six months to get up the courage."

"I was just practicing my lines. I have a poor memory, and I am not as verbal as she is."

Barnabas thought of something else. "Do you mind if I ask you a personal question?"

Sarah smiled, feigning outrage. "Well, Counselor, it just depends on what it is."

"I am not married, but I think it might be time to start thinking about looking for a wife. You guys seem to have the kind of marriage that I want to have. What is your secret?"

Sarah asked, "What's wrong with Stephanie?"

"I don't believe like she does. My lack of belief is a non-starter with her. In her words, she will not be yoked to a non-believer."

"How much do you believe?" asked Sarah.

"Given my experience, I just can't accept that God is the active kind of agent that the Bible claims, but Stephanie and her family obviously believe. I know that it is trite to say, but I only believe that Christ was a great moral teacher. People are just better off if they follow His teachings."

"Son, it is a good place to start," Kyle offered. "Just keep your mind open to the truth, and you'll be all right."

"But what has been the secret to your success?"

Sarah spoke for the both of them as she grabbed her husband's hand again. "Barnabas, learn that love is a choice and not an emotion. Be long on patience, gentleness, and forgiveness, and be short on anger and keeping score. Next to God, your wife is the most important thing in your life."

Kyle was nodding in agreement. Sarah squeezed his hand and said, "It is time to go or we are going to be late for court. May God's blessings be on you, Barnabas."

"The best of luck to you," Barnabas said weakly.

He heard them close the door to his office. It was 8:40 a.m. An anxiety overcame him, and he wasn't sure why. At first he thought it might be that they would be depressed if the judge dismissed their suit, but clearly they were prepared for that. He thought about his own future and realized it was unlikely that he would get married and be fortunate enough to have a relationship as strong as theirs. But he knew that that was not the reason for his anxiety. Then it occurred to him. Kyle and Sarah Williams were both getting older, and it was likely that one of them was going to die first. It was going to be difficult and very lonely for whoever remained. That would be a sad day.

He thought about his life. The best people he had known were his mom, Stephanie, Sam, Ruth, Jennie, Professor Paulus, and only for a few minutes, Kyle and Sarah. But there were other kinds of people: his dad, the driver that maimed his mother, Bill, and clients like Jessie Nicks. Nancy could have helped her friend in need but couldn't bring herself to do it. Clearly, joining the Frederick firm wasn't going to make him become a self-absorbed people-user and likely murderer like Bill, but was he being honest with himself if he ignored Stephanie's warning that there would be a cost that could not be measured? She was right; the only reason he was going to take the job was because of the money.

The simple facts were that Kyle Williams had invented that thing, whatever it was, and North American had stolen it from him. Silva and Bill had become murderers so that it could be stolen. Was he going to help and attempt to be part of the solution, or was he going to ignore them and join the very firm that was helping North American get away with theft?

Barnabas looked at his watch. It read 8:53 a.m. If he sprinted, he could make it in five minutes. He raced down the stairs, not waiting for the elevator, and ran the six blocks to the federal courthouse. Judge Kruger's courtroom was on the tenth floor, and he knew he would have to wait for the elevator. The security guard, recognizing him from the Abbott trial, waved him through. He squeezed into an already-full elevator and walked into the courtroom with the clock above the judge's bench reading 8:59 a.m.

Kyle and Sarah looked up and were startled to see him running into the courtroom. They were sitting alone at a table, and Barnabas took a chair beside them. Kyle looked at him with a puzzled expression.

Barnabas whispered, "It's against my better judgment, but I changed my mind."

"Thank you," said Sarah. "Whether we win or lose, I don't think you are ever going to regret this."

Barnabas said, "It may already be over. If she doesn't give us a continuance, she could enter judgment against you right now."

Barnabas had not looked at the lawyers seated at the other table, but he knew from his peripheral vision that there were three of them. He looked up. On the far left was Christian L. Frederick III, who glared at Barnabas with venomous eyes. Next to him was Bill, of course, whose smirk turned into a Cheshire grin.

Next to Bill was an older attorney, approximately sixty years old, whom Barnabas did not recognize. Barnabas concluded that he must represent Century Coal. And next to Century Coal's attorney, he saw a familiar face. It was Stephanie. She was smiling at him in a way that he had never seen before, like he had just won an award for bravery. *Bravery or stupidity?*

Barnabas immediately understood why Stephanie's e-mail stated that she had a conflict of interest. He had not looked at Century Coal's pleadings. If he had, he would have noticed Stephanie's name on them.

CHAPTER TWENTY-ONE

Barnabas didn't have long to ponder what was happening as the clerk pounded the gavel and announced, "All rise." Everyone stood, and in walked Judge Kruger. She looked over to the plaintiff's table and was surprised to see Barnabas.

"Please be seated," she said.

She looked over at Barnabas and smiled. "Mr. Mitchell, I didn't know you did patent work. Do you always enter your appearance the day of the scheduled hearing?"

Barnabas decided to make a joke of it, hoping to get Judge Kruger into a good mood.

"I didn't know I did patent work either, Your Honor. And to answer your question, I decided to get into the case just ten minutes ago."

Judge Kruger decided to keep the courtroom mood light. "Don't tell me you are going to ask for a continuance on the defendant's motions, Mr. Mitchell."

Everyone knew that he had to ask for a continuance, so Barnabas attempted to inject more levity into the situation while at the same time acknowledging that he was at the judge's mercy.

"Your Honor, I know that I am risking being held in contempt of court by asking for something that you have instructed me not to ask for, but my clients have diligently attempted to find another attorney, and I guess I am the only one dumb enough to represent them."

Judge Kruger smiled. Clearly, it helped that she knew him. She turned to the other table.

"Mr. Frederick, what is your position?"

Frederick rose, and with a slight edge in his voice stated, "Your Honor, our motion has been pending for over three months. Justice delayed is justice denied. This is clearly a last-minute attempt to delay the inevitable. We oppose a continuance."

Judge Kruger nodded and then looked at the other attorney, the one whom Barnabas did not recognize. "Mr. Clausen, what is Century Coal's position?"

Clausen rose. "We agree with North American. When Century agreed to pay for a license, we did our homework, and North American was the only inventor claiming a patent. This suit caught us totally by surprise. The uncertainty surrounding this claim needs to be put to an end."

Barnabas was about to rise, but Judge Kruger lifted her hand, and he kept his seat.

"I agree and disagree. I'm not going to enter any judgments without giving Mr. Mitchell at least some time. How much time do you need, Mr. Mitchell?"

Barnabas rose. "I'm new to this case. Frankly, I am not skilled in this area of the law. Can you give me forty-five days, Your Honor?"

Judge Kruger did not bite. "You're wrong by half, Mr. Mitchell. Have something on file in the next twenty days. I am going to take up the motion in twenty days. I'll see everyone then."

She stood, giving everyone else permission to rise. Barnabas looked over at the other lawyers. Frederick shoved his papers into his briefcase. Barnabas walked over to Frederick and, extending his hand, said, "Mr. Frederick, I want to thank you for the opportunity—"

But before he could finish his sentence, Frederick turned on his heel and walked off, refusing to accept his hand, refusing to say anything.

Clausen, Century's senior attorney, wasn't far behind him. Bill couldn't help but attempt to goad him. "Barney, you turn down an offer with the best firm in the city to take on a case that no other lawyer will take. One thing I had always thought about you was that you were smart. But you can add stupidity to your other issues. This has got to be one of the dumbest things I've ever seen in my life."

"Bill, what I've learned digging in this file is that you'll do anything for money. I'm going to dedicate myself to representing my client. You have always been sloppy. I'm betting that you've made at least one mistake. When I find it, I don't think even your father's connections will be strong enough to protect you. You would have been better off keeping your mouth shut, but you can't help yourself, can you?"

Bill glared at him, mumbled something under his breath, and left.

Stephanie lingered, the last defense attorney remaining. She turned to Barnabas and spoke to him from across the courtroom. "I'll see you tomorrow. I would like to know the whole story." And she left. Barnabas had forgotten it was a Friday.

The courtroom was empty, and so much had just happened. Barnabas, Kyle, and Sarah decided to use the courtroom to talk.

Kyle started. "What changed your mind?"

"I really don't know. I'm still not sure I made the right decision. You know we have an uphill battle. I nearly flunked physics in high school, and I never took an engineering course in college. But I just couldn't abandon you."

"What's this going to cost?"

"Well, it might be over in twenty days. They have moved for summary judgment, and we have to convince the judge that you know how this things works in language that she understands. Further, we are going to have a big war about whether your conversations with Dawson come into evidence. It could get expensive, but you guys don't have any money."

"Look, we can take out a mortgage on the house, and the kids want to help out. We'll get you enough money so that you can keep going."

Sarah added, "Several years ago, I worked in an office, and I am willing to come into your office and help out, even if it is just answering the phone." She paused and asked, "Just what is summary judgment? I understand that the judge has the right to deny us a trial because she can enter a summary judgment, but how can they not have a trial? I thought that was what lawsuits were about. Our prior lawyers never bothered to explain this to us."

"It is something the courts invented ninety years ago. If the court does not think there is enough evidence as shown by affidavits to have a trial, the judge has the discretion to end it before trial."

"I don't see the point. Why isn't Scooter's word as good as theirs?"

"It should be, but because this is a non-jury case, the judge might be tempted to end it early and avoid a trial. She shouldn't, but she might be tempted. This trial may take two weeks, and she will be looking for ways, like most judges, to avoid a trial."

"While we are on the point, can you explain to me why we can't have a jury? They never explained that either."

"You only get a jury in certain types of cases, usually ones where the plaintiff is only seeking damages. In this case, you are seeking to have a patent declared invalid. You don't have a right to a jury in this type of a case."

Barnabas turned to Kyle. "How many boxes do you have on the case again?"

"Four. They're still in my trunk."

"Well, you had better bring them by the office this afternoon. I'll try and get through them this weekend. You might as well plan on coming in on Monday. We're all about to get to know each other really well."

Kyle and Sarah both chuckled.

* * *

Frederick had told Bill that Barnabas was going to take a job with the firm. Bill had lobbied hard for Barnabas to work in his section, but Frederick refused without telling him why. He had hoped that he could take advantage of Mitchell's work ethic, which would free him up for even more time on the golf course. Bill had the least amount of billable hours of anyone in the firm, but he had secured his position by assigning half of the patent royalties to the firm. By adding the patent royalties into his billings, he was in the top ten percent of the firm's income producers.

When Williams filed his patent infringement action, he and Silva had spent five hours one evening being grilled by Frederick and Oxnard, but they were prepared because they knew that the grilling was coming. They had an answer for every question thanks to Silva's expertise. Because neither Frederick nor Oxnard understood the engineering, their explanations had held up. Bill thought that Frederick actually believed them, but it was obvious that Oxnard had his doubts.

It was so typical of Mitchell to turn down a plush job at the firm and throw away his career to take on this case. It was decisions like this that would keep Barney defending DUI's for his entire legal career.

Bill had been over the case with Frederick hundreds of times. It was almost airtight. He knew that Mitchell was tenacious, but Barney would never figure out where to look for the truth. Only he and Silva knew, and neither of them could or would give that up.

Out of the corner of his eye, Bill noticed Stephanie beaming at Barney, and he couldn't understand why. She was very easy on the eyes, and he had tried to hit on her during the course of the litigation. She showed no interest, but he had not made his most earnest effort. He knew that he had seen her before, but it had not clicked until that moment. Stephanie had changed her hairstyle since, but she was the girl who had beaten them in the moot court competition.

Barnabas and Stephanie Schultz had clearly developed a friendship since law school. At that moment, Bill decided that he was going to pursue her in a way that he had not pursued any girl before. He had never met a girl that he could not seduce eventually. Seducing her would be the ultimate victory over Barney.

CHAPTER TWENTY-TWO

Barnabas spent Saturday morning going over Kyle Williams' file. The four boxes were large and full of paper. Six depositions had been taken. Williams and Silva's were the first ones he read. In order for Williams to win, he had to prove that he had invented the device before Silva claimed that he did. Therefore, most of the two depositions focused on the timing of the competing claims.

Williams claimed that he started working on the device immediately after his wife had returned from the hospital. He had no receipts proving when he bought the old x-ray equipment, and the medical equipment business where he claimed that he bought the x-ray machine had declared bankruptcy. Purchase receipts had either been lost or destroyed. The owner of the business claimed to have a poor memory, but Barnabas wondered whether he had been bought off.

Even if Barnabas could prove that Williams had purchased the x-ray machine, that evidence would be far short of proving that he was the inventor. Dawson could have proven the case, but he was dead. Predictably, North American had invoices from a medical supplies firm that predated by several months the date that Williams had installed it on the miner. The Sharlot firm had taken the deposition of the records keeper for the supplier, but the witness could only testify that the records showed that an invoice had been sent, it had been paid, and the parts had been shipped. There were numerous ways that Bill and Silva could have planted false records. If Barnabas were going to do it, he would have bribed a tech that worked for the supplier to create a false entry. In any event, it was clear that Barnabas was dealing with powerful people.

If Silva were to be believed, the device was invented during a brainstorming session while he was at work six months before it was installed. North American's position was that they gave Williams detailed instructions as to how to install the machine on the miner. At that point, under Frederick's theory of the case, Williams understood how it worked. In his deposition, Williams had been able to explain in great detail the inner workings of the device. It was a small victory perhaps but still an important one; Frederick had conceded that Williams had the ability to build the device in his garage.

The attorney who had been assigned to the case from the Sharlot firm had both a law degree and a degree in electrical engineering. Those parts of the depositions dealing with how the thing actually worked were filled with technical terms, and they were indecipherable to Barnabas. From what little Barnabas could understand, Silva had a complete mastery of how it worked. Of course, this did not surprise Barnabas because Silva had taken it apart and was able to figure out how it functioned.

The file also revealed that Silva had never been convicted of a crime or charged with dishonesty. His contract with North American stated that—while he had to assign the patent to his employer—he retained sixty percent of the gross royalties as the one who invented the device. Silva assigned fifty percent of his interest to Bill. The Sharlot firm did not delve into this matter during Silva's deposition.

In addition, Silva got a $500,000 end-of-year bonus. Given the enormous profitability of the device, it would be difficult to argue that the bonus money was in actuality a payoff.

Williams performed well in his deposition, but it was clear that he was uneducated. In the end, Judge Kruger was going to have to be convinced that an uneducated man rather than a man who held a doctorate in electrical engineering had been the inventor. In order to make that finding, she was going to have to conclude that Silva was committing perjury.

On Saturday morning, Kyle spent three hours trying to explain to Barnabas in simple terms how the device worked. All Barnabas could conclude was that it did work. He just didn't know how, exactly.

Barnabas sat down and drafted a document called a request to admit, which he sent to Frederick:

> Admit or deny that the plaintiff, Kyle Williams, presently has
> the ability to build the device claimed to have been invented
> by your client that is the subject matter of this suit.

Under the federal rules of procedure, both parties had the right to send out requests for admission of facts. If North American denied the request, Barnabas was going to have Williams make another device, and the company would have to pay for the costs of the manufacture. It was not clear to Barnabas which would be more effective: forcing North American to admit that Kyle could make it, or making another device and admitting it into evidence in court. He finally decided to send out the request because there was no way that Williams could show in open court that any device he actually made—however impressive it might look—actually worked.

Before noon, Barnabas told Kyle to go home, and he met Stephanie for lunch. He drove to Bella Italy, arriving at 11:45 a.m. Some days the place was packed and others it was barely half-full. Barnabas could never figure out why there was such a difference from one Saturday to the next.

He ordered his usual, the ravioli. Stephanie arrived five minutes after he did with a big smile on her face. "Okay, tell me why you did it. I was convinced you were going to bolt for the Frederick firm."

"I told Kyle and Sarah that I wasn't sure that I made the right decision, and I'm still not. But they are such nice people. They didn't put any pressure on me, but I couldn't say no to them. Did you see Frederick glaring at me?"

"How could I not? I guess he is not used to people telling him no."

"You know, Stephanie, it could be over in nineteen days. We may not survive summary judgment."

"Why would you say that? I think you have enough to at least force a trial."

"Maybe, maybe not. But I guess we can't get into any detail. After all, you do represent one of the defendants."

"You're right. But I believe the day will come when you will not regret what you did. Hopefully it will be sooner rather than later."

"Yeah, that's what Sarah said. How long have you known them? Do you call him Scooter or Kyle?"

She laughed. "What a horrible nickname, but Sarah and he actually seem to prefer it. They started coming to church seven or eight months ago, and Sarah and Mom became friends instantly. I see them once or twice a week. As you know, our church is small, and the families are close-knit. Our pastor, Luke Davidson, makes it a point to get involved in everyone's life whether we like it or not. It is difficult to sit there in court under the circumstances. I even discussed with Mr. Clausen getting someone else to second chair for him. We don't anticipate doing anything other than listening. It is really between Kyle and North American. Century wants North American to win for no other reason than they don't want to have to renegotiate any deals."

"I understand. Well, if we survive summary judgment, I guess we will be spending a lot of time, if not together, at least in the same courtroom."

She smiled. "It will be fun to see you work. Maybe I can learn something."

"Yeah, and maybe they will be things that Clausen will tell you to forget."

She smiled again and touched his hand. "Barnabas, I want you to know that I am proud to be your friend."

* * *

As promised, Sarah started coming to the office to help out. Kyle was there most days as well, helping Barnabas organize the materials and looking for weaknesses in Bill and Silva's case.

The weekend before his response to North American's motion for summary judgment was due, Barnabas drafted his response. Frederick had answered "admitted" to the request to admit, which meant that North American conceded Williams' capacity to invent the device.

In his motion for summary judgment, Frederick had attached Silva's deposition. In response, Barnabas attached Williams' deposition and pointed out the portions where he testified to inventing the device and his ability to show how it worked. In addition, the response underscored detailed conversations between Williams and Dawson and highlighted when Williams had constructed the device. Because Dawson was senior-level management, Barnabas argued that it was not Williams' responsibility or problem that Dawson was not available. Barnabas argued that every conversation between Dawson and Williams should be admitted as evidence in Williams' favor. He concluded by attaching North American's response to the request to admit. In Barnabas' mind, Judge Kruger had to be impressed with the fact that even North American was admitting that Williams had the ability to make the device.

Frederick filed a reply to Barnabas' pleading, which admitted that there was a clear conflict between Williams' testimony and Silva's. Frederick argued that it defied credibility that Williams—without even a high school education—could have invented a device worth hundreds of millions of dollars. Frederick's response further argued that Williams should not be permitted to testify to what Dawson had allegedly said because this violated not only the evidence rules regarding hearsay, but also a rule of evidence called the dead man's statute.

The hearing was set for a Thursday. They all rose for Judge Kruger as she entered the courtroom. "Be seated," she instructed. Turning to Frederick, the judge said, "Mr. Frederick, this is your motion. I have read the pleadings, and there is no need to rehash what you have already argued. Do you want to add anything further?"

Frederick stood. "Your Honor, I will make a few brief remarks. I realize that there is a dispute in credibility between our witnesses and Mr. Williams. Usually, when there is a credibility dispute, summary judgment will not be awarded. However, you do have the discretion, when one side's evidence is so lacking in credibility on its face, to disregard it. This is such a case. We have the word of a man who didn't graduate from high school against that of a very well-qualified Ph.D. in electrical engineering. If this case were to be tried in front of a jury, no reasonable jury would accept Mr. Williams' testimony. Therefore, there is no need for even a bench trial. As to the words that Mr. Williams has put in Mr. Dawson's mouth, they are not admissible as set forth in our brief."

Frederick sat down, and Clausen rose. "Your Honor, Century Coal joins in the motion."

"Noted for the record," Judge Kruger said. She turned to Barnabas. "Mr. Mitchell, do you have anything to add?"

Barnabas rose. "Your Honor, I would like to speak to the last point. It is basic evidentiary law that the admission of a party opponent is not hearsay. While we are suing a corporation here, Mr. Dawson was not a janitor or even a truck driver. He was senior-level management. His statements come into evidence. As to Mr. Frederick's emphasis on the level of education of his witnesses vis-à-vis my client's, I guess I am somewhat offended by his position. As someone who did not go to an Ivy League school, I hope that Your Honor will give my arguments as much weight as you do

Mr. Frederick's. You know, even Lincoln didn't go to an Ivy League law school, and he turned out to be a pretty good lawyer."

Barnabas looked at Frederick out of the corner of his eye. He could almost see the steam coming from Frederick's ears.

Barnabas continued. "I am advised that Edison lasted only a short time in public school and had to be homeschooled. Einstein did graduate, but he was thought to be a slow student in his early years. Further, the court should note that even North American agrees that Mr. Williams is smart enough to make this invention. The best way to determine whether my client is telling the truth is by giving him the opportunity to convince you of that on the witness stand."

Judge Kruger looked around the courtroom and asked, "Anything further from any of the attorneys?"

There was no response.

"All right. I have given this matter considerable thought, and I am going to deny the motions filed by North American and Century Coal. I am loath to deny anyone a trial if they want it. I want to emphasize that the burden will be on the plaintiff. This is not the burden of more likely than not, but instead, Mr. Williams must prove his case by clear and convincing evidence. I urge the attorneys and parties to review their case carefully before we proceed to trial." Judge Kruger was looking at Barnabas. "I am entering a mediation order," she continued, "and I am referring this case to Magistrate Judge Franks to be concluded within the next two weeks. If mediation fails, trial will start thirty-three days from today."

She stood up, and everyone quickly rose to their feet. When the door to her chambers had closed, Sarah and Kyle turned to Barnabas with puzzled expressions.

"She is hoping that the trial will go away in mediation by having North American and Century buy you off."

"Will we be forced to agree with what the mediator says?" asked Sarah.

"No. If he is a good mediator, he will not try to force you to do anything. He may give his opinion as to our position, but if he does a good job, he will be doing the same thing with them as well. But his job is to try and get the sides to settle. He will work hard to do that."

CHAPTER TWENTY-THREE

The next day, Barnabas got on the internet and started searching for a witness. One of the main weaknesses in Williams' case was that Silva had a Ph.D. while Williams lacked even a high school education. Frederick had been pounding on that point, and Barnabas had to be prepared for more. He needed to do something to neutralize the argument, and the best way was to find someone whose credentials neutralized Silva's, someone who could take their side but who had manifestly better credentials than Silva.

After six hours of browsing, Barnabas believed that he had found the ideal person: Cynthia Anne Masters, Ph.D., British School of Technology, and Nobel Laureate in electrical engineering.

He called her office early the next morning, which was early afternoon in England, hoping to at least get a message to her, but she picked up the phone.

She had a clipped, demonstrably British accent. "Hello?"

"Dr. Masters, you don't know me, but I am an attorney practicing in the United States. I am in a world of hurt, and I am hoping that you could consider helping me."

"What can I do for you, young man?"

"I am representing a man who worked in our coal mines for over forty years. Are you familiar with coal mining technology, Dr. Masters?"

She laughed and said, "My father worked most of his life in the mines in Wales."

"Well, my client took existing x-ray technology, modified it, and put it on the miner. I really don't understand how he did it, but his device sends x-rays into the ceiling of the mine and the coal seam itself, and it measures the density of the formation. The x-ray readings are displayed on a remote monitor, and the operator, by looking at the monitor, can keep the miner away from limestone and rock shale and ceilings that are about

171

to collapse. The x-ray machine measures the hardness or relative softness of the coal. He created a transmission for the cutting head, and as a result, the bits do not break because they are not grinding on shale or limestone. Because the miner is always operating, output increases a minimum of ten percent a shift. The thing is worth at least five hundred million dollars."

"So what is the problem, young man?"

"His employer and a couple of others stole it from him and got a patent on it. I am trying to get the patent invalidated."

"So how can I help you do that?"

"His employer, North American Coal, has an electrical engineer who reverse engineered it, learned how it works, and then applied for the patent. My guy didn't even graduate from high school. I'm afraid that we are going to lose unless we can get someone with even better credentials to weigh in on our side. You are that person."

"What could I possibly do to convince a judge that you are right?"

"I'm hoping that you will consider reading the patent, reading the depositions, and even talk with my client on the telephone. Perhaps you can testify that my client knows what he is doing, that he has the understanding to actually invent the device, and if you can find weaknesses in the other side's deposition testimony, point those out."

"When do you have to have this done?"

"Trial is going to start in thirty-one days. Our budget is very limited, and we know that you must be very expensive, but it is possible, just possible, that you could tip the scales in our favor."

"Young man, I normally don't even consider doing what you suggest, but I must confess that I am intrigued by your situation. Let me think about it, and I will call you back this time tomorrow."

"Thank you in advance for even thinking about it."

Dr. Masters called the next day as promised. "When I talked with you yesterday, I had forgotten that we are scheduled to have a six-day family reunion starting in two weeks. I will have to drop everything I am doing to meet your deadline. I estimate that it will take me eighty hours to read your materials, get up to date on the literature, talk with your client, etcetera. I know that this is probably going to be cost prohibitive, but I must insist on getting paid five hundred U.S. dollars an hour for my time."

Barnabas gulped, hoping that she didn't hear him gulp. That was $40,000 she was asking for with no guarantee that she could even help them.

"That's a lot of money. I'm not sure we can raise it, but we are going to try."

"I'm sorry that I couldn't do this without a fee, but I just can't. Good luck to you, young man."

After talking with Dr. Masters, he sat down with Kyle and Sarah. "I have been trying to find a witness who can neutralize Silva's credentials. I have found one, but she will cost forty thousand dollars."

Kyle said, "I suppose we can put a second mortgage on the house if you think it is essential, but I hate to do it because we have been paying you nothing now."

"I can't tell you that it will guarantee success. It will help, but it helps us only marginally. I have thought about getting someone who also only has a Ph.D., just like Silva, and it would probably cost us far less, but I don't see Judge Kruger giving the testimony much weight if it is just one Ph.D. against another."

"Barnabas, we trust you. You make the decision," Sarah responded.

"I think you will be wasting your money right now. But I have an idea how we may be able to get Century Coal to pay for the witness."

Three days later, they arrived at the chambers of Magistrate Judge Andrew Franks for their mediation session. Frederick was there, along with a gentleman in an expensive three-piece suit who was introduced as the executive in charge of risk management for North American. Bill and Silva were there. Clausen was there with another gentleman dressed in a sport coat and tie. He was introduced as the president of Century Coal. Barnabas had hoped that Clausen would bring Stephanie along too, but apparently even Clausen didn't think they both needed to be there.

Judge Franks was a folksy fellow a full inch taller than Barnabas with a Texas cowboy drawl. He was even wearing cowboy boots. Judge Franks spent ten minutes talking to all of them in his courtroom. He explained how mediation worked and that he would be talking with all parties separately. Frederick and his team would be using Judge Franks' office, and Clausen and his client would be in a private conference room.

Meanwhile, the judge's law clerk ushered Barnabas, Kyle, and Sarah to the jury room. Judge Franks told them that he needed to take a bathroom break, and he reentered the jury room three minutes later. He started with Barnabas. "Mr. Mitchell, as you know, everything you say to me is confidential, and I will not share it with either North American or Century Coal or Mr. Silva or Mr. Cushman unless you give me express permission to do so. Please give me your candid view as to the strength and weakness of your case."

"Your Honor—"

Judge Franks interrupted. "You can skip the 'Your Honor.' Just call me Bob if it makes you more comfortable."

"Your Honor, I guess I would like to stick with Your Honor. I am not sure I can get used to calling you by your first name."

Judge Franks laughed.

"First, let me say that I am convinced that Mr. Williams invented the device. He wouldn't have cashed in his life savings and fought this thing for so long if this was some kind of fraud. I have been around him for the better part of a month, and there is not a dishonest bone in his body. If this comes across on the witness stand, we have a shot at winning this."

"What are the weaknesses in your case as you see it?"

"When the Sharlot firm first filed the case, I think they were confident that they could develop further evidence. Speaking candidly, I believe that Dawson's death was not a suicide, but there doesn't appear to be any evidence that can show that. The judge has ruled that Mr. Williams can testify as to what Dawson told him, but it is going to come down to who is more credible—Mr. Williams or the engineer at North American. The judge has made it clear that she is going to apply a clear and convincing evidence standard. I got the impression that she overruled their motions for summary judgment for the sole purpose of ordering mediation so that Mr. Williams will at least get something."

"Well, I have reviewed the case file," said Judge Franks, "and you seem to have a good handle on your case. So what is your offer? You are the plaintiff. You need to make an offer."

The three of them had agreed to start high, hoping against hope that their case would seem stronger to North American and Century than it actually was, perhaps even stronger than it seemed to Barnabas, Kyle, and Sarah.

"The device is being used in eleven mines currently with the potential of utilization in hundreds of underground mines throughout the world. We are willing to let them keep the patent in exchange for a twenty-cent-a-ton royalty on all coal mined from this day forward. As to back damages, we are looking for a settlement of ten million dollars."

Judge Franks smiled. "I'll say this, Barnabas, you've got guts. You know they are never going to agree to that, but I will go see what their position is."

With that, the judge left the room. Barnabas, Kyle, and Sarah sat and talked about the case for two hours before Judge Franks returned.

When he walked in, his face was somber. "I spent most of the time with Frederick. Of course, I can't tell you what he is telling me, but you will know from their offer what his level of confidence is. He says it is a firm offer and they will not pay a penny more. They will pay Williams one hundred fifty thousand dollars for a full and complete release of claims. I got Century Coal to chip in another fifty thousand dollars."

Judge Franks turned to Kyle. "You need to think seriously about this. A bird in the hand is better than ten in the tree. Given the strength of your case, you will be trying to get your own gold mine but without a gun or even a bow and arrow. You just don't have the ammunition to do it."

Barnabas watched Kyle while the judge was talking to him. It was clear from his expression that he understood what the judge was saying. The potential rewards with a trial were enormous, but why go forward if the chances were not any better than winning the lottery? And $200,000 could buy a lot of lottery tickets. Barnabas surmised that Frederick knew how much Kyle had invested in the case, and at least he could get that back plus a little bit of money for his trouble.

Barnabas was not surprised; in fact, he was grateful that Judge Franks had gotten them to come up with any money at all. Barnabas vowed that he would not pressure Kyle and Sarah one way or the other. If they were going to take this deal, he just didn't want them regretting it later. If they went to trial and lost, he wanted it to be their decision.

Barnabas spoke next. "I think my clients understand, but I calculated the damages here, and according to my calculations, the damages are just short of two hundred seventy-five million dollars. Why should they think seriously about letting it go for two hundred thousand?"

Judge Franks spoke directly to Kyle and Sarah without looking at Barnabas. "If your burden of proof was less, the case would be worth much more, but you have to win by clear and convincing evidence. Judge Kruger could issue an opinion that says that she doesn't know who is lying, but the burden of proof is on you, and you failed in your burden. It doesn't help that Dawson is dead and you have no receipts showing that you purchased the x-ray equipment. In the end, only a few people know the truth, and although it pains me to say it, this is not about truth. It is about who is more likely to win." Judge Franks paused. "Do you want me to leave while you think about it?"

Barnabas decided that he wanted Judge Franks to stay. Under the circumstances, Barnabas believed that Kyle and Sarah were going to lose, and he wanted to have Judge Franks available as a resource so that any decision would be made with full and complete knowledge of the risks of litigation.

"Please stay," said Barnabas. "If we need privacy, we will let you know."

Sarah spoke next. "I know he invented the thing. I saw him leave the house with it. That's got to count for something."

"Yes, but did you actually know what it was?" asked the judge.

"No, he never talks about his work until it is completed," she replied somberly.

Judge Franks nodded.

Sarah continued. "The way I look at it is that if we take their lousy two hundred thousand dollars, it is condoning theft and maybe even murder. I would rather go to my grave knowing that we didn't let them steal it, that we at least forced them to get on the witness stand and lie. We may not get justice in this life, but I shudder for them about judgment day in the next life."

Kyle intervened, putting his hand on hers. "Dear, dear, I wouldn't wish that on anyone, and you shouldn't either."

Her voiced flared slightly. "If you don't force them to go to trial and lie, it will just make them bolder. Someone has to stand up to them for no other reason than to protect future people like Scooter."

Barnabas thought about Bill, who had been getting away with whatever he wanted his entire life. He thought back to high school. Bill would have been better off if he had not escaped punishment back then. As he got older, Bill got bolder. Now it appeared that he was complicit in a murder.

Barnabas interjected with a thought, remembering what Dr. Masters had said about her fee. "Can we get Century to settle separately? We will give them a full release for fifty thousand dollars. Or do we also have to settle with North American as well?"

Judge Franks smiled, admiring Barnabas' creativity. "Not a bad idea. I will see what their thoughts are."

He was back thirty minutes later. When he entered the room, he was not smiling.

"The four of them seem to be bound together at the hip, even though I have them in separate rooms. It is all or nothing. They will not settle separately."

Kyle responded, "Then it is nothing."

CHAPTER TWENTY-FOUR

Two days later, Barnabas heard a fax come through on his machine. Jennie, Sarah, and Kyle were out to lunch, so he retrieved it himself. It was from Frederick:

Dear Mr. Mitchell:

I have to assume that negotiations broke down because of your advice. In all of my thirty years of practice, I do not recall such an irresponsible action by an attorney. I will do everything in my power within the boundaries of the canons of ethics to limit your ability to cause further havoc on your clients and on the legal system. I strongly suggest that you rethink your position. Call me if you come to your senses.

Christian L. Frederick III

Barnabas was stunned by the arrogance. It was a one-paragraph confirmation that he had made the right decision in passing on the job. He read it a dozen times at least, and each time he read it, his anger escalated. Since the bridges had already been burned, Barnabas figured he might as well bomb them, too. He faxed his response back:

URGENT!!!

Dear Mr. Frederick:

I am faxing you this letter to advise you that you must take immediate steps to increase your intra-office security! Earlier today, I received a letter purporting to be signed by you that contained the most asinine statements I have ever read in my life. I have confirmed that it was sent from your fax machine!

I am very truly yours,

Barnabas Mitchell

If there was one lesson he had learned, it was that he was not going to kowtow to the likes of Frederick or his ilk. Barnabas might lose, but at least he was not going to sacrifice his dignity. The trial was going to start in ten days, and Barnabas didn't know what he could do to win it.

That afternoon, Barnabas called the office of the detective who investigated Dawson's death. He was put through to Sheldon Vincent, Chief Investigative Officer. "Mr. Vincent, my name is Barnabas Mitchell, and I am hoping that you recall investigating the death of Carl Dawson three years ago. I am representing a party who believes that he would have been a strong witness for him. Could you tell me why you ruled it a suicide?

"Mr. Mitchell, I was just thinking about that case yesterday. I even spent a couple of hours going over the records."

"What can you tell me about it?"

"It is perhaps one of the strangest cases I have ever dealt with in my twenty years in this business."

"Do you think that it may not have been a suicide? There is a lot of money involved in this case. When you have that kind of money on the line, people will be tempted."

"I just don't know. What I can tell you for sure is that there was no note, and we have no idea how Dawson got the gun, if he did indeed get it. The fact that his wife had died and he had no other family, along with several people at North American claiming he was depressed, resulted in a finding of suicide. I was aware of the fact that Kyle Williams, who I assume is your client, claims that Dawson could have corroborated his claim to the patent, but Silva and Cushman provided alibis for each other. It is possible that the two of them overpowered Dawson since they were younger and stronger than he was, put a gun to his head, and pulled the trigger. I was investigating that angle when I got a call from the chief who instructed me to close the file."

"Do you still have the evidence?"

"You know, it was curious. A month after we closed the file, I get a call from someone in the mayor's office suggesting that I dispose of the evidence. It was highly irregular."

"So what did you do?"

"I took it out of the evidence room and stored it in a couple of file drawers."

"So what is in your file?"

"Not much. The contents of Dawson's office desk and his desktop computer."

* * *

Barnabas had lunch with Stephanie two days later.

She commented on his appearance. "Barnabas, I don't think I have ever seen you with so much anxiety. Are you going to be okay?"

"It feels like the days after my mother was injured. There is such a feeling of helplessness. Kyle and Sarah are good people, but I think Judge Franks is going to be right in the end. They are going to lose."

"Maybe I made a mistake sending them to you. You know I would help if I could."

"No, there is nothing you can do. You represent Century, and Century has taken the position that it wants Kyle to lose. I know that you are personally rooting for us to win, even though you are making all of the legal arguments why we should lose, but win, lose, or draw, my life has been better just being around them. I just hope I will be half the man that Kyle is when I am his age."

"Would it be easier if I begged off the trial? I have talked with an ethics expert, and he says that I don't have to disqualify myself from sitting in the trial. You know, I started on the file before our family even met Kyle and Sarah, but it may be better if Clausen got someone else."

"You're not going to do anything but watch. I don't see why Clausen even has you there other than to have his firm double bill the client. I can see and hear Clausen now. As soon as Frederick says anything, he is going to stand and say, 'We join in the objection,' or 'We join in the argument,' etcetera, etcetera."

"Clausen says that he thinks it will be good experience for me. I've done most of the legal work on the case. He says that if something unexpected comes up, he wants me there to consult with him. Clausen knows that you and I are friends, and it doesn't bother him or the client."

"Well, it is going to be difficult."

"You know that I will be praying for you. This has not been as easy on me as it may seem. It has to be difficult for you."

"Thanks," Barnabas said. *But I am going to need more than prayers.*

CHAPTER TWENTY-FIVE

On Tuesday, Judge Kruger conducted a conference call with Barnabas, Frederick, and Clausen. She, of course, spoke first. "Judge Franks told me that we are not going to settle. We are starting trial next Tuesday. Praise God this is not going to be in front of a jury. I've decided to bifurcate the trial. We will get the issue of damages only if I find for the plaintiff as to liability. Given that, how long is this going to take?"

Barnabas was not surprised but still not pleased about the judge's decision to bifurcate the trial, which meant that she was delaying her ruling on the question of damages. If Williams lost on the issue of liability, there would be no need to hear evidence as to damages. It would have been good for Williams if the judge understood the magnitude of the theft. The evidence would show damages in excess of $500,000,000. The judge's ruling was another indication of her opinion on Kyle Williams' case.

Barnabas thought about the judge's question. He had gone over Silva's deposition several times and decided that—except for a few points—he would not thoroughly cross-examine him. It was pointless. Silva knew how the device worked. Barnabas didn't, and he doubted that anyone other than Kyle and Silva did either. He was going to call Kyle, Sarah, and North American's corporate representative, expecting to be done in two days. But there was one matter that he wanted to pursue just for his own satisfaction.

"Your Honor, before I answer, I would like to extend discovery to take one more deposition of a party that has not been deposed."

"Are you asking for a continuance, Mr. Mitchell?"

"No. I know that the party is available. It is a party with whom I need not go through the intricacies of how the patent works."

Judge Kruger asked, "Okay, who is it?"

"I would like to take the deposition of the defendant, Bill Cushman."

Frederick interrupted, raising his voice. "Objection, Your Honor. Cushman is an attorney on this case. Anything he says would be privileged."

Barnabas was prepared for the objection. "Your Honor, somehow Mr. Cushman has become part owner of this patent. His expertise listed on the Frederick firm's website indicates that he has no expertise in patent law. I have done some research, and the nature of the fee arrangement between client and attorney is not per se protected by the attorney-client privilege. I think that the court is entitled to know just how Mr. Cushman came to have an interest in this patent."

Frederick came back hard. "With all due respect to Mr. Mitchell, this is a lot of nonsense. Everything that has transpired between Bill Cushman and Mr. Silva must be protected by attorney-client privilege."

The judge ruled. "It just so happens I dealt with this very issue last month. Mr. Mitchell is correct. It did seem odd to me that Mr. Cushman wound up with such a hefty percentage of this patent. It's relatively rare for the attorney to take his fee on a percentage, and I have never seen one where the attorney winds up with one-half of his client's interest in the patent. Mr. Mitchell, you may inquire about the following topics: how Mr. Silva and Mr. Cushman met, the details of their arrangement, and what work Cushman actually did on the patent, including communications with North American personnel. You may not inquire into communications between Silva and Cushman after they formally entered into their attorney-client contract. The deposition will start at nine on Thursday morning at Frederick's office. That said, how many days will you take, Mr. Mitchell?"

"Your Honor, Plaintiff's evidence is going to take two days. I have gone over our witness list, and I expect that I can be done on Wednesday."

There was a pause. The silence suggested that Frederick thought it was going to take longer.

Frederick spoke. "North American's case, along with Mr. Silva and Mr. Cushman's, will take two days at the most."

Clausen chimed in. "Century Coal does not intend to call any witnesses at this time but reserves the right to call witnesses depending on how the trial unfolds."

No one was surprised by Clausen's statement.

Judge Kruger closed off the conference. "We will start trial at nine o'clock Tuesday morning. We will break for an hour around noon, and we will go up to five p.m. if necessary, but I want to get done in no more than five trial days. I expect Plaintiff to be done on Wednesday, and I am giving North American, Mr. Silva, and Mr. Cushman two days. I will let Plaintiff put on some rebuttal evidence on Monday if Plaintiff has anything new to add. Have all your exhibits marked and exchanged at eight thirty Tuesday morning. Anything further?"

Simultaneously they all said, "Nothing, Your Honor."

Judge Kruger got in the last word. "See you Tuesday morning. Good luck to all of you."

* * *

Barnabas and Kyle arrived at the Frederick firm at 8:55 a.m. Barnabas would be naïve to think that Bill would crumble under cross-examination, but he felt that he had been around Bill enough that he could read his expressions. If Bill knew something, he was not going to admit it, but his expression might give it away. It might give Barnabas a clue about how to salvage the case.

Promptly at 9:00 a.m., they were ushered into an ornate conference room, and the court reporter, Bill, Frederick, and Stephanie were waiting for him. He had not anticipated her being there, but he was pleased.

The court reporter administered the oath, and Barnabas started to question Bill.

Bill sat through the deposition with his typical smirk. It took Barnabas fifteen minutes to cover the preliminaries, and then he turned to the guts of the case.

"How long have you known Mr. Silva?"

"About four years."

"How did you meet?"

"On the golf course."

"Did you develop a friendship after that?"

Bill attempted to be cute in order to distract Barnabas from his questioning. "What do you mean by friendship?"

Barnabas would not be distracted. "How regularly did you play golf after that?"

"Every weekend."

"Did you socialize elsewhere?"

"Yes, some."

184

"You are not married, are you?"

"No."

"And Mr. Silva isn't either, is he?"

"No."

"Did you and Silva go to parties together with your dates?"

"Yeah, that happened."

"And he has been a guest in your home?"

"Yes."

"And you have been a guest in his?"

"Yes."

"How did you first learn about the patent that is the subject matter of this litigation?"

"We were playing golf, and he told me that he had an idea that he was convinced would not only work but would also revolutionize coal industry production. He asked me if I was interested in helping him out in getting a patent."

"How long after that did it take for you to enter into a contract with him?"

"The following Tuesday."

"Now, did you talk with anyone in the firm's patent department before that Tuesday?"

Bill paused, and Barnabas knew that he was uncomfortable, but he could not lie, especially with Frederick sitting next to him. "No."

"Why not? Didn't you think it advisable to learn what the typical fee arrangement was for securing a patent?"

"As I said, Silva and I are friends. We share a lot of things on an equal basis, if you catch my drift." Bill broke into a large smile and chuckle.

Barnabas lied. "No, I don't catch your drift. Explain it to me."

"Let me put it this way—what's mine is his and what's his is mine."

"So you are not merely friends, but very close friends, true?"

"I guess."

"You trusted him in a way you would trust no one else, and the same is true with him?"

Frederick objected for the first time. "Objection, asking the witness to speculate about what someone else thought or believed."

Undeterred, Barnabas pushed on. "You can answer."

"I suppose that is true," said Bill.

"And if Silva asked you for help or a favor, you would do that without question, is that true?"

But Bill was prepared for the question. "There are limits to anything. But he would never ask me to do anything dishonest, unethical, or illegal."

Barnabas paused briefly and studied Bill. He knew from Bill's expression that he was lying. What conscience Bill did have was on display when he avoided eye contact for a moment and looked down at the table for a few seconds. It confirmed for Barnabas that Bill and Silva had indeed done something illegal.

Barnabas switched subjects. "Just what did you do to earn fifty percent of Silva's interest in the patent?"

"Well, I checked in on the patent section of the firm and made sure that they didn't let the thing languish."

"And how is the Frederick firm getting paid?"

Bill paused, not wanting to answer. "The firm gets thirty percent of whatever royalties I collect."

"And what was your royalty check last month?"

"Slightly less than four hundred thousand dollars."

Barnabas almost gasped. It meant that since the start of the case, there had been additional licenses issued. It also explained why the firm was willing to tolerate keeping Bill around.

Barnabas changed subjects again, and the change of subject caught Bill off-guard. "Did Silva ever mention to you a North American employee by the name of Carl Dawson?"

This time the pause was prolonged. Barnabas was surprised that Bill had not prepared an answer.

Bill lied badly. "I don't think so, but his name sounds familiar."

Barnabas wasn't buying. "Surely, as someone who is working on this case, you must have heard the name Carl Dawson?"

"I'm sure that I could tell you more if you could refresh my memory about why he is important."

This time the lie was palpable, at least to Barnabas, but he wasn't sure that it was so obvious to the others.

Barnabas addressed Frederick. "I think I'm done. Please let me have the room for five minutes to go over my notes."

Frederick grunted, and they all left.

Stephanie drifted in two minutes early. Barnabas looked up and smiled at her, and she smiled back. She was about to say something when Bill walked into the room. He couldn't help himself but attempt to goad Barnabas. "You know, Barney, there is something out there, but you will never find it, especially in less than a week. I just wanted you to go down knowing that it was at least theoretically possible for you to win."

Barnabas looked at Stephanie and then back at Bill. It was odd that he would say that in her presence. What was he attempting to accomplish? Obviously, he was hoping that she was impressed with his wealth, but did he really think that Stephanie would be impressed with the fact that he was concealing evidence? He looked over at her, and she had a quizzical expression on her face that he had never seen before.

When the rest of the group entered the room, Barnabas continued. "Mr. Cushman, while we were on break, you entered the room here before the others, except for Ms. Schultz, isn't that true?"

"Yes, that is true."

"And you volunteered something to the effect that—and I quote— 'there is something out there, but you are never going to find it.' Isn't that true?"

Bill smirked. "Yes, that is true."

Barnabas was surprised that Bill admitted it. "Well, Mr. Cushman, what is that something?"

Frederick's voice rose. "Objection. You talked with Mr. Cushman without me being present. You have violated attorney-client privilege."

Barnabas responded, "I didn't say a word to him. He volunteered it."

Still angry, Frederick said, "No way. I'm going to instruct him not to answer."

But Barnabas would not back down. "Let's get the judge on the line. We'll let her decide."

Frederick pondered his dilemma a full thirty seconds. Then he said, "Go ahead and answer."

"Yes, I said that, but I wasn't under oath because I wasn't before the court reporter. I was just toying with you, Barney. Just like old times. There is nothing out there." And Bill laughed.

CHAPTER TWENTY-SIX

Barnabas rehearsed Kyle's testimony four times and Sarah's testimony three times that week. Given his ignorance as to how the device worked, all he could do was ask layman's questions about it and let Kyle impress the judge with his knowledge. During rehearsals, he started with Kyle's experience as an inventor and finished with his conversations with Dawson.

Sarah was easier. She didn't know how the machine worked, and unfortunately, she couldn't testify that Kyle told her what he had been working on. He would just go out into his garage and "tinker." She did confirm that she saw him take a large, rectangular box to the mine one evening, which would have been around the time that both sides agreed that the device was installed on the miner.

Barnabas hoped that by the end of their testimonies, the judge would be impressed by their honesty and character. It was their only hope.

He got up at 6:00 a.m. as usual on Tuesday morning and went to his closet, looking at his choice of five suits. He picked the pinstripe one with a red tie and yellow shirt. He went over his trial notebook that contained the examination lines, assuring himself that he had overlooked nothing. Barnabas double-checked his exhibit list, which contained only eight exhibits, the original patent application with technical drawings prepared by the Frederick firm, the license to Century Coal, and photographs of Kyle's solar panels and vacuum system. He had the originals and four copies of all the exhibits.

Kyle had been so naïve. He just enjoyed working in his garage, but he never created any specifications or drawings. He had done it all in his head. *What could this guy have accomplished if someone had recognized his talent and forced him to go to school?*

Barnabas arrived in Judge Kruger's courtroom at 8:15 a.m. just as her deputy was opening the courtroom door. Kyle and Sarah arrived five minutes later. Promptly at 8:30 a.m., Frederick appeared, along with Bill and Silva and another gentleman. Barnabas assumed that the other man was Fred Stacy, the man who had replaced Dawson. One minute later, Clausen and Stephanie arrived. All of the players were in place. Other than the courtroom personnel, Barnabas didn't think there were going to be any spectators.

Barnabas rose and walked over to the defense table with two stacks of exhibits, one for Frederick and one for Clausen. He went to Clausen's end first. "Here are my exhibits. I assume that you don't have any for me, correct?"

Clausen grunted. "You're right, not since you have the license from Century." Stephanie just gave Barnabas a moderate smile.

He decided to ignore Frederick and put his exhibits in front of Bill. "Bill, do you have exhibits ready for me?"

Bill pulled a box off the floor that contained documents eighteen inches thick. "Have fun, Barney."

Barnabas was not surprised that Bill continued to call him Barney. It was the same Bill.

As he waited for Judge Kruger to come in, Barnabas quickly perused North American's documents. He had seen them all before. Many of them were phony memos between Silva and Dawson.

At 8:50 a.m., Silva came into the courtroom and sat in the back.

Right at 9:00 a.m., the bailiff came in and commanded, "All rise."

After Judge Kruger sat down, Barnabas remained standing, as he knew he was about to proceed with the evidence.

"I am very familiar with this case," said the judge. "I don't need opening statements unless Counsel really has something novel to say." Judge Kruger smiled. One thing Barnabas had learned in preparing the case was that the concept of novelty was important in patent law. Judge Kruger was making a joke, and he elected to respond with a modest smile. Neither Frederick nor Clausen seemed to get the joke, and therefore, neither smiled.

"Very well then, Mr. Mitchell. Call your first witness."

As Barnabas was about to speak, Frederick rose. Judge Kruger nodded in his direction.

"Your Honor, before we start, I move that witnesses be excluded."

Barnabas had expected the motion, and he had previously warned

Sarah that she would not be able to sit in the courtroom until she had concluded all of her testimony. Because Bill and Silva were parties in the case, they were permitted to remain.

Sarah left the courtroom with a frustrated expression on her face. As soon as the courtroom doors closed behind her, Judge Kruger looked at Barnabas and said, "Call your first witness."

"Plaintiff calls Kyle Williams."

Kyle was sworn in, and the most important case of Barnabas' career had begun.

"Your name is Kyle Williams, and you are the plaintiff in this case."

"Yes."

"How old are you?"

"Seventy-three."

"And your wife, Sarah, just left?"

"Correct."

"How long have you been married to her?"

"Forty-nine years, eleven months, and twenty days."

Barnabas noticed Judge Kruger smile. Their attempt to make Kyle human and likable was working.

"And how many children do you have?"

At this point, Frederick rose. "Objection, relevancy."

"It is just foundation, Your Honor, and it will speak to the amount of time my client had available to invent the device in issue."

Judge Kruger agreed. "Overruled."

"How old are your children?"

"The oldest is forty-five, and the youngest just had his twenty-eighth birthday."

"Do you have a nickname that they called you in the mines, and if so, tell the judge what it is."

"Scooter."

"How did you get that name?"

"When I was forty-two years old, I had a mine accident, and I had to have the lower half of my left leg below the knee removed."

"And what level of education do you have?"

"I didn't make it through high school."

"Why not?"

"I had to go to work. I was the oldest, and my father had died suddenly."

"Where did you go to work?"

"North American Coal."

"Have you worked at North American since high school?"

"Yes."

"You no longer work for them?"

"No. When this all started, I quit."

"Was all of your work in the underground mines?"

"Yes. In the early years I would work above ground in the tipple. But the rest of the time was underground."

"What equipment did you operate underground?"

"Well, again, in the early years, I did it all—roof bolter, buggy operator, mine examiner. But the last twenty-five years I was on the miner."

"Tell the judge what the miner does."

"It is a machine, typically with a thirty-two-inch cut, that extracts the coal from the seam."

"What happens when the miner shuts down for any reason?"

"You don't mine any coal. The miner has to operate if the mine is going to make any money."

"What are the reasons that the miner will shut down?"

"There are several. First, the ceiling can cave in. Second, you can break the bits in the miner by getting it off seam and into shale or limestone, or even if you press too hard against a hard seam of coal. Those are the main ones."

"I think the court understands about the bits breaking, but how does a cave-in slow you down? It sounds dangerous."

Kyle finished describing the basic details of the miner and then spent several minutes testifying how his device worked, how it minimized ceiling cave-ins, and how it prevented the bits from breaking.

Then Barnabas moved on to the increases in production, asking how much the device would increase production. "On a good shift, what is the total amount of coal the miners can extract?"

"More than ten or eleven thousand tons."

"Now, if we could switch gears here, prior to the device in question, had you invented other mechanisms and devices?"

"Sure, lots of them."

"Did you ever get a patent on any of them?"

"No. I didn't know how and didn't want to pay someone to do it."

"Tell the judge what you invented."

"Well, our house has an automatic vacuum system installed in the floorboards of each room. We have a solar power system that I made that is attached to the roof of our home. It saves us about seventy-five percent on our electric budget. I also made a device that measures air temperature and adjusts the carburetor on our cars. It improves our gas mileage."

"Have you ever had anyone show any interest in these things?"

"Yeah. About ten years ago, some management-type guy from Fountain Grove Labs came over, but I didn't trust him so I sent him away."

"Tell the judge how you invented the device in question before the court today."

Kyle provided Judge Kruger with a detailed account of his invention process.

"How many hours did you work in the mine during a typical week?"

"At the time I was working on this, I worked the first shift Monday through Saturday."

"What were the hours of the shift?"

"Seven a.m. to three thirty p.m."

"So when did you work on this device?"

"I would work on it a couple of hours two or three evenings a week, and three hours on Sunday afternoons."

"How long did it take you from start to finish?"

"Right about six months."

"How did North American learn about it?"

"I knew Carl Dawson, who was in North American's office."

"What was, or is, his title?"

"Vice president in charge of production."

"How did you know him?"

"He was the mine manager at the mid-valley number six mine for ten years while I worked there. I kept in touch with him over the years—you know, Christmas cards and things like that. When he came out to a mine I was working in, he would always look me up. He was a good guy, a strongly religious man, and I knew I could trust him. I believe he trusted me as well."

"How did you contact him?"

"I called him one afternoon and told him about it."

"How did he respond?"

"He said he would take it to the president of the company."

"Do you know whether he did?"

"I guess I don't know, but I believe he did because he called me back and told me he did."

"And what did Mr. Dawson say?"

"He said they weren't interested. They didn't think it would work."

"How did you respond?"

"At first I did nothing, but then I called him a week later and told him that the mine was shutting down for repairs and safety checks and that I could install it on a miner if I was given an evening. I could show them it would work."

"What happened next?"

"He called me back a week later and said they were willing to try it."

"When did you install it?"

"I remember very vividly it was January sixth three years ago."

"Who was there from North American?"

"I started at eleven p.m. Dawson was there for the first hour, and one of their engineers who claims that he made the device stayed up with me the entire night asking questions."

"And that was Mr. Silva, who is present in the courtroom?"

"Yes."

"How long did it take to install?"

"I was done by six a.m."

"Who operated the miner the first shift on January seventh?"

"I did."

"How many tons did you produce?"

"Just shy of thirteen thousand tons. I was very pleased. Even if you assume a maximum of eleven thousand tons on a good shift, it was a sixteen percent increase in tonnage on one shift."

"So how did North American respond?"

"Dawson seemed very pleased, and I was excited. The engineer just stood there passively. Then the engineer asked if he could take it with him to see how it worked."

"Did you let him do it?"

"Yep. The biggest mistake of my life. But I trusted Dawson. As long as he was around, I knew they couldn't screw me."

"Who did you talk to next?"

"Dawson came out to the mine about a week later, and he told me that the engineering department said they didn't think it would hold up."

"How did you respond?"

"Well, I figured that I was going to retire in three months anyway, so I told him to get it back to me. I planned to go to the other mines, and I was sure someone would take it."

"How did Dawson respond?"

"He promised he would bring it by in two weeks when he planned to be back in the area."

"Did he bring it back?"

"No."

"Why not?"

"Subsequently, I found out that two days after I talked with Dawson, he had died."

Barnabas paused for effect. He looked up. Judge Kruger seemed interested and attentive. It seemed that she liked Kyle well enough, but from her expression, it appeared that she wanted more.

Barnabas then went to the specifications on the patent and took Kyle through them. He answered the questions, but Judge Kruger's eyes glazed over as they got into detail.

They finished the direct examination at 3:45 p.m., and Frederick asked to start the cross the next morning, promising that it would not be long.

Frederick and Bill were the first to leave the courtroom, and Clausen stood next to Stephanie, helping her assemble her papers. Barnabas heard her say, "It's all right, Mr. Clausen. You go ahead. I can gather up the files."

Barnabas suspected that Stephanie wanted to speak with him. He sent Kyle and Sarah ahead, and he and Stephanie had the courtroom to themselves.

Stephanie looked up and said, "You did a good job today. You looked poised and confident. It's obvious that you have learned a lot since law school."

Barnabas was pleased because he knew she meant it.

"Looking back on it, I'm glad I spent that time in the public defender's office. I wanted to learn how to try cases, and I think I did."

They walked out of the courtroom together, both pulling metal dollies laden with legal files. They walked into the elevator together, and there was barely enough room for the two of them and the three boxes of files. As the elevator doors were closing, they saw someone thrust a hand between the doors, forcing them to open back up automatically. Barnabas saw Bill standing there with his ever-present smirk.

"Just got out of the bathroom. How are you two getting along? Barney, maybe you should get off so that Stephanie and I can ride together. It may look bad if your clients saw the three of us in the elevator together."

Barnabas guessed that Bill had waited outside the courtroom, hoping to catch Stephanie alone in the elevator.

"Bill, I'll take my chances."

For the first three floors, the three of them stared awkwardly and silently at the panel of floor numbers as they descended to the lobby. But Bill couldn't help himself, and he finally decided to say something to get under Barnabas' skin. "Did you try and look for it, Barney?" Then Bill got off the elevator and walked away, smiling to himself.

Barnabas turned to Stephanie. "Do you have any idea what Bill says is out there?"

"None whatsoever. He may be bluffing, hoping to get you riled up."

"I don't think so. I think that Bill does know something, but he is never going to tell me. That is for certain."

Stephanie's expression changed to the mysterious one that Barnabas had seen at the deposition. It was like a light bulb had gone off in her brain. Barnabas didn't know what she was thinking, and it didn't seem that she was interested in sharing with him. After exiting the courthouse, they said good-bye to one another, and Stephanie headed in a different direction.

Barnabas went to his office. He had an early pizza dinner delivered. Sarah, of course, wanted to know how it had gone. All Barnabas could say was that it went as well as could be expected. "The judge seems to like him, and that is the best we can hope for right now."

CHAPTER TWENTY-SEVEN

The routine was the same on Wednesday. Barnabas got up at 6:00 a.m. after falling asleep at 12:30 a.m. He arrived in court at 8:30 a.m. and went over his trial notebook. Sarah's examination was going to be short.

All the players were in place, and Judge Kruger entered at 9:00 a.m. She looked at Kyle. "Mr. Williams, you are still under oath. Please resume the witness chair," she instructed.

As Kyle limped up to the chair, the judge turned to Frederick. "Cross-examination," she said.

Frederick did not start strong, choosing to ask some technical questions that must have been planted by Silva. Barnabas scrutinized Judge Kruger, but it didn't appear that her ability to understand the device had increased from the day before.

But Frederick finished strong. "Mr. Williams, you claim that you got the x-ray equipment after your wife was admitted to the hospital."

"Correct."

"Which company did you purchase the equipment from?"

"Quality Medical Equipment Company here in the city."

"Do you have any receipts for the purchase?"

"No, that was over three years ago."

"Do you have anyone you are going to call who remembers you from that establishment?"

"No, the young man I dealt with no longer works there, and when we tracked him down, he said didn't recall me."

"Do you have any witness other than yourself that can verify that you worked on this invention?"

"My wife was there in the house when I was working on it."

"But you work in the garage all the time, true?"

"Yes, that is true."

"And you never told her that you were working on this invention, isn't that true?"

"Yes."

"So your wife can't verify that you were working on this invention, isn't that true?"

"Yes, I guess that is true."

"No further questions."

Judge Kruger looked at Barnabas. "Any redirect, Mr. Mitchell?"

"Just one, Your Honor. Kyle, has North American ever returned your invention to you?"

"No."

Frederick stayed seated, not moving. Judge Kruger looked at Kyle and said, "You are excused."

Judge Kruger looked over at Barnabas. "Please call you next witness, Counsel."

Barnabas rose. "Please ask the bailiff to bring in Sarah Williams. She is out in the corridor."

Sarah was brought into the courtroom, and she took her oath.

"Sarah, you are married to Kyle Williams?"

"Yes, for fifty years."

"And do you call him Kyle or Scooter?"

"Since I am under oath, I guess I have to admit to Scooter. It just kind of stuck. Not many men would continue to support their family after losing half of their leg."

"Now, you understand that your husband is claiming that he invented a device to increase coal production and that is what this suit is about."

"Yes, I know that."

"Has your husband invented other things while you were married?"

"Several."

"Which ones can you tell us about?"

"The ones I know best are the vacuum panels and the solar panels."

"Tell us how the vacuum panels work."

"It is not hard. He has installed a switch in every room, and you flip it on and it automatically sucks all of the dust and other items into the panels down into a dustbin in the basement."

"Are there any problems with it?"

"It definitely works better in smaller rooms that are contained, and when we had small children, you had to make sure all of the toys were off the carpet."

"What about the solar panels?"

"I have no idea how those work."

"How long have you had them?"

"More than ten years."

"Do they help?"

"The first year they cut our electric bill almost in half, and later on, after he tinkered with them, he reduced it another twenty-five percent."

"How often does your husband work in the garage?"

"He doesn't have much time, but the work in the garage is his hobby. It has been that way ever since I've known him. He would spend a couple of hours, usually late at night between nine and eleven. That would normally be a Monday, Tuesday, or Thursday because Wednesday night was church night. We tried to have a big family meal after church on Sunday, but he would usually spend the afternoon in his garage on Sunday afternoons."

"Did he always work alone?"

She smiled. "At times you wouldn't think so because he would talk to himself all the time while he was out there, but he was the only one in the family that understood what he was doing. He is a man that needs to have some time alone. He has always been that way."

Barnabas quickly glanced at Judge Kruger, and her expression conveyed that she liked Sarah.

"Now, do you recall approximately three years ago your husband spending a lot of time in his garage working on one of his inventions?"

"Yes. He was working on something during that time."

"What shift did he work during those months?"

"The first shift, the seven a.m. shift."

"Do you recall him taking his invention to work one evening during that time?"

"Yes, he said he had to work that shift, and I saw him put it into his truck."

"What did it look like?"

"It was a rectangular box with a dish and a monitor attached to it. I want to say it was three to four feet long and two feet wide. It looked like it was heavy, but I didn't lift it."

"No further questions."

Judge Kruger nodded to Frederick. "Cross?"

Frederick rose. "Mrs. Williams, your husband didn't tell you what he was working on, did he?"

"No one understands what he is doing. So the answer is no."

"And you understand that there is a lot of money at stake in this lawsuit?"

"Yes."

"Many millions of dollars, true?"

"Yes, a lot of money."

"And I understand that you are quite pleased with the vacuum and the solar panels?"

"They work fine for us."

"And you are not a rich family, true?"

"That is very true."

"Yet your husband has never sold any of these inventions or brought any money into the family for any of them, true?"

"It is true that he doesn't market himself very well."

"And you want this court to believe that all by himself he invented a device worth potentially millions upon millions of dollars when your husband's inventions to date have produced no income for your family?"

"All I know is that he is the most honest man I know. He would not lie."

"No further questions."

Judge Kruger looked at the clock, and noticing that it was about noon, banged her gavel. "We will take a break for the lunch hour and reconvene at one o'clock."

Kyle and Sarah went to lunch, and Barnabas remained in the courtroom going over his trial notebook. Stephanie waited until everyone else had left and then walked over to the plaintiff's table.

Barnabas looked up and couldn't help but smile. Stephanie asked, "Do you have any more witnesses?"

"Oh, I plan to call their corporate representative and cross-examine him about Dawson, and that'll be it."

"Do you think you are going to survive a directed finding?" A directed finding would mean that the trial would end without Frederick having to put on any evidence because Judge Kruger had concluded that Kyle's case was just too weak.

"I think so. It makes no sense for her to deny the motion for summary judgment and then give them a directed finding. It will only guarantee an appeal, and I think the judge wants it completely over."

"It would be a different case if Dawson were here, wouldn't it?"

"Sure would. But he's not, and while I don't think Bill was lying about something being out there, he wouldn't have mentioned it if whatever it was truly could be located."

"Well, Barnabas, I admire what you decided to do by taking this case. You are a winner in my book."

"Thank you, Stephanie. I needed that. But you had better go. It would be just my luck if Clausen came back into the courtroom and saw us together. "

"Oh, he knows we talk. But even if he didn't know and would object, I'm not sure that I'd care. Some things are more important than your job, and what you are doing here is one of them."

Everyone was back at one o'clock, and Judge Kruger, always punctual, opened the door to her chambers and walked into the courtroom. As she was sitting down, she looked at Barnabas and said, "Call your next witness."

"Plaintiff calls Fred Stacy."

Frederick, Bill, Silva, and Stacy all seemed surprised.

Hesitantly, Stacy rose and walked over to the witness chair and was sworn in.

Barnabas started to question him. "You are Fred Stacy, and you work for North American Coal, correct?"

"Yes."

"And you have worked in the corporate office for more than fifteen years, correct?"

"Yes."

"In fact, Carl Dawson was your boss, wasn't he?"

"Yes."

"And you now hold his old job?"

"Also true."

Barnabas had crafted the questions so that Stacy could only answer yes or no.

"You saw Dawson every day before he died, isn't that true?"

"Yes."

"He was a good boss to work for?"

There was a long pause, and it was apparent that Stacy didn't know how to answer the question. *Why is this so difficult for him?* Barnabas decided to let Stacy not answer. "Well, Mr. Stacy, when Mr. Dawson was there, there weren't any disciplinary proceedings pending against him, correct?"

"True."

"And no one said he was about to be fired?"

"True."

"And one day three years ago, you came to work and found him dead, true?"

"That is pretty much the case."

"And there was a finding of suicide, true?"

"That's true."

"But you don't why he would kill himself, isn't that true?"

"Well, he did seem depressed. Kinda lonely ever since his wife died."

"Did you ever go to him and tell him that you were worried about him?"

There was a long pause. "Not that I can recall."

"And you never went to anyone else in the company and expressed your concern, did you?"

"No, I didn't."

"Now, Mr. Stacy, what efforts has North American made to confirm that the death was by suicide?"

"We left it with the police."

"And you would agree that Mr. Dawson had valuable testimony that would have been crucial to the resolution of this case if he were still alive?"

Frederick stood. "Objection, calls for a legal conclusion."

Judge Kruger frowned at Frederick. "It is a bench trial. I'll allow it."

Taking his cue from Frederick, Stacy responded, "I guess I don't know. I'll leave that to the lawyers."

Barnabas smiled and pressed ahead. "But are you saying that North American Coal, with all of its resources, has no interest in confirming the cause of Mr. Dawson's death?"

Stacy squirmed, but he had no choice but to answer. "That's correct."

And then Barnabas asked the final question. "Isn't it true, Mr. Stacy, that North American Coal has no interest in confirming the cause of Mr. Dawson's death because it wants the answer to remain suicide?"

Frederick rose again to object, but before he said anything, Stacy said in too loud a voice, "That's not true!"

Barnabas decided to let things rest. "Your Honor, we have no more witnesses. I understand that all of our exhibits have already been introduced into evidence. If that is the case, Plaintiff rests."

Judge Kruger was obviously pleased. She had expected a full two days, but they were done by 3:30 p.m. She turned to Frederick. "I know what motions you are going to make, and I believe that the plaintiff has made out a prima facie case. I am going to deny your motion for a directed finding and note for the record that North American made the motion. Are you prepared to start your case?"

"Your Honor, I sent my witnesses away and told them to come back tomorrow."

"Are you going to be done in two days if we start your case tomorrow?"

"Assuming that the cross is reasonable, we will be done."

"Okay, we will start Defendant's case tomorrow."

* * *

They went to the office, and Sarah, as always, wanted to know what was going on.

"We survived their motion for directed finding, but that was no surprise."

"What is that?"

"It is the same thing as summary judgment basically. The defense will make the motion at the end of the plaintiff's case and argue that the plaintiff's evidence is insufficient. At least the judge thinks we have enough evidence to go forward."

"So why aren't you happy about this?"

"All we have done is show the judge what she already knew. But that is all we could do. Things are going true to form, and that is probably not good enough. As Judge Franks says, if Silva proves to be credible, the judge will likely throw up her hands and say we haven't met our burden of proof."

CHAPTER TWENTY-EIGHT

Thursday went true to form. Frederick spent all of Thursday with Silva, taking him through his credentials and somewhat tediously through all of the technical aspects of the invention. Frederick also spent an inordinate amount of time going over the calendar, showing that if Silva were to be believed, he had to have had the idea for the invention a full year before Kyle installed it.

Barnabas decided that Kyle was best served by having Silva on the stand for as short of a time as possible. He kept a close eye on the judge, and he decided not to make any objections. Judge Kruger was constantly interrupting and instructing Frederick to move it along.

Barnabas took up the cross-examination at the end of the day.

"Mr. Silva, how much were you making before the patent was issued?"

"Right at one hundred thousand dollars."

"And how much did your salary increase after you met my client?"

"I got a five-hundred-thousand-dollar bonus."

"That extra five hundred thousand dollars has now been built into your salary, correct?"

"Yes."

"And you own thirty percent of the gross royalties coming from the patent, true?"

"Yes."

"And last month's royalty check was in excess of four hundred thousand dollars, isn't that true?"

"Yes, that is true. But that is a small amount given what we did for the company."

"If you win this case, that four hundred thousand dollars will grow significantly, isn't that true?"

"I don't know the amount. I'm leaving it to the company to market it."

"But isn't it true that in terms of marketing the invention, you have only scratched the surface of all the mines that could use it?"

"I suppose that is true."

"How many devices have actually been installed on miners today?"

"My understanding is that North American is using them in eight mines, and Century is using them in three."

"But that is just a fraction of the market, correct?"

"Yes, I think that is true."

"Once this trial is over, the invention can be marketed to every coal mine in the world, correct?"

"Every underground mine. They don't use miners on strip mines."

"And since you claim to have invented this device while working for North American, you had to give part of the patent to North American, correct?"

"Yes, it is part of my contract."

"So North American didn't have to pay you a bonus at all, did it?"

"No. They are good folks to work for."

"Now, none of the devices being used in those eleven mines today is the one my client installed three years ago, true?"

"Yes, that is true."

"Where is that one?"

"That was just a prototype. We disposed of it when we commissioned the actual manufacture three years ago."

"Why didn't you keep it?"

"If we had known your client was going to claim that he made it, we would have kept it."

"But for something this valuable, why wouldn't you want to keep proof of every level of your invention?"

"Knowing what we know now, we should have."

Barnabas decided to drop it. Silva was too well coached, and it was obvious that he knew what they were talking about. Kyle had just been too trusting, and it was increasingly clear that that trust was going to cost him dearly.

PART THREE

Come to me, all you who are weary and burdened, and I will give you rest. Take my yoke upon you and learn from me, for I am gentle and humble in heart, and you will find rest for your souls. For my yoke is easy and my burden is light.

—Matthew 11:28-30 (NIV)

CHAPTER TWENTY-NINE

It was 8:00 p.m. on Thursday evening, and everyone else had left the office. Barnabas was going over the files, looking for a glimmer of what Bill said was out there. He was having no luck when he heard someone open the waiting room door.

"Hello?" a male voice shouted out.

The doors to the front of the building were supposed to be locked after 6:00 p.m., so Barnabas wondered how the visitor had gotten in. Most probably he had caught the door as someone was leaving. Barnabas went out into the waiting room and saw a familiar face. It was Jessie Nicks.

Barnabas felt his chest, hoping that his cell phone was in his shirt pocket, but he had left it on his desk. His stomach turned; he was not feeling good about his situation. He was alone, late at night, with Jessie Nicks, a man capable of hurting someone without any remorse. The last time they saw one another, Barnabas had made his distaste for Nicks apparent.

Nicks stood there smiling, and it was just like Nicks to smile when he was about to hurt someone. Barnabas had just decided to turn and run into his office to buy himself some time when Nicks spoke.

"Don't worry, Mr. Mitchell. I'm not here to hurt you."

Barnabas didn't know if he was being sincere or whether it was some kind of ruse to get him to drop his guard.

Nicks asked, "Do you remember me?"

"Yeah, I know who you are. You're Jessie Nicks."

Nicks nodded, and Barnabas tried to assume control by asking him questions.

"How long have you been out, Nicks?"

"Thirty-three days."

"Why are you here?"

"I won't be here long. I know you're busy. I'm here because I know I owe you an apology, and I wanted to get this off my chest."

"An apology?" Barnabas was dumbfounded.

"Yeah. Hard to believe, isn't it?"

Barnabas opted for honesty. "Yeah, it is."

Barnabas studied Nicks more closely, looking for any signs that would reveal his true motive. He sounded different, he looked different, but it was hard for Barnabas to identify how. If Barnabas were in control, he would have preferred that Nicks not be there at all, but he felt that he had no choice but to listen to what Nicks had to say. If Nicks were going to hurt him, he probably would have done it by then anyway.

Barnabas sat down and gestured toward a chair for Nicks to sit. "What have you been doing since you got out, Nicks?"

"I'm living in a halfway house, and I just found a job at a gym."

"Sounds like a good job for you. Haven't given up on the weights?"

"No."

"Nicks, I guess you are the last person on earth that I would expect to apologize to me."

"Well, I'm here to tell you that I behaved like a total, ungrateful, unmitigated ass. As the judge said, I should have spent twenty years in that joint, and I am out because of you. The entire experience must have been hard on your conscience. You gave me a chance to live a better life, and I assure you that I'm going to take it."

Barnabas had difficulty believing what he was hearing. It was the same Nicks he represented five months before, but he seemed to be a completely different guy.

"Okay, Nicks, I give. What's gotten into you?"

"I don't want to freak you out like I am some kind of crazy Holy Roller, but God got into me. Hard to believe, isn't it?"

"God got into you? Really? How did that happen?" Barnabas guessed that it was somebody like the prison chaplain that broke through, but he was astounded by the actual response.

"Four months ago, the Capshaw family came to visit me—all three of them. In fact, they came three times because I refused to see them the first two times they came. I was afraid to talk with them, afraid that they were going to tell me what they thought of me. Before the third visit, I learned that my best friend had been killed in a gang fight, and it forced me to start thinking. I decided that nothing would be lost by hearing what they had to say." Then Nicks paused, and he started to choke up. "They told me that they forgave me."

Barnabas could see the tears in Nicks' eyes and felt moisture in his own.

"I stayed in my cell for four whole days. I really didn't sleep. They forced me to decide what kind of person I was going to be."

"Well, Nicks, what kind of person are you going to be?"

"I will be satisfied if I can become just half as good as any one of them."

"How are you going to do that?"

"Get up every day, ask God what He wants me to do to be a better person, and spend less time thinking about myself. When I screw up, ask for His forgiveness and keep going. There is one thing her brother said to me that I will never forget."

"What was that?"

"He told me that we can never let them wear us down with their hate. We have to wear them down with our love."

Barnabas meditated on that thought for a moment. *How is it possible to wear someone down with love? I guess Nicks is a case in point.*

They talked for another ten minutes. Nicks discussed his plans, and then he left.

Barnabas went back to his office and pondered what he had just heard. He wouldn't have believed the changes he observed in Nicks without seeing it for himself. But he did see it himself. An hour ago, of all the people he had ever met, Nicks might have been the one he despised the most, even more than the man who had run into his mother or perhaps even Bill. But now he was forced to concede that Nicks was a better man than he was.

He thought about the Capshaw family. *How could they do it?* He'd seen them in the courtroom. Their grief was deep and real. He fully understood it. He had been there himself. Yet, they somehow had it in them to go to Nicks and forgive him. And Nicks hadn't even asked for it. He hated the man that had ruined his mom's life, and he didn't think he could ever get over that hate. He didn't want to get over it. That hate was one of the things that motivated him. The man didn't deserve Barnabas' forgiveness.

But the Capshaws' grief was every bit as real and deep as his, and yet, they were willing to forgive Nicks. They were better than he was, and in forgiving Nicks, Nicks had become a better man as a result. Truly, they had worn Nicks down with their love.

This had to be more than a belief system or a moral code. His mom, Stephanie, Ruth, Sam, Jennie, Sarah, Kyle, the Capshaws, and now Nicks—they had a peace, joy, and power that he was lacking.

Barnabas started to weep, but he didn't know why. He had not wept since his mother's funeral. He picked up his cell phone and dialed Stephanie's number. It rang ten times, but it went to voice mail. He didn't leave a message. He needed to talk with someone immediately. He tried Kyle next, who picked up after the second ring.

"Kyle, this is Barnabas," he said with a weak voice.

"Barnabas, is something wrong?"

"Yeah, things are not right. I know it's late, but I really need to talk with someone. Could I come over and talk?"

"What's this about, Barnabas? Are you well? Are you safe?"

"I'm not in any danger, although I thought I was. But I need to talk with someone about rearranging my life and my priorities."

"Barnabas, of course I would do that. But can I suggest we meet with my pastor? I'll be glad to introduce you. He is a good person to talk to, and I can be there as well."

"Kyle, I don't know him. I hate to admit it, but I'm kind of shy when it comes to this sort of thing."

"Barnabas, if you want to talk with only me that will be fine, but Pastor Davidson really is a very good man. You can trust him. I think he would be better at helping you think through these things."

Barnabas paused. He needed to talk with someone, and he trusted Kyle's judgment. "If you think it's best, I can meet with you and the pastor. Where should I go?"

It was raining, and it took him forty-five minutes to get to the church. It was 10:30 p.m. and there were two cars in the parking lot. He recognized Kyle's truck, and the pastor drove an older Ford compact car. The pastor heard him drive up and opened the front door as Kyle stood behind him.

Kyle did the introduction. "Barnabas, this is Pastor Luke Davidson."

They shook hands. The pastor spoke first. "Mr. Mitchell, can I call you Barnabas? It is good to see you again. Come in."

Barnabas was surprised. "I didn't think you would remember me."

"Why not? When I first met you, I knew that you must have been a special person in Stephanie's eyes or she wouldn't have invited me to come to church with her." He smiled. "As I recall, that Sunday morning was not one of my stellar performances, at least from your perspective."

Barnabas was trapped, but he liked Davidson's friendly style. "Your memory is very good. The problem was not with your message. It was with my attitude at the time."

Luke Davidson had not changed much from the last time Barnabas had seen him. If anything, perhaps his hair was a little grayer. He escorted Barnabas into his office where he had a pot of coffee brewing. Barnabas noticed that there was a large bucket in the corner on the floor to catch water that was leaking through the ceiling.

Davidson smiled as he saw Barnabas looking at the leak. "We need a new roof. Though what we really need is a new church. We hope to have the money raised by the end of the year to fix the roof. Tomorrow morning early, I plan to get up on the roof and locate the source of the leak. Can I pour you a cup of coffee, Barnabas?" the pastor asked as he poured one for himself. "How about you, Scooter?"

Barnabas was about to say, "No, I don't drink coffee," but then changed his mind. "Sure, I'll have a cup."

"Do you take it black or do you want cream and sugar?"

"I normally don't drink coffee, so I'll take it black."

Barnabas wanted to talk first, so he started while Davidson was preparing the coffee. "Pastor, I know that you don't normally work this late. I want to thank you for seeing me on short notice."

Davidson looked at Barnabas. "Barnabas, I've been doing this for twenty-five years. I've learned that in this job, there is no such thing as regular hours. One of the things I like about it is that it is not routine."

The pastor walked over to hand Kyle and Barnabas their coffees and then took the chair next to Barnabas. Barnabas expected him to dive in with something like, "Why are you here?" but he was surprised by what he said next.

"Well, Barnabas, I've been looking forward to this moment, and I wasn't sure that it would ever happen."

"Sir, I didn't think you even knew who I was."

"Barnabas, I like to be a hands-on pastor, and I try to become a member of the family of everyone who worships here if they are comfortable with it. You are warmly thought of by everyone in the Schultz family. Sarah and Scooter think the world of you."

"Well, I'm not feeling like such a special person right now, thank you."

Davidson pressed ahead, ignoring Barnabas' remark. "Barnabas—what a nice name. More parents should name their sons Barnabas, don't you agree?"

Barnabas didn't know what to think of Pastor Davidson. It was past 10:30 p.m., Davidson didn't know that he was going to be meeting with Barnabas until forty-five minutes ago, and it seemed evident that the guy was actually looking forward to having a long chat.

Barnabas knew that he wasn't going to sleep that night and that he was going to spend most of the next day just listening to Frederick continue with his questions. He had already decided that his cross-examination was not going to be extensive. He knew that he could get by on adrenaline. As far as he was concerned, Davidson could take as much time as he wanted.

"I never liked my name."

"Why in the world not? Barnabas was one of my favorite people in the entire Bible. From what I know, it is a good name for you."

"More than two years ago, Stephanie told me that she thought I was aptly named. I wasn't sure what she meant, and I forgot to ask her why she said it."

"Tell me how you met Stephanie."

"I met her and her parents at the same time. It was during a moot court competition in law school. Her team was better than mine, but she and her parents were very gracious winners. Looking back on it, I'm glad she won."

"But why did it develop into a friendship with her and her family?"

"It started to really develop when we studied together for the bar exam. It was an intense six-week experience. She became a good friend then. I ran into her father in court, and he invited me to come to lunch. He seems to think I was a better person than I think I am. It just feels good to be around them."

"But everybody tells me that you're a good guy. You gave up your youth to care for your mother. You have shown a lot of patience. And you took on Scooter's case when no other lawyer would. That makes you pretty good in my book."

"Now you are sounding like Sam, Ruth, and Stephanie. I don't think they know me as well as they think they do."

He laughed and responded in a jovial manner. "Maybe you should consider that they know you better than you know yourself. Those three people are among the wisest people that I know. Perhaps you should stop listening to yourself and start listening to them."

"They have been good to me, especially Stephanie. I dread the day when some smart Christian guy who meets her standards starts noticing her."

"Well, she's had her opportunities."

"Why has nothing worked out?"

"Why don't you ask her?"

"We have talked a little. She told me about some guy that had gotten out of the Navy."

Davidson laughed. "Yeah, I remember him. It didn't take her long to figure out that it would have been a bad match."

Barnabas wanted to get to the point, even if Davidson gave him all the time in the world. "Mr. Davidson, I really do appreciate your interest in me, but I'm feeling overwhelmed, and I wondered if we could move on to that issue."

"Call me Luke, please. So I can assume that Stephanie is not the reason why you are here. Tell me, what brought this on?"

"Five months ago, I represented a guy by the name of Jessie Nicks, one of the most despicable people I have ever met. He got drunk, rear-ended a young girl, put her in a coma, and it appeared that he had single-handedly ruined not only the girl's life but also her family's. He had absolutely no remorse for his behavior. A real nice piece of work. Later, the girl died, and he got charged with manslaughter. I got him off on a technicality, and he laughed in the courtroom while her family grieved about what had happened."

"Well, I can see why you disliked him."

"He came to see me earlier this evening at my office."

"Oh, really."

"He came to apologize."

"Really!"

"He said that he turned his life around after the family came to him and forgave him."

"Wow! What a nice story. So how did that make you feel?"

"Pretty lousy."

"And why?"

"I used to think that Nicks was a lowlife dirtbag, but tonight I had to figure that he is a better man than I am."

Davidson laughed. "Nonsense. He is not a better man than you are. The only difference is that he knows he has been forgiven, and you don't. But surely you must have met other people who have turned their lives around. Why is this guy so different?"

Barnabas paused, collecting his thoughts. "When I met this guy, he was the personification of the guy that put my mother in a wheelchair. He was a young punk, no remorse, an easy guy to hate. When he walked into my office, I was actually afraid that he was there to hurt me. But he was a totally different guy. He had no attitude. He was happy. There was a joy in his life, and I wouldn't have believed it without actually seeing it for myself. It is still difficult to see how it is possible."

"So you don't believe that people can change?"

"Sure, I believe it, but it's difficult to accept that it could be so dramatic. Today, he was confident. He loves life. Here is a guy just out of the penitentiary, but he doesn't seem too worried about anything. I find myself even envying him. Can you see how this can be a somewhat bitter pill to swallow?"

"Sure, I can understand, but why can't you accept the possibility that the same opportunity is available to you?"

"My mom took me to church every Sunday when I was a kid, but after her accident, we stopped going, and whatever faith I had just seemed to evaporate. One day, when I was around fourteen, I noticed that my faith was gone. I understood the Christian message, and I understood that many Christians that have a deep faith are genuinely happy people, but I didn't want to be happy and be living a lie. I prefer to be miserable and live in truth, you know what I mean?"

"I think so." Davidson thought for a moment and carefully measured his next words. He put his hand on Barnabas' shoulder and said, "Barnabas, did you ever think that maybe, just maybe, it is you who is living the lie?"

The words penetrated Barnabas' entire being like no other words had before. He had never asked himself that question. He was speechless. He sat for several minutes, contemplating the idea that he was the one living a lie.

"You're right. I have never thought about it that way. I guess I thought that I was at least being honest with myself, but it can't work both ways, can it? Either Stephanie, Nicks, my mom, my secretary, and other Christians are right and I'm wrong, or it is the other way around. But it can't be both, can it?"

Davidson chose not to respond. He elected to wait and let Barnabas speak again.

"Look, I know you are a good guy. Kyle never would have brought me here if that weren't the case. So what do you think I should do now?"

"I don't know. That's why I'm here, to help you think this through. But I think you know why you're here. You do know, don't you?"

Barnabas paused again. He knew, of course, that Davidson was right; he did know, but he didn't want to say it. "I guess I'm here to decide what to do about Jesus."

"Tell me, just what do you think about Jesus?"

"Well, when I went to church as a kid, I memorized a lot of Bible verses, but I guess I soured on Christianity when she got injured and her church friend abandoned her." Davidson shook his head, and Barnabas continued. "It is difficult to argue with Christ's teachings, but I could never bring myself to believe that He was God. I guess I thought that people like Stephanie and my mom were very good people, but they were basing their faith on fiction. Tonight I learned that a family sought out a man who had killed their sister and daughter and forgave him, and it changed his life. I know how those folks that forgave Nicks felt, but they have something going for them that I don't have going for me. And they gave it to Nicks. I wouldn't have thought what that family did for Nicks was possible."

Davidson interjected. "Barnabas, there are very few days of your life that you are going to remember vividly. This is one of them. You have an important decision to make, and I am here to help, but I can't and won't make it for you."

Barnabas paused. *Do I really want to do this?* He was no longer a boy going to church with his mother. The commitment had to be firm and final. There would be no going back. There could be no remorse, no second-guessing. No more using the past to justify his lack of faith.

"I'm reluctant only because I am not sure that I am capable of the kind of commitment that is required. I don't think I will ever be as good of a person as Stephanie is, for example."

Kyle, who had been sitting and listening the entire time, reached over and put his hand on Barnabas' shoulder. "Barnabas, understand that you are just starting a journey, and you are not going to get there in one day. Just open your heart to His leading, and He promises that He will take you as far as you are willing to let Him. He has promised that His yoke is easy, and His burden is light. Make that commitment, and you will never regret it."

Barnabas nodded, smiled, and said, "That used to be my favorite Scripture. Thank you for bringing it up." He paused again. "It's all happening too fast. I need some time to think. If I'm going to do this, it can't be equivocal in any way. It has to be firm and forever. I just need some more time. Though she might have felt different in this case, my mother always told me not to make hasty decisions. Can I think about it?"

"Of course. Neither Scooter nor I, and especially not the Lord, would want you to rush into anything."

* * *

Barnabas made it into his bed at 1:00 a.m. but barely slept. He would doze and wake up every twenty minutes. Every time he woke up, it was the same thought resonating in his head: *Barnabas, did you ever think that maybe, just maybe, it is you who is living the lie?*

He tried to clear his brain and go to sleep, but it was hopeless. When he turned on the light and saw that it was 5:30 a.m., he gave up and went to an all-night diner. His brain was in overdrive, his mind racing from his mother to Stephanie to Nicks to the Bible verses that he still retained. *Am I living a lie?* He had always suspected that it took a certain amount of faith to not believe, but now he knew it. His mom, Stephanie, Jennie, Ruth, Sam, Kyle, and Sarah were compelling witnesses. He had been able to explain away their faith in his own mind, but he could not explain Nicks. Nicks was a miracle. Of all people, he was like an angel that had been sent to him by God. But Barnabas knew that somehow it was not an accident that Nicks was the one forcing him to reassess his position.

Kyle had promised that Barnabas would never regret making the commitment, and Barnabas decided to believe him. It took less faith to believe than it took to not believe.

He was at his desk at 6:30 a.m. trying to concentrate on the trial, but he couldn't. Sarah and Kyle arrived at 7:15 a.m. and they walked into his office. "How was your night?" Kyle asked.

Barnabas opted for honesty. "Difficult, very difficult."

Kyle said, "You want to talk about it or do you want to be left alone?"

Barnabas responded, "All I know is that I don't want to spend another night like the one I had last night. The question has been burning in my head. Have I been living a lie? And I think I have been without knowing it. I have been surveying my life, and I have to conclude that I have been fighting God. I guess I have been angry with Him without even knowing it. Whatever it is that you guys, Nicks, and Stephanie have, I want it, and it is clear that it is Jesus."

"Do you want us to call Luke?"

"Kyle, I really like Davidson, but is that really necessary? I've been thinking about this all night. I think I know what to say. I just don't want to fight it anymore."

Sarah and Kyle both seemed surprised, but they nodded in agreement. Sarah said, "Do you want me to start the prayer?"

Barnabas smiled and said, "I don't think that will be necessary. I still remember some of my mom's prayers."

Barnabas brought his chair around his desk to where Sarah and Kyle were sitting. He held out his hands as he remembered his mother doing when she prayed. Sarah grabbed his right hand and Kyle grabbed his left. Holding hands with them, Barnabas prayed.

"God, it has been years since I have prayed, and I have been fighting you and rejecting you all of these years. But the time has come for this to stop. I come to you and confess that I have been in denial, I have been ungrateful, and I have not been open to your love and the gift of the sacrifice of your Son. I know that there are going to be many times that I am going to fail You, but give me the courage, patience, and love to press ahead, and I pray that I will do everything within my will to not bring You into disgrace. I confess Christ as my Lord and Savior. In the name of Jesus, amen."

Barnabas looked up and smiled at Kyle and Sarah. They both were beaming, and it was immediately clear to Barnabas that they had been praying for him for the last several weeks. Kyle rose and gave Barnabas a hug. "Are you going to tell Stephanie this morning in court?"

Barnabas thought about it. "You know, I think I'll wait until Saturday. There won't be enough time to talk this morning."

Sarah then spoke. "Barnabas, you are most vulnerable now. How do you plan to proceed?"

"I used to plan all the time, trying to think ahead, but to answer the question, I really don't know. I'm in the middle of Kyle's trial. That'll keep me busy. I guess I'll think about what's next when the trial is over. I know that several people will be happy about this decision, and I suspect that they have all been praying—Jennie and her family, you two, and the entire Schultz family, especially Stephanie. I'm going to have to be cautious about how I present it to her. She knows that I would like to be more than friends, but she has made it clear that it could never happen given her beliefs. I don't want her to think that she is the reason I did this. I think she respects me enough to know that I'm not doing this just to please her. I am excited to tell her, but I guess I am afraid that she will want to keep it just as friends."

Kyle chuckled. "Barnabas, Stephanie has too much class to doubt your motives for an important decision like this, but when it comes to women and love, I am inept. All I can say is if nothing is ventured, nothing will be gained."

"I guess you're right about that," said Barnabas.

Sarah asked, "Are you sure we can't call Pastor Luke? I'm sure he will be pleased."

Barnabas relented. "Okay, let's call him."

"Can I tell him you will be at church on Sunday as well?" Sarah asked hopefully.

"Of course, and this time tell him that I plan to stay awake during the sermon."

CHAPTER THIRTY

The trial started at 9:00 a.m. and Stephanie walked in at 8:59 a.m. with Clausen. Barnabas had no time to talk to her, but he felt a different energy and spirit. He looked over at Stephanie several times, already looking forward to their lunch the next day.

The evidence was the same, and he felt that the outcome would be the same, but it felt good to be there with Kyle anyway. For the first time in his life, he felt that God was in control. If God wanted to give a victory, He would grant one. If there were some other lesson to learn from the experience, Barnabas would learn it and move forward.

Frederick called several witnesses from North American's home office, proving up the records that supported their claim that Silva had invented the device. Barnabas chose not to cross-examine. Frederick was done by noon.

Judge Kruger looked at Barnabas. "Mr. Mitchell, are you going to put on any rebuttal evidence on Monday?"

"Your Honor, I would like to clarify a few points."

"How long is that going to take?"

"No more than an hour."

Clausen rose, and the judge turned to him. "Mr. Clausen, any evidence?"

"No, Your Honor, but I do want to say that I have another matter in state court on Monday morning, and given our limited nature in this trial, I am going to ask leave to have Century's interest represented by my colleague, Ms. Schultz."

Judge Kruger smiled and said, "Mr. Clausen, I'm sure that Century's case can be competently handled by Ms. Schultz all by herself."

Everyone in the courtroom smiled but Clausen. Barnabas stifled a laugh. They all knew—including the judge—that Clausen had been billing his client for two attorneys' time when only one would have been sufficient.

"Okay, we will finish up Monday morning. Have a good weekend, everyone." Unfortunately for Barnabas, the weekend proved to be anything but good.

It was 8:30 p.m. that Friday evening, and Barnabas was alone at the office. He was catching up on some neglected files that were in need of attention. He had not eaten all day, and he was hungry. He did a search online and found a list of restaurants near his office. He called the first three on the list, but none of them would let him order take-out. He was reluctant to call the fourth, Christos, because he had walked by it several times and knew that the menu was too pricey for his budget. But he was hungry, so he called anyway. The hostess told him that they would prepare a take-out dinner for him, so he ordered spaghetti and meatballs, the cheapest meal on the menu.

He walked in at 9:00 p.m. and approached the hostess. "You should have an order to go for Mitchell."

She smiled and him and disappeared into the kitchen. As he waited, he looked around the restaurant, and he saw her in the corner booth. It was Stephanie, and she was having dinner with a man about his age. He looked again, having difficulty believing what his eyes told him: the man was Bill, and they were holding hands in the center of the table. He was smiling at her, and she was smiling at him. Both were engrossed in conversation.

Barnabas was overwhelmed with emotions—fear, anger, worry, disgust.

The hostess returned. "One spaghetti and meatballs to go. That will be twenty-three eighty-eight with tax." Barnabas handed her a twenty and a ten and said, "I've changed my mind. Can I eat this in the booth over in the corner?"

"Of course. Do you want me to have the waiter bring you a plate and silverware?"

"No, I can use the ones you gave me in the bag."

The booths were embedded in the wall, and the side panels were six feet tall. By approaching from the side, Barnabas could slide into the next booth without being observed. He took the take-out into the men's room, came out thirty seconds later, and slid into the next booth. He hated himself for what he was doing, but he had to know what was going on. Perhaps there was an innocent explanation, but he knew he would not have the self-control to ask for it the next day at lunch.

As Barnabas slid into the booth, he could hear them clearly. Bill was saying, "What would you like to do tomorrow night? My dad owns a helicopter. Would you like to take a ride and look at the city lights at night? I'm told that it is very romantic."

"I would love to, Bill. I'm already looking forward to it."

"Are you going to tell Barnabas about us?"

"I will have to eventually, but I guess I'm going to be a coward and wait as long as possible. I'm afraid it might break his heart. I know because of your history with him that it'll pretty much end our friendship."

"He's a big boy. He'll recover."

Stephanie continued. "But I have to say, you're nothing like what I had pictured, the way Barnabas described you."

Bill smiled and shrugged in a boyish, innocent way.

"Have you picked out a church yet, Bill?"

"No, not yet. Is it too soon for me to start attending your church?"

"It probably is. I will have to arrange some way for you to meet my parents first. Is that all right?"

"Sure, we don't have to rush things. But just know that I am excited to be around you. I don't want you to do anything that will make you feel bad the next morning, and you know much more about the Bible than I do. But can I ask you a question about that?"

"Of course, Bill. Ask away."

"Where in the Bible does it say that premarital sex is wrong?"

"Well, I guess I never thought about that. There was the case of the Samaritan woman who was living with a man. It seems clear from the context that Jesus didn't approve of that."

"But wasn't that a case where she had had several husbands before? The woman clearly had a problem."

"Bill, the Bible specifically rejects fornication."

"But isn't it a matter of definition? Don't you think there is a difference between someone being promiscuous and a man a woman who truly love one another?"

Barnabas had heard enough. He was tempted to stand up and interrupt their conversation, but instinctively he knew it would be wrong. It had been wrong for him to eavesdrop, and it was time to leave. It would have been too difficult to hear more. He left the way he came, leaving his take-out at the table. He was no longer hungry.

He got up Saturday morning after spending the night in bed trying to sleep, but it had been hopeless. He hadn't slept for two nights. He felt like he had started out the week in hell, found paradise, and now he was back in hell again.

With his mom, her death had been gradual, and he knew it was going to come. The pain was deep, but it was not a shock. This time, the hurt was also deep, but the delivery was instantaneous. He wouldn't have believed it unless he had seen it and heard it with his own eyes and ears. He felt deeply rejected. Barnabas had always assumed that Stephanie was off-limits to him because of her religion. She had told him that. Just two days ago, Stephanie had told Barnabas that she was proud to be his friend, and now she was rejecting their friendship for a relationship with Bill.

Of all the guys in the world for her to start a relationship with, why did it have to be Bill? Maybe Bill is why Pastor Davidson dodged the question on Thursday.

Stephanie knew how deeply he despised Bill. Unlike all of the other women that Bill had gone after, Barnabas thought that she truly understood what Bill was like. When she first met Bill at the competition, she had rejected his advances and read him accurately. What changed? If she were going to relax her standards and start looking actively for a husband, why did it have to be Bill? Surely there were guys out there that met her other criteria and had better character than Bill. He had thought that Stephanie was the one girl who could see through him, but it was obvious that he was wrong.

Maybe Bill had had an epiphany like Nicks. Clearly that was the line that Bill was peddling, and she was buying into it. But it was just a line. There was no chance he was sincere. Bill was more lost than Nicks ever had been. Nicks had been a miracle. If it were real, Bill's conversion would be up there with the parting of the sea and having the sun stand still.

Bill had already told the studs the formula for seducing a Christian girl in law school. He hadn't forgotten his lines, and he was using them on Stephanie. He and Stephanie had been working on the same side of the case, so they had the opportunity to spend time together. She would have been a prime target for him. Bill was a charmer, and women loved his good looks and athleticism. The only logical explanation was that he had worn her down.

Maybe I should have told her about the bet Bill had made with the studs. He felt sick to his stomach. *Why am I the only one who can see through this guy?* He was not going to make the same mistake he had in law school; he decided he had to warn Stephanie about Bill. She was too special, even if he was only a special friend.

He waited until 9:00 p.m. and called Davidson. Luckily, he was at the church. "Pastor, it is difficult for me to say this, but something has come up, and I'm going to have to take a pass on Sunday."

There was a pause, and Barnabas could sense that Davidson was concerned. At last he spoke. "Barnabas, is it something that I can help you with? You know that it's my job."

"No, it's something I'm going to have to deal with myself."

"Barnabas, it's natural for someone in your position to have second thoughts. You are most vulnerable right now. Are you sure that we shouldn't talk about this?"

"Pastor, I just have to handle this one issue first. I'm not going back. Trust me. I need just a little more time."

"Okay, I'll trust your judgment, but I'll be praying for your situation."

"Thanks, Pastor. I know I'm going to need it."

* * *

Barnabas arrived at Bella Italy at 11:30 a.m. He wanted to be there first. If he got there before Stephanie, he could start talking while she was sitting down. If she had arrived first, she would probably be able to sense Barnabas' mood as he approached the table, and he didn't want her to say anything. He just wanted her to listen.

Every two minutes he glanced at his watch.

She arrived at 11:43 a.m. It was the shortest lunch they ever had. She smiled, and as soon as she sat down, he started to talk in as calm of a voice as he could manage. He didn't want to appear angry for fear that it would detract from what he was saying. "Stephanie, I need to talk for a few minutes without interruption."

Her expression changed from contentedness to concern. Immediately, Barnabas started in.

"What I am about to say is going to be very difficult, but I think it's necessary. I know that you're seeing Bill. I am ashamed to admit it to you, but I saw you two at the restaurant last night. I slipped into the booth next to you. I was there less than three minutes, but I couldn't stand to listen to any more. I shouldn't have done it, but I did. But actually, I'm glad that I did."

Immediately, the muscles in her jaw tightened, and her lips stiffened. She seemed angry. He had never seen that expression on her before.

Barnabas dropped his head. He couldn't bring himself to look at her. "I would like to talk after the trial is over. I'm asking that you don't move forward with Bill until then. Your relationship with him puts me in a very difficult situation. We have talked about this trial, and I suppose we have only talked about what is obvious, anyway, and I never saw Century as the real opponent. But now, I am wondering how much of my thoughts about this trial you have shared with Bill. That is why I think it best that we not talk until the trial is over. It will be over on Monday, anyway.

"I always knew the day was going to come when you were going to find someone, and that was going to require us to adjust our relationship. Frankly, I dreaded the day it was going to happen, but I guess I didn't know just how difficult it was going to be. But before I go, I just can't help but share my thoughts about Bill. Bill is the most selfish, narcissistic, self-centered person I have ever met. You may think that you know him, but no one knows him like I do. He is utterly incapable of putting someone else's interests ahead of his own. He uses people for his own enjoyment. He is not good marriage material. Whatever he may be telling you now about how he has changed, I wouldn't believe it for a second. He may tell you that I am jealous, and he would be right about that. But I would tell the same to anyone who I have any feelings for who was thinking of being with Bill in any way.

"And just one last thing about him that I never told you—when he was in his third year of law school, he once made a bet with three other guys for a substantial amount of money about which one of them could get a girl in our class into bed first. He won the bet. Looking back on it, I guess I should have told her about the bet. But let's just say it wouldn't surprise me at all if he has a bet of some kind going on about you right now.

"You have told me that you wouldn't marry anyone without your father's permission. Let me suggest that you get your father involved with this relationship sooner rather than later. I still consider you to be a dear friend, and I hope you understand that despite my own jealousy, I am concerned about your situation, and I think you are making a mistake. I am jealous, yes. But I am telling you because I am truly concerned about you. Also, I want you to think about Bill's deposition and the part when I asked him about Dawson. I think he is hiding something. Just consider that, please."

He was about to leave, but she stopped him. She had an edge to her voice. "You've got it, Barnabas. We'll talk on Monday. But here is something that you can put your mind to work on between now and then."

She reached into her briefcase and pulled out a sheet of paper. She then got up and walked out the door, clearly angry with him. The sheet was comprised of rows of numbers. He was suddenly and thoroughly confused. Why was Stephanie so angry? Was it because she had been caught? Why did she give him the paper? How did she get it? What did it mean? Barnabas studied the numbers:

22	6	18	18	23	8	21	
6	18	17	23	4	6	23	
4	15	8	27	5	18	21	10
22	16	12	15	15	8	21	
5	4	17	14	18	9		
18	15	17	8	28			
5	18	27	117	1			

As he drove home, Barnabas thought about what had happened.

He was not able to contemplate a set of circumstances that would result in something good coming out of her relationship with Bill. He had been harsh with her, but she was being extremely naïve if she thought she knew Bill. Hopefully one day she would thank him for intervening.

But what about the numbered paper? It was obviously some kind of code she thought was significant.

He went to a local church on Sunday morning and spent the afternoon trying to decipher the code. He thought that maybe the numbers simply corresponded to the letters of the alphabet, but that wasn't the case. He wasn't even sure that focusing on the paper was what he should be doing. He was tempted to call Stephanie, but he had told her that they should wait to talk until after the trial, and she had made it clear that that was what she wanted as well.

CHAPTER THIRTY-ONE

Barnabas did not arrive at the courthouse on Monday morning until 8:58 a.m. He wanted to avoid looking at either Stephanie or Bill. He walked in, sat next to Kyle, and stared down into his trial notebook. Kyle knew something was wrong because Barnabas had not been in church on Sunday. He gave Barnabas a reassuring grip on his shoulder.

The trial started at nine o'clock sharp with the clerk shouting out the familiar, "Oh yee, oh yee, oh yee."

They all stood, and in walked Judge Kruger. As soon as she sat down, she looked over at Barnabas. "Rebuttal?"

Barnabas stood, looked directly at the judge, and said, "Your Honor, Plaintiff recalls Kyle Williams." Kyle walked to the witness chair, and Judge Kruger admonished him. "Mr. Williams, you are still under oath."

He sat down, and Barnabas asked his first question. "Kyle, just to briefly remind the judge, you installed your invention years ago on North American's miner, and you ran the miner for a full shift?"

"Yes."

"Then what happened to your device?"

"I gave it to Dawson and Silva, their engineer."

"And how long was it before you realized that they had stolen it from you?"

"Two weeks."

"Did you ever get it back?"

"No."

"As someone who invented it, just how complicated is it?"

"Complicated? In what way?"

"How difficult would it be for Silva to figure out how it works?"

"Not difficult at all. That was the reason why he wanted it. He wanted to see how it worked."

"How long would it take for them to figure out?"

"Someone with good training should be able to figure it out completely in thirty to forty hours."

Barnabas paused. He was tempted to get into the technicalities again, but the judge had heard it all.

"Do you have any more questions, Mr. Mitchell?" Judge Kruger said wearily. Barnabas didn't have any more evidence, but he hated to concede defeat.

The judge repeated the question, this time with impatience in her voice. "Mr. Mitchell, do you have any more questions or any more evidence?" He was through; he had done all that he could. He decided that it was time to throw his Hail Mary.

Barnabas returned to the counsel table, pulled the numbered document out of his briefcase, and asked, "Your Honor, may I approach the bench with Counsel?"

Judge Kruger eyed him suspiciously but said, "Okay, approach the bench."

Barnabas approached along with Frederick, Bill, and Stephanie.

Judge Kruger looked at Barnabas. "Okay, what have you got?"

Barnabas placed the numbered document in front of her, and she studied it with a perplexed expression.

"Why is this important, Mr. Mitchell?"

"Your Honor, this document was given to me by defense counsel over the weekend, and I think it has something to do with the case, but I must confess that I don't know what it means. I would like more time to figure it out."

Barnabas looked at Stephanie, who had a blank expression on her face, but Bill, who was standing beside her, was glaring at her. He had never seen Bill so angry.

Then Stephanie interrupted. "Your Honor, Century has not rested, and with a few witnesses, I feel compelled as an officer of the court to explain this issue." Bill's glare intensified.

Surprised, Judge Kruger asked, "Century Coal wants to put on evidence? Are you certain?"

"Yes, Your Honor," Stephanie replied.

Frederick had been observing Bill's expressions and understood that nothing good could come from continuing the trial. He objected. "Your

Honor, this is highly irregular. There has been no showing that this is even probative."

Judge Kruger looked at Stephanie and asked, "How long is this going to take?"

"We should have it done in less than an hour."

"Okay, have at it. But this had better not turn out to be a wild goose chase."

"I understand, Your Honor."

Barnabas returned to the counsel table and looked at Kyle, who was curious about what was happening. Barnabas leaned over and said, "Stephanie is going to put on some evidence. It can only help us, but I really don't know what she is up to."

Because Sarah had finished testifying, she was permitted to sit in the courtroom. She was sitting in the front row, and she threw up her hands, held them up for a half-second, and quickly dropped them, clearly hoping that the judge had not noticed.

The rest of the courtroom was vacant, other than the bailiff, the judge's clerk, and the courtroom deputies.

Judge Kruger looked skeptically at Stephanie. "Okay, Counsel, call your first witness."

"Century calls Dennis Smith."

The bailiff called for Dennis Smith out in the corridor, and in walked a partially bald man about fifty-five years old with a hefty frame and an intelligent look on his face.

Smith was sworn in, and Stephanie began the examination. "Your occupation, please."

"I am a retired forensic examiner of computer software. I worked for the FBI for thirty-eight years. I retired last year."

"And how were you approached to be a witness in this case?"

"I got a call from your father late Friday evening asking me to help with an investigation."

"Explain to the court what a computer forensic examiner actually does."

"My job was to take computer hard drives, usually from laptops and desktops, and retrieve data."

"Now, what did my father ask you to do?"

"Friday evening, I was advised that the FBI had opened an investigation into the death of Carl Dawson, and early Saturday morning, I was able to retrieve Mr. Dawson's hard drive from his PC, which was in the possession of Detective Vincent of the DuPage County Sheriff's office. In conducting my examination, I focused my attention on the evening of Mr. Dawson's death. I noticed a shortcut to his e-mail account."

"Why is that significant?"

"His e-mail account was carl.dawson111@outlook.com. I was able to run diagnostic and retrieve his password, which turned out to be 39331946. Those numbers were the last four digits of his social security number and the year of his birth."

"Did you examine his entire e-mail account?"

"No. We just looked at the evening of his death."

"And what did you find that you concluded was significant?"

"His very last e-mail was sent just twenty minutes before the coroner said that he died. The e-mail was sent to the address scooter.williams777@gmail.com. The e-mail was in his trash folder and had been returned as undelivered. It was a perfect place to store the document. Most people don't look for documents in the trash folder."

"What did the e-mail say?"

"Nothing, but there was an attachment to it."

Stephanie handed Smith the numbered document. "Is this the attachment?"

Smith looked at it quickly and said, "Yes."

"Do you have any idea what it means?"

"No idea."

"One final question, Mr. Smith. Was there any evidence that other people had attempted to hack the e-mail account?"

"It is one of those things you can't say for sure, but I would answer in the affirmative. It appears that there have been repeated, unsuccessful attempts to access this e-mail. Also, the actual document had to have been created in the computer itself, but it seems clear that it was erased."

"No further questions. Century labels this document as Century Exhibit 1 and moves that it be introduced into evidence."

Barnabas stood and said with thinly disguised glee, "No objection."

Frederick stood. "I object. No showing of relevancy."

Stephanie responded, "Your Honor, you can reserve ruling until I connect it up if that would be better."

"I agree," said Judge Kruger. "We will reserve ruling. Call your next witness."

Stephanie barked out, "Call Tim Daniels."

Barnabas leaned over to Kyle and whispered, "Stephanie has found some evidence that really helps us. She is sticking her neck out for us."

"Why would she do that? I thought she was against us?"

"She told the court that she has an ethical duty as an officer of the court to bring out all relevant evidence, but I'm sure her boss is going to be pissed."

The bailiff summoned Daniels, and in walked a man in his mid-sixties, thin, and dark-haired with a smile on his face. It was clear that he had something to say, and he wanted to say it.

Daniels was sworn in.

Stephanie started with her first question. "Mr. Daniels, what do you do?"

"Presently, I am retired, but I believe the reason you are having me today is because I used to work for the NSA."

"And what did you do for the NSA."

"I was a code breaker."

"How long did you do that?"

"Over forty years."

"Handing you Century Coal Exhibit 1. Do you recognize it?"

"Of course. That is the document your father asked me to look at last Saturday morning. He asked me if I could break the code."

"And you have known my father for several years, so that is why he approached you?"

Daniels smiled. "And I have known you all your life, too. I was happy to help."

Stephanie smiled and pressed ahead. "Were you able to break the code?"

"Yes, it was really very simple. All you do is first take the alphabet and assign the letters to their corresponding numbers. The letter A is one, the letter B is two, etcetera. In this code, you then add three to the letter's numerical value and obtain its code value. For instance, A is one. When you add three, A's value becomes four. B is two, and when you add three, its value becomes five. This pattern continues until the end of the alphabet, with Z equaling twenty-nine."

"So what does the document actually say after the code has been deciphered?" asked Stephanie.

"No problem. It says 'Scooter, contact Alex Borgsmiller, Bank of Olney, Box 1171.' We found out that the last two entries—117 and 1—did not comprise a word since the code that I described to you contains neither 117 nor 1. It is the actual box number."

Barnabas looked over at Kyle and smiled. Frederick, Bill, and Silva sat uneasily.

Frederick rose to make an objection, and Judge Kruger showed him the palm of her hand, gesturing for him to sit down. She was clearly fascinated by what was going on. She turned to Stephanie. "Do you have another witness?"

Stephanie responded, "Call Scott Johnson."

The Judge interrupted. "Not Alex Borgsmiller?"

"Mr. Johnson will explain why," said Stephanie.

Scott Johnson entered the courtroom. He was in his mid-forties and had a peaceful countenance, but he seemed to appreciate the seriousness of the situation.

"Mr. Johnson, where do you work?"

"I am the president of the Bank of Olney."

"How long have you been the president?"

"About two and a half years."

"Who was the president before you?"

"Alex Borgsmiller."

"Why is he no longer with the bank?"

"He died in a tragic hunting accident about three years ago."

"Just how did he die?"

"He was in a deer stand during bow-hunting season, and he took a rifle bullet to the head."

"Was it gun-hunting season?"

"No."

"Did the person who shot him come forward?"

"No."

"Now, I served a subpoena on you yesterday, is that correct?"

"Yes."

"What did the subpoena require you to do?"

"I drilled open Box 1171, and I have brought the contents to you."

"What was in the box?"

"A DVD."

"Have you watched it or listened to it?"

"No."

"Has anyone else?"

"No."

"Do you keep records of who has looked in the box?"

"Yes."

"Who was the last person to open the box?"

"The box was opened only one time by Alex Borgsmiller who, it turns out, owns the box."

"When did you first discover that he owned it?"

"Two and a half years ago. A man claiming to be Alex's relative came into the bank and wanted access to the box. I didn't even know that Alex owned a box until this fellow arrived."

"Did he get access?"

"No. It was strange. I was pretty sure that I knew all of Alex's relatives, and I had never heard of this guy. He had identification, and he even had some family photos and the like. I asked him to wait while I went to my office to consider what I was going to do. I came back out twenty minutes later, and he was gone. Since then, no one has been back."

For obvious effect, Stephanie asked Johnson, "Do you see that fellow in the courtroom today, the one who wanted access to the box?"

Johnson took a moment, looked around, and said, "No."

Barnabas was looking at Bill and Silva. They managed to keep stoic expressions, and Barnabas thought, "They got someone else involved. I wonder how much they paid him. He might turn out to be the missing link."

But then Johnson volunteered, "But I did keep the bank's surveillance video. It sounds like it might be useful."

Bill look concerned, if not fearful.

Stephanie finished up her examination. "So, Mr. Johnson, would you please hand the DVD over to Judge Kruger?"

"Of course." He pulled the DVD out of his briefcase and handed it to the judge.

In a final act of futility, Frederick stood and exclaimed, "Your Honor! I think Counsel should see the DVD before it is published to the court."

"Nonsense," responded Judge Kruger. "Everyone in my chambers. We are going to all look at it together on my computer."

Barnabas' hopes rose. He tried to get Stephanie's attention, but she was ignoring him. Barnabas and Kyle were the last to enter, and just before he walked in, Barnabas took a deep breath, hoping to avoid the stench of the cigarette smoke. However, he was pleasantly surprised that the air was free of smoke and smell.

Barnabas and Kyle stood in the back. Bill and Frederick stood on the other side of Judge Kruger's office. Barnabas then walked up behind Stephanie and whispered, "I owe you big time."

She whispered back over her shoulder, "You sure do, but let's not get overconfident."

Judge Kruger put the DVD into her PC, found the right folder, and hit the play button. Immediately her screen was filled with the likeness of a man. Kyle whispered to Barnabas, "It's Dawson."

The voice was barely audible. Judge Kruger turned up the volume and started it over. They could all hear Dawson speaking on the PC:

> Scooter, if you are viewing this, it means that I'm dead and that you found the DVD with Alex at the Bank of Olney. I tried calling you, but I'm sure that my phones are being listened to. You need to take precautions for your own life. I have sent you a letter, but I think my mail is being monitored. I am being followed. I am afraid. I'm sure that Silva is behind it and that he is getting help, but I don't know who it is for sure. They are trying to steal your invention. I wouldn't have thought it possible, but when Silva first told me that we couldn't use it, it didn't make sense. I think he sensed that I didn't believe him. I am taping this video in the hope that they won't get away with it. I hope and pray that they won't be able to steal it from you. Again, if you are viewing this, it means that I am with the Lord in heaven. God bless you.

And the screen went blank.

Immediately, Frederick spoke up. "Your Honor, it is not admissible. It is hearsay. It is not subject to cross-examination. It violates the dead man's statute. There is no chain of custody."

Barnabas responded immediately. "It is an excited utterance. It's a dying declaration. It is a business record. Hearsay rule does not apply. The dead man's statute does not apply because he is not a party!"

Uncharacteristically, Judge Kruger shouted at them. "Gentlemen, enough!" She looked at Frederick and said, "I don't know if it meets the technical rules of evidence or not at this point, but it is going to come into evidence because I will find a way to let it in. Christian, do you really want to see this DVD on the network news while you are taking an appeal? You should consider this a chance to salvage something, but if you think you are being treated unfairly, we'll go back in there, and I'll rule. Do you really want that? I'm only doing this because Mr. Williams has waited too long for justice. I don't want any appeals. He needs to get paid for what you stole, and he needs to get paid now. Two people have died over this, and I am going to take away the incentive for anyone else to die. It is time to do something about that. Do you want me to go back on the bench and conclude this trial?"

There was a long pause as she stared at Frederick.

"I didn't think so," Judge Kruger said. "I suggest that you folks start talking. It is now ten o'clock. While there's lots of money involved, a settlement shouldn't be that complicated. We'll reconvene at three p.m. We have the jury room and two conference rooms available to you. The FBI is already involved, but I'm going to monitor this. This whole thing stinks. It's despicable. Go to work!"

Stephanie spoke up, and looking at Silva and Bill, she said, "I'll tell my father to keep the court informed."

Judge Kruger looked at her, nodded, and smiled.

Stephanie went to exit the judge's chambers first, and as she was about to walk through the door, she paused slightly, looked at Barnabas, and gave him a triumphant smile. Barnabas was the last to leave, and as he was walking out the door, he glanced at the judge, and she gave him a slight smile, too.

* * *

235

Frederick dealt with Bill abruptly. "You're fired. I suggest you lawyer up. Getting disbarred will pale in comparison to the criminal charges you are going to face."

Bill could barely control his fury as he got on the elevator and left the courthouse. When he got outside, he began talking to himself. "How could I have been so stupid? She was playing me the whole time, and I didn't even see it! Frederick thinks I'm going to jail, but at least I'll get out of that one." He pulled his cell phone out of his pocket and dialed his dad's number. When he heard his dad's voice, he said, "Dad, I need to come to your office and talk."

* * *

As soon as he walked out of the courtroom, Barnabas looked for Stephanie, but she was gone. He called her cell phone. It rang twelve times and went to voice mail. "Stephanie, it's Barnabas. Call me. There are a million things to talk about. The first will be my mea culpa. Call me, please."

He tried her direct-dial number at her law firm, but after five rings it defaulted to the receptionist. "Law firm," she answered.

"Hello, I am looking for Stephanie Schultz."

"I'm sorry, but she is in court."

"Look, I just saw her this morning in court. As soon as she gets in, ask her to call Barnabas."

The receptionist promised to have Stephanie call, but Barnabas was worried.

He next called Sam's cell phone with no better luck. It rang ten times, and Barnabas got his voice mail. "Sam, I'm desperate to talk to you or Stephanie or both of you. I'm going to be in negotiations, but I'm leaving my phone on. Call me."

Kyle and Sarah were standing close by, and they both shrugged. "We'll track her down soon," assured Kyle.

"Let's head into the jury room," said Barnabas. "We need to stake out our position. I never planned for this, and the judge wants us to try and get something done."

Sarah spoke up. "So what do you think happened?"

"It's really pretty obvious," answered Kyle. "I got a call from Sam yesterday, and he told me that there might be some hope. I didn't want to say anything in case it fizzled."

Sarah followed up. "But if this is Sam's doing, how did he get his lead?"

"He found out from Stephanie," said Barnabas.

"But how did Stephanie get the lead?" Sarah asked.

Barnabas looked at Kyle and smiled. "I guess we should let Stephanie tell us."

"Why don't *you* tell me?"

"It really is Stephanie's right to tell. Besides, I'd only be guessing."

Barnabas decided to change the direction of the conversation. "Kyle, Sarah, we have to figure out our negotiating position. Let's assume that you owned the patent all along. How much money would you have made off of it?"

"I figure that it boosts production a minimum of ten percent a shift, so you can assume at least two thousand tons per day per mine. This assumes only two shifts, but some mines run three shifts. There are eight North American mines using it, which means sixteen thousand additional tons per day. Assume that the mine is operating three hundred twenty days per year minimum, so you are talking about roughly fifty million additional tons for all eight mines. At today's prices, that is a total of two billion dollars in additional production per year. If you are generous in terms of additional costs for that much additional production, that's still a net profit of one billion dollars comfortably. If you let them keep half of that, the person owning the patent should receive a total of five hundred million dollars per year for the license for the company. That works out to one dollar for every ton they produce. Whatever you do, it is going to be a ton of money. Pun intended."

Barnabas thought it advisable to dampen the enthusiasm. "But the coal will always be there. Why is it more profitable to get it out early?"

Kyle replied, "The main reason is that they are increasing production with almost the same amount of labor."

"Is there any doubt that she is going to rule for us?" asked Sarah.

"She made that abundantly clear," said Barnabas.

Kyle gave Barnabas a vote of confidence. "Look, Barnabas, I'm sure you've heard people say before that it's not about the money, but it really isn't about the money. Squeeze them as hard as you can, but I agree with the judge—let's get this over with today."

"Okay, I've got my marching orders. Let's see how shaken the other side is." And with that, he left the room.

He called Stephanie again, and again he got her voice mail. He called the Clausen firm. The receptionist answered, and Barnabas asked for Stephanie. The receptionist responded, "I'm sorry, sir, but Ms. Schultz no longer works for this firm."

Barnabas' heart sunk. *They fired her! I can't believe it...but I guess I shouldn't be surprised.* Century wanted North American to control the patent, and she went directly against her client. But if she had access to evidence that had been concealed, she had an ethical duty to present it. She was in a tough position.

Barnabas then tried her home phone, but again there was no answer.

He knocked on the conference room door where Clausen was waiting.

"Come in, please." Clausen was just hanging up his cell phone. Barnabas looked at him and restrained a smile. "Are you able to talk or do you want me to come back later?"

"No, I can talk. I just got off the phone with the president of the company. He has been instructed to be available regardless of what is happening in his head office."

Barnabas hoped that Clausen would state his position first. "So, what are you willing to pay for past use and for the future?"

Clausen wasn't buying. "You're the plaintiff. Make a demand."

Barnabas wanted to see Clausen squirm. "We are going to require North American to sign the patent over to us, and we are prepared to assign it to you. My client admires your associate's honesty, and as long as she is representing Century, we feel confident that we are going to be dealt with fairly. We'll retain a royalty fee of fifty cents per ton, and Century will be able to at least double its money with further licensing. The way we figure it, the invention will be in every underground mine in the world within the next year if it is marketed correctly. Your company's net worth will increase dramatically. However, you can't license it to North American. We are going to make a separate deal with them. But this, of course, is contingent upon Ms. Schultz being involved. In addition, we expect Century to pay Mr. Williams twenty-five million dollars in damages. You should be able to get that back from North American."

Clausen turned white as Barnabas was talking. "I'll get back to you. Why don't you talk to North American while I run this by my client."

Barnabas left, knowing that Clausen was about to enter into a state of panic as he tried to talk with Stephanie. There was no way Clausen was going to have any more luck than Barnabas did in attempting to reach her. Besides, he would be shocked if he were ever going to get her to come back. He smiled.

He proceeded to the other conference room where Frederick was waiting. Bill and Silva were gone, and Barnabas decided not to make any inquiries as to their whereabouts. The meeting was professional but just barely cordial.

Barnabas started the conversation. "We want the patent assigned to Williams tomorrow. You can continue to use the device at a license fee rate of one dollar and twenty-five cents per ton, and we want to have ninety million dollars in cash wired into my trust account before the wire deadline tomorrow."

Frederick rose, attempting to control his anger. He was about to direct an outburst at Barnabas, but he caught himself. "That is much too steep. We need to keep the patent for starters."

Barnabas replied, "One would have be naïve to not understand that North American is about to have some major legal problems. Mr. Williams can't afford to let you keep the patent when there is a distinct possibility that your assets are about to be seized. You can't keep it. In addition, it violates Mr. Williams' sense of integrity to let you have it given the way you folks have behaved. The judge is about to rule that it is his, anyway."

"I'll have to call the president of the company."

Barnabas paused. "We can't let you keep the patent. It is much too dangerous. Mr. Williams will never give it to you."

Barnabas left the conference room, smiling.

He found Kyle and Sarah on their cell phones in the jury room. They looked up, and Kyle asked, "Any progress?"

Barnabas smiled. "I wasted some time by offering the patent to Century on the contingency that Stephanie continues to represent them. He doesn't know that I know they fired her. He is desperately trying to reach her now."

They both laughed.

"Have you been trying to reach her?" asked Kyle.

"More of the same. All the phones are off."

"Did you call her at home?"

"Yes, but it appears that the phone has been shut off."

There was a knock at the jury room door, and Kyle answered it. It was Clausen. He looked at Barnabas. "Can I have a moment?"

Barnabas got up and followed him out into the hallway.

"Of course Century would like the patent, but I can't guarantee that Stephanie Schultz will continue to represent Century."

Barnabas laughed. "You can't reach her either, can you?"

Clausen sighed. "Can you help us get her back? That's what you get when you make a decision while you're angry."

"That's between you and her. We'll consider assigning you the patent later, but we have to work out something today about your past and present use of the device. We know that Century was innocent when this started, and everything you pay us for up to today you can try to get back from North American. Wire us eight million tomorrow, and you can continue to use it for thirty cents a ton. That's fifty-five cents less than what North American is charging you. Now, I have one more condition."

"And that is?"

"We are going to insist on a thirty-thousand-dollar per diem charge if you are late with the money."

Clausen responded, "I'll get back to you in ten minutes." Clausen knew he was getting a sweetheart of a deal. He was back ten minutes later as promised. "It's a deal. The client said to tell you that they should have been rooting for you folks all along." Clausen and Barnabas shook hands.

Thirty minutes later, Frederick knocked on the door and called Barnabas out into the hallway.

"We'll sign over the patent, wire twenty million tomorrow, and we'll pay thirty cents a ton until the patent runs out. But we are going to need a confidentiality clause."

"Let me talk to my clients."

Barnabas walked into the jury room and smiled. "It's better than I hoped. It's kind of fun. I've never discussed these types of numbers before. As a politician once said, 'A million here, a million there...after a while you are talking about real money.'" They all laughed. "Let's hit them up for a little more. What do you say?" Barnabas suggested. They laughed again, but no one said no.

Barnabas went back to Frederick. "My client needs fifty million, and seventy cents a ton, which is less than what you charged Century. Also, we are going to need a one-hundred-thousand-dollar per diem charge if you are late with the money. Over the last three years, Bill and Silva have received almost thirty million in royalties. Grab their assets and monies. I doubt that you are going to have any resistance."

Thirty minutes later, Frederick knocked on the jury room door, and Barnabas talked to him in the hallway. Frederick grimaced and said, "Done." He walked away without offering his hand.

Ten minutes later, everyone was in the courtroom, and Judge Kruger walked in. Before the clerk could start her chant, the judge said, "Be seated, please."

Barnabas remained standing.

"I understand that we have a settlement," the judge said, looking at the clock. "And a full hour ahead of time. Good job, gentlemen. I assume, Mr. Mitchell, that you will do the honors as you are the only one standing."

"Thank you, Your Honor. The terms are fairly simple, as you suggested. As to Century Coal, Mr. Clausen and Mr. Frederick are going to prepare the papers for signature before nine a.m. tomorrow. They will be delivered to my office for my client's signature." And Barnabas repeated the terms while the court reporter transcribed every word.

Judge Kruger asked Clausen and Frederick if the agreement had been accurately stated, and they both acknowledged that Barnabas had accurately detailed the respective agreements. Judge Kruger rose and said, "Thank you, gentlemen. This matter is concluded."

Frederick was gone thirty seconds later, with Clausen close behind.

Barnabas felt like he was in a dream world; in twenty-four hours there would be fifty-eight million dollars in his trust account.

He leaned over to Sarah and whispered, "As soon as we get back to the office, we need to call the bank and tell them to expect a ton of money coming into my trust account. We don't want them rejecting it. Can you imagine it? They may have to make arrangements to handle that much money."

As Barnabas was gathering up his papers, the judge's clerk approached him. "Mr. Mitchell, the judge would like to speak with you in chambers." Dutifully, he followed her clerk into chambers, concerned why the judge would want to speak with him.

As soon as he entered, Judge Kruger looked up and smiled warmly. "Congratulations."

Barnabas was relieved that Judge Kruger didn't have something serious on her mind. "Thank you, Your Honor."

"Now that the case is over, I wanted to have this little chat with you."

"It is an honor that you are willing to speak with me."

"Mr. Mitchell, I hope you understand that until these final witnesses arrived, I had little choice but to rule against you. In my heart I believed your client, but sometimes you can't follow your heart because the law dictates otherwise."

"I agree, Your Honor. We were prepared for a loss. I was just hoping that you would not rule today."

Judge Kruger laughed heartily and said, "I suppose that I could have waited, but why delay things just for the delay, you understand?"

"Of course, Your Honor."

"Now, I want to make another point, if I may."

"Certainly, Your Honor."

"As a woman, I couldn't help but notice something that many male judges wouldn't. Now that you can afford it, maybe you can consider updating your wardrobe?"

Barnabas laughed. "I suppose I can do that, Your Honor."

"And finally, Mr. Mitchell, what do you make of Ms. Schultz's absence today?"

"Your Honor, my understanding is that she has been terminated."

"I was afraid of that. Is there something going on between you and Ms. Schultz? I realize that this is quite a personal question, but you must admit that what she did in court was quite atypical, even if she was ethically bound to come forward with evidence as an officer of the court."

Barnabas paused. *What a difficult question.* "I consider her to be my best friend, but I'd like to be more."

"It is so refreshing to see a young attorney put the truth before her own career. You are going to take care of your best friend, aren't you?"

"You've got that right, Judge. She is certainly going to be well taken care of."

Barnabas couldn't help mentioning the change he'd noticed in the office. "Have you given up smoking, Your Honor?"

"Tomorrow will be a month, but I've put on another fifteen pounds, so I'm forced to start my exercise regimen tomorrow. Thank you for noticing and asking. The best of luck to you and Ms. Schultz. Tell her that the both of you are welcome back in my courtroom anytime," the judge said, smiling.

Barnabas rose and walked into the courtroom where Kyle and Sarah were waiting.

With a surprisingly stern expression, Kyle said, "We have to talk about your fees." A queasy feeling came over Barnabas, and Kyle continued. "I figure that you spent a solid five hundred hours on this case, and because you did such a good job, we are going to double your rate to three hundred dollars an hour. That's a cool one hundred fifty thousand dollars for your trouble."

Barnabas stood silently. He realized that in his haste when he decided to take on the case, he forgot to get Kyle to sign a contingency fee agreement. *Such a rookie mistake! How could I have overlooked that?* Without a contingency fee agreement, he only had the right to charge his hourly rate. The $150,000 Scooter was offering was generous under the circumstances, but he had been counting money in his head that he did not have. Barnabas started to have a sick feeling in his stomach.

Barnabas then heard a loud, "Ouch! Stop that!" He looked over and saw Sarah pulling Kyle's ear sharply.

Sarah looked at her husband sternly. "That's not funny. I don't care how funny you think you are, if you expect to sleep at home tonight, you apologize for that bad attempt at humor!"

Kyle looked at Barnabas and laughed. "I just couldn't resist teasing you, but I prefer sleeping at home over any amount of money. It appears that there is going to be more than enough money to go around."

Barnabas smiled. "You had me. Wasn't a bad effort at all. Even under the circumstances, it was pretty funny."

* * *

They went to the office in a jubilant mood. Jennie instantly understood that they had won as soon as they walked in the door.

Barnabas announced, "Tomorrow we're going to shut the office down, and the party starts at two p.m."

But Barnabas' jubilance subsided as the afternoon went on. He kept calling Stephanie and Sam, but neither picked up. Every fifteen minutes, he called the Schultz's home phone but got no response.

By 9:00 p.m., he was desperate. He called Sarah, who was at home. "Sarah, I've been trying to reach Stephanie all day. No one in the family is answering the phone. Do you know anything? I said some things I should not have on Saturday, and I need to talk to her. Can you find out what's going on? Call me back if you learn anything. I don't care how late it is."

An hour later, the phone rang. It was Sarah.

"Did you find out anything?"

"Yes, I went over to the house. Ruth confiscated everyone's phone. They're talking about family matters. I stayed around for a half an hour and told them what had happened. They seemed pleased. They said they would get back to you."

But Barnabas wondered what they were talking about.

CHAPTER THIRTY-TWO

Barnabas got up at 6:00 a.m. as usual. He had been restless all night. He had started the previous day expecting to lose, burdened with all of the financial problems of operating a solo practice. By the end of the day, an agreement was in place that would give him financial security for the rest of his life. There was great irony in the fact that Christian L. Frederick III would be the source of that financial security. Barnabas knew that he wasn't an expert in God's ways, but the fact that God used the Frederick firm as the vehicle to deliver the money was not a coincidence.

But his thoughts again returned to Stephanie. *What is going on?* In his mind, he imagined the conversation that they would have, and he dreaded it:

Did you have such a low opinion of me that you actually thought I was capable of falling for Bill, of falling for his garbage? How could you have thought that? And to eavesdrop like that…what were you thinking?

Try and put yourself in my position. The very words coming out of your mouth confirmed that that was happening. How could I have thought anything else? How can you be offended? I definitely would have fallen for the line you were peddling to Bill.

As your friend, I was asking you to have some faith and trust in me. I was asking you to be a better person than Bill. Faith and trust mean that you don't make judgments about a person, even when it looks bad. At the very least, why didn't you give me the courtesy of asking me what was going on before you judged me?

He would have no answer for her. If he did talk with her, it would be stupid and pointless to do anything but apologize and admit that he had been an ass. She had stuck her neck out, worked to win the case, subsequently got fired, and he showed his appreciation by treating her like she was a traitor and, even worse, one of Bill's groupies.

It was easy to understand her anger. But was he going to get the chance to talk with her, to explain? Were they still friends? When she left the courtroom, she didn't seem hostile, but she clearly felt vindicated. Had something changed? Barnabas was tempted to get in his car and drive over to her house, but she already knew he was desperate to talk with her. He had to be patient, but it was eating him up. All his life, he had coveted financial security. Now that he was going to get it, he realized how meaningless it was.

Barnabas arrived at the office at 7:00 a.m., thinking that he was going to review several files that desperately needed attention, but it was impossible. He just sat and thought. He didn't want to start thinking about what he was going do with the money until he actually had it. Had Frederick come up with some last-minute strategy to renege on the deal? Barnabas didn't see how it was possible. If Frederick tried something like that, it was going to cost the client $100,000 a day. No, he was going to be a rich man by 2:00 p.m.

The first thing Barnabas was going to do was get out of debt, and the next, was find an accountant. There were too many cases where someone had won the lottery, and two years later they owed the IRS hundreds of thousands of dollars without the ability to pay. That was not going to happen to him.

But Barnabas couldn't shake his despondency. The price might have been too high. What was Stephanie doing? He had to talk with her, but she had frozen him out, and it was not like she didn't have any reason to do it.

Jennie arrived at 8:00 a.m. and Barnabas scolded her gently. "I thought I told you that we were shutting down today. The party starts at two p.m."

"You can't be serious. There is no way I am going to miss anything that happens today. Emily and Matt insisted on coming over right after school. You don't get many days like this. We are going to cherish it."

Kyle and Sarah arrived at 8:45 a.m. and Clausen arrived ten minutes later. The agreement was only ten pages, but it took Barnabas twenty minutes to read it. In the meantime, he heard Jennie greet someone else. Barnabas walked into his waiting room, and he smiled when he saw Oxnard. Barnabas should have known that Frederick's ego couldn't handle delivering the final settlement agreement himself—further evidence that Barnabas had made the right decision two months ago.

Clausen's agreement was in order, and Barnabas told Kyle to sign it. Clausen shook their hands and left. Frederick's agreement was twenty pages long, and Barnabas took a full forty minutes to read it. It had been well drafted. It did not vary from the agreement relayed to Judge Kruger the day before. Kyle signed off, and Barnabas handed Frederick's copy to Oxnard. Barnabas shook Oxnard's hand and stifled a smile.

Oxnard said, "Congratulations, Barnabas. I guess it's obvious you made the right decision. What are you going to do now?"

"Frankly, I am still in some kind of shock. I was fully expecting to lose. I have some fences to mend, and hopefully I will be able to do that. As far as professionally, I guess that I will keep practicing law."

Oxnard smiled. "Well, I hope we can cross swords again soon."

Barnabas laughed. "That would be fun."

Barnabas called his bank and asked a vice president to call him as soon as the money hit the account. The banker called back at 1:15 p.m. and he told Barnabas that fifty-eight million dollars had just been deposited into his trust account. Barnabas made the announcement, and everyone cheered.

Professor Paulus arrived at 2:15 p.m. just as Jennie was getting off the telephone with a pizza delivery place. Emily and Matt arrived thirty minutes later.

Barnabas tried to celebrate and share Kyle and Sarah's joy, but he was only feigning excitement. He was officially a rich person, but he felt empty. He had already learned the lesson that having money did not guarantee happiness.

At 4:00 p.m. Barnabas was finishing the last piece of pizza when they heard the office door open. Emily got up to see who was there. As she rounded the corner, he heard her say, "I'm sorry we are closed—oh, you must be her. Please come in."

Barnabas got up and went to the waiting room to see who was there. He turned the corner and saw Stephanie, Ruth, and Sam. Without thinking, he ran over to Stephanie and enveloped her in his arms. He held on tight.

"You need to give me a chance to breathe!" she exclaimed.

He didn't want to let her go. She had been such a precious friend, such a beautiful example, and in one courageous choice that had cost Stephanie her job, she had won the case for all of them.

He turned to Ruth and Sam and bear hugged them as well. He returned to Stephanie, grabbed her by the hand, and said, "Let's go into my office. I'd like to talk."

She smiled and followed him. He closed the door.

As soon as she sat down, she started to talk, but Barnabas interrupted. "Before you start, I need to say some things. I have rehearsed it all in my head, trying to make excuses and come up with rationale, but I have no excuse. I was wrong. You were the one who taught me how important faith and trust are, and the first time I was tested, I failed miserably. I feel ashamed. Yet, here you are. I hope that I will not make a habit of asking for your forgiveness. I will never jump to any conclusions again, and I will never make any judgments without talking to you first. I'm so glad you are here. I was afraid that you weren't going to give me this chance. I hope that we can still be friends."

She smiled at him and said, "That was nice. It was what I thought you would say but still nice. Of course I want to continue having a relationship with you."

He sighed in relief. She paused, collecting her thoughts. "Okay, how much of our conversation did you overhear?"

"When I came in, Bill was asking you to go on a helicopter ride on Saturday night. I couldn't listen anymore when he started on his definition of fornication."

She had a pained expression on her face and said, "That must have been hard. But if you could have held on for another ten minutes, you would have found out what he said that really got me started. Did you really think that I was falling for his lines?"

"I should have known better. You of all people would never fall for his BS, but you were doing a very good acting job, and you fooled me too."

She smiled delicately, but it was clear from her expression that she had been hurt by Barnabas' accusations. "I guess I should have understood that you actually thought I was falling for him. At first I was angry that you didn't know me better than that. I felt betrayed. But Dad and Mom forced me to look at what happened from your perspective. I guess I should have told you what was happening on Saturday, but we hadn't made contact with Johnson at that point. I promised Dad that I would not tell you anything until we knew for sure that we had the contents of the box. And remember, Barnabas, you were the one who insisted that we not talk again until the trial ended, remember?"

Barnabas knew that he was trapped. "You're right. I did it to myself."

Her countenance improved, and she managed a smile. "I was tempted to call you on Sunday evening despite your instructions, but by then I decided it was best to just do it myself. Besides, it didn't bother me that you were going to spend some time not knowing what was happening. But don't worry; Bill didn't come close to winning any bets, but I felt like Rahab anyway. The mere fact that I let him touch me makes me cringe."

Barnabas asked, "Rahab?"

She smiled and touched his arm. "You'll know what I mean someday, hopefully sooner rather than later. By the way, I'm a little surprised you didn't crack the code."

He conceded her point. "I tried, but I learned that code breaking is not among my talents. I'll never get a call from the NSA. So, what did Bill tell you that led to the e-mail and the box?"

As she immersed herself in the story, her mood seemed to improve. "Bill is so transparent. He made a couple of attempts to hit on me before you got involved in the case, but I shut him down. When the trial started last week, it was obvious that you weren't going to find what Bill said was out there, so after court on Wednesday I invited him to dinner. He was surprised, but by the end of the night, I knew he was going to ask me out again. When he did, I insisted that we go out on Thursday. We were running out of time.

"Bill is not as smooth as he thinks he is. He was willing to tell me just about anything to get what he wanted. By the end of the night on Friday, he told me that the solution had been in Dawson's computer, but the evidence was long gone and would have required an expert anyway. My theory is that Bill found the coded paper on Dawson's desk before he was murdered and either he or Silva erased the file from Dawson's computer. Anyway, that was what got us started.

"Bill and I were supposed to go out again on Saturday, but I called him on Saturday morning and canceled. We had a lot of work to do before Monday morning. I don't think that Bill understood what had happened until you produced the attachment with the code on it in court yesterday."

While she talked, it was becoming increasingly difficult for her to keep her composure, which surprised Barnabas since she was such a strong woman. She started to tear up. Obviously it was a difficult subject for her, so Barnabas took over.

"Tell me when you first told Sam about what you were doing with Bill."

"I waited until after our date on Friday evening. Honestly, I was afraid that if I told Dad before, then he wouldn't have approved and would have tried to talk me out of it. I didn't want to be talked out of it and didn't want to have a pointless conversation. I considered telling you what I was doing with Bill but decided not to for the same reasons. Besides, I didn't want to raise any hopes unless I knew that I would be able to deliver."

Barnabas noticed more tears, so he changed the subject. "So, you got fired?"

She managed a small laugh. "I guess I should have expected it. But the job wasn't that important to me, anyway."

"So you didn't tell Clausen about the e-mail?"

"Of course not. I didn't trust them to tell you. That's why I got Clausen to be elsewhere on Monday."

"Wow, you did that too?" Barnabas asked. He had never even considered that Clausen's other engagement had been part of her scheme as well. But he quickly continued. "Stephanie, don't worry about any ethics inquiries. There's not going to be a complaint from your client because they came out of this better than before. And you had no other choice but to proceed once you got the e-mail."

She responded in a quiet voice. "Well, there is no point in sugar-coating it—this last week I was being deceptive on several fronts." And then she switched the subject, and her voice got stronger, more forceful. "So, Barnabas, since you are charging me with keeping a secret, do you have any news? Do you want to tell me something?"

Her emotional intensity was building. He had never seen her in this kind of mood. She was on the verge of crying. He knew what she was referring to, and he wondered how she had found out. Pastor Davidson couldn't have been the source, so it had to be Kyle or Sarah. *Of course it was Sarah.*

"So when did Sarah tell you?"

In a soft voice she said, "When she came over to the house last night."

"Stephanie, why didn't you call me after you talked with Sarah?"

She was about to cry, and Barnabas couldn't ignore it any longer. "I'm not trying to make you cry, you know. Help me out...what can I do to help?"

She got out of her chair, sat down on the carpet, and leaned against the wall. "Come over here. Sit with me, put your arm around me, and give me some support, okay?"

He complied. And she started to talk. "I don't care how tough you think I am. This has been a very emotional week for me. First, I spent all that time with Bill, leading him on and living that lie. And here I am on Thursday night with that creep, holding his hand, and you're changing your life. Do you know how long I've been praying for this, and I don't even find out until last night? I guess I got what I deserved, but you're lucky that I didn't answer your call on Thursday because I may have just dumped Bill on the spot, and then where would we be now?

"And then I feel like there is hope and we begin to gather evidence, and we have our little chat, if you can call it that, on Saturday. And...how can I say it? You told me that you thought I was a naïve, hormone-driven tramp chasing after Bill. You really thought that, though, didn't you? And to top it off, just a little icing on the cake, you know, I get fired. Here you are, worth millions, and I don't have a job. So, can you appreciate that life has been like a roller coaster for me lately? Do you understand why I could have used less stress in my life? In some ways, you are just like my brothers. You guys don't have a clue. My mom warned me about what boys can be like. So just hold me and do your best, Barnabas."

Stephanie rested her head on his shoulder.

It was his turn to talk, and he knew that the right choice of words was crucial. It probably wasn't the right place to start, but he had to start somewhere, and it had to be positive. "Stephanie, everyone knows that there would have been no settlement if it hadn't been for you. You'll have all the money you will ever need, and you'll never have to work a day in your life if you don't want to."

"That was sweet, I guess, but you know that's not what I want."

"Look, we can form our own firm, on whatever terms you want. Is that something you would want to do?"

"We talked about that last night, and we thought you might want to do that."

"So why didn't you call me? You knew I was desperate to talk to you!"

"Mom's rules, remember? No cell phones during family meetings. Besides, I knew you were stewing, and it made me feel better that you weren't too exuberant in your newfound wealth. Just wanted to spread the misery around a little, okay?" She gently poked Barnabas in the ribs. "Besides, Monday was a very emotional night for us. I'm not even sure I would have been coherent."

Barnabas elected not to press the last comment. He decided it was better to let her do the talking. It was clear that she had more to say. She poked him again like he was dozing off. "So, what brought you around? You have to know that we have been praying for you for years. Why now?"

Barnabas told her the story about Nicks coming into his office and what happened afterward.

"What a story," she said. "So, it took an ex-con to get you to do it. Go figure. The Lord truly does work in mysterious ways." She gave a barely audible chuckle. "So, Barnabas, I have to know. Is this for real, or is it the result of an emotional encounter?"

It was not a subtle question, but Barnabas was glad she had asked.

"I see myself as having gotten on a train, and it has left the station. I really don't know where it's going, but I'm on it. I just have to trust that it's taking me to a good place. The train is going too fast for me to risk jumping off of it now. I don't see myself ever going back. Honestly, I was worried that you would see it as an effort to get closer to you, but it isn't. Your dad was right. He has always been right. It goes all the way back to my church, to my days as a kid, you know?"

She smiled. "I know exactly what you're saying."

"So, when did you start praying for me?"

"Remember after the competition I promised that I would pray for you? I kept my promise, but I suppose I started praying earnestly after

Thanksgiving. People who are indifferent don't ask the kinds of questions that you did. "

"So what did you pray for?"

"That God would put people in your life that are objects of His Grace."

Barnabas was surprised by her response. "Well, those prayers were certainly answered."

"I know," she said.

There was a pause in the conversation, and Barnabas weighed whether he should bring up the next subject or wait, but he remembered Kyle's advice: *If nothing is ventured, nothing will be gained.* The timing seemed right, but he struggled to begin. Barnabas sensed that Stephanie knew he was struggling, but the moment had arrived. He pushed ahead.

"Stephanie, remember when you told me about agape, phileo, and eros?" He knew that she remembered, but at least he was talking about the subject.

He was surprised by her sharp response. "So, you want to do this now? If you are going to do this, we are going to get up off the floor and at least sit in the chairs so you'll have to look me in the eye."

Her tone had abruptly changed, as if she were in court, ready for battle. Barnabas was taken aback. Stephanie stood up, grabbed his hand, lifted him off the floor, and dragged him back to the chairs.

As she sat down, she smiled at him in a way that bordered on laughter. She made him uncomfortable, which she seemed to enjoy. He opted for honesty and looked into her eyes. "Look, I am very bad at this, and I have had almost no experience with it. I actually thought that it might be too soon, so we can wait if you want to."

She stifled a laugh as he spoke. His tongue felt like it was frozen, and his words came with considerable difficulty. And she wasn't helping. She was enjoying his ineptness. She had warned him about this side of her personality, but he was surprised that she had decided to show it now, of all times.

"Now's fine, Counselor. What do you have to say?" she said coquettishly.

He looked at her in exasperation. "Look, this is difficult enough without you enjoying it, too. It's not easy, and you're not making it any easier."

"You're incompetence is really kind of charming. But you are a trial lawyer. You just won a huge case. You can think on your feet. It's not the time to get tongue-tied. It's time for you to man-up, Counselor, and spit it out."

"Look, we both know that that settlement was more your doing than mine, but I appreciate you giving me credit, anyway…and thank you for your support," he added sarcastically.

At this point, Barnabas resolved that he was not going to be deterred; this was his moment, and he was going to take it. In a strange way, by her obvious enjoyment of his awkwardness, she was reassuring him.

Stephanie continued to smile. "You're welcome," she said.

He went on hesitantly and grabbed her hand. "As much as I love you, the hope of a relationship with you is not the reason why I decided to become a Christian. And maybe I should have waited a few days to ask, but I would like to know if you have any interest in becoming more than friends."

It was not smooth—plodding at best—but at least he had taken the risk and said it. He had ventured, and he was now praying for the gain.

Her response was more natural. "I have been waiting for this moment. My mom and dad kept telling me to be patient and to keep praying. They were so confident that this day was going to happen. Dad kept saying that the values your mother gave you would bring you back to your roots. Of course I am interested in becoming more than just friends."

For the last two days, she had dominated his mind. He wasn't at all sure where he stood. Now, in a single moment, his anxiety changed to joy. He didn't know how much freedom he had to express his feelings, but he knew that this was a time to be bold. He closed the space between them, and when he noticed that her lips moved closer to his, he kissed her passionately.

She was giving herself to him physically, assuring him that her feelings were real. He had never experienced anything like it before. He didn't want it to end. But it had to end, and eventually it did. He realized that years of learning to persevere despite difficulties and deciding to be a person of character had been worth it.

He held her, not wanting to let go, savoring the moment. In a single moment, his future looked bright. He understood that it was the beginning of truly being yoked to her.

Barnabas released her, and almost by force of habit, he asked more questions. "You know, I wasn't sure that your response was going to be this positive. And I remember going to church after the bar examination. When did things start to change for you?"

She paused, choosing her words carefully. "I would like to talk about this in detail later, but you sold the family at Thanksgiving."

"But I was not a believer. You told me that the very next day. Did you ever consider relaxing your standards?"

"No, but that was when I focused much of my prayer life on you. Some pretty selfish prayers, but God answered them."

She smiled, and they started to talk. They talked about the trial, Dawson, Kyle and Sarah, and they lost track of time as they relived the events of the past week. Finally, she suggested that they end their time alone. "We should rejoin the party, don't you think? You are not being a very good host."

"I suppose you're right, but I could spend the entire night right here with you if you would let me."

She stood up, grabbed his hand, and pulled him up. "Come on, boyfriend, let's be sociable."

They opened the door and discovered that everyone had left. The clock on the wall read 9:15 p.m. They both laughed.

She said, "I guess everyone agreed that we needed to spend some time together. You are going to have to take me home. My parents and I came here together. They did this on purpose, you know."

They arrived at her house shortly after 10:00 p.m. and the lights in the house were out. She chuckled as he pulled into the driveway. He looked at her, curious as to why she was laughing. She looked back at him. "My dad never goes to bed before eleven p.m. Mom forced him to go to bed early."

He looked at her. "I don't get it. Why was it important that he not be up when you got home?"

"This is Mom's way of insisting that this entire evening be our time alone. It is her way of saying that she trusts you and likes you."

Barnabas walked her to the door, and they stood there and embraced and kissed for another half hour. Eventually, she looked up at him. "Okay, it is time for bed."

But Barnabas didn't want it to stop. "You know, I'm not very experienced at this. I still need more practice."

She smiled, but she was not buying it. "You're doing just fine. You don't need any more practice today. We can practice some more tomorrow. I have to get to bed early. You see, I am starting a new job and I want to impress the people at my new firm."

He responded, "I shut the office down tomorrow. Can I come over to your place?"

"Okay, I can wait a day to start working. Why don't you come over around noon? I'll make you some spaghetti."

"That'll be fine, but there is one problem."

"What's that?"

"I don't know where you live."

She laughed. "Call me and I'll give you directions."

On the drive to his apartment, he reflected on the events of the last week and then started thinking about his relationship with Stephanie—from law school to the bar exam, Thanksgiving to their lunches, and finally, the trial. He thought about his mother—whom he knew had prayed for him every day—and about Paulus, Jennie, Emily and Matt, the Schultz family, Kyle and Sarah, the Capshaw family, and finally, Jessie Nicks. He remembered Emily's promise to pray that his finances would improve, and he laughed out loud. He vowed that he was going to seek out Emily and start adding other things to her prayer list.

Things that had not been obvious before were becoming obvious now. Although he had left Stephanie just thirty minutes earlier, Barnabas felt compelled to call her. She picked up after the first ring.

* * *

Stephanie hadn't wanted him to go either, but the truth was that she was starting to get a little too aroused and suspected that he was, too. For the first time in her life, she was confident that Barnabas and she were united in purpose, wanting to go in the same direction.

She let herself in, and the house was dark, but she knew that her father was awake. She gently knocked on the bedroom door, and Sam silently opened it and peered out.

"You okay?"

"Much better than that. Is Mom awake?"

"I think she just drifted off. You want to talk?"

"Yes. So much to talk about. How about over a bowl of ice cream?"

Sam stepped out of the bedroom and quietly closed the door. They were eating ice cream at the kitchen counter three minutes later.

"So, what caused him to come around?"

"An ex-con."

Sam arched his eyebrows in disbelief.

"It's true. The guy was responsible for killing this girl, and her family members were Christians. They went out to the prison three times to tell him they forgave him. He finally met with them the third time."

"How was this guy able to talk with Barnabas if he was in jail?"

"Barnabas got him off on a technicality. He hated himself for doing it. That's why he left the PD's office."

"That's one technical argument he will never regret making. So, are you going to start working for him like we discussed?"

"Better. He says I will never have to work again if I don't want to."

"Is that what you want?"

"Of course not. You know that. He wants to form a firm."

"Is that premature? What if things don't work out?"

"What's wrong with practicing law with your husband?"

"He proposed and you accepted!"

"Not yet, but he's going to. It's just a matter of time, and we both know that." She laughed. "I've never been this happy. It couldn't have gone better."

"But it is so soon. How do you know he won't turn back?"

"If he were going to do it, he would have done it on Friday night. He may have felt betrayed by me, but he didn't turn his back on the Lord. No, his conversion is for real. He is never going back."

Then her cell phone rang. She looked at it and saw that it was Barnabas.

* * *

"You're not trying to come back and practice some more, are you?"

He laughed. "No. Did I wake you up?"

"What do you think? Given everything that has happened, it will be several hours before I will be able to sleep. Dad is still up, and we have been talking. He says hi."

"Say hello to him for me."

"So, why did you call? Can't this wait?"

"I guess it could have, but I just had a revelation that I wanted to share."

"Okay."

"You know, all those years that I was angry with God, fighting Him, convincing myself that He had abandoned me. He never did go away, did He? Mom prayed for me daily, and after she died, Paulus gave me support. He was a father to me, and then your family took over, and with the help of Jennie, Kyle, Sarah, the Capshaws, and Nicks, He was with me all along, wasn't He? I was just oblivious."

She responded with a heavy, "Yah think! You don't know how many times I was tempted to throw the book at you."

"What do you mean, 'throw the book'?"

"Do you want me to give you my list?"

"Sure."

"Well, let's start with the bar exam."

"What did I do wrong studying for the bar exam?"

"You never attempted to respond to my arguments. To you it was just an intellectual exercise, but I was attempting to get you to think."

"Uh-huh."

"Then let's move on to when you almost fell asleep at church, then your thoughts at Thanksgiving, and I don't know how many times during our lunches your mind seemed closed. I guess things that are so obvious to me were not so obvious to you, but we all knew that you were fighting God. It really was frustrating. And I was told to wait to raise this again, but since you're bringing it up, I was deeply hurt by your comments last Saturday."

"I'm so sorry. All I can say at this point is that I will do anything and everything to make it up to you."

"Oh, I know that. Dad and Mom kept saying that I should not lose patience. Dad insisted that you were going to come around. They said that God had a grip on you, and He was not going to let go. But you know the thing that I resented about you the most?"

Barnabas was overwhelmed with new information and could only manage a meek, "I give."

"You asked me about boyfriends. The truth is that I did meet a lot of guys in the last two years. I was constantly being introduced to guys by people at church and even a few other friends, but I was never really interested. You know why?"

"Let me guess, they weren't Christians?"

"No. That was generally not the problem. The actual problem was that I always found myself measuring them against you, and none of them measured up."

Barnabas was truly surprised. "Why would you say something like that?"

"You don't get it about yourself, and I doubt that you ever really will. Without even knowing God like you should, you've shown more character and love than any guy I have ever met. The truth is that I have been in love with you since we studied for the bar exam."

Barnabas felt compelled to respond. "Well, the truth is…for me, I think I fell in love with you the first time I saw you. I would have been an idiot to say it at the time, and I didn't want to say it later because I knew that you were never going to relax your standards. But it feels great to be able to say it now."

"Barnabas, I was not clueless, you know. I knew that you had always had strong feelings for me. The truth is that I was tempted to relax my standards, and there were times that I really did doubt that you were ever going to come around. It was frustrating for me that I was investing so much in you, and you just seemed to be so intractable. Don't you realize that Mom, Dad—even my brothers—and I have been praying for you every day? When Sarah came over last night and gave us the news, I couldn't help it. I…I just started to cry. This last twenty-six hours has been the happiest time of my life. The prayers, patience, and wait have been worth it."

"I'm dumbfounded. It really does make me feel special. As for me, my life turned around this afternoon when you came over. I shudder to think of where I would be if you had never come into to my life."

"Barnabas, thanks for calling. It proves that you really do get it. I think that this is such an important call. God bless you, and I love you— agape, phileo, every Greek word there is, even eros." She laughed when she said it. "But that will be exercised in moderation until a little later,

God willing. Dad is looking at me like I'm crazy, so I need to clue him in. See you tomorrow?"

She had said it all, so all he could do was reciprocate. "I love you, too. I look forward to tomorrow."

He made it home at 11:30 p.m. and crawled into bed. He had had little sleep for five straight nights, but his mind was racing. At 1:00 a.m., his mind gave in to his body. He slept through until 9:00 a.m. It was the first time in his memory that he had slept past 6:00 a.m.

CHAPTER THIRTY-THREE

Three months after their engagement, Barnabas and Stephanie drove to Bella Italy together. On the way, he raised a subject that she was not expecting. "Stephanie, I have been thinking about this a lot, and I would like you to read my journals."

She studied him intently. She was surprised by his request. "I don't think that's necessary. You don't need to show me. Don't feel like you have to tell me everything that has ever happened to you. It would exhaust my own patience and memory if I tried to do that for you."

He paused, pondering how to explain it to her. He pulled the car over. "I don't know if he will ever do it, but now that Bill has been forced out of the Frederick firm, he is under criminal investigation. There is no way of knowing what he is capable of doing. I wouldn't put it past him to try and pass something that he had read on to you. I think it would be best that you already knew it."

"I don't care to ever talk with him again. Just because he calls doesn't mean I have to take the call."

"Look, I know Bill better than you do. He is very shrewd. He can get himself on a case where you are on the other side. He is very devious, and if he wants to force you to talk with him, he can do that. I don't know what he read and how much he remembers, but we really do need to be prepared if he ever does call."

"Barnabas, have you thought that maybe you have lost a little perspective about Bill? Maybe he doesn't spend as much time thinking of ways to make your life miserable as you think."

"You're probably right. But there is another reason, even more important."

"Okay, give it to me."

"When I learned that he had read my journals, it was like he had stolen a part of my life that he had no right to. My journal is something

261

that if anyone has a right to, it's you. In my mind, it would deprive Bill of whatever victory he might have felt he had if you read them. You're probably right. It may well be that he will never call you, but it would make me feel better about knowing he had read them if you read them, too. It's like part of my soul will be restored to me. Do you understand?"

She smiled, nodding slightly, and said, "I understand."

They drove to the office after lunch, and Jennie was there. Barnabas asked, "Why did you come in on a Saturday?"

"I just got word from the PI, and I thought you would want to know ASAP."

"What did he find out?"

"They both live in Iowa, about fifty miles from one another. His name is Ted Rice, and he got out six years ago. They both are home every evening. Your dad doesn't drive a truck anymore."

Barnabas nodded and looked at Stephanie. "You know, I understand all of the reasons why I should do this, but I'm not sure that I can. I was really hoping that they wouldn't be found."

She took his hand and pulled him into her office, and they sat down together. "I don't doubt that it is going to be difficult, but you need to do this. Put this behind you and get on with your life."

Barnabas voiced the thoughts turning over in his mind. "One day there is a woman, my mother—strong, independent, loving—and the next day she is in a hospital, and when she gets out, she never walks again. I was forced to witness her slow death every day for seven years, all because some drunk kid had no thought, didn't care about anyone but himself. And Dad…we were okay financially, but he left us in terrible shape. You will never know what it's like to get up every morning wondering whether you are going to have enough money to buy lunch. Neither of these guys deserves a break."

"Of course they don't deserve a break, but neither do you or me. So why are you going to do this, Barnabas?"

He shrugged and forced a smile. "I know, I know. I'm going to do it because Jesus loves them, and I have no choice but to love them, too. Those are easy words to say, but it will be harder to do. Just don't expect me to like it."

Stephanie pulled him up, put her arms around him, and whispered in his ear. "The issue isn't knowing what to do—we almost always know what to do—the issue is having the love to do it. I will spend the rest of my life thanking God that you came into my life. I am so proud that I'm going to be your wife."

Barnabas responded, "Your gratitude to God and pride will never match mine."

Stephanie laughed and said, "Let's not compete over that one." She then asked, "Are you sure you don't want me to come along?"

Barnabas lightly touched her cheek. "No, Nicks asked to come along. If we get into a bad neighborhood, he actually may be more valuable to me."

She smiled at his little joke. "Okay. Take big, bad Nicks, but I insist that you take my car. Don't take yours. You are pressing your luck with that car as it is by driving around the city. Besides, the clutch is starting to slip. I'll take her in for maintenance."

CHAPTER THIRTY-FOUR

Barnabas relented and took Stephanie's car. He and Nicks left the next morning for Iowa. Barnabas chose to talk with Ted Rice first. For reasons that he couldn't fully articulate, he knew that it was going to be easier. He decided that he would simply go there that evening and knock on the door.

They arrived at his house at 6:00 p.m. It was a modest place in a poor neighborhood. Barnabas knocked and took a step back. Nicks waited in the car. Thirty seconds later, a man who looked about thirty-five years of age opened the door. "Yes, can I help you?"

Rice had deep eyes that were too small for the sockets in his face. It was as if his eyes had shrunk. Rice had long, stringy hair that was prematurely gray. His expression was not welcoming. Barnabas assumed that he distrusted strangers.

"Sir, you don't know me, but you may recognize my last name. My name is Barnabas Mitchell. I am not here to cause you any trouble."

The man dropped his shoulders and said, "So you're her son. I was told that she died seven years ago."

"Yes, she did, but I am here to put that behind us. Can I come in?"

"Well, you might as well come in. Whatever you want to get off your chest, you might as well do it inside."

Barnabas went inside and sat down on a chair that looked like it had been in storage for a long time. Rice sat down on a chair that needed new upholstery.

Rice spoke first. "Okay, Mr. Mitchell, what's on your mind?"

Barnabas had been rehearsing his words on the drive over and spoke slowly. "I'll be honest with you. For most of my life, I hated you. It would have suited me just fine if you spent your entire life in prison and died in there. I have a different perspective on life now. I don't know how much that event sixteen years ago has affected you, but it is not the real point of my being here. My mother was the type of woman who would want you to live the best life you can. I have no doubt that she is in a better place. You have served your sentence, and as far as I'm concerned, there is no reason for anger or bitterness. I wish you only the best."

Barnabas looked at him, and Rice's face did not reveal his thoughts. Finally, after a very long minute, Rice started to talk. "There has not been a day that goes by that I have not thought about that accident. And prison has not been the ideal place to change one's life for the positive. I guess that I believed that that was going to be my life."

Again he paused, but Barnabas sensed that he had more to say, so he waited. "Can I ask you something?"

"Sure, go ahead."

"What brought this on? It has been sixteen years. Why now?"

"It had been building up for some time, but the moment of change came when I was able to see for myself the compassion and unselfishness of a family who had lost their daughter and sister in an accident similar to ours. I decided that I needed to be more like those people, so here I am."

Rice nodded that he understood. "Well, Mr. Mitchell, I promise that you have given me a lot to think about. It would be nice to truly put this behind me."

"All I can say is that you don't need to be defined by your past. Work on where you are now, and move forward. Feel free to call me if you want to talk further." Barnabas reached out and gave Rice his card.

As soon as he got back to the car, Nicks asked, "How did it go?"

"It went fine. He seemed to appreciate it. It was good for me. I'm glad that I did it."

They drove over to Cedar Rapids the next morning and spent the day going over what Barnabas was going to say to his father that evening.

Shortly after 6:00 p.m., they got to the house. It was in a lower-middle-class neighborhood. The house was a little smaller than the one Barnabas had been raised in. Again, Nicks waited in the car. Barnabas rang the doorbell, and he could hear someone coming to the door. As the door opened, he recognized the man standing there as his father. He would have just had his fifty-second birthday. He was Barnabas' height, and it appeared that he had put on some weight from what Barnabas remembered of him at the funeral. His hairline had started to recede, but Barnabas didn't detect any gray in his light-brown hair.

From his father's expression, Barnabas knew that he recognized him, but he had to say something to get the conversation started. "Do you recognize me?"

"Yes, son, I recognize you."

His dad stood in the doorway, clearly struggling for something to say, so Barnabas decided to make it easier. "Can I come in for a minute?"

"Of course, of course, son, come in."

His dad opened the door, and Barnabas stepped inside. The living room consisted of a couch, table, television, and two chairs. While the spring-green paint was not peeling, it didn't look like the walls had been painted in several years. There was nothing hanging on the walls. There weren't even any books or magazines on the table. The room projected loneliness.

Barnabas sat down, and he looked into his dad's eyes. They were a dull gray and showed no sign of joy. Barnabas had rehearsed what he was going to say several times. "Dad, first I wanted to tell you that I am well and that I'm about to be married."

His dad interjected. "I know. I have been following your life from afar."

Barnabas was taken by surprise. "How have you been doing that, Dad?"

"It wasn't hard. You can learn a lot of things online. Lawyers are talkative folks. Recently, I located this fellow by the name of Oxnard who speaks to me occasionally. He seems to know what's going on."

Barnabas smiled. "Yeah, Oxnard is a good guy. I can see him doing something like that." Encouraged, Barnabas continued. "I think it is time for us to start a new relationship. I've no doubt that you regret some of the decisions that you have made in the past, and frankly, I'm not proud of the attitude that I have harbored toward you. But nothing positive can come out of that. Why don't we forget about the past and start something new?"

His dad had tears in his eyes, and he was searching for words. "I know that I have failed you and your mother. I am a weak person, and I never deserved her. I don't think that I will ever be able to make it up to you."

"Don't try to, Dad. I'm doing well now. I am about to marry a wonderful woman. Why don't we take it from here and not worry about the mistakes we made in the past? The important thing is how we can help one another now. Stressing out about the past helps neither of us."

Barnabas had no memories of his dad crying, and he could see that he was struggling to hold back tears. Barnabas decided that it was too much to ask his dad to begin showing his emotions, but he stood up anyway, walked over to his dad, and as his dad stood, Barnabas gave him a gentle hug.

His dad invited Nicks in, and they remained there the rest of the evening. It was the first real talk that Barnabas had ever had with his father.

CHAPTER THIRTY-FIVE

They decided to get married on a Saturday, and Barnabas learned the irrelevancy of the groom in planning a wedding. His job was to be wherever he was told and to speak when he was spoken to. He thought he had fulfilled his duties admirably.

It was a modest event at the church; Stephanie had refused to have a lavish wedding. Pastor Luke, of course, presided. As Barnabas waited for her to come down the aisle with Sam, he surveyed the audience. Ruth, of course, was in the front pew. He saw his dad in the front pew on the other side, and Professor Paulus with his wife were in the second pew. Kyle, Sarah, Jennie, Emily, and Matt sat together toward the middle. Toward the back, he smiled at Nicks and the family Nicks was sitting with. It was the second time that Barnabas had seen them. He had wanted them to come, but he didn't expect it. "Don't worry, I'll get them there," Nicks had assured him.

Barnabas had included a handwritten note in the wedding invitation. The first paragraph of the note read:

> You folks may not remember me, but I would like to explain to you why a stranger would invite you to his wedding. If it hadn't been for you, Jessie Nicks wouldn't have come into my life. If it hadn't been for Nicks, I don't believe that I would be a Christian today. I believe that I would have confessed Him eventually, but Nicks caused me to do it immediately. If hadn't been for Nicks, I would not be getting married. So, you see, the credit goes to you. Please come to my wedding.

CHAPTER THIRTY-SIX

She brought his journal, which was over four thousand printed pages, on their honeymoon, and quickly they got into the habit of reading in bed and then praying together. She would sit up in bed and read his journal. Early on, he asked questions about what she thought, and she would always give the same answer: "Let me finish first, and then I will let you know what I think."

The second time she gave the response, he reminded her, "Remember that they stop my third year in law school."

She patted his hand and said, "I know."

Eventually, he gave up asking her what she thought, but he would furtively glance over and attempt to read her expressions. They varied from smiles to sternness to anxiety to sadness. She was clearly engrossed in the subject.

About a month after they came home from the honeymoon, he felt confident enough to give her the liberty to stop. "Stephanie, I think I was too obsessed with what Bill may do. It is no longer important to me. You can stop if you want to."

She responded firmly. "Don't ask me to stop now. I need to know how this story ends."

He was tempted to say, "But you know how it ends," but of course they both knew that. She had started the project, and she was determined to finish it.

Five months after the honeymoon, he came home around 8:00 p.m. He had taken the bus after working late. She had left work earlier, taking the car. He had just celebrated his twenty-seventh birthday, and Stephanie had given him a three-year bus pass as a present. She was delighted with herself, and Barnabas was relieved that her gift was actually something useful instead of one of her usual pranks.

He went into the bedroom. He noticed that the bathroom door was closed, and he heard the bath water running. There was a large journal book on his side of the bed. It was a new one opened to the first page with a pen on top of it. She had written something. He sat down on the edge of the bed, picked up the journal, and began to read:

I've read every word, just as I promised I would. After I got started, there was no way that I could stop. I cried at times, laughed at times, and I was even afraid a couple of times to turn the page. And I will be honest—on a couple of occasions I was even angry with you, but it was good to think about you and your experiences. There is nothing in them that changes anything as far as I am concerned. If Bill ever does call, he will wish that he hadn't.

The worst part was the day you were cleaning out your mother's closet. Although I knew how it turned out, I never should have read that part while I was alone. It was frightening, but the most emotional part was the time between your mother's stroke and her death. There was such a convergence of emotions. I was sad, struck by your deep love for your mother, and I felt helpless that I couldn't do something about her pain. You were gone that evening when I read it, and I just started to cry, not fully understanding why I was crying. I had to talk with someone, so I called my mother. You told me that that was okay, remember? As I started to read it to her, she started to cry as well. Knowing you, I suspect that you don't understand why, do you? Let me just say that my love for you reached an even deeper level. I feel like I married the most special, lovable man in the world.

Why don't we start a journal together? Is it a good idea? It will be fun to read it together in forty years. You start.

Love,

Stephanie

He laughed at the reference to Bill. Bill had underestimated Stephanie more than once, and Barnabas believed that even Bill would not be so stupid as to try and intimidate either of them now, but he was relieved that she had read them. She had given him back his soul.

Barnabas smiled at her suggestion to start a journal together. There was so much to write about. He composed his thoughts, picked up the pen, and began to write.

CHAPTER THIRTY-SEVEN

They had been married for over six months, and he was sitting in Judge Kruger's court waiting for his case to be called. His was sixth on the docket sheet, and Judge Kruger called his case out of order, moving it up to third place. He was glad that Judge Kruger had done it, as he had been waiting there for more than an hour. The first case had gone unexpectedly long.

Judge Kruger usually had a businesslike, if not stern, expression on her face while she was on the bench, but this time she was in a joyful, if not playful, mood. Barnabas wondered why. The matter took no longer than five minutes, and Judge Kruger was in a hurry to get it concluded—looking at her watch, cutting his argument short before she ruled in his favor. As Barnabas was walking out of the courtroom, he turned on his cell phone. He saw a text message from Stephanie: *It is now 3:00 p.m. In Room 310 of the Ritz Hotel. You have until 4:30 to get here or I'm leaving.*

He looked at his watch. It was 4:25 p.m. The hotel was two blocks from the courthouse, and he was on the tenth floor. He stood in front of the elevators, impatiently waiting before one arrived. As he rode down, he looked up at the numbers above the elevator door as they slowly signaled his descent. As soon as the door opened, he raced past the security personnel and sprinted two blocks to the hotel. He ran up three flights of stairs and was completely out of breath as he reached the third floor. Looking at his watch, it was 4:33, and he was worried. He ran down the hallway to Room 310.

Just as he got to Room 310, the door flung open. Stephanie was standing in the doorway, laughing hysterically. Grabbing his hand, she pulled him over to the window. She had a perfect view of the two blocks between the courthouse and the hotel. She had purposely picked that room because she wanted to see him run.

"I have to tell you the truth. I left the message at four fifteen. I wanted to see how fast you could run if you were motivated. Very impressive!"

Still out of breath, Barnabas managed to ask, "But how did you know I was going to be getting out at four twenty?"

"Don't you remember that we tried a case there together? I got to know the judge's clerk. She's a friend of mine."

Exhausted and exasperated by what she had put him through, he responded, "Can we go back to being just friends?"

She approached him, grabbed him around the waist, and responded, "Not on your life. You are stuck with me now."

They learned a month later that that was the day they conceived their first child.

EPILOGUE

He had volunteered to give a two-hour lecture for a continuing legal education conference on a Saturday, and he wished he hadn't. When he had volunteered, he didn't know that Stephanie was pregnant. They had succumbed to temptation and asked to know the sex of their baby before the delivery. Her doctor told them that it was going to be a girl. They didn't give serious consideration to any names other than Alice.

Stephanie's due date was only four weeks away, and the conference site was a full three hour's drive downstate. A three-hour drive one way, another two hours of sitting, and a three-hour drive back—he wished that he didn't have to do it.

There were 250 lawyers in attendance, all getting their mandatory continuing legal education credits. As Barnabas got up to speak, he saw them both within the first minute. They were sitting on opposite sides of the room. Oxnard was sitting up front on the left-hand side, and Bill was sitting in the very back row on the right. Barnabas had been told that Bill had regained his license and that only Silva had been prosecuted. It didn't surprise him.

Barnabas wondered if he had anything to teach Oxnard, and he further wondered if Bill was willing to be taught anything at all. Oxnard gave Barnabas a barely noticeable wave, and Bill just smirked, his favorite pose. Bill didn't take any notes. Barnabas didn't know what Bill had been doing after Frederick fired him, and he didn't care. Bill must have found some job practicing law; otherwise, he wouldn't be at the seminar.

* * *

Bill did not know that Barney was going to be a speaker until he arrived at the conference that morning. His father had hired the best criminal defense and ethics attorneys in the country. He voluntarily gave up his license for

274

one year, and he pled to a misdemeanor in exchange for testifying against Silva. He had slightly more than ten million dollars in cash and assets when the Titanic had gone down that day. In exchange for assigning the cash and assets to—and agreeing not to testify against—Frederick, Frederick had given Bill a full release of claims.

One thing he had done to protect himself was plant the seeds in Silva's head about doing something regarding Dawson without actually saying anything. Bill had to admit to the FBI that Silva had told him about something on Dawson's computer drive, but that was the only evidence tying Bill to Dawson's murder. He admired his own cleverness by making it look like it was all Silva's doing. Eventually, Silva pled guilty to a mandatory twenty-five-year sentence in the penitentiary. At least Silva had been smart enough to send someone else to the bank rather than go himself, which saved him life in prison.

His father had hired Bill to be house counsel for one of his businesses, so he had to keep his license active. He knew that the only way he was going to make money practicing law was working for his father. He would never work for a firm or government agency given his background.

In the middle of all of his legal problems, his mother forced him to listen to her. She urged him to "reexamine your life and ask yourself some tough questions as to how you got into this situation." He couldn't do it. That would be like admitting that Barney had been right all along. He did promise his mom that he would cut back his drinking, which he understood meant cocaine as well. He would go a couple of weeks without alcohol or cocaine, which convinced him that he could go forever if he needed to. In the end, he knew that all he had to do was be patient, and in twenty years or so he would inherit his parents' fortune. He could do whatever he wanted whenever he wanted after his parents died.

As he sat and waited for Barney to speak, Bill knew that he could not give in to Barney for a moment. Barney might think that he had won, but there was no way that Bill was ever going to let Barney see any sign of remorse. He began to smirk when Barney got up to speak.

* * *

Barnabas finished his lecture at 5:00 p.m., the agreed time, and most of the lawyers filed out of the room. Bill was one of them. Oxnard, however, walked up to the podium and shook his hand.

"Barnabas, why don't you let me buy you dinner so that we can catch up?"

"Richard, I really shouldn't. Stephanie is eight months pregnant, and I should get home."

"Why don't you give her a call and see how she is doing? If she is all right, it would be a good opportunity to catch up."

Barnabas paused, picked up his cell phone, and dialed her number. She picked up after the second ring. "Hi, how did the conference go?"

"Fine, we just finished. Oxnard is here, and he wants to have dinner, but I wanted to see how you were doing first."

"Oh, go ahead. My mom is here. We are having a good time. Go ahead and have dinner with him. It will give us something else to talk about when you get home."

"You sure?"

"I'm sure. I'm doing fine. Go ahead."

"Okay. I should be home before ten."

"See you then."

Barnabas looked at Oxnard. "Where do you want to go?"

"It turns out that my uncle has a place down the road called, of all things, Oxnard's. Let's go there."

Barnabas gathered up his stuff and arrived at the restaurant twenty minutes later. Oxnard was waiting for him outside as Barnabas pulled into the parking lot. He thought it was odd that Oxnard was waiting for him outside. From the looks of the parking lot, the place wasn't full, but Oxnard would be able to get them a table even if it were. He walked up to Oxnard, who said, "Bill is at the bar drinking. Does that pose a problem?"

"Don't be silly. Of course we can eat here."

They spent most of the meal talking about old times, mostly about the Abbott trial. Barnabas knew that Bill had to be a source of irritation to the both of them, so he avoided bringing him up. Oxnard was genuinely interested in how Barnabas was doing and how many children he and Stephanie planned on having. Stephanie and Barnabas had talked about Oxnard before, and Barnabas decided to take advantage of the opportunity.

"Richard, how are you doing? Do you still enjoy practicing law?"

Oxnard decided to take his time before answering. "I have always liked practicing law, particularly the trial work. The office politics have gotten old, though. Very old. But I don't have any other options. My kids have another ten years to go before they all get out of college. I can't risk starting my own practice now."

"Richard, I'm sure that it doesn't surprise you that we now have more business than we can handle. We turn down more cases than we take."

"I'm aware. The word on the street is that you guys are doing well."

"Look, we don't want to ever become a mega-firm, but I'm sure that Stephanie would be open to bringing you on board. Unlike the place you're at now, you could develop your own client base, and I'm sure it won't cost you any money to leave."

Oxnard smiled. "Well, this is a real-life role reversal, isn't it? It would almost be worth it to see the expression on Frederick's face when I tell him I'm leaving." He paused again and said, "I'm surprised and flattered that you would even think of me. Let me think about it, if that's all right. I'll get back to you."

"Take all the time you want. Our offer will continue to be there."

At 7:00 p.m., Barnabas was getting ready to leave when he went to the men's room. He noticed that Bill was pushing himself away from the bar. It didn't appear that he had had anything to eat, and as he walked, he wobbled. *Bill is definitely in no condition to drive.*

As soon as Barnabas left the men's room, he went into the parking lot looking for Bill, but Bill had already left. Barnabas went back inside, thanked Oxnard for the evening, and headed back to his house, a place not too far from Sam and Ruth's and close to the site where the church was going to build a new facility.

As he was driving up Interstate 57 just past Kankakee, Barnabas noticed that traffic was at a halt, with both lanes of traffic at a complete stop. Whether it was an accident or something else, Barnabas had no patience to sit on the freeway waiting for traffic to clear. He was only 200 feet from an exit. He applied the brakes and was able to slow his car down enough to take the exit. He headed west for a mile and then turned on his GPS, which gave him an alternative route by taking the back roads.

It was dark, around 9:15 p.m., when he saw it. Barnabas was driving out in the cornfields. A new BMW had driven off the road and was in a ditch. The front end was destroyed. There were skid marks on the road, and the marks suggested that the driver had lost control. Barnabas pulled over and stopped his car. He walked up to the car. The air bag had not fully deployed. He opened the driver's door and saw Bill, unconscious.

Bill had not worn his seat belt. Barnabas pressed the overhead light in Bill's car, and thankfully, it came on. Bill had deep wounds on his forehead and bruising on his face. Barnabas checked Bill's pulse, and it was racing. His breathing was fast and shallow. He picked up his phone and dialed 911.

"There has been an accident on the county line road five minutes east of Route 51. The driver needs an ambulance."

"Hold on, sir."

As Barnabas waited, he grew more impatient. Finally, the man came back on the line. "I checked with all ambulance services in the area, and it does not appear that one will be there for thirty minutes."

"Thirty minutes! He can't wait that long!"

"There should be a police car there in less than fifteen minutes, sir."

"I don't think you realize the gravity of this situation. His life is in jeopardy."

"Sir, I have called every ambulance in the area. I realize that this is serious."

Barnabas paused. "Give me the number of the closest hospital."

Barnabas dialed the number. When the operator picked up, he said, "Give me the emergency room. I have an emergency."

There was a pause, and a voice came on the line. "Emergency room."

"I need to talk with a doctor immediately."

Ten seconds later, a male voice came on the line. "Dr. Tariq. How can I help?"

"Doctor, I am in the country. A car has gone into a ditch. The driver is breathing fast and shallow. His heart is racing. There are two deep gashes on his forehead. They say it is going to take thirty minutes for an ambulance to get here. I think he needs to get to the hospital now. Do you agree?"

There was a pause, but the doctor finally spoke. "It is a gamble if he stays and a gamble if you move him."

"What is the gamble if I move him?"

"He may have fractured his spine, and if you move him without waiting for the ambulance, you may cripple him permanently. On the other hand, it is obvious that there is stress on his cardio system that needs immediate treatment. Can you tell from where you are standing whether he has sustained any injuries to his neck or back?"

"Hold on."

Barnabas gently pushed Bill forward and examined his neck and back. "From what I can tell, there is no bruising or swelling or signs of impact that I can see."

"Well, it is up to you. I really can't tell you what to do."

Barnabas paused. "I'm going to move him. Give me directions to your hospital."

"It is a small, private county hospital. Get to Highway 51 and go north three miles. We are on your right just before you get into town. While you are moving him, try and support his back, especially his neck, as much as possible."

Barnabas hung up, got on his knees, reached into the car, and grabbed Bill by his legs with his left arm and by his mid-back with his right. Bill had to weigh a good solid 240 pounds, and Barnabas was not sure that he could move him. Gradually, Bill's body began to inch toward Barnabas, and one minute later, Bill was in his arms. Barnabas was not sure that he could stand, but bracing himself against the side of the car, gradually he was able to extend his legs. The hardest part was getting him out of the ditch, as the dirt was soft and wet, but slowly, Barnabas walked the forty feet to his car.

He was barely able to open the back door, and using the back seat to support Bill's head and shoulders, he pushed him gently inside. He fastened one seat belt around Bill's right arm and shoulder and another around his mid-section. He had to push Bill's legs up, as his body was too long to fit in the back seat fully extended. After the second belt was fastened, Barnabas leaped into the front seat and headed for Highway 51. He was at the hospital in less than ten minutes.

On the way, he called the hospital a second time and told them to have Doctor Tariq ready. As he drove into the emergency room entryway, two men and a woman wearing white coats were waiting with a hospital gurney. They had Bill out of the car in less than three minutes.

Barnabas had been in the waiting area for five minutes when a woman approached him with a clipboard. She had a cell phone in her hand.

"Sir, are you the one who brought the gentleman in?"

"Yes."

"We have no information on him. He had no wallet."

"I must have left it back in his car. His name is Bill Cushman."

She paused, and Barnabas could tell that she didn't want to ask the next question. "Sir, he has no insurance card and no money. I can't formally admit him without some form of proof that we are going to get paid. We can't afford to take patients who can't show the ability to pay."

Barnabas stared at her. "Are you saying that you are going to send him somewhere else unless you know he is going to pay you?"

She paused again. "That's putting it too bluntly, sir."

Barnabas was on the verge of showing the anger that was boiling inside of him. He stood up.

"Do you realize that this man is a lawyer and that his father is very influential? If anything happens to him because you don't treat him, his family is going to own this hospital. Is that what you want?"

The woman started to tear up. "Sir, I have a job to do. I'm a single mother with two small children, and I need this job. I almost got fired last month for allowing a patient to be admitted without trying to secure some form of payment."

Barnabas relented. "How much do you need in order to treat him?"

"We like to have at least two thousand dollars."

Barnabas reached into his wallet, pulled out a credit card, and said, "Do you take credit cards?"

"Of course."

"Run up as much as the hospital requires, and if you exhaust that, keep the details and run it again. Now, since I am paying for this, would you give me his cell phone?" She handed it to him without saying a word, and she returned with his card five minutes later.

Barnabas sat there and prayed silently for Bill. While he was in prayer, he sensed that a man was standing next to him. He was wearing a white coat. Barnabas stood, and the man reached out his hand.

"Hi, I'm Doctor Tariq. Do you know this man?"

"Yeah, I know him."

"Is he a friend?"

Barnabas paused, pondering the question. Then he said, "He is my brother."

As Dr. Tariq was leaving, Barnabas picked up Bill's cell phone. Luckily, it wasn't locked. Barnabas looked through the contacts. When he saw "Dad," he pressed the call button.

"Hello, Bill?"

"Mr. Cushman, this is Barnabas Mitchell."

"Mr. Mitchell, what are you doing with Bill's phone?" Mr. Cushman said sternly.

"Sir, Bill has been in a serious automobile accident about an hour and a half from you. He's in the hospital. I suggest you get down here immediately. I'll wait until you arrive."

Bill's father inundated him with questions on the phone, most of which Barnabas could not answer. Barnabas sat down and continued his prayers.

Bill's parents arrived at 1:00 a.m. His dad began shouting as he entered the waiting room. He approached Barnabas, who was still praying in the corner. "Where is my son? What did you do to him?"

Barnabas stood up, wondering whether he would need to protect himself from a physical altercation, when Bill's mom entered the room. "I didn't do anything to Bill. His car was in a ditch when I arrived."

"Don't think that I am so naïve that I'd believe that Bill is now in serious medical condition and you happened to be there by chance! Let me assure you that if there are any serious problems with him that I will sue you for everything you're worth."

Barnabas was tempted to finish the argument and put Bill's dad in his place, but he quickly rejected the thought. "Sir, my car is in the parking lot. I'll be glad to show it to you. I can show you where Bill's car is. I'm sure that it's still there. There are no skid marks from my car. I had nothing to do with this accident."

Bill's father accepted the challenge. "Okay, let's go to the parking lot and look."

At that point, Bill's mom stepped forward, put her hand on her husband's shoulder, and said, "We're not going to do it that way. As far as I'm concerned, we're fortunate that Barnabas came along. It's silly to accuse him of causing this. If he had been guilty of something, he never would have stayed here. He would have gone back and attempted to cover his tracks. We're going to sit down and begin to pray like he has been doing."

Bill's dad was surprised by the force of his wife's words, and before he could respond, Dr. Tariq entered the room. "Are you Mr. Cushman's parents?"

"Yes," said Bill's mom and dad simultaneously.

Dr. Tariq spoke slowly. "It is a wonder that he is alive. He broke five ribs. He punctured his spleen, and he lost two quarts of blood from internal bleeding. The blood tests show that his blood-alcohol content was .23. He shouldn't have been driving. He almost died." Then, nodding at Barnabas, he added, "You are very fortunate that this young man was there."

There was nothing left for Barnabas to do, and it was time for him to get home. As he was leaving, Bill's mom came over to him and hugged him. "Thank you. You saved his life."

"You're welcome. I will continue my prayers on the way home. May God bless you."

* * *

Barnabas did not get home until 2:30 a.m., and after his shower, he crawled into bed. Stephanie had been sleeping exclusively on her side for the last two months, and she was facing him as he crawled into bed. She awoke from a deep sleep, and she turned to her other side. She whispered, "Come and cuddle with me."

She loved to cuddle. She could sleep all night with his arms around her. He moved over to her, put his left arm under her head, and placed his right hand on her rounded stomach. She was even more beautiful because of her pregnancy. There was a color in her face that had not been there before. As she started to fall back to sleep, she said, "Did you get much accomplished?"

He smiled and said, "Yes, dear, I just got back from Samaria."

She was too fatigued to understand, so she said, "That's nice," and she drifted back to sleep.

As he lay next to her thinking about the events of the day, his right hand felt Alice kick. He smiled. Then he began to recite in his mind his

282

favorite Scripture: *Come to me, all you who are weary and burdened, and I will give you rest. Take my yoke upon you and learn from me, for I am gentle and humble in heart, and you will find rest for your souls. For my yoke is easy and my burden is light.*

And he fell asleep.

CPSIA information can be obtained
at www.ICGtesting.com
Printed in the USA
FSOW04n0034030117
29119FS